Lucy held out her hand to Sam Houston, who, resplendent in his Cherokee robe, bent to kiss her fingers.

He had charmed the two women by his attentions. They were much taken with the man's bearing, and entertained by his earnest asking of their advice in matters of chivalry and haberdashery. As for Houston, President of the sovereign republic of Texas, he returned to his capitol captured by Lucy —Lucy gazing in profile towards the Brazos river, Lucy draping green sashes across her slim arm for him to choose, Lucy saying that, surely, he would not receive her as he had Monsieur de Saligny.

He lay that night on his bed in a state of bewilderment he had known only once before in his life.

Terry Coleman is a novelist, historian, and reporter. His novel *Southern Cross*, set in the early years of Australia, was a worldwide bestseller. *Passage to America*, his history of immigrants, has gone through many editions. As special correspondent for the *Guardian* and the *Daily Mail* he has travelled to seventy countries. In 1988 he was named Journalist of the Year. *Empire* is his third historical novel.

EMPIRE

TERRY COLEMAN

Mandarin

A Mandarin Paperback
EMPIRE

First published in Great Britain 1994
by Sinclair-Stevenson
This edition published 1994
by Mandarin Paperbacks
an imprint of Reed Consumer Books Ltd
Michelin House, 81 Fulham Road, London SW3 6RB
and Auckland, Melbourne, Singapore and Toronto

Copyright © 1994 by Terry Coleman

The right of Terry Coleman to be identified as author
of this work has been asserted by him in accordance
with the Copyright, Design and Patent Act 1988

A CIP catalogue record for this title
is available from the British Library
ISBN 0 7493 1572 5

Printed and bound in Great Britain
by Cox & Wyman Ltd, Reading, Berks

The glory of the United States has already culminated. A rival power will soon be built up and the Pacific, as well as the Atlantic, will be component parts of Texas in thirty years from this date. . . You may laugh at these suggestions, but they are the results of destiny over which I have no control.

– Sam Houston
President of the Texas Republic
1844

For Wallace
Sett and Pattern

Contents

PART THREE

PART FOUR

Foreword

This novel is the story of the great American empire that never was, an empire which would today share the north American continent with the United States. In 1844 Sam Houston was president of the independent and sovereign Republic of Texas whose destiny, as he saw it, was to be a rival power to any nation on earth. He opposed annexation to the American union. He foresaw and feared that any further American 'aggrandizement' would lead inexorably to civil war between the states. On 24 September 1844, Houston ordered his secretary of state to accept a British and French offer to guarantee the independence of Texas against the United States and against the world, by war if need be. What followed was a struggle of the New World against the old. What happened is history. History was within an ace of going the other way.

PART ONE

Come to the Bower

Sam Houston rose from his place at the head of the table. At which the band of four violins, two pipes, and an ancient deep-noted wind instrument called a serpent, broke into the melody of 'Come to the Bower I Have Shaded for You'. He was plainly taken by surprise, and stood gazing shaggily round at the singing faces of his friends as everyone took up the tune of this love song, and those who knew the words sang them. He bowed his head and then, since the tumult continued, turned to the band and motioned them to stop. Joe Runyon, the first fiddle, grinned straight at Sam and defied him, whipping up his band to a louder pitch, until the cheers drowned everything out and at last there was silence, and Houston faced the two hundred men gathered on a warm evening in the late spring of 1840 in the ballroom of the Tremont Hotel at Galveston, Texas.

'Gentlemen. In responding to your toast ...,' he said, and, having got that far, and having raised a great hand and the great glass in it, was greeted with laughter, and cries of 'Empty,' and then chants of 'Fill, fill, fill. Fill the general's glass.' He and his friends had dined well, on venison and plover and swan, and drunk well too. 'Fill, fill,' came the cry again. A girl took a magnum of Rheims champagne from the hogshead of ice in which it rested, ice shipped from New Orleans for the occasion, crossed to Houston's side, and refilled his glass. It held the better part of a pint. She curtseyed to General Houston, and the company, delighted by the evening and delighted by everything, was delighted again at the sight of the two of them together, Sam Houston and this strange girl.

Sam stood six feet four inches tall, a commanding, courtly
figure in a blue broadcloth coat, with lace at his cuffs and at
his high collar, looking, as the fancy sometimes took him, like one
of the Founding Fathers of 1787. So he stood, with his large head
erect and his features lit by eagle grey eyes, holding out a heavy
hand-made glass which in his grasp looked tiny – to be filled by
this girl. She was a young German with long yellow plaited hair,
black-skirted and with a broad red band at her narrow waist, an
immigrant off the boat from Hamburg, five feet nine or ten in her
low peasant heels, as tall for a woman as he for a man. He looked
down on the girl's shining head as she bobbed to him, caught her
eye as she raised her head, and gallantly raised the glass to thank
her.

'It is four years,' he said, 'since the army of the Republic of
Texas moved up the slope of the field of San Jacinto – to that
melody. We had two fifes to play it then. [Cheers.] And a drum.
And Santa Anna's army scattered, and Santa Anna ran in his shirt
[laughter], and our republic was born – free from Mexico, free of
the world, one of the nations of the world. And Generalissimo Santa
Anna, president of Mexico, Napoleon of the West [more laughter] –
no, gentlemen, enough of him. Except. Except this. This is not a
thing that has come into my mind since, but it comes to me now,
and I'll tell you. The day after the battle – among the ruins of his
army, and his own life not safe, though I spared it . . . '

A voice was raised in the room: 'Should've hung him, General.'

'No, my friend. He was useless dead, but useful alive. Alive he
could call his other armies off, which were coming up. I spared him so
he could call them off. He did call them off, with orders I saw written
and sent on the spot. But gentlemen, the thing that came to my mind
this moment, was this. We surveyed the field, he and I. Six hundred
of his army lying unburied, and only nine Texians dead. And Santa
Anna, Napoleon of the West, coolly looking at the matter, and coolly
looking at his dead, said to me, very civil, "General Houston, had I
the power, I would prevent even the birds from flying to Texas into
Mexico." And his meaning was, he would not, if he could stop it,
have even birds with free Texian spirits come to Mexico, let alone

men with free Texian spirits come there, who had just cut up his army, and taken Texas for themselves.'

A roar of happy applause filled the room.

'One other thing, gentlemen, apropos. After the battle – you will remember, those who were there – we were scattered to the four winds, scattered in pursuit, scattered over miles. But wherever three or four of us were gathered together, after it was settled, we thought of nothing but eating and drinking. The day was ours. We lived. We ate. We drank.'

The ballroom was silent, the men leaning back in their chairs or hunched forward, nodding their heads at the recollection – because it was true.

'Well, gentlemen, we have eaten tonight too. And since this is not a cold-water-doin's [renewed laughter], we have drunk a drop, or two maybe. [Lasting cheers.]'

The toast to which Houston had risen to respond was, 'Texas, Free, Sovereign, and Independent.' After a short speech of three quarters of an hour in all, he proposed one of his own to 'Texas and her friends, first among whom I name the Kingdom of France.'

The toast having been drunk by all present, each in half a pint of champagne, Jean Pierre Isodore Alphonse Dubois, comte de Saligny, French chargé d'affaires to the republic of Texas, arose to answer. This was going to be good for a laugh. When Texas first saw him the year before he was plain Alphonse Dubois. Since then he had first added 'de Saligny', and then advanced himself to the nobility by adopting the rank of count. He was the son of a French provincial tax collector. His only distinction was that he happened to have been, for a while, at the same school as Prince Ferdinand, son of Louis Philippe, king of the French, who favoured public education. No one in Texas held it against a man that he should call himself count if he liked, just as few minded much that he had paid for his first lodgings with counterfeit bills, since it was well known that the bills had first been palmed off on him. It was good experience for the chargé d'affaires of a European power.

Saligny began. It was a great honour for him to represent in this young republic an ancient power, France, which, having sixty years before been the first nation to recognise the independence of the young United States of America, had in 1839 been the first European power to recognise the independence of the still younger Republic of Texas.

Moderate applause. The assembled company had heard all this before.

'And,' said Saligny, 'as I look round at the assembled gentlemen in this magnificent room, I can only marvel at the resolute Texian character [cries of 'Hear, hear'] which, once it has undertaken a project, will hang on like grim death, against storm and tempest, and move heaven and earth to build such a fine hotel as this in which we meet this evening, a hotel to sleep two hundred, a hotel where two hundred can feast, a hotel built, as we all know, gentlemen, on land which only last winter was a stinking swamp.'

An incipient cheer, encouraged by such turns of phrase as 'move heaven and earth' and 'fine hotel', emerged as little more than a low growl. The inhabitants of Galveston did not consider that their swamps stank.

Saligny did not notice, and was off again. 'I shall now allude to a delicate matter, gentlemen, but it is one on which I have confidence we shall be in perfect agreement.' Here he raised his own glass of champagne, showing it to the company. 'I speak of Champagne wines, gentlemen, one of the greatest gifts of France to civilisation. Now, gentlemen, a diplomatist must not go beyond his strict instructions, so I do not here speak for the king [laughter], but rather for myself and I hope for other gentlemen here. It so happens that on a case of a dozen bottles – and I should think, gentlemen, we have killed more than a bare dozen this evening [ribald laughter] – but let us take one dozen bottles: on that dozen, gentlemen, there is a duty imposed, on importation into this republic, of two and one half dollars.'

Groans and cries of 'Shame' rewarded Saligny, who then, encouraged to the point of rashness, fell into the pit he was digging for himself.

'This is, of course, a matter I can properly take up only with President Lamar . . .'

And then Saligny was howled down.

Bar two or three, every man at dinner was a Houston man, and Lamar was his enemy. The day before San Jacinto, Mirabeau Buonaparte Lamar had been a private. Conspicuous bravery brought him promotion overnight, and he fought the battle as a colonel. The first elected president of the Texas Republic was Houston, but the constitution provided that no man could hold that office for two consecutive terms, so in 1838 Lamar became president. In that office he debauched the currency, drove the Cherokees from Texas into Arkansas, maintained a navy which Houston thought useless, wrote and published verse, and taxed Champagne wines. On the night of the dinner at the Tremont, when Saligny so unwisely invoked his name, Lamar was still president. His Texian navy – a sloop, a brig, and three schooners – lay in Galveston Bay. And he was planning to send an expedition five hundred miles inland to Santa Fe, to gain for Texas the trade of the Santa Fe trail and to encourage a rebellion against Mexico in that city. So Lamar was president, a decent man, but bankrupt and reckless and ill. Few doubted that Sam Houston would soon be president again.

Forty-three other toasts were drunk. To Liberty. To the United States. To Dr Ashbel Smith and his seventeen new cows, to which Dr Smith replied with a toast of his own to the gentleman, whose name he regretted was unknown to him, who had sold two town lots in Galveston in order to buy cherries from New Orleans, for his wife. This led to the toast, 'To the ladies: may they all be cherished with cherries.' Then more toasts still. To the fecundity of the Franco-Texian connection and to Queen Maria Amelia of the French and her eight children – a toast Saligny was by then too drunk to take offence at, let alone make any reply. Then to Her Britannic Majesty Queen Victoria, with whose ministers Texas was negotiating a treaty of recognition and trade, and might her recent marriage be as blessed with offspring as that of Maria Amelia. At which a few less politic members of the gathering began a scattered rendering of a low ballad entitled 'Aboard the *British Queen*', which was ostensibly about a steamboat of that name.

Sam Houston, leaning back in his chair with an arm round

the waist of the German waiting girl, asked where she was from and, when she told him, proposed a toast to Hanseatic Hamburg. He turned to ask the girl her name, but she had slipped from his side and was back standing near the door, and would not look up when he called to coax her back.

Near Houston, but out of earshot in the buzz of the room, sat Dr Ashbel Smith, whose new cows had been toasted, and next to him Dr Anson Jones, both physicians, and a Colonel Bee, all friends of Sam. All had seen the passage with the waiting girl.

'Sam soon goes to be married in Alabama?' asked Bee.

Smith, who had kept a clear head, nodded. Jones muttered something indistinguishable about Lamar.

'He will not,' said Bee, 'live with his new wife six months. I never knew a man more totally disqualified for domestic happiness.'

'Lamar?' asked the befuddled Jones. On principle he drank little, and therefore in practice got easily drunk.

'No,' said Bee. 'Sam.'

'Sam,' said Jones, 'doesn't mind how completely Lamar lets the country go to ruin. So's people can say, "Gone to the dogs. Must have Old Sam again." And Old Sam's drunk.'

Smith, who loved women and loved Houston, turned first to Bee, whom he knew to be no fool. 'Maybe not six months. But I hope you're wrong, Colonel. I have known Sam be a very constant man.'

Then Smith turned to Jones. 'Sam is no more drunk than I am. And if he were, Sam drunk is worth a hundred Lamars sober.'

After a shaky last rendering of 'Come to the Bower', sung unaccompanied because the band had long gone home, those that could rise from the table did. It was past midnight. Sam Houston called for water, and motioned Smith to go with him to his sitting room, which looked clear out over the dark bay. There was no moon, but it was a night of brilliant starshine, a night so untypically clear and free of haze that the setting stars were cut cleanly in two by the horizon. On a table in the window lay a map of north America, from Maine to Oregon, from the Floridas to the peninsula of lower California. As they looked out on to the bay they looked south-south-east.

'It has struck me,' said Houston, 'that the Gulf of Mexico is somewhat in the shape of a horseshoe. At one heel of the horseshoe is Cape Florida, over there,' – gesturing to his left, towards the darkened south-east. 'And at the other heel', gesturing straight before him, 'is Cape Catorche, near Yucatan. And the opening of the horseshoe, the opening of the Gulf into the Atlantic and the Caribbean, is defended by the island of Cuba.'

Smith looked up at the starshine and waited.

'And round that Gulf,' continued Houston, 'lie some of the finest harbours in the world – Tampa, Mobile, New Orleans, Sabine, Galveston, Tampico, Vera Cruz.'

'Yes?'

'And where are we?' Houston asked suddenly.

'Where are we? As we stand here now?'

'Here. As you and I stand here, we are at the toe of the horseshoe. At the toe of that great horseshoe lies Texas. On the coast of Texas, level prairie. One hundred miles inland from the coast, high rolling prairie – the richest soil in the world. And timbered valleys. In the south oranges and sugar cane, in the middle region cotton, and further north wheat. But think of the horseshoe. See it in your mind. Think of Galveston here, eight hundred miles from Cuba, seven hundred from Vera Cruz.'

'I see it,' said Smith. 'It is vast.'

'It is not vast,' said Houston. 'It is a bay. It is a beginning. See it not as a gulf but as a bay. Then the lowland prairies and the inland prairies we both know become no more than the surrounds of a bay. Beyond those surrounds is a far greater hinterland.'

He took his gaze from the darkened sea outside the windows, brought his right hand down hard on the map spread out on the table, and held it there.

'See.'

'That,' said Smith, 'is half the continent.'

Sam Houston raised his spread palm from the map and began to trace a direction with his forefinger. From Texas he first moved overland north and west.

The girl came in with a pitcher of water and glasses. Houston was so absorbed he did not see her. She waited.

'But that,' said Smith, 'is just where Lamar will go, where you have condemned him for thinking of going, and where you say he will lose his army. That is Santa Fe.'

'I shall not take it with armies. I shall people it. Santa Anna will then fail to take it back with armies, and in failing lose his armies.'

From Santa Fe, Houston's hand moved south of the Rockies, and the west and north, until he had taken in all the western continent, stretching to the Californias and the Pacific.

'There,' he said, 'under my hand, are the true Halls of Montezuma. I was made to revel in the Halls of Montezuma.' This was no triumphal statement. He said it as matter-of-factly as he then asked the girl to pour him a glass of water. She watched him sip. For the first time since she entered he saw who she was. Tossing back his head, he emptied the glass. She refilled it, gave it back to him, curtseyed – another bob of that bright head – and left.

Smith did not stay much longer. He did not demur at Sam Houston's rehearsal of his destiny. He knew that Sam in his entire life had been changed or influenced by only two human beings. One was Andrew Jackson, Sam's ancient mentor and once president of the United States. The other was his long lost first wife, lost before he ever came to Texas, but remembered and remembered. Smith knew Sam always carried, in a pocket next to his heart, a letter from Jackson when he was president. It had been written when Houston, in the darkest days of his life, had left Tennessee and roamed west and south. Houston had showed this letter to Smith and only to Smith. They had shared a room in the days when Smith was surgeon-general to the Texian army, and often talked long into the night. Smith remembered part of the letter, not word for word but near enough. As he remembered, Jackson wrote:

'When we parted I saw you on the brink of happiness, and rejoiced. You were about to be married to a beautiful young lady of accomplished manners and good family, and of your own selection. You held high elected office and the affections of the people of Tennessee. So you may judge my grief in receiving from you a letter dated Little Rock, Arkansas Territory, saying you were an exile from your country. It has since been communicated to me that you had in mind the illegal enterprise of conquering Texas and setting yourself up as emperor of that country. I really thought you deranged to have such an enterprise in view, particularly when it was to be achieved with the help of the Cherokee Indians. Indeed, Sam, I cannot believe that you have any such chimerical visionary scheme in mind, that would injure your country and tarnish your fame.'

Smith had some of the phrases of the letter by heart. As for the rest, that was the sense of it. Well, the marriage to the lady of good family and accomplished manners had taken place. It had been brief. Because he had lost her, that woman was still in Sam Houston's heart. He had conquered Texas from the Mexicans, though not with the aid of the Cherokees. Texas was a sovereign republic. Houston would soon be president again. And he had, that evening, looking out over the dark bay, revealed the destiny he still pursued.

Most of the revellers were gone, those at any rate who could walk or be helped to walk. From the top of the grand staircase Smith could see, down in the lobby, two members of the Texas senate and the acting attorney general sprawled asleep in leather armchairs. From a distant wing of the hotel came the laughter of men and the protest of women's voices. As he was about to descend the staircase, Smith looked back and saw the shadow of a skirt enter Sam Houston's rooms.

Next morning, towards eleven o'clock, Smith sat on the verandah of the Tremont taking coffee, served by the tall girl of the night before. There were three like her at the hotel, all from Hamburg – the other two neither so tall nor so striking, but all dressed alike in black skirts which revealed their ankles, and all wore wide red waistbands. Smith noticed women. A man who would sell land to buy cherries for his wife would naturally have Smith's admiration. Some years before, when he lived in France, where he studied medicine for a year because the medical schools of Paris had succeeded those of

Edinburgh as the best in the world, he had loved the spirit of French women. He still remembered – and shuddered at the memory as he had shuddered at the time – the occasion when a fellow doctor, a Frenchman, conducting Smith on his morning rounds of the hospital, had drawn back a bedsheet to show the fine form of a young woman as she lay there. She was very fine, but the sensibility of Ashbel Smith, as a man and as a doctor, was offended, because the woman was dying. He had covered her himself, and walked away, not giving a damn for the ridicule of his medical colleagues.

It was Smith who coined the epigram about Texas which *The Galvestonian* had quoted in one of its tri-weekly editions: 'Taxes light, soil fertile, climate delicious, ladies scarce.' Any woman in Texas was soon sought as a wife. No American woman in Galveston would work in a hotel or a bar, so the Tremont hired from among the immigrant girls. Two were French, whom Smith knew well. The three Germans were new to him. The tall one in particular had a lovely gravity. As she leaned across to pour him more coffee, Smith's forehead was within a few inches of the red waistband where it met the girl's white shirt. The crispness of the shirt, its stretched folds where it covered her as she leaned, the warmth of the woman – all moved him.

'What is your name?' he said.

'Helga Becker.'

And at this moment the strong tones of Sam Houston carried from the lobby, where the innkeeper was, as he hoped, making sure of his money by personally presenting the bill. Houston never shouted. He was a man who did not need to raise his voice. But his voice was warm with indignation.

'To five dozen bottles whiskey – seventy-five dollars American,' read Houston. 'To twelve dozen magnums Rheims champagne – three hundred dollars. To four hogshead New Orleans ice, shipped and chopped . . .'

'Excellency,' began the innkeeper, but Houston cut him off: 'I do not dispute that, sir.'

'To breaking one dozen whisky tumblers and fifty-six champagne flutes?'

'Excellency, I can produce the shards.'

Houston glared at the man, laughed, passed that over, and read on, finishing with, 'To breakage of one bedstead etc.'

'What is this "et cetera",' Houston demanded, and, before the unhappy man could attempt an answer, carefully placed the bill on the counter, smoothed out the paper, took a pen and dipped it, and then, while the innkeeper stood by in petrified silence, wrote across it in his bold looping hand, 'The liquor, wine, and ice are admitted. The broken flutes and tumblers also, though excessive. The rest I will never admit, as I am satisfied it is unjust.'

He rode off.

That afternoon at the Tremont, Ashbel Smith met Joe Runyon, the principal fiddler of the night before, who called by appointment. He came to collect his twenty dollar fee for playing, at General Houston's particular request, the tune of 'Come to the Bower' which had, in the eyes of all at the dinner, so clearly taken the general by surprise. Joe was an old political friend and would have done it for nothing, but the general, who knew Joe had four children to feed, insisted on the fee.

This done, Smith took the innkeeper aside, agreed a less extortionate rate for the drink consumed, waved the man's other explanations aside, not wanting to know about other breakages or et ceteras, and paid the rest of the bill in full.

2

Lucy on Lammermuir

In the August of that year, half way the other side of the world, just
north of the border between England and Scotland, Lucy Moncreiffe
and her cousin Richard pursued each other in the ravine of Herriot
Water.

'Courting, do you say?' said her father, when he was indirectly told this over breakfast by Lucy's older sister Sarah. It
was something he perfectly well knew himself. Sarah had only
told him to sound him out and know what was in his mind. So he
sipped his tea and folded his newspaper before he roused himself
to say more. *The Times* of London that he held in his hands was
two days old because Herriot House was two days from London
by the fastest route. For that matter the news of the China war
he had been reading had taken three months to reach London
from Canton. So what hurry was there over another two days, and
what hurry to enquire into the substance of his daughter Sarah's
remark?

But in the end he put his paper down.

'Courting, father,' said his daughter. 'He's in a rage for her
– all the people say it.'

'You're all of seventeen, Sarah?'

'I am.'

'And therefore old and wise? Richard in a rage for her? What of
your sister? Is she in a rage for him? Do the people say that? Has
she said it?'

'I have eyes to see, father, that Lucy is happy with him.'

'And you have sense, I hope, to know she is younger than you. She is what – fifteen . . . ?'

'Sixteen, sir. All the people say they are handfast, and that there will be a wedding before the end of harvest.'

'Sixteen then; and the lad Richard only waiting the offer of a ship to be away?'

It was true. Lady Lucy Moncreiffe – Lady Lucy by courtesy because she was a daughter of the thirteenth Earl of Moncreiffe – was sixteen. Her cousin Richard, who was twenty-two, was a lieutenant in the Royal Navy. He had been for two years on half pay without a ship, and unless he wished his career to end there and then would certainly take the first place that was offered. His cousinship was distant. He too was a Moncreiffe, but from the cadet branch of the family, with no lands or title to his name. Except by luck or his own extraordinary effort he would never have either. He was the third son of a baronet and, both his elder brothers already being married and already having sons, his rank would remain that of esquire all his life. The earl was not a proud man. He knew very well there was no damned merit about his hereditary rank, and that a thirteenth earl of Moncreiffe was unlikely, unless by the Grace of God, to be more able than a thirteenth Mr Brown. At the university a thirteenth Mr Bailey, the son of a crofter, had deprived the earl of the one thing in life he had ever really coveted, the rector's prize for Latin verse. So, as his people said, the earl was neither prydy nor haughty. He stood on no ceremony. But he was proud of his line and of his daughters, and could hardly be unaware that the daughter of a Scottish earldom dating from 1231 was several cuts above a young man who did not even have a claim to his father's baronetcy – and that baronetcy itself, as the earl saw it, a poor recent thing dating no further back than 1685.

'He is a Moncreiffe, father,' said Sarah, 'and a proper man.'

'He is a proper man. I see that. He is also a Moncreiffe, and that, girl, is also to his credit, but half the men on my lands bear that name.'

This was true. The earl was surrounded by kinsmen. His house servants and his steward, his factor and his attorney, his gamekeepers and his shepherds, half of them bore the clan name. He happened to be the head of the clan. He was known and referred to not as the earl, not as his lordship, but as the Moncreiffe.

Still, the earl was proud of his spirited daughters, and if anything prouder of the younger, so he did ask, as he went back to his newspaper, 'Where's Lucy?'

'After her man.'

'This early?'

'Early and late. She is with him by the Water. That is what Jeannie said.' Jeannie was Lucy's maid, who was chaperoning the two cousins.

The earl grunted, reflecting that Jeannie loved her young mistress and would let her come to no harm, and that Richard Moncreiffe was a man who knew his duty, and a devout Christian – too devout for the earl's liking, who was no religious enthusiast – but an honourable Christian man. The earl returned to his newspaper and to China, where it was reported that HMS *Wellesley*, 74 guns, on station in the Pearl River at Canton, was playing havoc with the war-junks of the Heavenly Dynasty.

Herriot Water, except in its highest reaches on the heights of Lammermuir, is no torrent, and where Lucy and Richard walked that morning it flowed almost as slowly as the Pearl, though unlike the Pearl it was transparently clear. The ravine of Herriot Water was nowhere very steep. But Jeannie, though a young woman, only five years older than her mistress, did not want to go scrambling down banks, and muck and mire her frock and her boots. So she remained on the bank above, while Lucy and Richard scrambled down to the river, he finding his footing and then drawing her after him, holding out a strong arm to steady her. They came to a ledge six feet above the water, and stood for a moment. He was a well-made young man, five feet ten inches tall and broad with it, with the blue eyes that go with the reddish curly hair of his kind. He was a Moncreiffe, but his father had taken a Highlander as his wife, and Richard's looks favoured his mother. Lucy was an unmistakable Lowland Scot. Her hair was black and she let it fall round her shoulders. Her eyes were a candid green, and the eyebrows above them dark and distinct. Her

nose was of the sort then called retroussé, which meant it was small
and turned up at the end, and her mouth was wider than was thought
proper by the best portrait painters of the day. Her skin was naturally
pale, but took a touch of brown from the sun. To be brown was not
ladylike either, but often Lucy could not be bothered with her parasol,
and that morning had left it with Jeannie on the bank. Lucy's looks
were not fashionable, but her face would have appealed to Raeburn
– a man who had painted both her late mother and grandmother,
as he had in his time painted half the aristocracy and genius of
Scotland. Lucy was not often called pretty, but there were few who
did not see that she was sometimes beautiful. She was slender and
tall, really no more than five feet five inches, which was taller than
most women, but appearing taller because of her slenderness and
because of a certain carriage of the head.

The two of them stood on the ledge. Before them was a steep
scramble down to the water. 'Go down and help me,' she said. He
did, and she looked down at him and at the water, and then took
off her shoes and tossed them to him. Then, leaning against the
bank, she raised one foot and then the other, and rolled off first
one stocking and then the other. This was necessary if she were
to keep her shoes and stockings dry, but did she know what she
did to the man waiting beneath her? Raising her head after taking
the second stocking from her foot she saw his eyes on her, smiled
down at him, and called out, 'Catch them then.'

She had a bold voice, which carried to Jeannie, who replied
from above to the call.

'Nothing,' replied Lucy, and then, rolling the stockings loosely
into a ball, called to Richard again, 'Here,' and he caught the flimsy
ball tossed down to him and stood with the scented stockings in
his hands. They were warm from her body. All his senses were
bewildered. Then she slid down, more lightly than he had, and he
caught her by the waist. They stood together on the pebble beach,
a foot wide, that was formed by a bend in the river. He held her
and she stood still in his arms. Those who are always chaperoned
soon learn what can be accomplished in an unseen minute.

The air was warm, and his body warm against hers. Her bare

feet were cooled by the Herriot Water as it ran under her soles and between her toes. She separated herself from his arms, and looked down. Both saw that the water lapped at the hem of her cotton dress. He knelt in the water, held her by the ankle, gathered a handful of water in his right hand, sprinkled it over her feet, and kissed them.

'The first-footing is mine,' he said. They both knew what he meant. He was claiming her as his wife. There was a ceremony on the marriage morning when the women friends of the bride washed her feet as she set out for the wedding, as they would later that night undress her and brush her hair, readying her for her husband before they left the two alone. Down by the Herriot Water he was putting her in mind of all this.

The Moncreiffe was right when he said to himself that Richard was an honest man and a Christian. He was more right than he knew when he had slight doubts about Richard's enthusiasm. Young Moncreiffe saw God in everything. Scottish Calvinism had passed the Moncreiffes by, or they had passed it by. The Roman Catholicism of the Stuart kings, or its undeclared remains, still lived among the Moncreiffes. But to Richard not only the communion wine, which was the blood of Christ, was holy, but so were the earth and the sky, and the birds of the air and the flowers of the field, and the trees and their fruit – and so was the body of Lucy.

So it went on through that summer. When he knelt to kiss her feet she was touched, but could not allow him to kneel. She simply could not allow it. She ruffled his hair and raised him to his feet. They scrambled to the top of the bank again, and he held out her shoes for her to step into. Jeannie looked narrowly at his trousers, which were sodden from the knees down, and Lucy laughed. There was no way for Richard to restore her stockings in Jeannie's presence, so he kept and cherished them.

Through the frequent hot days of a Lowland summer, exploring the old locked-up rooms of Herriot house, or in the ruins of an abbey church, he continued his impassioned, chaste pursuit of Lucy, and she pursued him, all in unchaperoned minutes. Once Jeannie, having lost them in a maze of disused rooms, found them in the chamber where a king and queen of Scotland were supposed to have slept one night on a visit three centuries before. It was a room where grey dust-covers had fallen into tatters to reveal more tatters of red velvet upholsterings beneath. Young Moncreiffe was sitting upright in a carved, high-backed chair, gazing at the bed across the room on which Lucy lay alone, with one arm flung across the bed and another covering her eyes. She was asleep. At Sunday morning service in the chapel of Herriot House – a service attended by the steward and the servants but never by the earl, Richard and Lucy sat in the family pew together with only their hands touching – but to them, in their elated state, this touch was everything.

They roamed the moors and the house. In an attic they found the model of a frigate of a century before, a shipwright's model two feet long. The timbers were intact but the rigging had fallen to tatters. He showed her the geography of a ship – the prow, the stern, the fore, main, and mizzen masts, the quarter deck and sterncastle. And as they wandered the moors they learned, in a state of covered chastity, the geography of each other. She had no brothers, but she had lived her life close to the boy and girl children of her father's tenants, and had observed the animals on their farms. She had seen a stallion put to a filly. So one day, as they stood embraced, while he was entranced, it was she who, feeling him hard against her, said, 'Your prow?' He drew away and they walked on.

It was about then that Jeannie took it on herself to remind her betters of the etiquette of the matter, saying bluntly to Richard, 'You'll be asking the Moncreiffe?'

Richard did ask. The Moncreiffe gave his daughter and his blessing. The foy was held, the feast to celebrate a betrothal. The dreaming bread was distributed: the wedding cake cut before the wedding, and a part given to each single woman on the estate, who wrapped it and slept with it under her pillow, and dreamed. The next day was the foot-washing, and the wedding and the vows, and the scatter, where Lucy stood at the church gate in her wedding gown and scattered sweets and coins to be dived and scrambled for by the children of the house and the parish. Then Lucy was put to bed by the women, who withdrew and left her for Richard.

Next morning at first light, as they lay with each other still awake, they heard the clink of the mason's chisel on the door beneath them, through which they had come into the house after the wedding of the day before. When they rose at midday they saw carved in the lintel what they knew they would see – the initials of their names and the year of their marriage, the last in a long list of such dates. Herriot House had seen a hundred foot-washings, beddings, and comings-in through that door. There the inscription was – RM-LM 1840.

Richard had written his bride a letter which he asked her to read on the morning of her wedding day. He wrote: 'I have made a resolution to ask a gift of you, so that I may show to you and to God that, intense though my love is for your body, I love it most deeply as an expression of your soul. And therefore, when we are married, will you consent to remain for a month in my arms a virgin bride? Shall we not then feel, as we lie clasped together, that there is more in store for us, and that what we then feel is only the dim shadow of a union which shall be perfect?'

Only Lucy ever read this letter. Whether she made her husband the gift he asked of her, and remained for a month his virgin bride, cannot be known except indirectly by the awed account of John Moncreiffe, a shepherd, who was walking one evening in the late September of 1840 in the foothills of Lammermuir, two miles from Herriot House.

It was a week after the wedding at the big house. The shepherd was following the track to his cottage. He was hungry and intent on his supper, getting along fast and not looking about him, and would not have seen what he did unless his eye had been attracted by a patch of colour in a shallow glen to his left. It was only thirty yards off as he glanced down. He saw the bare and slender back of a woman lying with a man. It was the glimpse of a moment. He never forgot the slenderness, the arch of the woman's back bare down to her hips, the ripple of the backbone which was clear to see, the shape of the shoulder blades beneath the flesh, and then the arch of the arm as she threw back her head and her dark hair. He did not see the man, whose lower limbs were enclosed by the woman and by the red and green squares of a cloak of the Moncreiffe tartan. This was the colour that had first caught his eye. As if sensing his presence, the woman raised her head and looked the passer-by full in the face. He turned away and moved on home.

As he told his fellow shepherds the next morning, 'She naked from the long neck to the cleft of the body, and the small back moving. There's a fortunate man, and Christ I wish it were me.'

'Gallantish?' said his friend.

'A bold warm-hearted woman,' said the shepherd.

'It was sunset?'

'Sunset and bitter cold, but she made nothing of the cold.'

John knew the woman. He would not say who she was but it was agreed that her boldness, and her making nothing of the bitter cold, made a man proud to be a Moncreiffe. The Moncreiffe who saw it had gone home to his supper and amazed his wife with a zest she had thought long gone.

As for the man with the woman, it was agreed some smaller share of the credit must go to him too, and that he would soon get a child by her.

But by the February of 1841, when Richard Moncreiffe left to join HMS *Calliope*, a twenty gun sloop, as second lieutenant, there was no promise of a child. After he joined *Calliope* at Greenock, Richard wrote to Lucy, looking forward to their reunion, which had to be two years off. 'Then we will go up, and undress and bathe, and kneel down in our night dresses, and then you will extinguish our light and open your arms to me and clasp me, and spread out each limb that I may lie between your breasts all night, and we shall praise God alone in the dark night with His love enclosing us, and our joy made by Him a more perfect delight.'

And she replied, in the last letter he received before he sailed for the India station, 'Yes, yes, all that. And Lammermuir, and your cloak in the heather. So yes, but before you return, I'll be with you now, in your narrow cabin. Look, here I am in our bed at Herriot now, really only a half without you. So I'll think myself with you

now – and you must think it too and that'll make it so. I'm with
you in *Calliope* and your bed is so small we must lie inside each
other – that's what.'

3

Ten Million Acres
of Blue Sky

Alexander Hamilton Treaze laid out his wares on the mahogany centre table in the lobby of the Houston city hotel. Four farmers and a boatswain in the Texian navy gazed down as he opened first one baize-lined case and then the other. Each case held two pistols. He took one pistol from its case, held it balanced on his palm, and exhibited it as an object of beauty, slowly moving his extended arm in an arc so that each man enjoyed a full view of the beautiful weapon he was offering.

'None of you gentlemen will need me to name for him the parts of a pistol. The barrel – four, five, or six inches in length, at your choice. The calibre, thirty-four. But the principle of this pistol is new, and is based, as you will see, on the automatic rotation of a cylinder by means of a pawl on the hammer engaging a ratchet on the cylinder. Five shots in the cylinder, gentlemen, five.'

He waited for this extraordinary information to take its effect. His customers all knew it was a five-shot pistol. That was why they had come to see it. But to see the weapon before them, and hear it talked of before them, was confirmation of all the wonder of the thing.

'The stock,' Mr Treaze continued, 'is of sound black walnut, high grade finish, such as will fit your hand, sir,' – this to a tall farmer – 'as well as you see it fit mine. Take her, sir.' At which he placed the pistol in the large hand of the farmer.

'It is not loaded, sir, but I do not expect you to take my word for that. Break her, sir.'

The farmer did so. The barrel swung forward on its hinge, exhibiting the chamber of the pistol.

'Five chambers, to take five shots. This, gentlemen, is a revolving pistol manufactured by Colt's Patent Fire Arms Company, of Hartford, Connecticut. No better pistols sold anywhere on the globe. In use in all climates, and especially in Texas – and I need give you no greater recommendation than that. As manufactured for officers of the Texian Navy which was, gentlemen, the first military outfit in the world to possess a revolving pistol – before the United States Army itself. As used for two years by the Texas Rangers, whose confidence in the weapon is so unbounded that they habitually face odds of five to one. Patented in the United States, England, Prussia, and France, but more sold these last three years in the Republic of Texas than in the entire world beside.'

It was true. This was the Colt company's standard patter, but it was true. Mr Treaze's territory had been New Jersey and New York. Then he had come south to Louisiana, and still paid frequent visits to New Orleans which remained a big market, but his happiest hunting ground was now Texas. He was familiar in the hotels and bars of Galveston, San Antonio, and the new and much smaller city of Houston. And he knew he had already made a sale. When he put that piece of machined steel in a man's hand with a practised firm smack, as he had put it in the farmer's hand, he knew he had a sale – if the man could pay. Times were hard, harder now in Texas than even in northern states, and he had never known times so hard there. But a man needed a revolving pistol, against Indians, against fellow settlers more lawless than himself, and against Mexicans. Or rather, in reality, more against the constant fear of Mexican incursions than against Mexicans themselves. There were raids, but they were only occasional. But what was constant was the fear. Texas was apprehensive of Mexico.

All three farmers and the sailor handled the gun. All weighed it in their palms. All spun the five-shot chamber. While they were handling the pistol, Mr Treaze kept up his background patter. The great beauty of the weapon, he stated again, was the revolving principle. But there was a second uniqueness to the pistol. This was that the barrel, the cylinder, the hammer, the tumbler, the tumbler spring, were all interchangeable with those of any other Colt pistol – an advantage of machine production unknown to your regular hand-made pistol. And Mr Samuel Colt, he murmured, Mr Colt the inventor, was from the city of Paterson, New Jersey, just across the North River from New York city. Did they know what the principal product of Paterson had been before Mr Colt made his invention? Silk, gentlemen, silk. Which he liked to think accounted in a small way for the silky smoothness of the steel weapon they were at that moment handling.

The big farmer asked the price, the salesman named the great figure of twenty-five dollars, and before anyone had time to demur at this great sum, he was explaining that Paterson, New Jersey, was a city founded by no less a gentleman than Alexander Hamilton, which accounted for his own name, gentlemen, which was Alexander Hamilton Treaze – he, like Mr Samuel Colt, having had the good fortune to be born in Paterson, New Jersey.

But twenty-five dollars was eventually demurred at.

'It is not twenty-five dollars for a pistol,' said Mr Treaze, 'but twenty-five dollars as the price of preserving your life and your children's against the Comanchee, or against Santa Anna. When a man can get off five shots to the murderer's one, then he has five times the chance of life.'

This always went home, not so much because of the danger from murdering Comanchees, since that danger was not immediate and present – though three men had been scalped in Houston city one night the previous winter – but rather because each of the four men standing in the lobby knew that the pistol he already possessed and carried at his waist carried only a single shot. So the beauty of a pistol with five shots in a revolving chamber was a great beauty. And each man had held this wonderful thing in his hands.

Two farmers drifted off. They did not have twenty-five dollars in any form, or anything near it, and a good ordinary pistol could be bought for ten. The first farmer and the sailor remained. Mr Treaze reminded them that another great Samuel, Sam Houston, had proved the efficacy of Samuel Colt's revolving pistol. Mr Colt

had made him the present of a pair, which he had tried out against a
mark pinned to a tree at twenty yards, and had said they were better
than any he ever had, and the best weapon in the world.

The farmer and the sailor hesitated. The sailor asked to handle
a pistol from the second case.

'The blued steel?' asked the salesman, and then handed over
a blued pistol, removing it carefully from its box, this time not
smacking it into the man's hand but holding it out in his two palms
to be taken like something precious. The sailor broke the pistol, spun
the chamber, closed the pistol, aimed it at the ceiling and then out of
the window, taking a bead on the head of a dummy swinging in the
breeze outside a tailor's shop. Then he offered twenty dollars, not a
cent more. Mr Treaze smiled, shook his head slowly, and declined
with expressions of great regret. He then replaced the two pistols in
their cases, closing the lid of the blued pistol with finality.

'Twenty-five then,' said the sailor, 'but for the blued one, mind;
and not a cent more.' Mr Treaze hesitated, weighed up the offer,
looked narrowly at the sailor as if admiring a man who knew how to
make his way in the world, and then, after this agreeable sideshow,
accepted with a firm handshake.

The sailor then offered Texian redbacks, laying on the table
bills printed on one side of government paper with the back left
plain red.

This broke the deal. Mr Treaze regretted, but the redback
had been worth only fifteen United States cents the year before,
and was now down to three.

The sailor, who perfectly well knew this, offered exchequers
instead.

Mr Treaze was willing to inspect these. They were also bills
drawn on the government of Texas, but paying interest at ten
per cent a year, and, because there were fewer of them, much
less reduced in value.

'See,' said Mr Treaze, 'your redback is a hussy.' He demonstrated
that the three dollar redback carried the engraved portrayal not only
of a steamship but, in the middle foreground, of a woman with her
left breast bare.

'And your fifty,' he said, taking such a bill from a pocket where he kept it for this purpose, 'has a woman bare as to both breasts, and bare altogether, the full length of her, except for a wisp of mist in the middle.'

But the exchequers, as he pointed out, were engraved with chaster women, altogether clothed, the ten dollar woman resting on a Roman pillar, and the twenty bearing a shield with the Lone Star of Texas on it. He would take the exchequers, but at fifty per cent of their face value. Fifty Texian dollars in exchequer bills for twenty-five dollars US.

It was done. The sailor happily carried off the blued Colt whose full asking price, as it happened, was precisely the same as that of its grey-steel companion – twenty-five dollars US. After a drink Mr Treaze sold a grey Colt to the farmer for twenty-two dollars US, made up of ten discounted Texian exchequers, two American silver dollars, and an assortment of French francs and Mexican and Spanish silver coins also heavily discounted in the salesman's favour.

The farmer went back that night to his wife near San Antonio, and to his farmstead which had three months before been looted by Mexican skirmishers. But he and his neighbours were better armed and prepared now. The Mexicans would not get away so easily a second time. So he was going home to plant more corn. The farmer had a second reason to induce him to recover his strength, to arm himself and to retrench. His wife's brother was one of the few who had escaped from the Texian expedition sent by Lamar to Santa Fe, sent by Lamar who had been confident his men would be welcomed as saviours, who had not dreamed they would be opposed not only by Mexican soldiers but by the civilian inhabitants, and who, above all, had not foreseen that in a desert his men would die for want of water. Lamar had expected his expedition to bring back silver, gold, and furs. Instead he lost five companies of infantry and one of artillery, three hundred and twenty men in all, and twenty-one ox wagons.

The night the farmer returned home with his new Colt, Sam Houston, whose name had helped sell the Colt, was trying to get both his private secretary and the Texian Congress to see sense. He was having a hard time of it.

'Sir,' said the young Mr Washington Miller, 'as I see it a great drama is in progress.'

Sam Houston was in a mood that night not for drama but for prudence. But since he had dictated to Mr Miller only a few weeks before a letter in which he told Santa Anna that before the Mexican banner should ever again float over any part of Texas, the Texian Lone Star would display its bright folds over the isthmus of Darien, he allowed Mr Miller to continue for a bit. Mr Miller's thesis was that the first act of the drama had been the seizure by the thirteen colonies of their independence from England; that the second had been the seizure by Texas of its independence from Mexico; and that the third would be the conquest of Mexico itself.

Houston sat back and said nothing.

'General, I am not raving, I am in earnest.'

'The more raving for being earnest, Mr Miller. If I had four or five thousand disciplined men . . .'

'The Congress offers you fifty thousand.'

'Disciplined, Miller, disciplined. I said disciplined men. The Congress passes a law enabling me to place myself at the head of the Texian army in the field. What army?'

'Sir, Congress gives you power to conscript a third of the male population.'

'Dreams, Miller. A chimera. How do you conscript one third of all the men? Would they come if you called? Suppose they came, could you feed them? Suppose you fed them, could you arm them? Suppose you armed them, where would you lead them? March them to the city of Mexico – and what then? What state would their boots be in then? What state are their boots in now? How could men with naked feet talk about marching to Monterey and the city of Mexico? It is all done by *thinking*. Lamar *thought* he could take Santa Fe. Congress *thinks* it can take the city of Mexico. It is thought of the same quality.'

Mr Miller desisted for a while, and suggested to his chief a glass of whisky. Houston declined.

'Cold water doin's these days, sir?' asked Miller cheerfully, and was silenced by a glare. Sam Houston had not taken strong liquor since he married his new wife Margaret the year before. The whisky was there for his guests. The general let himself be ruled by Margaret's temperance convictions, but sometimes found it hard to be ruled.

Miller continued with the assured insensitivity of youth. 'Mr Van Zandt says in the House that foreign capitalists would be eager to buy millions of acres of land to pay for the war . . . '

'I thought I knew Van Zandt, and now he promises me what he calls a field for glory which has no parallel since Napoleon crossed the Alps. And others agree with him. Does Mr Van Zandt recall what happened to Napoleon? Do those others? Does the Congress know what it is doing when it happily legislates itself into the possession of the whole of New Mexico, just like that – when Lamar could not even take Santa Fe? Does Congress know what it is doing when it appropriates to itself half the rest of all Mexican territory besides, everything south and west of the Rocky mountains? More conquest by profound thinking? Conquest with a pen? A congressional joke, I take it?'

'No, sir.'

'No sir indeed. Congress, like you, is the crazier for being in earnest. To think I would entertain it, Congress must think me as snarlish mad as a half-starved dog. Let us wait, Miller, wait. All things will come. Let us nourish ourselves. Then let Santa Anna come to us. Then we shall see about the third act of your drama.'

'General . . . '

'Enough. You will now draft my message to Congress vetoing that bill. You will say that I, as Executive, am opposed to any dictatorial powers being conferred on any person such as are proposed to be conferred on me. You will mention to the Congress what I have just told you about boots and bare feet. You will say the land they propose to sell at such a vast profit would be unsaleable at any decent price if all offered at once. You will say the whole proposal is unconstitutional anyway. I do not know whether it is, but neither does the Congress. And you will end with this remark, word for word. "The entire bill, gentlemen, is a resolution to appropriate ten million acres of blue sky, and conferring dictatorial powers on the north wind." Do you have all that?'

'Yes, sir,' said the miserable Miller. 'Why north wind?'

'Miller,' said Sam Houston, 'get on with it. Let me see it in an hour, so that Congress shall have it tomorrow.'

Congress received the veto message. Congress debated. Citizens eager for easy conquest presented themselves in a mass before Sam Houston's porch. He heard them out and then gazed at them in silence. What, said the chief spokesman, were the general's orders, now that he knew the true spirit of the people? What should they do? Houston spoke four words: 'Go home. Plant corn.'

What Sam Houston was doing was watched far off. When he heard the news, Andrew Jackson, once president of the United States and more than any other man Houston's instructor and protector, wrote from his retirement in Tennessee: 'I hope your Congress had not the design, in passing that bill, to disgrace you, regardless of the injury an offensive war would entail upon the Republic, if it didn't destroy it by making Texas an easy conquest for Santa Anna, after all your resources were consumed. By your veto you have saved your country, and yourself from disgrace. Stand on the Defensive.'

So Sam was prudent. He did not invade Mexico. And he patched up the quarrel with the Indians, which Lamar had made so bitter. The Comanchees you could do little with. He knew that. But he had spent three years of his life with the Cherokees, and they trusted him. He appropriated five hundred dollars from the Republic's treasury, to be spent on gifts for the Cherokees, from their brother Sam Houston. It was politic. Besides, his years with the Cherokees had entered his soul. Could he trust Mexico? He could not. Could he trust his own Congress? He could not. But, as he frequently said, he knew of no Cherokee yet who had ever broken his word to Sam Houston.

4

Woodshavings
and Christian Powers

By that autumn Sam Houston was on the defensive for sure.
More Mexican raids had forced him to move his capital eastwards
from Houston city to Washington-on-the-Brazos, which was a city of
thirty run-down shacks. It was there, on a darkening evening in early
September, that one stranger asked another stranger where lodgings
were to be had, and in this way the representatives of two powers
made each other's acquaintance.

'A set of rooms, you say?' said the American, a small, wizened
man in his late fifties, about whom the only brightness was that
of his intelligent eyes. 'Well now, sir, the senators sleep on the floor
of the senate chamber, which is over the grocery.' He indicated a
shack to their left, from which came the steady buzz of conversation,
drinking, and gambling. That shanty, like all others in the settlement,
was picked out by lines of light where the illumination of oil lamps
within shone through unplugged cracks in the unseasoned timber
walls.

'Ah,' said the enquirer, a middling-tall man of about forty in a
blue coat and floppy white hat. He slapped at a mosquito feeding
on his cheek.

'Yes, sir. The senate itself, in full session, in the exercise of its own
senatorial prerogative you might say, arrogated to its own members
the use of the chamber floor. They bring their own blankets, you
understand. You have a blanket, sir?'

'No.'

'Neither had I, when I first came. You are British, sir, from
the sound of your voice?'

'I am.'

'And I from Kentucky. And the House of Representatives, sir, appropriates to itself a bar-room over Hatfield's gambling saloon.' He gestured towards another source of noise, bustle, and light.

Then he pointed out another log hut as the department of war, and then another which used to be the carpenter's shop but was now the department of state. Through the timbers of each building the same cracks of light appeared.

'An abundance of government,' said the newcomer. 'But no hotel?'

The American laughed. 'No hotel. No set of rooms. No room of any description. What is your line of business, sir?'

'I am Captain Elliot, of the Royal Navy.'

'Then I know you by reputation, sir. And I am Judge Eve.' The little judge seized the captain's hand and shook it with honest warmth. The captain was once again struck, as he had often been struck in the weeks since he first landed at New Orleans and then made his way first to Galveston and then up the Brazos valley to the city of Washington-on-the-Brazos, by the endless inquisitiveness and endless generosity of the Americans and Texians he met.

'And now, Captain,' said the judge, 'I have no set of rooms to offer, but I do have a shed which will be as commodious for two as for one, and I shall be happy to share it.'

In this way Charles Elliot, a post captain in the navy of Her Britannic Majesty Queen Victoria and British chargé d'affaires to the Republic of Texas, met Judge Joseph Eve, late of the Kentucky House of Representatives and then, because he had campaigned for the right candidate in the American presidential elections of 1840 and was owed a political favour, United States chargé d'affaires to the same Texian republic. They stood together on a dirt track, defending themselves as best they could from midges and mosquitoes, on the edge of a group of shacks called a city, which was the capital of the Republic to which both were accredited.

Elliot's horse was stabled, Elliot and Eve dined and drank together at Hatfield's, and then both retired to the judge's shed and lay down in their day clothes on the judge's commodious mattress of wood shavings. They conversed by the light of a tallow candle. Elliot smoked his pipe, which kept the insects away but at one point very nearly set fire to the wood shavings. Eve coughed but did not complain of the tobacco smoke, which was good of him because his lungs were weak and easily irritated. This was one reason why he had been sent to Texas, where the climate was thought, by northern politicians who knew nothing of it, to be as mild as Italy's.

Eve confessed to the political favour he had been owed, but then, he said, other men were owed as much and more. He was overwhelmed by what he regarded as his good fortune.

'Fact is,' he said, 'I've never had anything to do with diplomacy. Don't know the slightest thing about it. Don't know what I'm supposed to do here. I've been a military man. I've been a judge. And you're a naval man. And we're both here.'

Elliot puffed at his pipe. A naval man, Eve called him. He held his post captain's commission, and if he lived long enough would become an admiral by right of seniority, even if he never saw another ship. It was already twelve years since his last command, and he had spent those years as a servant of the foreign office. Still, he was happy to be considered a naval man. And he admired his companion's frank innocence. He had not commonly known diplomats to be so plain spoken. He would have admired Eve the more if he had known that when the judge first exclaimed he knew him, it was because of the entertaining abuse of Elliot which the American papers had reprinted from *The Times* of London. *The Times* had damned Elliot's appointment as rank rotten, called him a bungler unfit to run a respectable apple stall, accused him of an uninterrupted series of diplomatic fooleries in his previous career, remarked by the way that he was out of his mind, and said that a new nation like Texas deserved better than to be sent a lunatic whose talents, if he ran true to form, could be relied upon to spoil everything for a good half century to come. Eve had read all this, and thought little of it. The tone was familiar to him. As a colonel, as a judge, as a member of the Kentucky House of Representatives, and on his own appointment to Texas, he had been praised in similar terms.

Not that *The Times*'s opinions had much bothered Elliot either.

What really had stung was the prime minister getting up in the House of Commons and declaring that he knew nothing to show that full confidence might not be reposed in Captain Elliot's integrity and ability. This was, said the prime minister, a spontaneous intimation on his part. He knew as he said this, and Elliot knew, that it was not the truth, and that the statement was made in answer to all sorts of spontaneous abuse of Elliot, not only in *The Times* but in and around the House.

In his shed, Judge Eve went on: 'You see, my wife was ill, and she wanted to come to Texas for the sake of her health. She'll be coming on later, and I'll meet her in Galveston. So some relative of hers in Washington arranged to give me this post. It lets us travel in some comfort. Lets us live in some comfort, you see?'

Elliot thought of the grim journey from Galveston to Washington-on-the-Brazos and wondered what Eve would call discomfort.

'Where were you before this?' asked Eve. 'I did read of it, but can't rightly recall.'

'China,' said Elliot. He had indeed been British plenipotentiary in China. He had taken the island of Hong Kong for the Crown, and represented it as a jewel of empire, only to be told by a furious foreign office that he had taken a barren, useless rock.

'See, I'm not at all unhappy with my appointment,' said Eve. 'Not so far. But if some real difficulties came up I don't know I should be able to handle them. Then I guess I should have to say it was my friend the president of the United States' fault, because he'd be to blame, having made me a diplomat without consulting me. Without even consulting me. I just came home one night and my wife had a letter for me making it so.'

Elliot was not a self-deluding man. But it had never before occurred to him to admit to himself, let alone to a stranger, that he owed his successive preferments to the connections of his family, whose members had filled the offices, among many others, of secretary to the Admiralty and governor general of India. He had been born in a palace in Dresden where his father was British minister. He knew his family possessed what was called 'interest', influence in high places, and had accepted what this interest brought him.

But here was the innocent and good-natured Eve freely admitting he had got where he was through a bit of political patronage. And listening to him, Elliot reflected briefly, and for the first time, on the probable reasons for his own appointments.

'Now as to Sam . . . ' said Eve, and he talked well into the night about General Houston, whom he had known for twenty years, speaking of the general's dashing days, and of the general's character now reformed by the refined influence of a new and Christian wife. 'There were plenty,' said Eve, 'who did not give the marriage six months. Well, more than two years now, and not a restive murmur from Sam, not that I've heard.' He finished with the advice to his colleague and rival that the best time to see President Houston was the morning.

'Best in the morning. And earlier now than you'd ever have seen him up and sober in the old days.'

So at nine o'clock next morning, Captain Elliot sent a message to the presidential mansion asking leave to present his credentials. He received an immediate reply that the president would receive him, without ceremony, at any time he chose.

Elliot asked the president's messenger what time would best suit the general, and received in return a shrug.

Eve, overhearing this, simply said, 'Any time. You'll find him now.'

Elliot had not been able to bring all his baggage on from Galveston. His large trunk remained there. He did not have with him the laced and frogged court dress in which he would normally have presented himself, or the plumed head-dress. He made do, and it was in the mere dress uniform of a post captain, with two gold epaulettes and his old-fashioned bicorn hat, that he appeared at the door of the mansion. The black boy at the door stared at this apparition and jerked a thumb round the back of the one-storey building. Elliot walked round in the mud and found a man shaving on the verandah. He enquired again for the president. The man stood upright with the razor in his hand and lather still on his face. He was six feet four inches tall, and he was undoubtedly Sam Houston.

The accustomed ceremony of a lifetime does not easily desert a man, even in circumstances where it is absurd, so Elliot saluted,

removed his hat, and held out the papers which were his credentials.
Houston put down the razor, wiped the lather from his face, and
gravely, in shirtsleeves, received the offered papers and put them
aside.

'Leave that to Jones.'

'Jones?'

'Dr Jones, my secretary of state.' Then Houston apologised for the
lack of any decent place for Her Britannic Majesty's representative to
stay. Washington-on-the-Brazos had been the capital for only a month
or so. Captain Elliot would see that the presidential mansion was a
makeshift. A verandah. Two rooms, one his office, the other his and
his wife's bedroom. And a dog-run.

'A dog-run?' asked Elliot.

'A dog-run between those two rooms, from front to back of the
house. A door at the front and a door at the back, and the passage
between left open to the air, so we catch any breeze that's going.
And, I suppose, so a dog may run through if he pleases.'

Houston indicated a bench, and they both sat.

'Mr Addington,' said Elliot, remembering a message he had
been instructed to give, 'asks to be remembered to you.'

'Addington,' said Houston thoughtfully.

'He is now at the foreign office in London, but was once
at our Washington legation. Remembers happy times, and asks . . . '

'Addington,' said Houston, suddenly recalling the name, suddenly
all animation. 'Oh, many times. Many nights together on the town.
Oh, larks! Many years ago.'

And he told the tale of nights twenty years before when he
was a young congressman from Tennessee and Addington was a
secretary with the British mission. 'Late theatres, late suppers, dark
nights warm all night until dawn. Larks.'

And all the while the president of Texas, in shirtsleeves, and
the chargé d'affaires of the greatest power on earth, in the uniform
of a naval captain, talked small-talk and regarded each other with a
most wary respect. At a first meeting, neither would touch on any
matter of consequence. Both knew that. Houston well understood
that Great Britain's recognition of the sovereignty of Texas would

give him more weight in any dealings with the United States. And Elliot knew that an independent Texas – independent above all from the United States – would be a source of abundant cotton, cotton free from American tariffs. And, though he had never been plainly told as much, he knew there was more than cotton to it. An independent Texas was for England a convenient check to the inconvenient territorial ambitions of the United States. So he knew Texas was not the derisory posting the world thought it must be for a diplomat. It was not China. He had not advanced his career by his course in China. Texas was no promotion. But he remembered that the foreign secretary, Lord Aberdeen, had seen him before he left London, as he bothered to see few men going to serve abroad. He had said nothing much, only this: 'I asked to be shown everything we had on Texas. We had a few scraps of paper. So you see, Elliot, it's not so much what Texas is as what it becomes. I'd rather it did not fall to America. Good morning.' And for Sam Houston, whichever way Texas went and whichever way Sam Houston went, much might depend on the good offices of Great Britain – or might not.

So he made small-talk with cordiality, apologising again for the savage state of the place and the lack of any lodgings fit for a gentleman. They would mend this. In the meantime Captain Elliot was staying with Judge Eve? They would have much to talk about, the two diplomats. Now the Frenchman, Saligny, said Houston, had not yet presented himself at the new capital, and was probably at this moment in New Orleans, which he unaccountably seemed to prefer to any Texian city. But Eve was good company. He had known Joe Eve, oh, as far back as he had known Addington. Would Captain Elliot convey his regards to Mr Addington?

Elliot took his leave and returned to Judge Eve with a peculiar request. He had with him, for the greater security of his correspondence with London and with Her Majesty's ministers at Washington and Mexico City, a cypher and a decypher. These papers he was to carry on his person where this was possible and prudent. At other times he was to deposit the same in a case provided. His written instructions called this an oak case, but the word 'oak' was crossed out and 'tin' substituted, the foreign office having run out of oak containers. He had had oak in China. But at any rate this box, for the greater security of its contents, came with 'an apparatus' for screwing it to the wall or floor of the apartment in which it might for the time being be placed.

Now this was awkward because Judge Eve, as American chargé d'affaires, was in every way Elliot's rival in Texas. The interests of their governments were bound to conflict. But Elliot asked if a corner might be found where he could screw down this strong box, tin not oak, to contain his small valuables – his watch, his exequatur from the Texian government when it arrived, the document which would request all Texian citizens to allow him to carry out his functions as chargé d'affaires and consul general. Elliot said nothing about the cypher. Eve made light of the request, smiling at the extravagance of the box when Elliot smiled, and a corner was found to screw it down. They screwed it down together. Eve at once wrote to tell his own government. Elliot for his part always carried the cypher upon him. The box remained screwed to the rough floorboards of the two diplomats' commodious shed, as a reminder to them both of the secret nature of their honourable calling.

Elliot heartily wished to get away from Washington-on-the-Brazos, back to the relative comfort of Galveston, but while Sam Houston stayed on the Brazos so did he. It was his duty to get to know the man. He could not avoid hearing the talk. Everyone talked of Sam here as everyone in Galveston had talked of him. But Elliot also observed the president, watching him at the races which were one of the few diversions the town had to offer, and taking tea with the president's wife. Her name was Margaret. He wondered that so timid and pious a woman could subdue so vital a man, but he saw that she did. Elliot sat at her tea parties and observed Sam Houston sitting silently with a tiny porcelain teacup poised in his great hand. Margaret sat with her needlework, or played the guitar. General Houston talked of procuring an ox-cart to bring her piano over from Houston city.

By an oil lamp, Elliot encrypted a despatch to Addington in London. He said he had given Mr Addington's good wishes to

Sam Houston, whose life, he was bound to say, from all he had heard from many sources, had for long intervals been strange and wild. 'Habitual drunkenness;' he wrote, 'a residence of several years among the Cherokee Indians, begetting sons and daughters; and then a sudden reappearance on this Texian stage with better hopes and purposes, but still with unreclaimed habits. Finally, however, a new connection with a young and gentle woman brought up in fear of God, she having been conquered no doubt by his glowing tongue but in good revenge making conquest of his habits of tremendous cursing, and passionate love of drink.'

Elliot paused in his composition. All true, he reflected, all true; and yet. And so he continued, conveying to his masters at the foreign office the other side of General Houston, going on to give a picture of a man who was more than a lapsed libertine and more than a tamed husband. 'Nevertheless, whatever he has been, it is plain that he is the fittest man in the country for his present station. His education has been imperfect but he possesses great sagacity and penetration, surprising tact in the management of men trained as men are in these parts, and is perfectly pure handed and moved in the main by the inspiring motive of desiring to connect his name with a nation's rise. And as to these strange Texian people, they jolt and jar terrifically in their progress, but on they do get, and many of them prosper too, under circumstances when our people would starve and die.'

It was late in September that the bad news came. Judge Eve had left for Galveston to meet his wife, Margaret Houston had gone further east to stay with friends, and an intimacy had grown up between president and chargé d'affaires. They sat on the verandah of the shanty of the nation's capitol, the president whittling away at an ash stick and Elliot talking about the sea. Elliot loved the sea, and Houston loved to hear talk of places he had never been. Elliot was embarked on the tale of his first command, in the Caribbean. She was a little schooner, he a lieutenant, the ocean off Guadaloupe whipped up in a gale. . . But he never reached the climax of his story because four dirty men riding exhausted horses galloped up to Sam Houston. San Antonio had been raided again, this time not by skirmishers but by a Mexican army of a thousand men under a French mercenary general. The Mexican artillery was said to have fired on a white flag. Mexican troops had marched up to the courthouse, and arrested judge, jury, witnesses and all. Then they had held the city for nine days.

While Elliot was still with Sam Houston, while the dust from the riders had not yet settled, a mob assembled in front of the presidential verandah. One man yelled: 'Truth is, you are afeared to do anything, you damn drunk old Cherokee.'

The man was drunk himself. Houston glared. But the mob laughed. The country was aflame for revenge. This time Houston knew he had to send men in pursuit. He chose as commander Brigadier General Somervell of the Texas militia whom he had known for ten years, and who had served in the Texas senate. He was an officer who would do nothing wild. But still Houston had to send two regiments, seven hundred men, when he knew he could spare none.

Elliot encrypted more despatches. For two weeks he did not see the president. Then he received a summons to attend General Houston, the first he had ever received. This was no casual invitation, brought over by a black boy, to stroll over and take tea. This time the secretary of state sent a colonel of militia to demand Captain Elliot's presence in an hour's time.

Elliot went. He had mistaken his man again. This time the formality was all the other way. Captain Elliot presented himself in his plain blue coat and floppy white hat. He was ushered into the presence of President Houston who, for the first time in Elliot's experience, was wearing the full uniform of a major general of the Texian army, with sword at his waist and lace ruffles at the neck and wrists. Houston stood by his desk, silent. Elliot stood facing him. The president did not ask him to sit. Nor did he sit himself.

Elliot waited.

Houston began, speaking as if he had rehearsed the form of words. He requested and required the intervention of Great Britain, as a Christian power, not against Mexico but against the savage inhumanity of the Mexican attacks, which were directed not against the Texian army but against the civilian men, and the women, and the children of Texas.

Elliot thought himself as well informed as Houston about the course of the French general's army. He knew of nothing atrocious in that officer's conduct of the raid on San Antonio. But he listened. When Houston fell silent, Elliot began the formal recitation of an assurance that he would acquaint Her Britannic Majesty's foreign secretary with the president's request.

Houston cut him off and began to pace the room.

'My friend,' he said, 'you will have heard much talk of the annexation of Texas to the United States?'

Elliot said he had. Judge Eve had candidly laid bare to Elliot his conviction that Texas would be better off all round if she were sheltered under the eagle's wing of the United States.

'Now,' said Houston, 'a good half of those I converse with are in favour of the measure. And nine tenths of those who favour it, do so on the grounds that it would give us peace. Mexico would not send a French general to attack the United States. So, if Texas were a constituent state of those United States . . . You follow me?'

Elliot assented.

'Then,' said Houston, 'on this point of our national existence I feel well satisfied that England has the power to rule.'

Elliot bowed.

Sam Houston threw himself into a chair in exasperation, half rose again to unbuckle his swordbelt, placed it on the table, sat again, looked up at Elliot, and motioned him to sit. Then Houston sat back with the smile Elliot had often seen in their brief acquaintance. 'Friend,' he said softly, 'to defeat this policy – this policy of annexation – and to bring peace to Texas, it is only necessary for Lord Aberdeen to say to Santa Anna, "Sir, Mexico must recognise the independence of Texas." Like that. Santa Anna would be glad of such a pretext. He cannot now, for the sake of Mexico's pride, let Texas go. He must maintain a claim to Texas which he does not want to maintain. It costs him too much in treasure. He has other uses for that treasure. No doubt he has his own personal uses for it. But given that pretext, having heard those words from Aberdeen, he could then say to the Mexicans, "You see how I am situated. I cannot go to war with England, our last friend. Let Texas go."'

Houston paused, but had evidently not finished. Elliot waited.

'In all these matters,' said the president, 'I may be mistaken. But I am honest in my convictions that Texas and England would both be benefited by this course. Time will tell the tale.'

Houston sat back and spread out his arms with the open palms towards Elliot. Elliot smiled. He remembered writing in an early despatch to England of Houston's glowing tongue when it came to winning himself a wife. Now he heard Houston speak in the same tongue, in another cause.

'Lord Aberdeen,' Houston repeated slowly, 'need only say to Santa Anna . . . ' He rose, moved over to Captain Elliot, put an arm round his shoulder, and left the rest unspoken.

They parted. Elliot wrote more despatches. Houston went straight to the office of his secretary of state, where Jones had before him a draft of the first, formal part of the speech that Houston had made to Elliot. 'Date it this day,' said Sam Houston. 'Date it as from Washington-on-the-Brazos, and direct it to the department of state at Washington-on-the-Potomac. Write that out in full.'

Jones did so. And thus the government at Washington-on-the-Potomac, as well as that in London, was appealed to as that of a Christian power, and asked to intervene not against the Republic of Mexico as such but rather against the savage inhumanity of the Mexican attacks on Texian civilians, women and children.

5

Grey Ghosts and
the House of Godoy

One morning in the late spring of the following year, in London, a light carriage turned into a street of modest houses of the early eighteenth century, and came to a halt. It was an ordinary street, like a hundred others in London, a street of four storey brick houses with white painted sash windows set in red brick facades. That morning workmen were patching the brickwork on two houses on the northern side of the street, and that also was ordinary, because the houses were already one hundred and fifty years old and had been shoddily built in the first place. It was Downing Street, where, just along from establishments which were boarding houses – boarding houses for gentlemen but boarding houses nevertheless – the prime minister of Great Britain had his residence. Other houses in the street, having been brought up from time to time by the Crown, accommodated the Treasury, the Colonial Office, and the Foreign Office. In such a street lived the ministers of the greatest power on earth, and from there they exercised their vast authority.

A maid got down from the carriage first, and then a lady in a grey silk dress. It was a very English spring day. Occasional shafts of sunlight penetrated the clouds and illuminated the intermittent light rain, which was so light that for most of the time it was no more than a fine mist whose droplets shone when they were caught in the odd ray of sun. The maid was urging her mistress inside out of the rain, but she shook her head and stood looking up and down the street. She had not been there before. The sun, coming out again, caught the grey silk of her skirt and made it shine. Then the sun went in and the sheen disappeared, leaving the dress plain grey again. The lady was in mourning, not the full mourning of unrelieved black paramatta wool and unrelieved black crape but the half mourning of grey silk and purple crape which was permitted a widow after eighteen months. At her throat she wore a pendant of jet on a silver chain. Two doors away the bricklayers on their ladders stopped work and looked down at her. A young man, catching her eye as she looked up at the fitful sun, touched his cap. She smiled at him.

'Ma'am,' insisted the maid, who was waiting at the open door.

The lady entered the house almost at the same instant that an old gentleman, who had been told of her arrival, came into the hall to greet her. She ran across to him, called him uncle, and kissed him. He was George, fourth earl of Aberdeen. The house she had entered was the Foreign Office. Lord Aberdeen was Her Majesty's principal secretary of state for foreign affairs, the Aberdeen to whom Sam Houston had addressed his appeal as to the representative of one of the Christian powers of the world.

He had known her since she was a girl. He still saw her as a girl, and she was. She had been married and widowed, and was still barely eighteen. He was not her uncle but her great uncle. And she was Lucy Moncreiffe, in mourning for her husband Richard, who met his death only a month after arriving in the far east.

They did not speak about that. Her great uncle had commiserated with her in her grief, but that was something which no longer darkened quite every moment of her day for her. She was recovering her spirit.

'Lucy,' he said, when they were seated in his room, 'that cherry we planted by the southern wall. Remember?'

'Five years ago?' she said.

'Or six.'

She remembered. She had been a girl in short frocks. They planted a cherry tree by a wall where it would get all the sun that her great uncle's Scottish estate could offer. It was too far north for a cherry to flourish, but they planted it in hope. They planted it together, as they had planted a hundred other trees. He had taught her how. Aberdeen's second passion, after archaeology, was the forestation of Scotland. His friends said he and his foresters had planted fourteen million trees. It was not a figure capable of proof, but no one who knew the earl disbelieved it. If he did a thing he did it well. His friends said, 'Ask him to go a mile with you and he'll go two.' As a young man he had found only limes and Scottish firs on his lands. He had planted oak, cedar, walnut – even, in a glasshouse, eucalypt from New South Wales. Lucy remembered the cherry. They had planted it together. He held the sapling upright while she arranged the roots as he had often shown her – ensuring that the stronger roots lay facing the direction from which the wind would come, and then packing the earth in around them with her fingers.

'I remember,' she said.

'It flowered. So far north, it flowered. There will be fruit from it yet.'

'Yes.'

But Lucy's answer showed the earl – who was sensitive to the changing states of a woman's heart: had been to his late wife's sensibilities and now was to Lucy's – that talk of planting trees in hope, and of flowering, brought back to her the memory of her husband as surely as if he had spoken Richard's name. He was right in his instinctive feeling. She saw herself at that moment as two girls – one girl, the younger, kneeling to bed the seedling in the soft earth, the other, three or four years older, raising a man, who was going to be her husband, who knelt to her by the Herriot Water.

So, the earl told himself, no more talk of trees. A moment's silence lay between them.

'Grand tour, Lucy?' he said.

'Oh yes,' she said, sitting up straighter, then leaning towards him as she spoke, telling him more fully what she had mentioned in her letter of a few days before, when she reached London from Scotland, that she and three friends were proposing to embark on a grand tour. There was her friend Adelaide, with whom she had practically grown up, a neighbour's daughter who had married a tea merchant from Bristol. Twining by name. He was a man who had always travelled a lot. Less since he married Adelaide. But he was now determined to show her the world. They would be accompanied by Twining's unmarried brother, who was a good amateur yachtsman. They wanted Lucy to go with them too.

Aberdeen approved.

'It will revive the spirit,' he said. He rose to his feet, went to the window and looked out over Horseguards Parade. In his mind he saw the great cities of Europe he had known so well as a young man – Paris, Berlin, Vienna, Florence, Rome, Naples, Athens. He knew Lucy had several times visited Paris and had once, the year before her marriage, spent some months in Italy with her father and sisters.

'Lucy,' he said. 'See Athens. More than any other city I have always remembered Athens. "Athenian Aberdeen", I have been called.'

She smiled. She knew it well.

'But I have no Greek,' she said.

'Oh, there are no longer any Greeks. There are those who now live in Greece, but they are not the Greeks we know about. Those Greeks are long gone, but Ancient Greece lives on.'

'In its ruins?'

'More than ruins, Lucy. In spirit. No one will ever explain it to you. I cannot explain it to you. It is something you must feel for yourself. Then you will know.'

'We are thinking,' she said, 'of the Gulf. The Twinings wish to go yachting in the Gulf.'

'The Gulf?'

'Of Mexico. By steamship to Jamaica and then to New Orleans, and then yachting in the Gulf. We shall go to Texas and Mexico.'

Aberdeen turned from the window and looked at his great niece. He saw she was determined on new worlds, and knew better than to oppose her. He could only warn where a warning might help. But the nearest he had come to America was forty years before, when he had declined a posting to the mission in Washington because his wife was ill. He knew no more about the United States, Texas, or Mexico than his agents told him in their despatches. On his understanding of that information he founded the whole foreign policy of Her Majesty's government towards those countries, and he knew very well how slight that understanding was. Hadn't he just told Lucy that she could not understand the Athenian spirit until she saw Athens? The Gulf. What did he know of the Gulf?

He rang the bell, and told the footman to find Mr Addington, who had at least once served in Washington.

Addington listened while Lucy repeated the itinerary of her grand tour.

'Forgive me, Lady Lucy, but is all this wise? I mean Texas and Mexico. We have for the moment brokered a truce between those two nations. How long it will last I can have no knowledge. Until one side or the other believes its interests lie in breaking that truce, I should think. Texas is, at best, disputed; and as for Mexico . . . '

'What of Mexico, Mr Addington?'

Aberdeen replied for him. 'A nation, Lucy, bound to us by strong ties of friendship and so on – that is by the fact of its owing our bankers millions of sterling which we must hope will one day be repaid by that friendly nation. The Mexicans did propose a year or so back that we should take Upper California in lieu of the debt, but we declined. Too much trouble. Always having to send a frigate to bail out colonists who have enraged local sensibilities. And never mind local sensibilities. Think of those of the French, who want nothing for themselves on that Pacific coast, but would be put out if we had something. Not worth the candle. How many millions are we owed by Mexico, Addington?'

'About nine, sir.'

'Nine million. Now, Lucy, to assist any hope of repayment, we conciliate that friendly nation as far as we decently can. You see? We can, for instance, arrange this Texian truce because Mexico, at the moment, finds itself indisposed to lay out more money on incursions or invasions, military honour for the moment having been satisfied. This is an indisposition we encourage, because Mexico not wasting money on war will be the more able to repay some of those millions owed to us. So, as I say, we conciliate as far as we decently can. The French, now the French a few years ago bombarded Vera Cruz to encourage the repayment of debts. What happened? Santa Anna fired hardly a shot in return, and then, when the French sailed away, claimed a victory.'

'But,' said Lucy, 'I should not be trying to recover a debt from the Mexicans.'

Mr Addington looked at the ceiling and began to frame a careful reply.

Aberdeen was blunter. 'Lucy, Lucy. Think. Yellow fever often, bloody flux always, roguery and bandits everywhere, and fifteen revolutions in the last twenty years or so.'

Lucy, keeping her eyes on Aberdeen as he spoke, saw his right hand emerge from his coat pocket. While he waited for her reply she saw that he held in his hand two acorns, which he rolled in his palm. It was involuntary with him, and a sign of impatience she knew well.

'Still planting great oaks, uncle?'

It was a long habit of Her Majesty's principal secretary of state to plant acorns here and there on impulse, dropping them as he walked and gently pressing them in with his heel, to encourage the growth of oaks and provide timber for the ships of Her Majesty's navy.

'One planted in St James's Park this morning as I walked across,' he said, 'to replace a tree the wind brought down.'

They understood each other. Aberdeen saw her to the carriage himself. She had promised to avoid Mexico. He had promised her letters of introduction to Her Majesty's governor in Jamaica, to the consul in New Orleans, to the British chargé d'affaires in Texas, and to President Houston.

As she leaned forward to kiss him he saw again – as he had seen the moment she arrived – the stain on her neck where the rain, and the warmth of her body, had caused the dye to run from the purple crape which trimmed her grey silk dress, and stained her throat.

She waved from the window as the carriage drove off.

'Do you think, sir,' said Addington, 'that she knows Captain Elliot is in Texas, and who he is?'

'I know her, Addington. She is very dear to me. I know her too well to dream of asking. But she knows.'

To travel in Texas, Lucy needed a passport. Her friends the Twinings had already got theirs from the Texian legation in London, in St James's, between Berry's the wine merchant's and Lobb's the bootmaker's. But there a young clerk informed Lucy that the chargé d'affaires to the Court of St James was also accredited to the French court, that he had just left for Paris and was not expected to return for another three weeks, and that only from him could she obtain the document she needed. The party planned to leave within two weeks, so Lucy wrote ahead to the Texian chargé, and crossed to Paris to meet him. It was a city she had often visited, and known since childhood. It was there she was fitted for her first long dresses, at Baudin's, only three years before. The same couturier had made her wedding clothes.

The first morning of her visit, Jeannie dressed her. Lucy was still in half mourning. First the grey silk dress – the fitting bodice slipped on as she held out her arms, then the wide skirt held open for her to step into. Then she sat so that each stocking could be rolled on to her foot, fitted at the ankle, and then smoothed up to her knee, and the garter fastened. This had been done for her all her life – by her nurse, her governess, and then her maid. Jeannie had dressed her mistress for seven years – as a young girl, a young wife, and a young widow. It was all familiar. The silk stockings were called grey ghosts, grey stockings to go with her grey dress. Grey was a colour of mourning, and even a woman's stockings went into mourning. In Paris, as she sat to be dressed, with her legs apart, and as Jeannie knelt before and attended to the fitting of the grey ghosts, rolling them over the ankles and fastening the garters on her mistress's thighs, Lucy, sitting with the folds of the silk skirts raised to her hips, was invaded with the sense that it was her husband Richard kneeling before her.

She sat still. Then she stood abruptly. The image returned to her at moments throughout the day.

It was a memorable day. She met Dr Smith, the chargé d'affaires, in the public rooms of the Hotel Meurice where he had both his legation and his lodgings. This was Ashbel Smith, sent by Houston because they had shared a tent and many confidences. The goodwill of London and Paris were essential to Houston, and he trusted no man more than he trusted Smith. And besides, Smith knew Europe and spoke French well.

She sat waiting in the reading room, heard him enquire for her of a servant at the door, and observed him as he crossed the room towards her – a slim man no taller than herself, with thick chestnut hair, wearing a black dress coat and carrying a silver-tipped cane and white gloves. He introduced himself, warmly shaking her extended hand. She noticed the man's hazel eyes. She felt the firmness of his handshake. She had also noticed, from a couple of sentences over-heard as he asked for her at the door, that he was easier in French than she was, and she was herself much better than competent.

They chatted. Smith was a man who, without setting out to do so, unconsciously entertained a woman. He told her he had just come from Mass at Notre Dame. Not that he was any kind of Roman Catholic, but had she ever heard the glorious sound of a choir of seven hundred boys' voices?

She feared she had not. She supposed his diplomatic duties must be demanding? 'Oh, in this city particularly. The diplomatic corps is large, and the universal diplomatic custom is to play cards between two and six every afternoon. It is one's diplomatic duty to know one's colleagues, so it is necessary to devote many hours of each day to the playing of cards. Which demands a great deal of a man. No doubt it hones the judgment.'

And had he known Paris long? 'As chargé d'affaires, I have been in Europe only a year, and that time has been divided between France and England. But yes, I do know Paris. You see, I lived here some years ago, before I ever saw Texas, before I could very well have told you where Texas was.'

'But surely you are an American, Dr Smith.'

'I am a Texian. I *was* an American. I studied medicine at Yale. That is in New England. Plenty of New England Yankees in my undergraduate days could not have pointed at Texas on a map. To this day plenty could barely tell you where Texas is. Somewhere down south and west. After Yale, when I was still an American, I came to Paris, because in Paris there were the best hospitals and the best physicians in the world, and I wished to learn from them. Paris has for me the effect of magic, even though I first saw it during an epidemic of cholera.'

She exclaimed.

'That was ten years ago,' he said. 'I learned a great deal about cholera. Do you know, I sometimes still walk the hospital rounds in the mornings, the early mornings, by candle light. I must keep up with my first profession. So here I am, playing piquet with plenipotentiaries in the afternoons, and in the mornings walking the wards.'

'Then how long have you been a Texian, Dr Smith?'

'Since I went to Texas.'

'The mere going there is enough?'

'Oh, the law of Texas calls a man a Texian when he has been there six months. He is supposed to swear before a judge that he wishes to become a citizen. Now Texas is vast, and has few judges to go round, so the custom is, if you are there, and don't persist in calling yourself an American, or a German, or a Frenchman, you are considered a Texian. Anyway, I was a surgeon with the Texian army, and that was more than enough to make me a thorough Texian. Now, because I speak some French, here I am as Texian plenipotentiary.'

He had told her who he was. And she? He knew she and the Twinings wished, as Mr Twining had put it when he had come to the London legation two weeks before, to go yachting in the Gulf. That was all he knew, and he did not ask to know more. She sat before him in her mourning, and that told him something. A great deal.

It was not that he gazed at her. But she felt his eye rest for a moment on her crape, and said openly: 'My husband was in the navy, Dr Smith. On the India station.'

Lucy always had a bold voice. It was the bolder and steadier as she said those words.

'I am sorry,' he said. For a moment he said no more. Then he whisked her away to Texas.

'You will see prairies clothed with long grasses, and, among the grasses, flowers. It is as if the countryside is enamelled with flowers. And tomatoes grow spontaneously, and wild plums, and wild grapes, and blackberries. And there are pecans.'

She did not know what a pecan was, not even whether it was plant or animal. So he told her what it was, a kind of nut unknown to Europe. 'And grapes growing wild for the picking, and wild horses to be had for the rounding-up. And as to other animals, turkey, partridge, deer, buffalo. All under skies of a transparent clearness. What strikes a visitor first, what struck me first, is the open champagne nature of the country.'

She laughed at the extravagance of the description. She liked the man. He told her it was his ambition, when he returned to Texas, to grow miles of sugar cane and lay out a thousand miles of railroad. And now, he said, looking outside, it was a fine spring day in Paris, warm, and the air perhaps not so transparent as in Texas, but the sky blue enough. Should they sit outside for a moment, in the sun? Would she take a glass of champagne?

She would. The sun and the champagne warmed them. Lucy was almost gay, until out of the blue her present gaiety brought back to her mind other occasions of gaiety, and the very warmth of the sun through her dress reminded her of former moments of a different warmth – many moments, deep or wanton, or deep and wanton – which were still vivid to her. The more aroused her senses were by this recollection of past warmth, the more chilled she then was by the familiar but always sudden realisation that came upon her, that these things were all past and gone. She was cast down by her gaiety. The image of that morning, as she sat to be dressed, returned again with a force which distressed her, and took all her spirit to dismiss. But she summoned her strength to bring herself back to the present and to the boulevard, and sipped her champagne and looked up at the plane trees.

Smith was a man observant of women. Lucy dissembled well, but she could not hide everything, and he saw something and guessed more. He led her into more talk of prairies. She was grateful, and came back to life.

They were sitting, with a view down the rue de Rivoli, when an old man came slowly down the boulevard, stopping here and there, taking an exact interest in the objects displayed behind the plate glass windows of the shops. His black coat was rusty and worn and frayed, and too long for the fashion of the day. He came alongside Smith and Lucy, and greeted Smith with a bow. Smith returned the greeting with an inclination of the head, which was civil but not an invitation to remain. He did not wish anyone to make a third to himself and Lucy. But the man did remain, until Smith, if he were not to be uncivil, had to present him to Lucy: 'Don Manuel de Godoy, duc de l'Alcudia, principe de la Paz. Lady Lucy Moncreiffe.'

Prince of Peace. He had been given that title by the Crown of Spain at the end of the previous century, when he had contrived a treaty between France and Prussia.

Godoy bent to kiss her hand and then, when he spoke, showed a charm unexpected from an old man who had been shambling along looking in shop windows. 'I am prince, madam, of a peace long forgotten, that ended a war forgotten even longer. And it was all fifty years ago.'

But his eyes lived, and his features, though those of a man nearly eighty, still had the remains of beauty. Lucy knew of him. Who would not? She had no idea, though, that he was still alive. He was a great figure, but a great figure of two ages before. First minister of Spain, generalissimo of the Spanish empire, lover of the Spanish queen – a man vanquished by the collapse of Spain and by the disgrace and death of his royal mistress. A prince in destitution remains a prince of sorts. Once presented, he had to be offered a chair and a glass of champagne, and was told of Lucy's grand tour.

'So, Texas,' said Don Manuel – as enchanted by Lucy's first acquaintance as he had always been by that of any woman of poise, or wit, or even sense. 'You will go to Texas? You will see Texas. That is more than I ever did. Now Dr Smith has heard me tell this before, but out of his courtesy he will allow me to tell you?'

Smith smiled.

'So, madam, Texas forty years ago was a province of Spain,
and at the Spanish court I was fortunate enough to have done
the king and queen some small service. In consequence of this,
His Most Christian Majesty the then king of Spain bestowed the
province on me as a gift.'

He paused to sip his champagne. She could not take her eyes
from him. He sat upright, almost in profile to Lucy, his brilliant
eyes from time to time resting on her but for the most part, while
he spoke, regarding the clear sky as if he were reading his story
from it.

'It was made to me as a gift, to be an appanage of the House of
Godoy. Texas was to be mine. Two thousand soldiers were embarked
in transports to garrison the province, and a thousand horses, and two
thousand girls from the orphan asylums of Spain . . .'

Here he turned his head, caught Lucy's eye, and, attributing a
question to her, answered it. 'The girls to comfort the soldiers and
to breed.'

Godoy surveyed his now empty glass, which Smith did not
offer to refill.

'But then,' said the prince, 'Napoleon invaded Spain and there
were other uses for the soldiers and the horses, and I dare say
for the girls, so the transports never sailed. And now here I am
in Paris as you see me, and Texas in the course of a few years
became Mexico's, and now I gather is partly Mr Smith's. And he
will, I dare say, have been promising you prairie grapes and wild
horses?'

At which Lucy laughed. The prince turned pleased eyes upon
her face, then gravely rose, kissed her hand again, and took his
leave, saying as he did so: 'Madam, your brief acquaintance has
given me more pleasure than you know. Young people do not know
such things. I wish you well in my province of Texas.'

Then, nodding amiably to Smith, he continued his walk down
the boulevard, on the way back to his fifth floor attic in the rue de
la Michodière. While he was telling Lucy the story he had the bearing
of a prince. As she watched him walk away he turned again into a
shuffling old man. She had seen in his lapel the tiny red ribbon of

the French légion d'honneur, an award also from two ages back. Smith told her: 'It is all he now has. It brings with it a pension of a few thousand francs, on which he lives.'

'And is what he says true?'

'Only he would know that now. He has told the tale often enough. Anyone who could deny it is dead. But we must see to your passport.'

So, leaving Jeannie where she had been fretting all morning, in the servants' basement, Lucy went with Smith to his legation, in a sitting room of the hotel. She sat, looking round at his books. A Cyclopedia of Practical Medicine, the works of Shakespeare in four volumes, the works of Voltaire in fourteen, a Treatise on the Cholera Morbus, and a slim volume with a title in Greek she could not read.

'The New Testament,' he told her. 'I always think that to read it in the English translation is like seeing Julius Caesar in a sixteenth century doublet and a beaver hat, instead of in a toga and wearing a laurel crown. But wax, I need wax.'

He needed wax for a seal. Finding none, he went to look for it in an adjoining room which, as she could see through the open door, was his bedroom. She could see the end of a bed, a coat thrown over the back of a chair, and, next to a life size statue of the Venus de Milo, an anatomical skeleton hanging from a hook in the ceiling. Smith rummaged, and then returned with wax and a sheet of parchment, which was already made out.

Lucy read: 'In the name of the Republick of Texas, Free, Sovereign, and Independent, to all whom these presents shall come, I, Sam Houston, President thereof, send greetings.' And so on, down to: 'Given under my hand and the Great Seal of the Republick on the —th day of ——, in the Year of Our Lord 18—, and in the Year of the Republick the —th.' Then followed the Houston signature, with a flourished rubric twice the depth of the name itself.

'I have a stock,' said Smith, and filled in the name and quality of Lady Lucy Moncreiffe, and the colour of eyes and complexion, asked her height – five feet five inches – and inscribed that too, and then certified in the blanks that it was the third day of May in the Year of Our Lord the one thousand eight hundred and forty third, and of the Republick of Texas the eighth. Then he added his countersignature, and with wax and candle consummated the whole document.

Sam Houston's was the grandest signature she had ever seen.

'Does it look like the man?' she asked.

'It does.'

Smith and Lucy had brightened each other's day. But for his respect for her grey silk and purple crape, he would have embraced her, or so he told himself. He offered her his hand, and conducted her back to the boulevard and to her maid.

When she was undressed that night, Lucy remembered again the morning's image. She also remembered Mr Smith whom, but for her grey silk and purple crape, she would have kissed in affection. She remembered Godoy's gallantry to her. She knew it was a small thing. He would say the same to any young woman, but his compliment pleased her.

As she stood in the nightdress which had just been slipped over her head, and when she had shaken out her hair and was quite ready for bed, she touched with bare toes the stockings her maid had draped over a stool.

Jeannie said: 'Have done with the grey ghosts, ma'am. It's time.'

Lucy nodded. That night she cried bitterly. She did not sleep until the small hours. When she woke next morning, Jeannie was already back from Baudin's with a dozen pairs of white stockings in netted Chantilly lace.

6

The Mier Diezmo

<hr>

By then the fate of the seven hundred men Houston had unwillingly sent after the Mexicans was well known in Texas. They had pursued the invading soldiers south from San Antonio, never catching or even catching sight of them. Near the Mexican border the pursuers were themselves caught by the onset of winter. The days were still hot but the nights clear and bitterly cold. They shot deer and cured the skins as best they could, to make winter clothes. At the border town of Laredo discipline broke down, and two companies left camp and looted the defenceless town. Kurt Neumann, who had come out two years before from Germany to settle in Texas, and had gone with the expedition for the pay, because he could find no work in Galveston, wrote to his sweetheart back in that city: 'Men broke down doors and ransacked houses and took everything that could be taken, even the blankets from the women's beds, which was wrong. The general ordered the goods returned, but most were not. Even the officers laughed at him.'

General Somervell pressed on over the Rio Grande but his army was now straggling and reduced to five hundred men. He ordered a return. Three hundred men defied him, saying they had not come this far for nothing. They elected their own officers, and struck off on their own. Neumann went on because his company did, and they were men he knew. He sent his first letter back with those who withdrew with the general, adding a postscript that he would take his chance, though he was ill at ease. They all thought the Mexicans must turn and fight some time. They aimed to take the border town of Mier. He would be back with his sweetheart in two months at the outside.

Somervell, returning to Sam Houston, told him: 'Some good men did go on, and I could not make out why. But two thirds of them were adventurers. Their object was plunder. They had nothing at home, in fact no homes to go to, and many went forward because there was nothing for them elsewhere, and being so far from home they had no fear of my authority, or yours.'

'Brigands,' said Houston.

Three days before Christmas these three hundred Texians, brigands or not, entered the main square of Mier demanding rations for twelve hundred men, in particular ten sacks of coffee and forty sacks of flour, tobacco, blankets, and shoes. The mayor, fearing from the size of the demands that more Texians were hidden in the countryside around, promised the supplies, but played for time. The Texians waited in their armed camp. No tribute came. On Christmas day, on a dark and drizzling afternoon, the Texians went back to take what had not been brought to them, and ran into Mexican regular troops. In the uncertain light neither side knew the strength of the other. The town of Mier was a maze of narrow streets and adobe houses. Texian irregulars and Mexican troops fought house to house and roof to roof. By the light of the following morning, out of food and water and down to their last few rounds of ammunition, the scattered Texians saw the drawn up ranks of Mexicans and for the first time realised how badly they were outnumbered, ten to one. If they fought on, the struggle would be hopeless. If they ran, they would be cut down before they reached the Rio Grande, which was four miles away. Even if they reached the river, they would be shot in the water. If they crossed, they would be pursued and ridden down.

They surrendered on the Mexican general's assurance that they would be treated honourably. They were given food, and sat on the ground eating. Then new trouble overtook them. The Mexican soldiers, having spent all morning bringing down from the flat roofs of Mier the bodies of their dead comrades, began to lay them out in the square, on the side where there was shade. The lines of bodies grew longer. A young captain made a count. No fewer than six hundred corpses in blue and white uniforms were lying there. Only thirty Texians were dead or wounded. At close quarters Mr Colt's

revolver was a deadlier weapon than the long barrelled muskets of a
Mexican army modelled on Napoleon's infantry of thirty years before.

The number, six hundred, was spoken aloud. A growl arose
from the Mexican guards. They levelled their long rifles at the
prisoners, wanting to finish them off with bayonets there and then.
The younger officers were of the same mind. In the hubbub, the
Mexican general stepped from his quarters in the city hall out on to
the balcony. He had been disturbed at dinner and carried a glass of
wine in one hand and a linen napkin in the other. He surveyed the
carnage laid out before him, and glanced at the groups of Texians
menaced by the bayonets of his men. The Mexican soldiers looked
up at their commander. The Texians sat in silence. A sergeant
guarding the general, standing beside him on the balcony, called
out to him: 'Kill the devils.' All in the square heard him.

The general looked coolly at the sergeant, and struck him hard
in the face with the napkin.

'Devils, yes. I see I gave my word to devils. But it is my
word. Bury the dead.'

Some of the Texians spoke Spanish and understood these words.
All, whether they understood the words or not, knew, as they looked
up at the grim faces of their guards, that though their lives were for
the moment saved, they would have no easy time of it.

As the general turned away from the square and moved inside, a
corporal dashed a billy can of water from Neumann's hands. 'There
was no more water for us that day,' he wrote in one of the letters
he continued to write to his sweetheart, 'nothing to drink and no
blankets, and no food either, and I cannot say I thought the man
wrong who, seeing so many laid out dead on the stones of the square
who would never drink another drop, knocked the can from my lips.
When we saw so many were laid out, we thought ourselves dead men
too.'

Then they were marched away as prisoners into Mexico. They
asked for their blankets, cooking pans, and other possessions to be
brought from the camp they had left outside Mier, before coming
into town. Their captors fetched these things, but kept most for
themselves, and all the blankets. And yet the Texians were allowed

to keep the little money they had in their pockets. That was not taken
from them. Then they were marched ten, twenty, sometimes thirty,
miles a day. They slept without blankets on nights of sharp frost. Or
they could not sleep and built brushwood fires which flared up in
a minute and then died, leaving them chilled again. When they were
lucky they slept in sheep pens, which gave them some shelter against
the cold northerly winds. As they were driven through some villages
the men and women watched with sullen enmity, but in others with
no more than curiosity. In one town, some of the women pitied them
and brought out scraps of food. At the next, an hour further on, the
women howled hatred and called them animals. In one large town
the bells rang, and the soldiers were feted and the prisoners along
with them, as if they all were part of a holiday show. They were
allowed to spend what little money they had to buy rice and beef.
That night they ate cooked meat for the first time in two weeks,
and slept in a cow byre, on filthy straw but in the warm. A man
from San Antonio, settling among the straw and dried cow dung,
pawed the ground and bellowed like a bull. The guards laughed at
his antics. The townsmen came to see. Other Texians pawed the
ground as if in a bull ring.

'It was a mad show,' wrote Neumann, continuing the endless
letters that he wrote on scraps of paper and carried with him unsent,
'but it earned us each a cup of beer. I never knew before that the
human heart could be so changeable, as the hearts of these Mexican
people have been to us. Yesterday a handsome woman, young and
mild-faced, and with nothing but good to hope for from life, came
up as if meaning well, and then spat at me. Then today an old man,
seeing I had nothing against the sun or the rain, took a ragged hat
off his own head and put it into my hands.'

Having been marched to the Gulf, to the town of Matamoros,
five hundred miles east of where they started, they learned they
were to march west again and then south to the City of Mexico.
Several men wept. Now they were marched bound two-and-two
with leather thongs. They began to plot escape. The leader was
a Scot called Cameron, a tall, wiry man who had retained more of
his strength than the others. One dawn they rose, ate what breakfast

there was – boiled rice and weak coffee – and walked over to the stockade where the soldiers had stacked their rifles. It was still not full light. Cameron said in a quiet tone, as if he were remarking that it was a fine day, 'Well boys, we will go it.'

The guards were drowsy and taken by surprise. Two hundred prisoners seized a hundred rifles, eighty horses, enough water for several days, and made off north towards Texas. They walked for two days without stop, taking turns to ride. Mexican cavalry in small groups appeared on the horizon, and then disappeared.

'To avoid them,' wrote Neumann, 'and the reinforcements they might bring up, we left the road and broke away into the mountains. Then it went hard with us. We found no water for man or horse. We feared to light fires in the cold night for fear of showing ourselves to pursuers. One horse died and, since we could not feed or water the others, we slaughtered them. Some horses screamed when they saw the knife. Many men drank the hot blood that spurted into the cans we held out, and everywhere, but I could not. We cut our saddles into shoes now, but we had no one who knew how to make them and they did not serve well. We cut up the horses and each man had ten pounds of horse meat, but it was a burden to carry. It rotted before we could eat it, though some ate maggots and all, but then our water was gone, and our rifles too heavy to carry further so we let them drop. Then in a valley we saw before us a squadron of Mexican cavalry. They did not move but waited for us, and we went up to them as if to our best friends and only hope. They stood, and then two men came and gave us water as we straggled up. Then we were bound again. The rawhide cut into our wrists because all our limbs were swollen. We were prisoners again. It had all been for nothing. But not a man there that was not glad to be taken again, and bound, because of the water. We had been two days without water. A Mexican told me the mountains we went into were called Tierra de Muerte. He said that was death country, and if we had kept to the road we would have got clean away. Then we were marched back the way we came, until in four days we came to the place we had escaped from. My feet were cut to pieces by the rocks. As we came into this place, which was called Salado, we saw a whirlwind which lifted the earth from the ground and climbed like a great coil of rope tossed into the air. It was a mile off. When we got to the place it had been, trees were standing on one side of the track but stripped, broken, and uprooted on the other. A Mexican officer, seeing us amazed, because I had never seen the like, laughed and said Santa Anna would do the same for us. I thought he was in earnest.'

Neumann was right. The officer who laughed was a colonel newly arrived from Mexico City. His horse was well-groomed and fresh. His blue uniform was unfaded and his silver epaulettes bright and untarnished. The rest of the officers stood apart from him, seeming in awe of him. They did not address him except in the way of duty.

The commanding officer of the garrison, who had treated the prisoners as moderately as he could before their escape five weeks before, shunned the new officer. The few Texians who had any Spanish picked up a rumour that they were all to be executed. Cameron went to the commanding officer and challenged him. 'I thought,' he said, 'that we were in the hands of a gentleman and an officer, not a murderer.' The Mexican lowered his eyes and did not reply. Then he rode off, wanting no more to do with that day's business.

It was already late afternoon. The light would not last much more than an hour longer. One hundred and seventy six Texians, all who had survived the march, the escape, and the ordeal in the mountains, stood bound in pairs and surrounded by Mexican rifles. The new colonel spoke. His Excellency Antonio Lopez de Santa Anna, commander in chief and president-dictator of the Estados Unidos de Mexico, had determined that the Texian brigands, on account of their murderous conduct at Mier and their contumacious attempt to escape from their merciful captors, should suffer death.

This was translated by one of the Texians. His comrades maintained an unbroken silence.

However, His Excellency, in the exercise of his clemency, had commuted this sentence to a more merciful one. Here the interpreter had trouble following the colonel, and asked him to repeat a passage.

'Diezmo. Diezmo,' said the colonel.

The interpreter looked for help to a Mexican lieutenant he knew spoke passable English. The young officer hesitated, perhaps for the right word in English, perhaps because he did not want to say it aloud. 'Decimation,' he said.

Still the Texian interpreter did not understand. The Mexican lieutenant then told him rapidly in Spanish what was intended. The interpreter stared at him, then at the colonel, and then told his comrades. 'Boys, they mean to shoot one in ten of us.'

A clay jar was brought. Into it a sergeant poured one hundred and fifty-nine white beans, which the colonel said he had already counted himself. Then the colonel dropped into the jar, one by one, in the presence of them all, seventeen black beans. He ordered the prisoners to come up in turn, two by two. The jar would be held above their heads. Each man would reach in and take a bean. Those who drew white would be spared. Those who drew black would be shot.

Cameron's name was called first. He was the leader. The sergeant held the jar high so that a man could reach it only with his fingertips. The black beans had been poured on top and hardly shaken. Cameron was meant to draw black.

'Well,' he said, 'let's be at it' – and reached up and with his finger tips drew a white bean.

The third man, Neumann's company commander, drew the first black. It took fifteen minutes for all the men to draw.

'Johnny Trewin,' wrote Neumann immediately afterwards, 'when he drew the second black, said well boys he never in his life had failed to draw a prize. When it was my turn I spoke against it, saying the jar was held so high my fingers could reach no bean, white or black, and the jar was lowered till I could touch, and it was white. When all had drawn, those that had black beans were untied and led apart. It was almost sunset, and we could go to them and speak with them. Johnny said, "They only rob me of forty years," but to make sure they should rob him of nothing else, gave all his clothes to his friends, keeping only his drawers. They offered a priest, and two men accepted, but the others laughed. One said he would speak to his God himself, not through any descendant of Montezuma's, and was cuffed about the head for his insolence. The Mexicans offered food, not to us but to those about to die, and all refused, having no stomach for it, except Richard North, who we called Mary Anne, him being so slight and we never expected to last through any trouble but he lasted through the lot until then, and he said he would certainly have no stomach for anything after, but since he had not eaten for a month he would have the bowl of mutton stew then, which he did, and ate it.'

Then the condemned men were separated and taken away.

'We only heard,' wrote Neumann, 'and could not see because they were taken behind a wall ten feet high. There was a pipe and a drum which the Mexicans played for their own comfort for it was no comfort to us. And while this dirge was wailing the shots came, and some men screamed, and the shots went on so they could not have hit them cleanly. Then another dirge, and more shots, and not so many shots this time because the soldiers told me they stood closer the second time. They shot them in two goes, nine first and the other eight after. The first time they shot three minutes in all, and the sentry on top of the wall was sickened by it and swayed and all but fell off.

'Then it was dark, and they did offer us the mutton stew. One man refused, but I was hungry and ate it. We all but one did eat. And after we had eaten an officer came and asked me my name. I was afraid and would not say it, thinking he had another black bean, for me. He saw this and told me my name. You are Kurt Neumann, he said. Then he gave me a purse, and it was from you. It was twenty silver dollars. And there was your letter saying it was to ransom me. The lieutenant said it would not ransom me, but it was mine. Sweet love, I did not know you had twenty dollars to send, and I thank the kindness of your heart. It had gone from Galveston to Matamoros on the Gulf, and safely, and now this officer, who had been there, sought me out and brought it to me.

'I did not say to him the others had robbed us of our blankets and of our freedom – though, it is true, never taken the money in our pockets – but he saw it in my face and said nothing more in English but spoke in Spanish, something about his honour, and pulled himself up very straight. But he saw in my face that seventeen honest Texians lay dead behind that wall, so said no more and went away. I think of you always, and long for you, and do not understand this honour. I pray to rejoin you soon in the Lands of Promise, but sweet heart I shall be longer than I thought.'

All this was known throughout Texas by mid-May of 1843. And Kurt Neumann's letters, which he entrusted to various Mexicans, always did, eventually, reach his sweetheart, who was Helga Becker of the Tremont Hotel in Galveston.

7

Beautiful Crescent

Lucy stood on the deck of the schooner *Kingston* gazing towards the golden dome that had been visible on the horizon for an hour already. They were coming into New Orleans, and the dome was the only feature that stood out from the flat landscape. The breeze from the Gulf of Mexico caught Lucy's long muslin skirts and extended them before her like a lateen sail. With her left hand she held firmly on to a ratline of the fore-rigging. With her right she held back the dark hair which the breeze blew back across her forehead and over her eyes and face. She loved the sense of the moving breeze on her and round her. It helped cool her, but still the humid heat was everywhere. She could feel the dampness in the small of her back, where the thin fabric of her dress clung to her.

'That is the cathedral?' she asked the American pilot standing beside her.

'Nope.'

'That dome,' she repeated. 'I saw it from miles out, the first landfall, before we took you on board.'

'See it from fifteen miles out in the Gulf,' said the pilot. 'But ain't no cathedral. The cathedral in New Orleans burned down years ago. Still a ruin. The monsignors can't stir themselves so much as to clear the rubble. That dome's the new Saint Charles hotel. Now the old Saint Charles burned too, but why, we had a new one up in a year, which whips the old one. In a year ma'am. Go Ahead's our motto. Sleeps five hundred; and I guess, ma'am, that whips any hotel in Europe.'

'I am sure,' she said, 'that it does.' They had hove to and

taken the pilot on board only ten minutes before, and already he had announced that his own yacht, which a good American yard had built in three weeks, could whip the *Kingston*, and that though he had heard of London fogs, he guessed a Mississippi fog could whip those any day.

The Twinings and Lucy had crossed from Plymouth to Jamaica by mail steamer, calling only at Funchal. In Jamaica they had joined the Twinings' schooner, which her crew had sailed out from England ahead of them. She was of two hundred tons, too small, said the senior Mr Twining, since the whole purpose of the excursion was to allow the ladies to recover full health and vigour, to afford Mrs Twining, or Lucy, a comfortable passage of the Atlantic. This was probably true, but on the passage from Jamaica to New Orleans both Lucy and Mrs Twining, in spite of their supposed fragility, had shown themselves better sailors than the gentlemen. The crew were amused to see this, particularly since the young Mr John Twining had a considerable reputation as an amateur yachtsman. But that was in English coastal waters, and in regattas for which the crew had a friendly and deep contempt.

From England to the Gulf had been a passage of more than four thousand miles. Mr Lindsay Twining, the elder of the two brothers, had visited the United States before, in the tea business. To his wife Adelaide, and to Lucy, and to Mr John Twining, New Orleans would be their first landfall on the continent of North America.

The *Kingston* eased into the Mississippi.

'You could fairly say it whips the Thames, ma'am,' said the pilot, addressing Lucy. He did not ask it as a question.

'You have seen the Thames?' said Lucy.

The pilot owned he had not.

'Well then,' said Lucy, looking down at the warm, thick river, 'you could fairly say this whips the Thames for muddy sluggishness. Any day.'

The pilot was not at all put out by this, but drew the attention of all the English on board to the richness of the port's commerce, to the sea-going ships anchored in tiers five deep along the riverside, to the immense cargoes of baled cotton being loaded, and to the innumerable casks of sugar and molasses waiting on the dockside.

'See those flatboats, ladies?'

There was no avoiding the sight of these craft, which were gathered in their hundreds.

'Rather like a larger sort of punt,' said Adelaide.

'From New Orleans, ladies,' said the pilot, 'those flatboats, that you call punts, can navigate twenty thousand miles of river – the Mississippi, the Missouri, the Illinois... And great steam-boats besides make great voyages up river.'

The pilot, who was determined to extol the beauties of his country, then drew the ladies' attention to the rich carriages driving along the levee, and to the unexampled beauty of the ladies of the city of New Orleans. The city, as he pointed out, indicating with a sweep of his arm the curve of the river, was in every way the beautiful crescent it was justly reputed to be.

As they were disembarking, and the pilot was taking a farewell glass of rum with the master of the schooner, the American turned to Lucy, and, severally addressing her and Mrs Twining and Jeannie who were standing in a group together, remarked that he guessed they'd be putting up at the Saint Charles.

Mrs Twining replied that they would be.

'Well then, ladies,' said the pilot, 'you will have the sight of yourselves in the largest mirrors in Christendom. Five great mirrors in the lobby. And in every suite, ladies, looking glasses that whip those in any other establishment whatsoever, and wherever.'

He raised his glass to them. They thanked him civilly. The man laughed uproariously.

All those in the Twinings' party were British, but the first man to leave his card at the Saint Charles, the next morning, was Alphonse, comte de Saligny, chargé d'affaires of His Majesty the king of the French. He asked them to do him the honour of being his guests at the opera. If they consented, he would send carriages for the ladies and gentlemen.

He did send his liveried servants, with two carriages, and while they were making the short drive to the opera, Saligny's head man, a sort of major domo, conversed as familiarly with Lucy and the older Mr Twining as if they were his equals, whom he had known for years. He cheerfully told them the old opera house had burned down too.

'A lot of fires,' said Twining, who was as much astonished by the familiarity of the man as by the inclination of New Orleans to burn down. The cathedral? The former Saint Charles hotel? And now the opera?

'The old opera, sir,' said the man, 'was already grander than any opera house in Europe. Now the new one . . .'

'Built in a year?' asked Lucy.

'From foundation stone to the gilding of the last cherub on the last box on the fourth tier, ma'am, six months and a day. As splendid as the old house, and better being new, and known as the New American Opera.'

At the opera Saligny received them in full diplomatic fig, plumes and all, though in the United States he had no official standing whatever. By his side stood a magnificent woman whom he presented as Natalie de St Aubin. She was as much entitled to the name of de St Aubin as he was to that of de Saligny or to the title of count, and indeed he had conferred the prefix *de* upon her himself, the better to fit her for her social position as his mistress. But there was no doubt about her exotic beauty. Both the Mr Twinings felt it. Both men had been in Louisiana a day, but both had already learned, from conversations with American gentlemen in the smoking rooms of the hotel, what needed to be known about the New Orleans tradition of *plaçage*. Any man who could afford it, kept a Creole mistress and set her up as grandly as he could in the old French town of the Vieux Carré. The Creoles were the descendants of the French who had come out to Louisiana when it was French, or to the French islands of the West Indies. The Creoles were those born in the colonies. They were white, but over the generations had interbred. The most beautiful and most desired of all women were those who, from somewhere back in the generations of the previous two centuries, had acquired a quarter or one eighth strain of the blood of the elegant Woloff women brought out as slaves from the furthest western coast of Africa. Saligny had found himself such a woman. Her head was held elegantly on a long neck, her sinuous walk was all elegance, and her silk dress, though extraordinarily bright by the standards of either London or Paris, set off her rich darkness of skin. But then, as both Lucy and Adelaide could not help remarking, in New Orleans all the ladies were brightly dressed.

The opera was *Elisir d'Amore*, sung by an Italian company, but it was the evident custom of the better class of patrons to pay little attention to what was played or sung on stage. Many gentlemen greeted Saligny in the grand foyer and on the wide stairs as his major domo conducted his party to a large box which, like most other boxes in the house, was designed to give its occupants the greatest privacy. The box was protected from the gaze of those in the pit by an elaborate gilded grille. The theatre itself was brightly illuminated throughout the performance, the house lights never being dimmed. The box on the other hand was softly lit within. The result was that those in the box could clearly observe the perambulations, constant visitings, and goings and comings of the greater part of the audience, or even, if they wished, watch the stage. But the hoi polloi in the house could not see into the box.

'A fine house,' said Mrs Twining, who did look through the grille to see into it. She did think it fine, and she, living in London, was used to Covent Garden and Drury Lane.

'They are proud of it,' said Saligny. 'I preferred the older one, which was less, shall we say, brash? They were absurdly proud of that, saying it was grander than the Paris opera.'

'And was it?' asked Lucy.

'It was bigger. They made it to be bigger. I know the architect of this theatre, who first had to remove the ruins of the other. He said it was a mercy it burned down before it had time to collapse. He said it could have fallen down on the heads of an audience at the next high C. The pillars of the facade had sunk two feet into the earth, and there was nothing but swamp beneath. Nothing in the way of foundations. The whole city's a swamp. I have seen a man dig in a spade and strike salt water eighteen inches down.'

'But you choose to live here,' said Lucy, 'rather than in Texas?'

'I do,' said Saligny, 'when duty permits me to do so.' This

was a sore point with him. He had twice been rebuked by Paris for failing to reside in the country to which he was accredited, and for preferring the luxury of New Orleans to the rawness of Texas.

'Are there no opera houses in Texas?' asked Mrs Twining.

'One, in the head of an Italian, who keeps it there along with grand plans for avenues, parks, palaces, and ceremonial fountains. But his plans are in any case for the city of Houston, and President Houston, after whom that city is named, has lately refused to live there for fear of Indians and Mexicans, and has moved his capitol to a spot nearer his own part of the country, in a village, or settlement, which he calls Washington.'

The younger Mr Twining said he had heard President Houston was a man to reckon with.

Natalie de St Aubin did nothing without elegance. She laughed elegantly. 'The comte will tell you how to reckon with him.'

At which Saligny launched into his tale.

'When I first went to present my credentials, and went to the capitol, which in those days was in the city of Houston, I waited outside for a moment, expecting to be received by an aide de camp. There was no aide. There was no guard. There was no ante room in which to wait. I entered. And there stood a man whom I recognised from his description to be the president. He was standing on a table.'

Neither Lucy nor any of the Twinings had warmed to Saligny, but at this account it was hardly possible not to smile.

'On a table,' Saligny continued, 'wearing an Indian robe. I affected to notice nothing unusual, and presented myself as the envoy of the king of the French. He looked at me with those grey eyes. They are fine eyes. "You come," he said, "to represent a king. Now I shall show you the wounds of a true republican." At which he threw open the robe – and the ladies will forgive me when I say the robe was all – and there were his scars. Which he got, he said, in the war of 1814 against the English.'

'Ah,' said the older Twining, looking in concern at his wife Adelaide, but her amused eyes had met Lucy's. He was surprised to see that both women, far from being affronted, were hard put to restrain laughter, laughter moreover at Saligny's expense. As for

Lucy, Twining could understand. But Adelaide? He told himself there might be more to his wife than he thought.

'But now,' Saligny went on, 'the president has in some part reformed himself. This is due, I believe, to the influence upon him of a young, gentle, and god-fearing wife.'

'Effrontery!' thought Mr Lindsay Twining. 'The fellow receives us with his undoubted mistress and then dares to talk piously of the influence on Houston of a god-fearing wife.' But he was Saligny's guest, and said nothing. In any case Natalie was by then taking up the tale of President Houston's misdemeanours.

'Young she is. Certainly twenty years younger than Sam Houston. And so was his first wife, who they say was eighteen when she married him and still only eighteen when she left him.'

Mr Twining senior – who had married Adelaide when she was eighteen, and who knew Lucy had married younger still, though not to a much older man – was about to remark that a great difference in age did not necessarily mean a great difference in sensibilities or sympathies, but Natalie was not to be stopped.

'All his women are much younger. It is his taste. And there are those who say his new marriage is bigamous into the bargain, his first wife back in Tennessee having been shuffled off with a Texian divorce which was no more than Houston's own presidential decree scrawled on a bit of paper for himself, when he wanted it. And all this quite apart from his Indian squaws.'

Saligny by now had observed that both the Twining men were looking pointedly at the stage, and that Mrs Twining and Lucy were saying nothing, but he could not catch his mistress's eye and warn her, and so this lovely woman continued in a soft voice to recount Sam Houston's Indian adventures. There was in truth little malice in what she said. In Louisiana as in Texas you were either for or against Sam Houston. Besides, he was a man whose exploits bred anecdotes. They were the common coin of New Orleans drawing rooms. So, with no other wish than to entertain her lover's guests that evening, as she had entertained many others, Natalie continued with a story so old that it had long lost its sting, except to those hearing it for the first time.

'To this day, you can tell where Sam Houston travelled in Cherokee country by the presence of grey-eyed Indian children. And you can tell, moreover, whether he went on foot or rode horseback.'

'I do not see . . . ' began Twining the younger. He was about to say, as gently as he could, that he did not see this was any concern of theirs. Natalie misunderstood him.

'You do not see how one can tell? Well, Mr Twining, you find grey eyed children ten miles apart if Sam Houston walked ten miles in a day, and then stayed the night. You find them forty miles apart if he rode, and then rested.'

An intermission between acts saved them.

For the rest of the evening Lucy and the Twinings sipped Saligny's good wine and, in between applauding occasional arias, kept the talk firmly away from President Houston's private life and as firmly as could be on the tea trade, which Twining senior knew intimately, and on the American and Texian duties on tea, on Champagne wines, and on this and that.

It was Lucy who, when excise matters were wearing a bit thin, asked Saligny his opinion of the Mexicans' barbarous conduct in the matter of the Mier diezmo, of which they had learned when they reached New Orleans the day before.

'In a strange way,' she said, 'which I cannot explain, and which is not rational, it would have been less calculated if all the prisoners had been killed. It would have been terrible, and, in any rational sense more terrible. And yet this decimation – so carelessly random, so careless of life. I have an uncle who knows his Roman history, and I can hear him saying that this has the tinge of some crime of the last emperors who were a degraded lot.'

Mr Lindsay Twining looked at her and his look showed he shared her compunction and sympathised with the distinction she made.

'All that,' said Saligny. And the Frenchman, considering his point, appeared a man of more substance than he had seemed all evening. Vanity and an inclination to tattle do not mean a man is devoid of all sense. 'But I must suggest another way of looking at the affair. Such

an atrocity – it is an atrocity – is the sadder because in my belief it
is useless when directed against people like the Texians. It will fail
utterly to achieve its only conceivable purpose.'

'Which was?' asked Lucy.

'To deter, however barbarously. But it will not. Among people
accustomed to regarding the life of a man as a play-thing, and the
chances of war as a game – I mean the Texians, and you will see
that I am right – such an act, so far from intimidating them, so far
from turning them back, will only stir them up and drive them on.
Look, the Texians are reckless, and they will just exact an even more
bloody retaliation. President Houston knows this, and has disowned
these bands of adventurers, brigands is as good a word as any, who
prowl the Rio Grande and loot the Mexican border towns.'

'Surely his writ runs that far?' asked Mr John Twining.

'I don't know that it does. It doesn't run as far as the quarter
decks of the sloop and a brig he has for a navy. But,' said Saligny, the
opera and its twelve curtain calls having come to an end, disregarded
by most, 'more of that another time.'

Their carriages took them back to the Saint Charles along a
mile of roads lit by gas lamps, through a night that was still hot.
As she stepped down on to the wooden sidewalk in front of the
hotel, Lucy distinguished, in the warm air, the scent of frangipani,
daphnes, and something she could have sworn was violets.

Jeannie asked how the evening had gone, whether the gentleman
from France had a head on his shoulders, and whether his lady was
as beautiful as she had heard from one of the other maids in the
hotel.

Lucy said: 'The opera – we heard very little. Saligny – I really
do not know. His lady – yes, quite beautiful, in her way.'

She then saw, again, what the Mississippi pilot had meant by
his raillery about the greatest mirrors in the world. The mirrors
in the lobby were vast, running the whole height from floor to
ceiling. As you mounted the stairs it was impossible not to see
yourself reflected from at least two angles, in at least two mirrors.
The same was true of the looking glasses in her suite of rooms. At
home, a looking glass to Lucy was a thing held in the hand. Here

at the Saint Charles the gilt-framed glasses in her rooms never left her form unreflected – dressing, undressing, or lying thoughtful in her bed. Along the hotel corridor Adelaide, with her husband, had made the same discovery. Both she and Lucy now understood very well why the Mississippi pilot had laughed aloud when he informed them that the Saint Charles's mirrors were one of the wonders of New Orleans.

Mr Lindsay Twining saw himself in the dim light lying embraced by his wife Adelaide, and considered for the second time during this brief visit that there might be more to her than he had thought. Lucy fell asleep to the faint sound of dancing which continued in the ballroom below.

8

Galveston Island

They remained a week in New Orleans, and then set sail for Texas. During the passage to Galveston, sailing westward across the Gulf, Mr Lindsay Twining was again prostrated by the movement of the *Kingston*, and was nursed by Adelaide. Lucy spent most of the daylight hours on deck, accompanied by a most attentive Mr John Twining, who fetched books for her when she wished to read, offered her frequent iced drinks and fetched those too, and in the meantime did his utmost to entertain her with his yachtsman's observations on the strength and direction of the wind and the course they were taking, and by translating for her the orders of the officers to the sailors and the helmsman.

'Hold your luff,' from the master.

'Aye aye, sir,' from the helmsman.

And John Twining was delighted that Lucy should understand his explanation of this manoeuvre. He was much taken by Lucy, and told himself she was an apt pupil.

Galveston, when it came in sight, was an island so low lying that a clump of three trees was pointed out as a landmark. And as Lucy saw as they crept in to their moorings, it was a city not yet recovered from the latest hurricane. She counted a dozen houses blown over on their sides and left there. The church had been propped upright but the windows not yet reglazed. But merchantmen from Liverpool and Bremen lay in the harbour, trading finished goods for cotton. A barque from Hamburg was discharging bewildered emigrants clamouring for their baggage which was being swung up from the hold. The Twinings' party settled at the Tremont, which was upright and prospering. Indeed the whole city, in spite of the wreckage everywhere, was bustling with commerce.

'It is a prosperous ruin,' said Lucy, surveying the blown over houses from the Tremont verandah.

'No ruin, ma'am,' said an American gentleman, leaning back at full length in his cane chair, tilting it back on its hind legs as far as it would go without falling over altogether, and with his own legs stretched out before so that they rested in the verandah rail in front of him. 'See, we aim to put up an *en*tire new house inside a week. Say four days.'

Lucy was now used to being addressed by complete strangers, something that her friends, standing beside her, could not bring themselves to accept so easily.

'Indeed?' she said. 'An entire house?'

'Piles, frame, floor, walls, roof. Yes, ma'am.'

'Then why not prop up those houses we see there? Why not prop them up inside, say, *two* days?'

'Better build new. Strip off the board that's usable, move down the street to another lot, build new and bigger.' The man rose to his feet, tipped his hat to the ladies, and slowly walked away.

They had arranged to see the island on horseback, all except the older Mr Twining who, still feeling the motion of the Gulf, did not wish to feel the movement of a horse beneath him. The Tremont had recommended a Captain Carey who rented horses at fifty cents a day. He was due to bring three horses over personally at two o'clock in the afternoon. The horses did appear, in charge of a tall, grizzled black. Mr John Twining looked the horses over and found them acceptable, and then walked round testing the saddles and the girth straps.

'Now I've seen to that, sir,' said the black slowly and with much good nature. 'Two ladies' saddles, one gentleman's. I've seen to all the fixings.'

'It seems you have,' said John Twining, when he had satisfied himself. 'Where's Captain Carey?'

'I'm Captain Carey, sir,' said the black.

'Ah.'

Captain Carey assisted Mrs Twining to mount. Mr John Twining helped Lucy.

They set off at a walk along the beach, which was the only promenade the island offered. Captain Carey went with them as guide. Yellow larks skimmed above them. From the marshes a hundred yards inland geese rose at their approach, and the occasional white swan.

'Plenty game,' said Captain Carey. 'You was thinking, sir, how come a black man like myself has three horses to rent?'

'Not at all,' said Mr Twining.

'No, sir? Well, sir, from the age of eleven I had a shotgun, of sorts. My mother was a family Negro, see, brought from Virginia when Master came into Texas twenty years gone. I was a boy then, and my mother called me Carey. Plain Carey. I was a slave, sir, but we rested on the Lord's Day, and Master said what a creature did on the Lord's day was between him and his Maker, not between him and his master. So I come to the shore and lay in wait for game, in the long grass. Plenty game. I was a good shot, sir. Twenty cents for a goose, twenty-five for a swan. Snipe and plover too. Then I got me a rifle, of sorts. Two dollars for a deer. I shot two deer in one day, once.'

Mr John Twining, who had shot small game birds in England, but had never bagged a deer, or even got close to a deer, looked with interest at the black. He had for that matter never conversed with a slave before. Not that Captain Carey was a slave any longer, as they soon discovered.

'And so,' he said, 'with my hunting I earned a quarter here and a dollar there, and I saved, until I had a thousand dollars.'

How freely, thought Mr Twining, these Americans and Texians talk money. Like most Englishmen, he never talked about money. It wasn't done. But, he thought, it must have been a momentous sum for a black man.

'And then,' said Captain Carey, 'I bought my freedom.'

They jogged along. All three visitors were moved by the story of a man who had bought his freedom. Mr Twining was ashamed of his reflections of the moment before. It had been a hugely momentous sum to the man. He leaned over, seized the black's hand, and shook it heartily.

The man looked round at the three of them, and broke into a wide smile. He said: 'I thank you. And you see, when I had my freedom, and enough over to buy one horse – and then hire it out until I had enough for a second, and then a third – they called me Captain. And Carey was my name, so I was Captain Carey. Now mind, sir and ladies!'

He called out his warning as they came to a bleached carcass, or rather one third of a carcass, of a horned beast. The horns, the skull, and a few ribs were all that showed above the surface of the reeds to their immediate left. It was a cow, he told them, that had strayed and sunk into the swamp, up to its shoulders. When the people heard its bellowing they came and tried to haul it out. But it sank in further, so they shot it. Then they tried to raise it but still could not, so all that beef went to waste.

'There is nothing but beef to eat at the Tremont,' said Adelaide. 'No mutton. No pork, though there are pigs enough around in the streets.'

'Which pigs,' said Captain Carey, 'you would not want to eat, ma'am. Nobody does, leastwise not as I know. See, the pigs clean the place up. Those pigs are scavengers, and living on dead dogs and snakes like they do, they taste of snake and dog.'

Having learned this, they rode on.

The clouds had cleared. The day was fine. A breeze tempered the heat. The beach of firm sand stretched ahead. Lucy broke into a trot and then a canter. She loved to ride. A path veered to the left from the beach, and her horse, given its head, followed it. Behind her she heard Mr Twining call out, but took no notice. Then the deeper voice of Captain Carey called out. She glanced back, saw the others three hundred yards behind her, waved back, and let her horse run on.

Mr Twining made as if to pursue her, but Captain Carey forbade it. His tone of command was unmistakable. 'Stay here. Stay with the lady,' and, leaving Mr Twining and Adelaide on the beach, he went full gallop after Lucy. But her horse came to a halt before he could reach her. Then, standing still, it reared and she, riding side saddle, barely kept her seat. Captain Carey, seeing this, reined in and came up cautiously at a slow walk. When he reached her, her horse was calm, and stood lifting its left forefoot. Lucy, looking down, saw that the horse had put his hoof through a human skull. Looking around, she saw that everywhere she was surrounded by human fragments – bones here, there a tuft of hair breaking through the surface, and there again splinters of rotten wood that had been a coffin.

Captain Carey dismounted, and led both horses back to the beach.

Lucy, being led as she had not been since she was a child, said to the man: 'That was foolish of me.'

'The storm,' he said. 'The soil is sparse enough anywhere on the island, and mighty thin there. Never could do more than scratch a grave out in that grave ground, and then the storm came and shifted what soil there was. I had reckoned to give it a wide berth.'

Neither Captain Carey nor Lucy told the others. What they had seen remained between them. No point in distressing the other lady, he said. She nodded, and kept the scene of carnage to herself. Mr Twining and Adelaide naturally concluded that the man had pursued Lucy to stop a bolting horse and she let them think that. They returned quietly by a dirt path which skirted many newly built houses. From each house came a sweet scent. It was the cedar wood, said Captain Carey, which was the easiest to bring over from the near mainland, and was everywhere used for cooking fires.

Next day the Texian navy returned to its home port. The sloop *Austin* and the brig *Wharton* stood off in the channel, near the wharfs. Shore batteries saluted the vessels. Pinnaces, launches, and small boats of all kinds, filled with cheering citizens, rowed out to the vessels. Crowds assembled on shore. Half the town went down to the waterfront.

'What is that flag the sloop is flying?' asked Lucy.

The master of an American merchantman told her. 'The battle flag of Texas. Looks mighty like the stars and stripes. The stripes are there all right, but if you look you'll see, where the twenty-six stars for twenty-six states are on the American flag, just the one white star of Texas. At any distance you can't tell. Looks like the stars and bars, and I'd say a Texas ship, if she were to fall in with a Mexican squadron at sea, would be glad of the mistake.'

But the man who spoke was an American. The Texians on shore were gathered to welcome their navy after a splendid victory over Mexican steamships. They had known the news for a week and regarded it as a salvation, since they were convinced that the steamships would otherwise have bombarded Galveston. The crowds called again and again for the commodore to appear. Sailors leaned over the *Wharton*'s rails and caught bouquets thrown up to them. Two young officers waved from the quarter deck of the *Austin*, but there was no sign of the commodore. The mayor sent a message of congratulations and proposed a civic banquet. The commodore replied by letter, regretting he could not come ashore unless it was to surrender himself to President Houston.

All this came out in dribs and drabs of news, gossip, and rumour. It was only human that two men, seeing their women in the crowds, jumped overboard from the *Wharton* and swam to the wharf, where they were cheered ashore. Then the city sheriff himself went aboard the *Austin* and assured the commodore that he had no warrant, no authority, and not the slightest wish to arrest him. Moreover, he wouldn't, if he had a warrant in his hand signed by Sam Houston himself. Then Commodore Moore came ashore to great rejoicing.

'What is all this?' asked Mr Lindsay Twining, who had now recovered enough to take over the leadership of his little party, and had sought out the British consul and his wife. Mr and Mrs Consul Kennedy were taking dinner with the Twinings and Lucy at the Tremont while the whole town rang with celebration around them.

'May I suggest you might try a Vox Populi,' said Kennedy, handing Mr Lindsay Twining the card which set out the Tremont's specialities in aperitifs.

Lucy took the card from Mr Kennedy and read aloud from

it: 'Vox Populi there is. And Virginia Fancy, Knickerbocker, Cock Tail. What is Cock Tail?'

'Mostly gin, ma'am,' said the waiting girl standing by their table, 'with rum, and . . . '

'Now, Kennedy,' said the elder Twining again, 'I take your point about *vox populi*. I hear the voice of the people outside. But what is all this? These ships come home. They are received with much clamour. The commodore declines to come ashore, talking about arrest . . . '

'Because,' said Kennedy, 'it was Lamar's navy. President Houston has always thought it useless. He determined to sell the Texian navy six months ago. It was then at New Orleans. He sent a commissioner to New Orleans to sell it. The commodore, not wanting his ships sold under him, preferred to go privateering in the Gulf, encouraged by funds from some New Orleans merchants who hoped he might take great prizes to be shared with them. He was encouraged also, it is said, by the very commissioner who was sent to sell him up. And the Texian crews had not been paid for two years, so the balance of opinion was in favour of not being sold up before they at least went and had a go at what Mexican ships they could find, and took what prizes they could. They did find Mexican ships, and there was an engagement. With what result I don't know. Both sides claim a victory. But the prizes the Texians took cannot have been much, since I gather from talking with two officers this afternoon that they and the men have still not been paid.'

'So the commodore has disobeyed his orders?'

'You could say so. A month ago President Houston had the city papered with posters accusing him of fraud, desertion, piracy, and murder. I am not certain who was supposed to be murdered. The posters were all torn down by the citizens, who regard the commodore as a hero. That is the jubilation you can hear in the street and outside the liquoring halls. They do not admire Houston one bit, and that is the growling and murmuring you can hear.'

'We have heard little good of the president,' said Adelaide. 'At New Orleans that Frenchman, Saligny, had nothing but ill to say of him.'

'If you should see the president, Mrs Twining, you will find he will have more than a little good to say of himself. And you will find him persuasive. Most do. If he were here tonight, he would very likely talk them round. Sometimes I think he could even talk them around to loving his precious Indians. Did you see that letter of his that was published in the Galveston newspaper?'

'His message to the Indian chief?' said Mr John Twining. 'I did see that.'

'Yes,' said Kennedy. 'Now Flacco is a chief he has known for many years, and his son died. So it is in order for the president to say that his heart is sad and grieves for Flacco, and that the birds are silent – even though Texians would prefer their president not to write like an Indian. But then he signs himself "Thy brother, Sam Houston." And that's unwise, because most people loathe the Indians.'

'Are they,' asked John Twining, 'as blood red as they are painted?'

'I do not know. I have met few Indians, and I have met those few here in Galveston, not on the prairies when they were coming at me for my scalp. I just say it is unwise to love them so openly. And then there are those Mier prisoners, too.'

'Those who were decimated in Mexico?' asked Mr Lindsay Twining.

'The same. Houston did not want to send men into Mexico. He ordered them back. They refused. They went on. He disowned them. So far he has all the right on his side. But then you get this wretched affair of the diezmo, and all Texas is outraged, not by Santa Anna who shot them but by Houston, because he will not, and could not, send an army to rescue the nine out of ten that were not shot. That girl from the hotel who was serving us just now . . .'

'The one,' said Lucy, 'who was telling us about Cock Tail?'

'That one. She is German. Her sweetheart, who is also German, is with the Texian prisoners. He escaped the diezmo. He writes to her, and, Lord knows how, she sometimes receives the letters, by way of neutral ships out of Vera Cruz, or somehow. There are others like her, with men in Mexico for whom Houston will do nothing, and almost certainly can do nothing. She can hardly be a partisan of Houston, can she?'

'And where is Captain Elliot?' Lucy asked after a long pause in the conversation.

'Ah,' said Kennedy, who did not always see eye to eye with Elliot, who as chargé d'affaires was his superior. 'He's in Washington.'

'Washington?'

'On-the-Brazos, with Sam Houston. He and the president are thick as thieves.'

Late at night, when they had all talked long after dinner, they all walked out on to the portico in front of the hotel. There, on the corner, suspended from a lamppost, a straw figure of Sam Houston burned brightly.

'Well,' said Kennedy, 'that does not quite mean what it would in London. What with the navy, the Indians, and the Mier prisoners, the president is up to his neck in trouble. But burning someone or other in effigy is a frequent recreation. I have seen Houston burned before, and then a few months later he was elected president. If he pulls off some treaty now with Mexico, or slaughters a few Mexicans in some skirmish, he will be a hero again. Good night.'

Lucy was about to go inside when she saw, standing on the sidewalk illuminated by the flames licking at the effigy of Sam Houston, the tall, straw-haired girl who had served them at dinner. She watched the girl, and felt a strong fellow-feeling rise in her, for a woman whose man was in danger. Lucy had known that helpless fear. The memory of it had never entirely left her, and had returned sharply that afternoon when she stumbled on the bones, and hair, and rotten wood.

She went up to the girl.

'Forgive me,' she said.

The girl turned, and recognised her.

'I have heard that your man is a prisoner in Mexico. And I am sorry. And I wish him well, and you.'

The girl inclined her head and gravely answered, 'Thank you.'

Then she turned her eyes back to the blazing figure of Houston. Lucy went inside. She did not know and could not know half of the turmoil in the mind of Helga Becker.

9

The Birthright

After sunset, on the verandah of the Texian capitol, General Houston and Captain Elliot talked empires. Behind the capitol the slaves were at supper. In Hatfield's gambling saloon more ready money, in United States silver dollars, was changing hands in one evening than would be needed to pay the salary of Houston's cabinet for a year.

They sat by the light of an oil lamp. A curtain of muslin netting, weighted down with bird shot at the hem, helped to keep off the midges and mosquitoes. The tobacco smoke from Elliot's pipe helped too.

'Dear Captain,' said Houston, 'I do congratulate you on this vindication of your Chinese policy. The Celestial Empire is vanquished. Now I must admit, as any man half-honest would have to admit, that there's a tinge of envy in my congratulations. It must have been a splendid theatre in which to play a part. I should love to have played a part there. The whole of China opened up, and according to the plan suggested by you. Canton, Shanghai, Amoy, open to the trade of the civilised world. I shall have a word with our Galveston merchants. We must send a ship to Shanghai now it is open and safe – and you, my friend, are the man who began to make it so.'

China had been much on Captain Elliot's mind since the newspapers from Galveston and New Orleans had arrived at Washington-on-the-Brazos that morning bringing news of a victory won months before by a fleet of thirty-four British men o'war over a collection of imperial war junks.

He had come over that evening, as he often did these days, to take a glass of wine with a man he now regarded as a companion and friend. He found, as he feared he would, that Houston had devoured the same reports of the treaty imposed on the Chinese and the indemnities extracted from them. Not only that; the president also had his big globe out on the verandah, and had found on it those cities which would now be open to the west. He had been unable to find Hong Kong, which also figured largely in the newspaper reports.

Elliot showed him. 'General, see where Macau is marked? Now, come east a hairsbreadth, and there's the island, too small to be seen even on that splendid globe of yours.'

'What does the name mean?'

'I was told something like Fragrant Harbour. Fragrant it was not, but it is a magnificent harbour.'

'And Canton I did find but have lost.'

Elliot indicated the Pearl River and traced its course a hundred miles inland to Canton.

'I can never hear the name of Canton,' he said, 'or see it on a map, without hearing the voice of my interpreter there. A strange high voice for a man who was so big in his body. A huge man for a Chinese. I heard his voice in my head earlier today when I read the same reports I see you have read. There he would be, translating some edict of the emperor conveyed to me by the commissioner, Lin. Lin was the emperor's man in the Canton province. "Be speedy, be speedy," my poor man would say, translating the insolent edicts which always ended with those words, telling me, the Foreigner, to be speedy to do the emperor's will. And the man's voice would be trembling and apologetic as he read the emperor's words, as if he thought himself insolent to retail such words to me. I can still hear his voice as he translated with such deference the emperor's threats to the Foreigner Elliott, the Taipan Elliot, the Source of Evil, who was to be driven back to his own country, and his contemptible forces extirpated. And always, at the end of each edict, "Be speedy, be speedy." I can still hear it.'

'I read this morning,' said Houston, 'that it was you who first blockaded Canton, two years ago, and then spared the city. I knew you were in China, but I did not know you did that. Now that was a fine thing – to have such power, and show such magnanimity.'

'It was not a thing I was praised by everyone for doing,' said Elliot.

'It wouldn't be. Thousands have never forgiven me for not shooting Santa Anna when I had him in my hands. And since this Mier affair, tens of thousands more have newly discovered they never forgave me for letting Santa Anna live. But it would have been barbarous to kill him in cold blood, and besides I had everything to gain by keeping him alive. But to spare a whole city, when you had a fleet that could destroy it, now there's a fine thing.'

'I was not the commander in chief of the fleet, merely the civil power.'

'But the fleet obeyed when you ordered it to withdraw?' said Houston. 'Therefore, if you had seen fit to give other orders . . . ?'

Elliot could not rise to this. He could not answer this question. He had possessed all effective power over a squadron of men o'war, but he had been driven out of China. Driven out not by the Emperor but by the political interest of the China merchants in London who were enraged at his having previously handed over twenty thousand casks of their opium at Canton. This was before his fleet arrived from India, and before he had the Chinese at his mercy. The Chinese demanded the opium, and he had no choice. He ordered its surrender to prevent a massacre of the Europeans in the city. He gave the merchants receipts for their opium, and the British government later paid them for it. But they still accused him of acting like a mandarin enforcing the Chinese law upon them, and of failing in his duty as British plenipotentiary. Then he had returned with the fleet and blockaded Canton. He had done well enough, but because of the opium he was replaced and brought home.

But he could tell Houston none of this. They were friends. But between a head of state and the chargé d'affaires of a foreign state there can be friendship but never intimacy. The first interests he represented were always those of his government. It was his duty to preserve a distance, and therefore, certainly, it was his duty to say nothing that could suggest his recall from China had been anything but proper.

Houston saw this. He did not know the whole story. He could not even guess at it. But he felt Elliot's reticence and in part understood it. His feline instinct did understand such things. So he poured Elliot another glass of the good French Bordeaux that had come up from Galveston that morning with the newspapers, and said he would be sorry to see poor Joe Eve go.

'Judge Eve?'

'He came out here for his wife's health. Now she is blooming but he has been ill for two months. So ill that he has been recalled.'

'Then I'm sorry for it. He was kind to me when I arrived here without a bed or even a blanket.'

'Margaret is unwell too. Sam junior thrives but she does not, and so she will stay east for a while longer.'

Elliot nodded.

'I am sorry,' he said. And he was. Houston's son, Sam junior, then two months old, was a child who would thrive. Margaret, though in the opinion of all she had reformed her husband, was a woman who looked too fragile for the life of the Texian frontier.

Houston took another glass, and then mentioned that he would be most obliged for the captain's opinion on a document he had received that day.

'It is,' he said, 'a naval matter, which needs the knowledge of a naval man to make head or tail of.'

He placed in Elliot's hands the report of a surveyor who, after two days' negotiations with the commodore at Galveston, and having bribed the boatswain, had got himself on board the *Austin* and examined her fabric.

Elliot read it over. 'To be fitted out for sea, would need entirely new bulwarks, new lower masts, new fore and cross jack yards, new sails in part, all running and part of standing rigging; a part of her sails, from going so long without drying, have become so mildewed that they would not be fit for use. On board her are five hundred charges of powder, which would not answer to be taken to sea.'

He had never seen such a catalogue. He said nothing.

'Captain, if she were a vessel of the British navy, what would you say to that?'

'That she had been five years in the tropics, twelve months without sight of land, with the carpenter and sailmaker dead, and half her people besides.' He did not add that all her officers would be court martialled and all her ratings dismissed.

Houston kept his face expressionless.

'When was this vessel built?' asked Elliot.

'Two years ago, at Baltimore.'

'All the Baltimore vessels I have seen have been well built, and some superbly built,' said Elliot, handing back the surveyor's report. He did not ask what the vessel was, and did not want to be told. He could not fail to know that she was either the Texian sloop or one of the two brigs he had seen the year before at New Orleans, when all had been ship-shape. Something had gone badly wrong since then. The report read like that of an old, neglected, badly officered, undercrewed, slummocky merchantman. All that, however, did not make her officers pirates. Houston's proclamation to that effect had been tactfully ignored by the navies of France, England, and the United States, all of whom had disregarded his appeal to all naval powers to arrest the vessels of his navy wherever they were met with on the high seas. Elliot had no intention of being drawn into that matter, or into the president's quarrels with his commodore.

Houston tossed the surveyor's report aside and embarked on the idea of empire. 'Now the celestial empire of China,' he said, 'proved in the end powerless because it claimed too much, because it claimed to rule a tenth of the globe when in fact the emperors had not the means to rule much beyond their principal cities. Would you say?'

'That, and the determination of the emperor and his mandarins to keep all barbarian foreigners from all trade with the celestial empire. And their determination, against all the evidence, not to see that a frigate could blow three war junks out of the water with one broadside.'

'Yes. But the empire that concerns me is that of the United States. There is such an appetite for conquest that one end of the union cannot hope to know the other, let alone share the same real interests. Already, what has Massachusetts in common with Georgia, let alone with Michigan or Arkansas? To be blunt, how much common accord has there ever been between New York and Virginia? But now there is talk of the Floridas as a state of the American union. Indian territories are taken. All talk, all movements, on the part of the United States seem to me to indicate an eye to empire, and an empire that will rupture in the not too distant future.'

Houston had not been this explicit before. Elliot listened. Then he said: 'General Houston, you were born an American.'

'Just so. I was born an American. I served in the army of the United States, and in the Congress of the United States. I know the Americans. I know their generous daring. I know their genius. I know their excitability. I know their love of dominion, this endless appetite for the extension of their territory. There is already in place a Union so vast that the founding fathers could never have imagined it. If they had, they would have provided against it in the Constitution. Add to it further, and it will stretch itself to breaking. And then there will be war.'

Elliot put out a hand, touched Houston's globe with one finger, and slowly spun it. 'My colleagues in the United Kingdom will be interested to know your opinions on this subject,' he said. 'With your permission I shall convey those opinions to them.'

Houston watched the globe, and then stopped it with his hand, leaving it so that as the two men sat side by side in the lamp light it was the continent of North America that lay between them.

'That continent,' he said, 'includes the Texas Republic, and my opinions are, therefore, also of interest to the representative of Great Britain in Texas. The continent of North America, the whole continent, is regarded by the people of the United States as their birthright – to be secured by policy if they can, by force if they must. They cannot realise that Texas and the United States now form two nations. Texas is entitled, by her darings, her sufferings, and her privations, to an independent place among the nations of the world.'

Elliot drew on his pipe: 'For a while now Great Britain and France have recognised that you are indeed two nations. And though poor Judge Eve said often enough and plainly enough that the United States and Texas ought to be one nation, his very presence here as chargé d'affaires was proof that they were not.'

Houston sat silent for a moment and then rose. 'Elliot,' he said, 'I have a ceremony to attend to, and should be grateful for your company. Martha is marrying Peter, and since I have known Martha since she was two hours old, and since I named her, I have promised to give her in marriage.'

He took a covered lantern and led the way to the slaves' shanty. The two men walked towards the sound of a lively fiddle and the aroma of roast mutton and fried chicken. At the door they were greeted by the bride's mother, who called Houston Mr Sam, and then by the bridegroom, a young black who called him Master. Then they entered, and the girl Martha came shyly over to him, and then threw herself into his arms, embracing him.

The whole ceremony was something Elliot remembered for many years, most of all for the part Houston played in it. He had seldom seen the president so much at ease – certainly more at ease than he was at his wife's tea parties. Then there was – and Elliot felt he could only use this word – the *paganism* of it all, and Houston's ready acceptance of that paganism. Elliot had gone expecting a form of Christian service and words spoken by a minister of religion. But Houston's giving of the girl in marriage was just that. He took her by both hands, led her to her bridegroom, and delivered her into the literal embrace of her man, who took her head in his hands and then ran his hands down her body, from her throat to her waist and hips, and then to her feet. Then she took possession of him in the same way and with the same gestures. The formal act of marriage was the pair's jumping over a broomstick held out for them by Sam Houston, at which a cry arose from the assembled slaves, and the pair were put to bed on the instant in the same room, behind a mere screen.

The happiness of it all was plain. They had feasted on mutton, which Elliot knew from his own experience was a rare delicacy. They had eaten chicken, which was also none too plentiful, and Houston was obviously content that they should eat his mutton and his chicken. He was happy at his entire part in the whole ritual. He

was happy to be Mr Sam, happy to embrace this girl, happy to hold
out a broomstick for her and her man.

'How old is the girl?' asked Elliot.

Houston asked the girl's mother, who, after reckoning it out,
answered that Martha was thirteen.

'Thirteen,' said Elliot. He was shocked.

'Come, Captain, what was the marriageable age of Roman citizens?'

He knew that as an educated Englishman – that is to say an
Englishman educated only in the classics – Elliot would know that
the Roman age of consent for a girl was twelve.

Elliot did know, and conceded the point. 'And when they have
children, will you own those children?' he asked.

'In law, yes.'

'This is the law of Texas you are speaking of, not Rome?'

'It is. But I would no more sell mother and child apart than
I would forcibly separate a white mother and child. I do own the
child she already has and would not separate them for the world.'

'She already has a child?'

'It is the custom. A man and woman want children. They wait
until they know the woman will bear children. Either until she is
with child, or, more often, until the first child is a few months old
and thriving.'

Houston said his goodnights to the blacks, leaving them to
their revels, and he and Elliot walked back.

'Come on Elliot, you and I are a world apart in such matters.
But what of it? Does it erect a barrier between us?'

'I could not own slaves myself. I could never accept any form
of slavery – even as benevolent as yours is over your people. But
I shall not hold anti-slavery meetings. That is not my business. If,
as captain of a British ship, I intercepted a vessel carrying slaves
at sea, I should free the slaves, impound the vessel, and see the
master tried for piracy. But the laws of Texas within the Republic
are not my business. On principle I refuse to own slaves or hire
another man's slave to work for me as a servant, and that costs me
dear because white men in Texas seem mightily disinclined to act

as anyone's servant, unless for great wages. So I pay high for my principles. And I pay high with my own money since the foreign office in London, while approving the reason I will not hire slaves, declines to compensate me for the inevitable results.'

Houston laughed. Elliot had not heard him laugh aloud before. Strange that so demonstrative a man should often smile but never laugh. He threw an arm round Elliot's shoulder and they returned to the verandah.

He offered more wine but Elliot declined, preferring just his pipe. In the presence of his wife Houston took no alcohol. While she was away he still drank no spirits, but did permit himself wine. That evening he had taken a great deal of wine.

'You know, Captain Elliot, you are seen here, by those who want annexation at any price, as the personification of British double dealing, turpitude, greed for trade, greed for power. The spectre of Great Britain, and the spectre of Elliot – perhaps I should say the spectre of the Taipan Elliot – will be conjured up, and so will every ridiculous humbug which the crazed imagination can marshal. All for the purpose of alarming Texas, exciting disorder, and producing suspicion of England. You will hear it said that England will exact, as the price of any treaty of support, a solemn covenant from Texas to abolish slavery. This will be said often. It will be said to compel Texians to look to the United States, and only to the United States, for their salvation.'

'I have heard something of the sort.'

'From the Texian Congress?'

Elliot nodded.

'And I,' said Sam Houston with real warmth, 'can do nothing without Congress. Congress is always of two minds. One mind one day, the other the next. I can do nothing while Congress is in session unless I slip in quickly, interposing myself between its two minds. The Congress says it wants peace – and so will take annexation with the United States at any price, and damn our national independence. The Congress, still in the search for peace, wants to make me a dictator and invade Mexico – and I veto the bill. So the government is often at a standstill. This is what we have come to with these wonderful republican theories.'

Elliot did not betray himself by any change of expression. He sat back and drew on his pipe again. But here was Sam Houston, a man who had spent most of his public life in the service of two republics, and now he spoke like this?

'I tell you, Captain, you are lucky to have a monarchy in England. I wish to heaven we had. Things would be better very soon. But it will come. Not in our day perhaps, but for our children. The entire world will soon be undeceived by the example of events in the United States. And between ourselves, Captain, I am convinced that there will not exist, in fifty years' time, a single republican government on the face of the earth.'

10

The River of
the Arms of God

'The forest,' exclaimed Lucy, 'is an ornamental shrubbery on the most gigantic scale.' She and Jeannie were looking up from the back of the flatboat at a magnolia whose branches formed an arch eighty feet over their heads. They were at the confluence of the Brazos and Navasota rivers. Either side of them, on the river banks, grew elm, oak, walnut, and other trees she had never seen before and could not recognise.

Lucy leaned her head far back, holding on to her wide straw hat with one hand, and with the other catching Jeannie's shoulder for support, as she arched her back from the waist to see as far as she could into the tops of these extraordinary trees.

'What is that?'

'Hackberry,' said the boatman, 'the one whose fruit you see the birds eating, and the paper mulberry next to it, the smaller one, because there's paper made from the soft inner bark.'

'Smaller?' she said. The tree was all of fifty feet, but compared to the hackberry it was small.

'And persimmon,' said the man, 'that we get a dye from.' He reached up, plucked one of the lower leaves as they drifted by, and placed it in her hand.

'Furry,' she said.

'And with fruit like plums,' he said, 'only bitter yet. Be sweeter later on in the season. See there, like plums.'

'Orangey-coloured plums, then,' she said.

Nothing was ordinary. All was extraordinary. She knew trees. Her great uncle had taught her to know them. There were many she had never seen, but the most astonishing of all were the familiar trees that grew there, in the bottom land of the Brazos, to an amazing size. At home she saw magnolia most often as a bush. Here it was a forest tree.

But then, the previous two days had been a constant amazement. After the flatness and desolation of Galveston island – that island of sand and swamp and bones and dead wood – the journey up the Brazos had taken her and her companions into a country that was all alive. The first day was by river steamer, the second by flatboat.

On the first day a new settler from Georgia, hearing from their talk that Lucy and the Twinings were British, harangued his fellow passengers as if they were a political meeting, arguing forcibly that the best course for Texas was to become a British colony. His reasoning was that since Georgia had flourished longer as a British colony than as a state of the United States, then that was the natural order of things.

'Ha,' said a tall farmer, looking contemptuously up and down the ragged figure of the Georgian. 'Damn British might want Georgia, but not with you as part of the deal.'

The Georgian spoke on through the laughter. His audience, who were mostly American but with some Germans among them, grew scornful. Whether or not the British would have the Georgian, the rest were not interested in cultivating a colony for the British queen and would have none of her. The orator grew heated, and he would have ended up thrown in the river if the first of the day's miracles had not occurred. A herd of wild horses appeared. They were fearless of the belching steamboat, trotted alongside, and were startled only when the captain blew his steam whistle. Then the whole herd broke into a gallop and flew off into the distance with manes and tails streaming, leaving a trail of dust that rose high and then slowly settled.

'And I did not believe him,' Lucy told Adelaide. 'Dr Smith told me about wild horses. I thought it was an entertainment. I thought it was a wild horse story to entertain me. But they are there – a hundred of them.'

'Make tough eating, though,' said an American, who had continued to lean on the rail, chewing tobacco, throughout this apparition of beautiful horses, and gave no sign that he saw anything remarkable. When the animals stampeded away he spat once again on the deck, which was already slippery with tobacco juice.

Then a panther appeared, slipping silently along the bank, leaping into the lower branches of a post oak, following the boat and its passengers with an unmoving stare. After that the abundant wild pigs, routing in packs, caused no sort of stir.

'Savager than your cougar,' said a hunter coolly. 'Kill a man. Come at you with tusks. Bold.'

'Like boars out of a story,' said Adelaide. 'Like boars on some tapestry, being hunted, goring hunters.'

'Good eating,' said the hunter, at which another American enquired whether the first speaker had ever, as he once had, shot twenty deer in a day. Receiving no reply at all he repeated his question to the younger Mr Twining, who had to admit that the largest creatures he had ever shot were game birds, and the largest of these were geese. And some pigeons, he said.

'Pigeon,' remarked a third man, offhand. 'Now I surely recollect bringing down eighty-seven pigeons with one blast.'

'Really?' returned Mr John Twining, after the slightest pause. And although, as he and all the British party were rapidly discovering, English and American were two distinct languages, he found that this pause, as much as the one word he spoke and the intonation with which he spoke it, revealed that he was expressing disbelief, a disbelief which offended the American.

John Twining and the American stood facing each other. It was the wisdom and quick thinking of Mr Lindsay Twining, those qualities which had made his fortune in tea, which saved the day.

'It was,' he enquired, 'a double-barrelled shotgun you were using, sir?'

The older Mr Twining had even learned the use of the American 'Sir', a word rarely spoken among Englishmen who were equals but uttered, as it seemed to him, every fifth word by the Americans and Texians he had met.

'It was, sir,' said the American. The elder Mr Twining nodded in understanding, as if to say that of course explained everything. His younger brother took his cue and nodded in turn. Honour was satisfied all round.

Now it happened that they were approaching sundown. Not ten minutes after this exchange, out of the western dusk, appeared a distant flock of birds, which turned into a distant cloud of birds, which became a cloud of birds that was nearly upon them. The cloud grew until it darkened the setting sun. Everyone on board gazed up at the beating of wings as this cloud passed over the steamboat.

'Pigeons by God,' said Mr Lindsay Twining, holding Adelaide close to him as the last of the birds passed over and veered south.

'Passenger pigeons, yep,' said the American.

'Even I,' said the younger Mr Twining, 'could bag twenty of those with one shot. Not eighty. Not fifty, not I. But twenty perhaps.'

'With a double-barrelled gun, sir?' said the American. Both Mr Twinings laughed, and friendship was altogether restored. And Mr Lindsay Twining, still holding his wife by the waist, was finding her growing dearer to him by the hour, and himself growing by the hour more grateful to this American and Texian trip in the Gulf that was bringing about so happy an issue.

Next day there were the bisons. The remaining passengers had left the river steamboat and were now on board a flatboat, one of the sort Adelaide had called a punt when she saw them at New Orleans. Most of the Americans and all the Germans had stayed at the overnight stop of San Felipe, one of the original Texian settlements, which now had more than fifty houses. One of the remaining Americans was the man who had brought down eighty-seven pigeons with one blast of his shotgun. He was now on the friendliest terms with the British, and had appointed himself their guide, keeping up a constant commentary.

The land was now prairie, broken occasionally by islands of trees, but the greater part of the landscape was prairie of a lushness unknown to the Twinings' European eyes. Where the river banks were low the grasses rose above the passengers' heads, so that they were surrounded by green.

'Mulatto prairies,' said the American.

'Mulatto?' asked Adelaide.

'On account of the dark richness of the soil, ma'am. Soil like a mulatto woman, if you'll pardon the way of putting it. Part that tall grass with your hands, ma'am, as you safely could without harm to the softest skin, and you would find no stones, not a pebble. Dark soil. Soil like a woman. Not surpassed in fertility by the far-famed lands of the delta of the Nile.'

Adelaide coloured. The American continued to expound the richness of the country. During a short break in his recital a dull sound was heard in the east, at first no more than a distant resonance. Then it grew until they could no longer hear the lapping of the water along the sides of the flatboat.

They all listened intently. All conversation ceased. The air was full of the sound.

'Cattle running,' said the older Mr Twining.

'Tcha,' exclaimed the American, who had been observing with amusement the intent faces of the British party. Cattle it was, of a sort, as he had very well known. He felt himself cheated out of his native right to explain the mystery. But he still had his revelation to impart.

'Bison,' he said.

And they were. As the ground rose to the right of them they saw a sea of running beasts. The American whooped in triumph. Adelaide and Lucy laughed aloud at the splendid sight. The two Twining brothers gazed in awe.

'There's your cattle,' said the American. 'Bison.'

'They are more marvellous than the horses,' said Lucy. 'A thousand of them? Five thousand?'

'No such beasts in Europe,' said the American, announcing that as a fact.

'But,' said Lucy, 'there is no dust. Where is the dust? There was dust with the horses.'

It was, the American explained as if to children, the nature of the country, the nature of the land. The wild horses had raised dust from terrain that was rich. Granted it was rich. But that was the day before. Compared to this, yesterday's soil was friable, apt to blow away. That soil was not your rich mulatto soil.

'Your mulatto soil, ladies, this blackland prairie soil here, gentlemen, is not soil to be puffed away, not even with the pounding of twenty thousand hoofs, not when the beasts are running on a carpet of prairie grass eight feet tall. No sir.'

They ate a lunch of roast squirrel, which the boatman said you could hereabouts pick off the trees, and they were floating through the heat of the afternoon when Lucy recalled another miracle which Mr Smith had promised but which she had not yet seen. She asked about the wild flowers which, he had told her, enamelled the prairie.

The American nodded casually, as if she had asked him to satisfy her curiosity in the matter of a trifle.

'Now the bison raised no dust, ma'am?'

'No.'

'But they flattened the prairie. You saw the trampled grasses lay down flat? Now, come winter, all your tall grass prairies die down, and lay flat, and the land is covered with a grey-green mat. And come spring, that mat is covered with your primroses, squaw weed, bluebells, snow on the prairie. Those are your flowers. And as to enamelling the prairie, why, I never saw enamel. But it is as if ten thousand men had walked over the prairie, in a line, scattering petals broadcast.'

As they turned a bend in the river and saw the shanties of Washington-on-the-Brazos, and prepared to part, the younger Mr Twining offered the man a gold sovereign. The American scarcely glanced at it, leaving John Twining with the offered coin still held out in his hand.

'I showed you my country, sir,' he said, 'as I expect you would show yours, to strangers.'

The Brazos, as they ascended it, had been reddish, muddy, and brackish. Now, at the point where the Brazos met the Navasota, the waters of its tributary flowed clear, limpid, and shallow. The arching magnolias, eighty feet high, were reflected on the clear river bed.

Next morning Mr Lindsay Twining's famous tact misled him. The

appointment he had requested by letter was with the president, but
wishing to act strictly according to protocol he presented himself first
not at the presidential office but at that of the secretary of state. This
was a mistake. He could not know that all protocol demanded was
that he and his party should turn up at Sam Houston's verandah.
Dr Anson Jones, having kept him waiting for twenty minutes, was
anxious to impress upon Mr Twining that the affairs of the Republic
devolved almost entirely upon himself, and that this was in particular
true of all foreign matters.

Mr Twining, in a long commercial life, had met the likes of
Dr Jones often enough. He knew it would defeat his purpose to
say outright, or indeed to say in any way however subtle, that he
and his people had no interest whatever in talking to Dr Jones. He
could not say that their only business was with General Houston, the
world-known man. So he smiled and made small talk and temporised.
Then after fifteen minutes of civilities he mentioned that his letter
had been addressed to the president, and that it was therefore only
civil of him to request that the president should be informed of his
presence. Dr Jones regretted that the president was much occupied
with the preparations for a visit to the Cherokees, but stated again
that he, Dr Jones, was at Mr Twining's service.

'Ah,' said Mr Twining, and was leaning further back in his
chair, becoming every moment more affable and every moment
more determined to get past this man Jones as he had got past
a hundred other obstructive subordinates, when he had a stroke
of luck. Mr Miller, the president's secretary, entered. Mr Twining
in a moment mentioned his letter to the president, and in another
moment was on his feet, smiling back at Dr Jones, and accompa-
nying Mr Miller. He was greatly assisted by the undoubted fact that
Miller had a low opinion of the secretary of state, and habitually did
everything he could to thwart him.

A meeting was arranged. Mr Twining and party would come
along to see General Houston in thirty minutes' time.

When the two Mr Twinings, Adelaide, and Lucy kept their appointment they were given chairs on the porch, from where they could
hear murmured conversation between Miller's voice and another.

Then they were shown straight in.

Sam Houston was standing with one hand poised on the terrestrial globe which he had used to demonstrate matters of empire to Captain Elliot. He was not wearing uniform of any kind, or clothes that could serve as the civilian dress of the president of a republic, but only a Cherokee robe.

He stood there like a monolith, quite still, with his great head held high, and wearing this robe of red, indigo, and gold. It was true he was not standing on a table, but Lucy's mind went back to Saligny's description of his own first meeting, of Sam Houston in his Indian robe, of the robe thrown back to reveal the general's republican wounds, and of the robe being all there was.

She spoke first.

'You will not,' she asked, 'receive us as you did Monsieur Saligny?'

At which she could have sworn he was for the moment confused.

Both the Mr Twinings stood unspeaking, taken back by these words of Lucy's. Adelaide glanced sideways at Lucy and saw a smile on her lips. She also saw, more quickly than her husband, that all would go well with the president.

Houston surveyed the four visitors before him, gazed at the girl who had uttered those words to him, and smiled a slow smile.

'Ha!' he said. 'Saligny. No. You require my word? You have my word.'

Then, while being civil to the men by addressing occasional remarks to them on foreign affairs, international trade, and the various qualities of tea, he concerned himself almost exclusively with the two women, gallantly kissing their hands and engaging them most earnestly in conversation about the colour of a ribbon. It was only the colour of a ribbon they talked of, but it was not small talk. He sat with them, drawing his chair close to theirs, leaning forward, turning from one to the other, listening carefully, looking each in the eye. Miller, standing behind the president, observed the absorbed circle of heads – Houston's shaggy chestnut mane, Lucy's shining black hair, and the gentle mouse of Adelaide's. He had seen it all before. Houston, both with men and with women, had this gift of absorption in whatever he was for the moment doing, and the gift of drawing others into the aura and atmosphere of his own intensity. This is a great gift in a politician. Miller had seen it when he knew it was policy on Houston's part. He had seen it when he knew it was real. He had seen it when he was not sure whether it was policy or real. He thought this was real – and it was over the colour of a ribbon. Sam Houston charmed them, and they were charmed by him.

'You see, ladies, I am a friend to order in the Republic, and therefore I have started an order of chivalry – to create some reward for the worthy, as we have little cash, to encourage gentlemen in preserving order.'

'That,' said Lucy, 'is what I have always thought English and Scottish orders of chivalry were all about in the first place. A reward in lieu of cash. Convenient for the monarch.'

'Yes. And the order is my creation, d'you see, not the Congress's, and those who hold it shall be called the Knights of San Jacinto.'

'That is the patron saint of Texas?' said Adelaide.

'That,' said Sam Houston, 'is a patch of ground on which there was a battle, at which Texas won its independence from Mexico. San Jacinto. Now if Napoleon could create his légion d'honneur, and Iturbide, the Mexican, his order of Guadaloupe, I ought to be able to give gentlemen ribands to wear over their coats. Now, ladies, what are the principal orders of Great Britain? I ask because of the colours.'

'The Garter,' said Adelaide, 'and the Bath, and . . .'

Her husband made no suggestions of his own but watched with a mounting happiness to see his Adelaide happily engaged with the president.

'And of those British orders,' Houston asked, 'which is the senior?'

'That,' answered Lucy, 'depends on the holder and where he finds himself at any moment. In England, the Garter. In Scotland, it would be the order of the Thistle. I am a Scot.'

'Then, Lady Lucy, you will have worn the sash of the Thistle?'

'No, General, I would not. They are not for women.'

'There is nothing for the ladies?'

'A king's mistress might get a duchessdom. It has been known. But no orders of chivalry.'

'Ah,' said Houston, brought up sharp by this reply. 'Ah –
but the colour of the sashes of the orders you have mentioned?'

'Blue for the Garter,' said Adelaide.

'Scarlet for the légion d'honneur,' said Lucy. 'Though I have
never seen the sash worn, only the rosette which a man wears in
his lapel.'

'See, ladies, the first recipients shall be the Texian chargés
d'affaires at the courts of London and Paris, though that's one
man, and Brussels and Hamburg. They will be received with other
ambassadors who are loaded down with orders but will have nothing
to show for themselves. So Dr Smith is one of the first . . . '

Lucy raised her eyes to Houston's. She had been thinking of
Paris, where she had seen that scarlet rosette in Godoy's shabby
coat, and seen it in the company of Ashbel Smith.

'I have met Dr Smith,' she said, and told him how and where.

'He was well?'

'Flourishing,' she said.

'I had almost determined on green,' said Houston, 'but the
point is, which green?' He took from his desk a leather folder and
opened it to show specimen ribbons, all in silk satin, all in different
greens. The folder was stamped with the name of a New Orleans
haberdasher. The order was a matter that had been for some time
in his mind.

He lifted the ribbons with his broad fingers. Lucy instinctively
took them from him with her light hands, arranging three ribbons
over Adelaide's forearm and three over her own, and then lifted
them to the light. Such was the tableau in the presidential chamber
of the Texian capitol – Houston, now standing, seriously regarding
the ribbons displayed for him by the two women, the two Englishmen
looking on, and, discreetly by the door, the president's secretary.

Houston could not decide.

'What month was San Jacinto?' asked Lucy. 'What season? What
shade was the grass?'

That way it was settled. Spring green. A small rosette to be
worn in the buttonhole of the coat over the heart, or, with court
dress, a broad sash to be worn over the left shoulder.

They were with him for nearly two hours. Houston invited them
to accompany him on his visit to the Cherokees. Mr Lindsay Twining
declined with much regret, saying that the rigours of such a journey
might be too much for the ladies. Houston nodded. Of course. The
truth was, it was a reply he was coming to expect, no matter whom
he asked. Saligny had declined a year before, with smiles but quite
adamantly. Even Captain Elliot, asked two days before to come on
this same visit, had excused himself, pleading business which would
keep him in Galveston. Well then, said Houston, since they intended
to return cross country, by way of Houston and then down Buffalo
Bayou to Galveston, he hoped to have the pleasure of their company
again in one of those cities. And he knew they wished to meet Captain
Elliot, and had hoped to find him at Washington-on-the-Brazos. But he
had left two days before, taking the route they meant to take, and so
they might meet him in Houston city too.

The president came out with them into the heat of the day.
A hundred yards away Lucy saw the high magnolia under whose
branches she had first arrived at Washington. In a moment of silence
she could just hear the waters of the river.

She stood gazing towards the magnolias. The broad brim of
her hat shaded her eyes so that Houston could see only her cheek
bones and then her chin and throat.

She asked, 'Why is it called the Brazos?'

He said, 'The Spanish called it El Rio de Los Brazos de Dios –
the River of the Arms of God. There is a tale that they were dying
of thirst, and then found this river here.'

Lucy held out her hand to Sam Houston, who, resplendent
in his Cherokee robe, bent to kiss her fingers.

He had charmed the two women by his attentions. They were
much taken with the man's bearing, and entertained by his earnest
asking of their advice in matters of chivalry and haberdashery. As for
Houston, he returned to his capitol captured by Lucy – Lucy gazing
in profile towards the Brazos, Lucy draping green sashes across her
slim arm for him to choose, Lucy saying that, surely, he would not
receive her as he had Monsieur de Saligny.

He lay that night on his bed in a state of bewilderment he

had known only once before in his life.

All the women had to share one cabin and one bed. Lucy and Adelaide, sharing a mattress of wood shavings with Jeannie, answered her questions about that afternoon's meeting with Sam Houston. They laughed together about the Indian robe. They talked drowsily about the spring green that had been chosen from all other greens to be the ensign of the order of San Jacinto. Lucy told them about the River of the Arms of God.

They lay for a while in companionable silence.

Then Lucy spoke. 'You know . . .'

Her companions stirred. Both were almost asleep despite the woodshavings which had worked their way out of the mattress and into and under their clothes.

Lucy raised herself on to one elbow.

'Do you know,' she said, 'I swear the man is shy.'

11

Retail Invasion

In the Fall of 1843 the affair of Texas was in the minds of great men in London and Washington. But in London, Lord Aberdeen, as foreign secretary, found his time rather more taken up by the old Duke of Wellington, who was fretting over the dangers of a French invasion. The great duke, the conqueror of Napoleon at Waterloo, had never forgotten the French. Now, in his middle seventies, he was still in the Cabinet as commander in chief, and often rode his grey horse alone to Downing Street.

'I could not,' he told Aberdeen one fine morning, 'raise two regiments to repel the French if they came.'

'What more can I say, Duke,' said Aberdeen, 'than that I have never known friendlier times between us and the French. There is an entente . . .'

'Damn ententes,' said the duke. 'How many regiments has an entente?'

He was as tired of Aberdeen's talk of his celebrated *entente cordiale* with France as Aberdeen was weary of the duke's constant reiteration that Waterloo had been a damn close run thing. *Entente cordiale*, thought the duke, was a fine phrase, but he was damn sure that Aberdeen, having invented the phrase, put altogether too much faith in the substance of the idea it expressed. Aberdeen, for his part, wished the duke would realise that Waterloo, though a damn close run thing, was almost thirty years in the past. Each man, in spite of these irritations, esteemed the other. When they walked together to Parliament, as they often did, older gentlemen, meeting them in the street, raised their hats and told their sons and daughters, 'That is

Wellington and Aberdeen.' The young people were awed to hear it.

'Her Majesty,' said Aberdeen, wishing to reassure the duke further, 'is about to visit the French king.'

'The queen,' said the duke, 'may do as she pleases – or is it as you please?'

Aberdeen assented with a gesture.

'Yes,' said Wellington. 'Just so. Can think of no reason why she'd want to see the man herself. Happier with her own man. Three children in three years?'

The earl assented again. The duke rode off alone, pondering the indefensibility of the southern coast of England. England did possess, as his colleagues in government sometimes reminded him, a navy ten times the size of France's. But ships were not all. He was an army man.

Towards four in the afternoon, as he was about to leave Downing Street – since the foreign office of Great Britain, in those days of its greatest power, kept civilised hours – Aberdeen glanced through the Texas correspondence which a clerk put before him. There were four letters.

First, Captain Elliot on the United States' sense of God-given right to the American continent. Nothing there that he did not already know from his minister in Washington. Then Houston's views on monarchy. Well, no odds to Britain whether she dealt with foreign presidents or foreign monarchs. In Aberdeen's time, France had been a kingdom, a republic, and an empire, and was now a sort of kingdom again – though a sort of quasi-republican kingdom, where the monarch was styled king not of France but of the French. Again, no odds to him.

The second letter was from General Arthur Wavell. Aberdeen knew him. His commission as a general was Mexican, but he had previously served with the British in Bengal. Wavell had been in Texas, and had observed the American immigrants who were now pouring into that country.

'So dangerous a people never before existed,' read Aberdeen. Well, Wavell's Mexican masters would say that, wouldn't they?

'They penetrate, subsist and conquer where others would starve.

When apparently at rest they are watching the wild bee to his hive, which they call a bee tree, and fatten on the honey; they track the reptile or beast to his pool or stream, where they entrap or shoot it.'

Aberdeen, being a good classicist, liked a sounding phrase.

'Reptile or beast to pool or stream,' he repeated to the clerk. 'Acknowledge the general's kindness.'

The clerk slid the third letter before him. It was from a traveller known to Aberdeen since their early days at university together. Richard McNeil – he read the signature and remembered the man. It crossed his mind that many people seemed to be travelling in America these days. Where, he wondered, was Lucy? But anyway, what this man wrote would be worth the reading. He had been a fine botanist in his day, but now seemed to be making a study of man, particularly of American man, whom he called gain-seeking, eager, and fitted beyond the rest of mankind to carry out a kind of surreptitious warfare against the territory of neighbouring states.

Aberdeen finished the first sheet, held up his hand for the next, and read on: 'They rove widely and lawlessly, taking the land for their own and therefore for the country of which they are citizens. They conquer whole provinces as the cuckoo steals a nest. It is not necessary for the United States to invade territories with armies to take them. There is no need for that sort of wholesale invasion, when American settlers do the work piece by piece, retail as it were. America grows ever vaster by this kind of retail invasion.'

Retail invasion. Aberdeen thought that well put.

'Now,' the writer continued, 'if Texas flings away her national existence and makes herself subservient to the policy of the United States, the increase of Washington's power will be as rapid as the decay of its defenceless and ungoverned southern neighbour, Mexico. More than twenty years have passed since that country threw off her allegiance to Spain, and during that time the decline of the nation has been inconceivably great and rapid. The result is pitiable. The country is now as defenceless as it was in the days of Montezuma. Another Cortez might march within a hundred miles of the capital without hindrance. Mexico is there for the plucking.'

All this chimed in with what the British minister in Mexico had been telling Downing Street for years. Aberdeen continued to read.

'But Texas independent,' his correspondent went on, 'is peculiarly fitted to interpose, as it were, the keystone of an arch between the United States and Mexico. By ensuring the independence of Texas, Great Britain and France may hope to maintain the balance of power in North America. There, as well as in Europe, a universal dominion would be dangerous. The only check to the rapacious encroachments of the United States will be found to consist in the establishment of another energetic and independent power to share the dominion of North America. Such a power we may still hope Texas may become.'

Aberdeen put down Richard McNeil's long letter.

'Retail invasion,' he said.

'Sir?' enquired the clerk.

'Never mind. Write Mr McNeil a formal acknowledgement and let me have it. I shall wish to add a few remarks of my own.'

The fourth letter was from the British minister in Mexico City himself. Prisoners from Texas, having first been put to work building a road near the city, had now been imprisoned in the fortress of Perote. Aberdeen replied instructing the minister to use his best efforts to see the prisoners were decently treated, and to communicate to Santa Anna that Her Britannic Majesty's government would be gratified to hear of their early release. And in doing this, the minister was to act together with the French minister in Mexico, keeping him fully informed. Aberdeen would do whatever he could to assist Texas to maintain her independence, but the entente mattered to him above all other things, and he would do nothing on the American continent unless in concert with France.

The administration in Washington had meanwhile sent a new chargé d'affaires to Texas, where he was flagrantly exceeding his authority and offending the Texian government and the chargés d'affaires of both Britain and France. He was William Sumpter Murphy, another

major general of militia, this time from Ohio. Having met Charles
Elliot in Galveston he assumed an instant familiarity, publicly slap-
ping the captain on the back and referring to him in bar rooms as
Charles, as if they were lifetime acquaintances. Elliot for his part
disliked the man as instinctively and as much as he had liked his
predecessor.

At first meeting Elliot had expressed his real regret at the
illness, and then the death only a few days before he was due
to leave Galveston for home, of poor Judge Eve.

'Well, sir,' Murphy replied, 'but for his dying I wouldn't be here.
And I aim to make a mark with General Houston, which Joe Eve
did not.'

There was no diplomatic answer to this falsehood, or to the
coarseness of its expression, so Elliot said nothing.

Saligny, who had at last brought himself back to Texas after
months in New Orleans, was so offended that Murphy failed to
call on him that he wrote despatches to Paris on the boorishness
and uncouth dress of his American colleague. And Murphy had
shown himself to be boorish. It was the finest harvest in Texas within
memory, and Murphy took the opportunity to throw a Thanksgiving
dinner, a sort of harvest supper. Most Texians had never heard of
Thanksgiving. Nor was it a festival celebrated in Murphy's home
state of Ohio. But he had heard of its being celebrated in the
New England states and gave his dinner, inviting the chief men of
Galveston. He drank a great deal of whisky, and, when a toast was
proposed to him and to the United States by the mayor of the city,
happily toasted himself, and in whisky too.

Then he replied to the toast.

'Dear fellow citizens,' he began – and for the chargé d'affaires of
the United States or any foreign power to address in such a manner
the citizens of the sovereign and independent state to which he was
accredited was an insult, suggesting, as the mayor later put it to his
wife, that Texas was no more than a pocket in the American cloak.

These opening words were received in silence.

Murphy at first looked down as if to deprecate his slip of the
tongue, but then gazed defiantly round the room and said slowly:

'And why should I *not* say fellow citizens? Who will prevent me from calling you fellow citizens? America is the mother and Texas the daughter. There is no closer and no more sacred relationship.'

There was scattered applause at this, but it was quickly stifled. Murphy had misjudged his audience. Most of the residents of Galveston, particularly those Americans just off the boat from New Orleans, would happily cheer on annexation, particularly after a few drinks at an American diplomat's expense. But Murphy had invited the élite of the city, the mayor, the shipowners, the merchants, who were to a man supporters of their own interests, which would best be served by an independent Texas. It was true that some among them had welcomed Commodore Moore when his navy returned to the city, but that was because they believed he brought them a Texian victory, not because he had crossed Sam Houston. True, they had not suppressed the burnings of Houston in effigy which had followed that night. But then, they had not the power to stop the mob, and had remained prudently indoors.

Replying to his toast, Murphy ploughed on, ignorant of all this.

'No tyrant on earth,' he said, 'shall stop me calling you fellow citizens. We are all free men. Tyrants may trample upon the children of liberty, but will never overcome them.'

The banquet ended earlier than expected. Some of his guests left with no more than the most formal thanks. Even Murphy, drunk as he was by then, felt this coldness and took it as an insult to the United States. One of the departing guests tried to enlighten him.

'General Murphy,' he said, 'you must understand why we are unconvinced that our being swallowed up by the United States, and thereby indeed becoming your fellow citizens, would be greatly to our good.'

'And why not?' demanded Murphy.

'Because Galveston is now the principal port of a republic which is on its way up. We are getting to prosper, and for the first time. You have seen the ships and the docks. You have seen the goods we now bring in. You have seen the cotton we ship out. Except on champagne, which is something your French colleague cannot forgive us for, our

duties on everything brought in are lower than those imposed by the
United States. That is why ships come here direct from Hamburg,
Liverpool, Rotterdam.'

'Many more ships come into New Orleans. What have you to fear
from the embrace – and I advisedly term it an embrace – that the
American people offer?'

'Just that,' said the merchant. 'Come annexation, which the
Lord forbid, and duties will be slapped on, and the port at which
all goods enter will be New Orleans.'

'Happy days,' said Murphy.

'No, sir. Because what would Galveston then become but a
tributary port to New Orleans. Good night.'

He left Murphy expostulating.

But Murphy, finding his way out into the cooler air of the
street, found there an audience more to his liking. They had hung
around listening to the speeches, and stayed in the hope of Murphy
standing them drinks, which he did.

Then he was in his true element, making a stump speech
late at night by the light of flares.

'Do you see the ship I came in, lying at the quay. The *Flirt*,
gentlemen. The United States Schooner, *Flirt*. Well gentlemen, the
United States does not merely flirt. The United States will be an
urgent wooer. The *Flirt*, gentlemen, is merely the first of an American
fleet that will lay an honourable siege to Texas – a siege, gentlemen,
I mean, to the hearts of Texians, to win Texas as a consort.'

Encouraged by a cheer from the ragged crowd, Murphy went
on to hint that Sam Houston, a brave man and an American, was
so beset by the English ambassador – he meant Elliot – that he
had lost his judgment and would be seduced into selling Texas for
money.

He begged his audience, to whom at that moment he stood
another round of hard liquor, to look the facts in the face and
calmly review them. Why had he promised them an American fleet?
Did they know? Did they understand? That American fleet would
sail in order to reach Galveston before an English fleet from the West
Indies, whose imminent departure he had learned of, on the best

authority. Did they wish to see an English fleet anchored in Galveston Bay?

He waited for the many cries of 'Never, never,' to die down.

'We shall come, gentlemen, with a force that will show the stars and stripes to the world. The English, too late, may then come with their fleet, and that English fleet may loll in the bay and see the sacred flag that protects Texas – and that English fleet will then sheer off and run.'

More cheers from the crowd, all of whom would have been typified by Aberdeen's third correspondent, and by Aberdeen himself, as retail invaders.

'Show the English more than flags,' yelled a sailor.

'Now you hear the voice of Texas,' shouted Murphy, pointing out the man. 'And I am with you, sir. If it were up to me – I tell you this – I should call down American men o'war which would show the English more than flags. But we have not much longer to wait.'

When word of the Murphy's toast to fellow citizens and of his night harangue in the street got to Sam Houston, he cursed. Saligny reported Murphy was deranged. Elliot kept silence. But the word according to Murphy spread, so much so that when two weeks later a United States brig of war put into Galveston with despatches for him, the American lieutenant who delivered them said drily, in the slow drawl of South Carolina: 'Well, sir, the word in New Orleans is, that an English fleet lies in that bay.'

Murphy took the despatches and glowered.

The lieutenant scanned the empty bay.

'The word in New Orleans, sir, on the best authority – they do say your authority, General – is that fifty British sail lie in Galveston bay. Now, I don't see that, General. Do you?'

12

The Jewels of
Perote

—————————

'And now for the adjustment of the jewellery,' said Feargus in his Irish lilt, and the Mexican blacksmith, already tipsy on mescal though it was only mid-morning, grinned broadly.

Kurt Neumann held out his right hand while the smith examined the link in the chain that shackled him to Feargus Mullin. The Mier prisoners were now chained in pairs, one man's right wrist to the other's left. So that each in turn should have his right hand free, the shackles were changed round once every three days. The Mexican officers approved, thinking this ensured that their blacksmith would inspect the chains regularly. They were proud of their vigilance over these wretches who had already escaped once.

'Besides,' said the Mexican lieutenant overseeing the operation, addressing the two prisoners, 'we are as humane as is allowed by the articles of war.'

Mullin grinned at him. 'Si si, tenente. Veramente. Gracias.'

It was one of Mullin's unlikely Irish accomplishments that he spoke a mix of Spanish and Italian. 'As how would I not?' he asked, when the Texian prisoners enquired, 'with me having worked two years on railroads in Spain and Piedmont, before crossing the ocean to make my fortune, which has landed me here in such fine company?'

It was Mullin's turn to have his right hand freed, and that day he intended to write a letter, to the president of the United States, no less. Like many Irishmen, he wrote better English than most Englishmen. He had turned the letter over in his mind, rehearsing the phrases.

But before the letter there was the matter of the chains. It was another of Mullin's accomplishments that he was a competent blacksmith. He had picked up this trade on railway works, where it had freed him from the greater labour of shovelling twenty tons of muck a day. It was an accomplishment he had not revealed to the Mexicans, who would have had him at work repairing the rusting iron cannon, grilles, and other fittings of the crumbling fortress of Perote. This was a grim, star shaped fort at the foot of a mountain on the road between the city of Mexico and Vera Cruz, in which the surviving one hundred and ninety Texian prisoners were held.

'Walls thirty feet thick,' said Mullin, who from his railway days was also an expert on great building works. 'Now I've seen many viaducts and many bridges, and now I've seen Perote. Now from the slovenliness of it all, I can tell you it will all fall in a heap one fine day. Rotten stone, rotten grouting, mortar falling away, and the stones themselves laid all of a heap anyway. But it will fall down in God's good time, which may not be in ours, and walls thirty feet high and fifteen thick, even rotten walls, are not to be torn down by bare hands – or even tunnelled through. D'you see?'

He said this, and had often said it, to Texians and Americans who wanted to be up and out of Perote.

'Men,' said Feargus, 'men, now we'd tear our hands to pieces, and break our backs, and kill ourselves dead, half starved that we are on potatoes and scraps of tripe. Rather put our minds to other ways of easing ourselves.'

So they had talked and decided on the letter to the president. But, before that, Feargus had his mind on another kind of easing – that of the wrists.

The Mexican smith was a peasant. 'You tribe of How-de-do's or God-damn-me's?' he asked Feargus, these being two expressions he had so often heard the prisoners utter that he took them for their tribal names. It was a serious question to him. Having seen many of his fellows killed at Mier by the daring hardihood and better marksmanship of the Texians, assisted by Mr Colt's revolving pistols, he thought of them as a race with supernatural powers.

'What's he say?' asked an American.

'He takes us, poor simple creature that he is, for a tribe of white Indians with the power of gods. He believes there are two such tribes, and if he means Americans and Texians he may be right. He wants to know if we are the tribe of God-damn-me's, or the other.'

Loud laughter from the prisoners caused the guards to look round, but then they shrugged and went back to their habitual torpor.

Feargus slapped the smith on the back, and he joined in the merriment. 'Now then,' said Feargus, producing a small bolt of metal from his pocket and coaxing the man. 'I'll show you.' The Mexican at first did not comprehend at all. Then he shook his head and refused. Feargus produced a wad of tobacco. After more talk, the smith took the metal from him, and did as the mad Texians wished. A group of ten prisoners watched. First the smith changed round the chains on Kurt Neumann and Feargus, and then he attended to those on four other pairs of wrists. Each time he knocked out the iron pin joining the two handcuffs, and each time replaced it with a new pin made from the metal given to him by Feargus.

When he had finished he waited. Feargus gave him a second wad of tobacco. He was satisfied, and left.

'Now boys,' said Feargus, 'we must black it over. He took a piece of charcoal and showed them all how. He had persuaded the smith to replace the iron pins that secured the cuffs with new pins made from lead. They blacked the lead with charcoal until it was indistinguishable from iron.

'Now,' he said. 'By day we wear our Mexican jewellery as we always have. Come night, we knock out the soft lead pins, and a man can at least turn in his sleep without tearing the arm off his neighbour. Come morning, we ease the pins back.'

Then there was the letter, to which they all contributed phrases here and there. Feargus did the writing, in a clerk's hand his father had taught him back in Galway.

* * *

To His Excellency John Tyler, President of the United States of America, Washington.

Sir,

Your memorialists [the prisoners were certain that petitioners in official correspondence styled themselves memorialists], being captives in a foreign land and in great distress, and being abandoned by the Hon. Sam Houston, president of the Republic of Texas, who has cast them aside and will give them no succour, even to forbidding his generals and officers to offer the same in any wise, call in their humble judgment on you, sir, as commander in chief and first magistrate of a nation whose vicinage both to Texas and Mexico authorises you to intercede, as does the morality common to all Christian nations, such intercession being by all your memorialists most earnestly requested and desired.

The composing and writing took two hours. The letter, as it was finally agreed, ended with these words:

We being Texians, the loins of your manhood, speaking the same language, professing the same religion, upholding the same law, striving always to advance the mighty rush of the same civilisation and race, call upon Your Excellency's power and goodwill, invoking Your Excellency's beneficent and mighty protection and aid, such being the earnest wish of us all suffering here in chains and in the vile prison of an alien and maleficent enemy.

This done, and the letter put safely aside until they could bribe a courier to put it on board ship at Vera Cruz, they paraded to celebrate, willy-nilly, the saint's day of the fort in which they were imprisoned. This was Saint Carlos' day, the fort having been built seventy years before in the reign of the Spanish king Charles IV.

The image of San Carlos, carried by four peasants, was paraded in the plaza of the fort, followed by five priests under a canopy, then by seven musicians, then by the officers of the fort and the citizens of the nearby town, each of the officers bearing a candle. After fifteen paces the procession stopped, when the priests prayed and all the others knelt. After another fifteen paces the procession stopped again. And so on, until the image was paraded at all four corners of the fort.

Only Feargus, being Irish and Roman Catholic, knelt by instinct and custom when the Mexicans knelt. The other prisoners were forced to their knees by the guards. At the fourth kneeling, Kurt Neumann was unwise and defiant enough to look his guard in the eye as the man forced him down with his rifle butt. Neumann was not a religious man, and only in the presence of such ceremonial Roman Catholicism did he feel himself a protestant, but his look was taken for insolence and he was dragged off to solitary confinement.

As the blacksmith knocked the pin from their shackles to take Neumann off, Feargus prayed that neither the smith, nor the colour of the lead pin when it was knocked out, would give them away. In the scuffle, no one noticed. As Neumann was led away, Feargus stooped and pocketed the lead pin.

Later, in the approaching dusk which came early at that time of year, Feargus did what he could to comfort Kurt Neumann through the grille, three inches square, which gave on to his cell. As Neumann looked out he could see, beyond Feargus, the wife of one of the Mexican sergeants walking across the plaza.

He and Feargus exchanged glances.

'I will see,' said Feargus and went across to the woman who stood smiling, hands on hips, as he spoke to her. Then she darted away. A minute later she reappeared, having changed her hat. This one was larger, having a broader brim decorated with fabric flowers. They watched her light figure as she came up to them. She motioned Feargus into the shadow by the wall, and put up her hands to unpin the hat.

'God,' said Feargus, 'the raised arms of a woman. There's a sight to raise the spirit of a man who has not had a woman in months.'

She did not understand his English. She unwound from the brim of her hat the gut of a cow tied at both ends, like a long, broad sausage. It was this that the fabric flowers had concealed. But there was no way this brandy-skin, because that is what it was, could go through the narrow double-bars of the cell window.

Many of the Mexican women sold brandy in this way. It was

forbidden. Most of them, at this point, would have shrugged and gone on their way. The sergeant's wife did not.

'Wait,' she said.

She flew off and returned with the dry shell of an egg. With her fingers she broke it in two, and then into quarters. She took one quarter, poured brandy into this narrow drinking vessel, and with her slender hand held it through the bars for Neumann to drink from, refilling the fragment of shell so that he could take a sip at a time.

He thanked her. She took the coin Feargus offered her, dipped her head, looked round her, and was away.

'A frisky, handsome, laughing woman,' said Feargus. 'You have a woman, in Texas?'

He knew Neumann had. They had been chained together for weeks. Until today's innovation of the lead pins, they had been shackled together day and night. On the days when his right hand was free, Kurt wrote incessantly. Feargus could not help seeing what he wrote. He could not understand the German but could very well understand the passion behind so much writing.

'I have,' said Kurt Neumann. 'She is tall and bright-haired. And Christ, that she were in my arms, and I in my bed again.'

Back in Galveston, standing in her shift at an attic window at the Tremont, in the small room where she slept, Helga Becker gazed out over the roofs and back lots of the city. It was two o'clock in the morning of a late November day. On the deal table in the window lay the last letter she had received from Kurt, a week before. She had read the pages many times.

'It is night and cold, so I remember you warm. What do the chains on my wrist matter if they remind me so clearly of the times when it was late and I ought to go, and you held me by the wrists, and held me down to keep me longer?'

Looking over the roofs she remembered those times. Kurt laughing as she held him by the wrists, letting her keep him. Then Kurt holding her by the waist after she had dressed and he really must

go, and the warmth of his hands through the stuff of her dress and
through the broad waistband the Tremont girls wore. And then she
remembered General Houston who, watching her loosen that same
broad red band from her waist, had one night called her wonderful.

Behind her a drowsy voice said, 'You will get cold.'

She did not turn round but shook her head. At night she
untied her yellow hair and let it fall to her hips. In the window,
her splendid hair caught what light there was.

'Come back.'

She came back. The young man who called her, a boy of
nineteen, had landed that day, or rather the preceding day now,
a sailor ten weeks on the passage from Bremen in the barque
Königsdorf. He had heard her say a few words in German to one of
her fellow maids at the Tremont. Bremen is near Hamburg, which
she had left three years before. They knew the same countryside.
On the quay they walked together in the dusk, he dared to touch
the inside of her forearm with a hand that trembled, and she had
brought him up to her room.

13

English Gold

Sam Houston, dressed in his full 1787 finery, addressed a crowd-ed meeting in the Presbyterian Church at Houston city. The rings glittered on his fingers, the white ruffs stood out clearly at his wrists and throat, contrasting with the black velvet of his coat, and he was at bay.

For half an hour, standing in the pulpit where the minister stood on Sundays, he had reasoned with the members of his audience. 'My congregation,' he had called them when they indicated at the beginning of the evening that they wished him to go into the pulpit rather than speak from the body of the hall. The sitters in the pews listened silently. The trouble came from the loungers leaning on the pillars. He humoured them at first but then a man called out to him, 'Don't believe you, Sam.'

Houston turned to face the man.

'See, Sam, we have it on good authority . . .'

'Good authority?' said Houston, with deadly cold in his voice.

'Bill Murphy says so everywhere, and I reckon his word is good enough for us.'

So, there it was stated for the first time to Houston's face, that the American chargé d'affaires was putting it around in Galveston that he was selling Texas for a bribe.

'Gentlemen, and ladies, for I see there are some ladies, it is not, in a diplomatic manner of speaking, possible for the representative of a friendly neighbouring nation to be considered a scoundrel. Diploma-cy does not allow me to consider him as such. Friendly nations do not send scoundrels abroad to speak for them. It is a formal impossibility.

And if, by some wild freak, quite contrary to the whole nature of diplomacy, such a man were to be sent abroad, it would ill befit the president of a sovereign state to take notice, the slightest notice, of the mutterings of such a scoundrel. I talk, you see, in hypotheses.'

'Second nature to you, Sam,' said another voice.

Then Houston became angry. He put his head down and glared at the heckler.

'So be it,' he said. 'The head and front of the charge against me is that I have taken a bribe? That I am to sell my country to England? That I am to be governor-general of the British colony of Texas? And all this for five thousand pounds sterling? I have sold my country for English gold? That is it?'

'That's about it, Sam.' This from a third man.

'A rotten treasonable conspiracy, yes? Well, a conspiracy takes two. It takes two to conspire. England and Sam Houston you say. First consider England. What has England done against this country? Helped secure a ceasefire with Mexico. How many more Mexican raids have there been this year? None. And as to our becoming a colony, I question very much, my friends, whether England would have us if she could get us. Why should her exchequer expend five thousand, or five hundred, or fifty, to get what she does not want? But England is to swallow us up? Very well. Look at it. We are all to be sold, like a parcel of beggars and slaves, into the mercy of England? England don't want you in my opinion, gentlemen. She has a great many mischievous and unruly subjects of her own. If she had Texas at this moment, she would be glad to be rid of us. So why this passion against England?'

'More against you, General,' came the voice of the first lounger from his pillar.

'I have compromised the government, you say? Sam Houston has sold Texas?'

'Benedict Arnold,' came the cry from a man by the door.

Houston stood silent for a moment, mastering his anger, surveying the people in the pews, letting his gaze scan the whole church while he digested this charge of treason. Then he turned to the man by the door.

'Friend, your challenge to a duel will have to wait its turn. There are others before you. I make it a rule to deal fairly with all calumniators in turn, so you will have to wait.'

There was laughter at this. Houston cut it short.

'I am the Benedict Arnold of Texas? I am the man to betray Texas as Benedict Arnold betrayed General Washington to the British? But even then, his price, if I remember right, was twenty thousand sterling. I give that much for your Benedict Arnold' – at which Houston raised his left arm and contemptuously brushed the dust off the black velvet of his coat.

'And I give that for such talk.' He contemptuously brushed the other arm. Three hundred pairs of eyes watched as the dust, illuminated by the oil lamps either side of the pulpit, rose, fell, and dispersed in the light.

'I cannot remember when there was not such talk of buying and selling Texas. I have no monopoly of being accused. I have not that honour. Three years ago, friends, President Lamar was so convinced that the United States was buying Texas from Mexico, with American gold, that he sent a protest to Washington-on-the-Potomac, where it was laughed out of court.'

More laughter.

'But what of me? The charge is English gold. I have demanded that you should examine the English part in this chimera, why she should want us. But what now of my part? Look at the motives or inducements that could be furnished to Sam Houston by European emperors or kings – or queens. I will not be modest. Say a million in sterling. But a million I could not take with me beyond the grave. Innuendoes and rumours are propagated among the people of Texas that there is a Caesar in the land, who would arrogate to himself all power. There is a call for a Brutus who would rid his country of the tyrant. Last year, only last year, the Congress pressed upon me the powers of a dictator, and I vetoed the bill and was damned for it. I vetoed the bill because I would have *no* dictator in the land. Now I am said to be Caesar and there are calls for Brutuses to cut me down. Where are these Brutuses and of what nature, these Brutuses leaning on pillars and skulking in aisles, or standing by the door where they can slip out mighty quick? I should say brutes rather than Brutuses, myself.'

When he had finished he had brought the people round, and was cheered from the meeting. The loungers had disappeared from their pillars and left into the darkness.

Among his audience, in a pew at the back, had sat the Twinings and Lucy. The ladies he had seen were Adelaide and Lucy.

'Is he not fine?' said Adelaide. She was excited. Her blue eyes shone, her colour was heightened, she no longer wore her hair up but let it fall to her shoulders, and she took her husband by the arm, looking up as she asked this question.

Mr Lindsay Twining looked at his wife with admiration. He liked her new spirit more than he could say, more indeed than he thought it would be proper to convey to her, in words at least. He did convey it in other ways. They were happier together than they had ever been. But he could not approve of General Houston's style of oratory, thinking it close to demagoguery. So he said, 'Yes, yes,' in a tone which did not at all go with those words. It was Lucy who answered Adelaide, saying the general had certainly carried the meeting. The younger Mr Twining agreed with her.

Their carriage took them back to the Houston Hotel. They had again missed Captain Elliot, who had left the day before their arrival, leaving a note for Lucy saying he hoped they might meet in New Orleans. But this was a pleasant time of year. After the summer heat, the cool evenings of the present season were congenial to Europeans, and they stayed longer than they had planned.

In the hotel lobby they saw that the president's party had arrived before them. Houston saw them, and raised both arms aloft, inviting them to join his group. Mr Lindsay Twining was all for making a polite gesture of thanks, and declining. He had already embarked on the gesture, raising his hand and smiling, when Adelaide moved towards Houston, taking the whole party with her.

'Mrs Twining, Lady Lucy,' said Sam Houston, rising, and kissing their hands. He bowed to the Mr Twinings. He introduced the congressmen from Harris and Brazos counties, and his young attorney general, and announced that Lucy had met Mr Ashbel Smith in Paris.

'But I see no English gold,' he said. 'Surely you are the bringers of English gold?'

The congressmen laughed. Lucy smiled, and as she did so Houston caught her eye.

'You smile, Lady Lucy. I wish others would. See, those who murmur about English gold in Galveston are as certain sure about it as if they saw it counted out into my hand. As sure as if they were here now,' – he put out his hand to her – 'and saw you, knowing you to be English, take the sovereigns from a carpet bag and count them from your hand into mine.'

As they stood there, he holding out a hand to her and she facing him, they were instantly back into that strange intimacy, that circle of attraction, which it was his gift to create. She had felt it at their first meeting, when she and Adelaide and Houston had all three bent their heads together as they attended to the colour of a ribbon.

She drew herself back almost imperceptibly. Houston sensed this and let his hand drop.

'And yet, General,' she said, 'I have heard you fought against the British in the war of 1812. People have told me that. Yet the same people who know that, now accuse you of taking English gold?'

'I was very young. I saw the White House smouldering. It can only have been a few hours after the British left, who had burned it down. So I never saw the British at Washington. I had already got my wound.'

She saw that, before he as much as mentioned a wound, he had put a hand to his shoulder. She saw that it was an unconscious thing with him, as if he were remembering, before he spoke about it, the pain of the wound.

He saw her eyes on his shoulder.

'Oh,' he said, 'that is the way it was easiest when my shoulder was a bit smashed. It was easiest to walk or stand with a hand on my shoulder. I suppose to steady myself. But having fought the English is no defence now against these calumnies hurled at me,

no defence against these accusations of taking English gold. Do
you know, those who fought then are often the ones least bitterly
opposed to the English now. Those who have known a war, know
enough never to want another.'

'I can see that is true,' she said. 'I can understand the not
wanting war.'

'But that, you are saying, is not the point I was making? And
no, it is not. I think it is this. When you have fought against an army,
and met some of those men afterwards, as we did, there is a sort
of camaraderie between you, because you have fought, in the same
cause though on different sides, and have shared a common danger.'

'And have perhaps shared the same wounds, some of you?'

'Perhaps. At any rate, it is those who are younger and have
never seen an Englishman who are most suspect and mistrust
England now. Except . . . '

She waited.

'Except for my old chief General Jackson. Andrew Jackson, who
became president of the United States. I was a third lieutenant under
him in that war. I first met him then, and have known him ever since.
We were in Washington together, before I ever came to Texas. He was
my mentor. I was a junior congressman from Tennessee. He was
the senior senator from Tennessee. Now we write. We write all the
time.'

'You were saying he was an exception . . . ?' said Lucy. 'You
said, "Except."'

'See, he fought the English in 1812. He was a general in that war.
He won the greatest battle of the war. But *he*, unlike so many others,
does not possess quite that sense of camaraderie I spoke of with the
old enemy. And that is strange. You might expect a man who routed
an enemy, as he did rout the English at New Orleans, to forgive and
forget. And he may have. He may have done that. But he has never
ceased to be wary of England. Not that he would have anything to
do with this nonsense about English gold, but he watches England.'

Mr John Twining, the younger, approached Lucy, saying that
his brother and Adelaide wished to make their farewells to General
Houston.

'You are going?' asked Houston.

'Yes,' said Lucy. 'Tomorrow. To Galveston and then New Orleans, and then home.'

The farewells were said. Mr Lindsay Twining and Adelaide retired. Mr John Twining remained with Lucy. Houston saw that they too would soon go. He saw that he was about to lose Lucy. He cast about for anything to detain her.

'You have seen Mr Elliot?' he asked.

'By the time we reached here he was gone. He has kept a day or two ahead of us.'

'And I do not think you will find him in Galveston now. But he will winter in New Orleans, and you will see him there.'

'I hope so.'

Mr John Twining was hovering. Houston could not bid goodnight to him without losing Lucy. She saw this. The shawl she had worn in the cool air outside, and had shrugged off in the heat of the hotel, was in her hands. She let it fall to the floor. Mr Twining, as she expected, recovered it for her.

'Thank you,' she said, smiling at him. 'Could you give it to Jeannie, whom I see waiting for me on the stairs?'

He went to give it to Jeannie, pushing his way through the crowd to reach her. For a short minute Houston and Lucy were alone. In the crowded lobby, in its fug of tobacco smoke, surrounded by the noise of political chatter, isolated in a sense by all this, they were briefly alone.

A man may clutch at straws. Sam Houston clutched at the straw of hope she had given him when she sent her companion away.

'Lucy,' he said. It was momentous. He had never before called her by her simple Christian name. He would not have done. It was not done. The convention was rigid. They did not know each other well enough. The invitation to do so should in any case have come from her.

'Lucy, before you leave America altogether, will you go to see General Jackson?'

'How can I?'

'He would be delighted to receive you. I should be delighted for you to see him. I love the man.'

'But he is wary of England. You told me so. Why should he wish to see me? Why should any visit of mine be congenial to him?'

'Wary of England, yes. Of an individual Englishman, or an English lady, no. He is an old man, still a great man. Still a power in the land.'

As he said this he heard his words and wondered at their futility. What was it to her that Jackson was a great man and a power in the land?

The two stood quite helpless.

'Take the three rivers from New Orleans,' said Houston. 'Up to Nashville. He is very near Nashville. The three rivers. Anyone will tell you how.'

She looked down. She said, 'I will remember. I will try.'

They were an island in the throng and in the babble, but a score of men had their eye on General Houston, waiting their opportunity to slip in and approach him about this matter or that – an overdue major's commission for a generous contributor to the last election fund, a country postmastership for a cousin, an endorsement as senator for a place that had fallen vacant.

They were in public. In saying goodbye to Lucy, Sam Houston allowed himself a gesture that could appear innocent only in public. He touched, with an upward movement of his hand, a strand of her hair. This was seen by all around as mere Houstonian gallantry. Only the two of them knew it for what it was.

As she left him, two office seekers hove in to make their requests. They had chosen an unfortunate time. Houston nodded and nodded but hardly heard them. The hand that had made that gesture was raised to his wounded shoulder. He was recalling the letter he received only that morning from his wife Margaret. 'Oh when I think of the allurements that surround you I tremble lest they should steal your heart from God. There is something so bewitching in the voice of fate.'

She had in mind the allurements of office. He, at that moment, had only Lucy in mind.

Next morning Sam Houston went early, leaving for Lucy a letter of introduction to General Jackson and the briefest of notes for her. 'Go to see him. It would be a great service to me. I told you I love the man.' She saw again Sam Houston's grand signature, with the flourished rubric twice the depth of the name itself. As Ashbel Smith had told her in Paris, it was like the man.

PART TWO

14

The Purposes of
the Heart

Back in the bustle and brilliance of New Orleans, all the members of the Twinings' party reflected happily on the good success they had enjoyed, and on the many pleasures of their long trip.

Yachting in the Gulf – Mr Lindsay Twining had called it that when he first proposed their tour. It had turned out to be much more than that. They had made of it a grand tour in a new style of their own. They had all travelled in Europe before, in France, Germany, and Italy. Many of their friends and acquaintances had done the same – the sights of Paris, Dresden, and Vienna, the antiquities of Venice, Florence, and Rome. But here they had done much more – the crossing of the Atlantic, the sights of Jamaica, the beauty of New Orleans, and the discovery, in Texas, of a country wholly new and unformed, which yet promised to become one of the great nations of the world. No single one of their acquaintances had made such a tour. And they now intended to finish off their grandest of tours in the grand manner, returning by way of New York. They had been warned of the severity of the New York winters, but did not comprehend what they were told, Mr John Twining saying that he supposed it would be like London in a cold snap, and Lucy that nowhere could be colder than Edinburgh in winter.

They were all happy in New Orleans. The winter was mild. The sun shone. Mr Lindsay Twining and Adelaide had grown closer throughout the tour. Mr John Twining was in such high spirits that he had even forgotten the sea sickness which had prostrated him on the passage out. And Lucy's spirits, as all the others agreed, had recovered splendidly. She appeared her old self again. In all respects the grand tour was a triumph.

Then two events in one day changed the face of all Lucy's expectations.

After breakfast, she and Adelaide sat in the principal room of the St Charles Hotel, which at that time of day was pleasantly quiet, and exchanged reminiscences of their journey.

'Dear Lucy,' said Adelaide, 'oh, that straw bed at the Texian capital.'

'I'm pretty sure it wasn't even straw,' said Lucy. 'Woodshavings. They came through the ticking. I disentangled some from my hair in the morning.'

'And I too – from my hair and other parts of my person. I remember. Woodshavings it was. And how we talked, those two nights.'

So they had. Their two nights at Washington-on-the-Brazos were the only two the women had slept together – Lucy, Adelaide, and Jeannie. There had been only two beds. The two men had taken the other.

They laughed. Lucy's bold laugh roused a Yankee traveller at the other end of the salon, who looked across at them over his paper, tried to listen for a while, found their speaking voices too low to follow, and went back to the New Orleans *Picayune*'s comments on the state of the cotton markets.

'Lucy, I have something most fortunate to tell you.'

Lucy sat upright and waited.

'I have thought it for two weeks. Now I am certain. I am with child.'

Lucy leaped up and kissed her dear friend. Adelaide had been married more than three years, and there had been no sign of a child for her. It had been a sadness, but one about which she had not talked even to Lucy for some time, nor even to her husband. She had resigned herself, but now it was to be.

'I have thought it for two weeks, and should have thought it before then if I had the wit. I found a doctor two days ago, from Edinburgh, who practises here. He told me I had very good cause for hope. He said he could hardly think of better cause for hope, but certainties were for God not him. However, he said, obvious signs aside, which I would soon detect, I should soon know it myself. I would *know*. No rational thing, he said, just instinct. He had never known the instinct play a woman false.'

'And now you know?'

'I know,' said Adelaide. 'I have longed for it.'

'Perhaps our grand tour has helped,' said Lucy.

'More than perhaps.'

And Lucy and Adelaide, sharing the same thought at the same moment, thinking how much closer their travellings had brought Mr Lindsay Twining and his wife, both laughed again. The Yankee stirred once more, and this time heard Lucy say, 'A great deal more than perhaps, I'd say.'

More laughter from the two ladies.

'English,' said the Yankee to himself. 'Mad.'

'We have,' said Adelaide, 'been much drawn together, Mr Twining and I. And it has been a wonderful thing, this drawing together, for the purposes of the heart.'

That afternoon, while Adelaide rested, and while Mr Lindsay Twining stroked her brow and made much of her, Lucy and Mr John Twining took a stroll into the French Quarter. They walked down Chartres Street, towards the ruined cathedral which no one, in all the bustle and constant rebuilding of the city, had thought to restore. Some of the burned walls had been pulled down to make the ruins safe. Mr Twining, offering his arm, guided her along a rough path made through the rubble. In what had been the centre of the nave, she sat on a block of stone, one of the few sizeable pieces of rubble that had not been carried away to patch up houses and walls all over New Orleans. She sat and looked through the wrecked facade across to the Place d'Armes, where French and Spanish regiments had drilled for two centuries, in the days before Louisiana was American.

John Twining stood before her.

'We shall not,' he said, 'now be returning by way of New York.'

'No,' she said, 'that would not be wise.'

After Lucy was told the news that morning, so was the younger

Mr Twining, by his proud elder brother. Mr Lindsay Twining had
himself consulted the Edinburgh doctor about his wife's condition.
The strong advice was that the climate of New York in winter was
severe beyond the imagining of anyone who had not experienced it.
The doctor had experienced it and was firm that New York was
no place for Mrs Twining to go at this season. Besides that, the
shortest passage home should be taken, and that was the way they
had come, to Jamaica and then direct to England by mail steamer.
It was decided.

'Shall you be sorry?' he asked.

'Sorry to miss New York? I had not considered it. I am delighted
for Adelaide.'

'And I, for her and for my brother.'

'As for what I shall miss, most of all it will be Texas. I shall
remember Texas.'

'Ah,' replied Mr Twining, in a way which showed his opinion
of that country differed from hers. 'Why would that be?'

'I should be hard put to say *why*.'

'Not for its comforts.'

'No, Mr Twining, not for that. Perhaps the strangeness of
the place. No, better, the spirit of the place.'

Young Mr Twining did not comprehend, but he had more
important matters on his mind. He waited, summoning his forces,
and then addressed her.

'We have been much together these last few months.'

She nodded abstractedly.

'Lady Lucy,' he said, 'there is a matter I can no longer delay
putting to you.'

She understood. She uttered no word and made no movement.
She sat in the winter sun among the ruins while he made a proposal
of marriage. She heard his serious voice, and knew this was a serious
matter to him.

She let a long moment pass, and then suggested they should leave
the cathedral and walk across the Place d'Armes. He offered his arm
again, and she took it. She looked straight ahead. On their slow walk
he excused himself if he appeared hasty. He hoped, however, that

he would not be thought too precipitate, since it was now – and he did put this gently – two and a half years since her bereavement. He assured her of his complete sincerity. That was something she had never doubted. She now saw Mr John Twining's many small attentions in a new light – his always pleasant conversation, his real concern for her when her horse, as he thought, bolted at Galveston, his frequent offering of his arm, his picking up of his shawl in the lobby of the Houston Hotel when she dropped it. She told herself with a lively sense that she had not then treated him well – he could not have known what was in her mind when she did that.

Once on the Place d'Armes they were in sight of the sluggish Mississippi. He continued to murmur sincerities. She walked by his side. He did hope, he said, that he had not approached her too soon. If it was too soon for her to think of marriage, then he hoped . . . She heard the hope in his voice, and remained silent. The fact was that she had not once thought of remarrying. She had not once, since Richard's death, thought of any marriage except hers to him. Moreover, it was alien to her entire nature to think of any second marriage which was not, in *its* nature, as wholehearted as her first. She had not known, when she became a wife, that hers was a marriage of rare good fortune. She had since seen that it was. More than that, not only had she never thought of Mr John Twining as a husband, she had hardly thought of him at all.

It was his misfortune that, in beginning his proposal to her, he had remarked that they had been much together. Those were words to describe his brother and Adelaide, whom she had seen much together, whom she had watched as they came much together. Adelaide's news that morning had moved Lucy. She could not help thinking of the child she never had by Richard. Adelaide was her dear friend, and Lucy was happy for her. She had never thought of Adelaide as vivid, but she had said of her marriage, as Lucy could have said of hers, that husband and wife had been much together and that this was a wonderful thing for the purposes of the heart.

It was hard on Mr Twining that his own proposal was encouraged by the same news which had brought Lucy's marriage so strongly back to her. But whatever he had said, whenever, and in whatever manner, it would have made no difference. She could not have him. She had not thought of him. She had not noticed the man.

She spoke the one thought of the many in her mind which was both true and would not wound him.

'I have not at all considered marriage. And I cannot do so.'

Then she lifted her eyes to his for the first time since his proposal. She thanked him for his proposal, and for having made it with such consideration. She was truly sorry. She had not thought of marriage. Mr Twining stood in dumb confoundment. She kissed him swiftly on the cheek, asked him for his arm, and they walked back to the hotel together.

Later that same week the venerable Henry Clay of Virginia held court in New Orleans. It was a modest kind of court, in a hotel sitting room, and the hotel was not the St Charles but the older and less fashionable St Louis, in the middle of the French quarter.

Mr Lindsay Twining, wanting to meet a man who for many years had been a United States senator and had twice run for the presidency, had enquired and been told that Clay's meetings were open house. Anyone who wished – so long as he was decently dressed, wasn't drunk, and wasn't a damn Democrat – could turn up at the St Louis after dinner, most any evening that week. So the Mr Twinings, and Adelaide and Lucy did so. Lucy, having expected some sort of formality, found none. It was what she would have called, back in England, an 'At Home'. There were perhaps twenty people in the room, which was warmed by a log fire of scented wood. The senator sat in an armchair, stretching his long legs before him, entertaining at the same time half a dozen Louisiana politicians and a pretty girl who was dressed as if for the opera in a black gown which left her shoulders bare.

Lucy took a chair at the side of the room, where she could see Clay's face, and watched and listened. She saw his silvery hair, his white gloves which were carefully laid over the arm of the chair, and the unopened snuffbox which he held in the long fingers of his left hand. She saw him take no snuff. It was a tableau. It was as if snuffbox, gloves, the relaxed pose of the long body, the erect carriage of the silver head, and perhaps even the young woman with her astonishing bare shoulders who knelt before him on the rug regarding him with unbroken admiration, were all items of Clay's theatrical personality – his props. The gentlemen were assuring him that he was their undoubted choice, indeed the undoubted choice of the whole United States, for the Whig candidature in the next year's election for president. They could assure him of that. The kneeling young woman cast further adoring glances at the senator. The gentlemen renewed their assurances. He accepted these attentions with grace, but also as his due. The conversation then turned to a man, also a sound Whig, who had recently married, and had taken care not to marry too intelligent a wife.

Lucy and Adelaide, sitting together, could not catch all the conversation, but they could hear the senator. It was strange, but Clay, speaking in the quietest voice of all those in his circle, was the most easily heard.

'This friend of yours who married,' he said, 'in making his choice, was careful then, would you say, to avoid the terrible consequences awaiting a man who, having married a clever wife, and coming home in need of mental rest after a day spent in the arduous pursuit of, shall we say, commerce or government, is greeted by a lady who has opinions of her own on such matters, and moreover utters them?'

None of the gentlemen surrounding the senator dissented. They readily admitted that the man of whom they spoke might have made such a choice for such reasons.

'Yes,' said Clay. 'What such a man wants is a wife who will be a soft pillow on which to lay his head?'

Lucy could not say whether he spoke with irony or not. If he did, it was not apparent to the courtiers around him.

'What do you say, my dear?' asked Clay, raising a hand to touch the bare shoulder of the young woman dressed for the opera. At the moment of this touch, Lucy felt the eyes of Mr John Twining upon her. She turned away, and so did he. Since the proposal they had been most delicate of each other's feelings.

The young woman also agreed with the senator, though it was difficult to make out what she agreed with, and at this Clay, as if searching for something else to speak of, and yet not making that apparent either, looked into the fire and began a brief discourse on timber, complimenting Louisiana on its ilex which burned so brightly, and on its cedarwood which so scented the room. The senator knew his forest trees well.

Lucy then recognised the scent as that she had first encountered on Galveston island when, after her ride on the beach, she had passed the new houses, each with woodsmoke rising from its chimney. By the fire in the St Louis hotel, the political gentlemen were readily accepting this compliment to Louisiana as a compliment to themselves.

Then the group around Clay changed, introductions were made, and the senator was addressing a tall man in a blue coat. He was the most plainly dressed man in the room but obviously of consequence. Lucy gathered this not from anything in the man's demeanour but from the knowing murmurs of those around her. This was Captain Charles Elliot, Her Britannic Majesty's chargé d'affaires in Texas, the man she had sought there, and now at last had found in Louisiana. She had only that day discovered where he was staying in the city and left a letter for him at his lodgings. This was her first sight of him.

He was even quieter in his talk than the senator, but she gathered that he was indirectly asking Clay's views on Texas.

'That may be so,' she heard the senator say. 'Either way it may be so. I have heard often enough that all Texas is wild for annexation. Perhaps you have heard so too? For myself, I have not been in Texas. You will know Sam Houston's mind better than I. What? You say I have known him for twenty years? Oh, more. But it is a mind difficult to know. And a mind, besides, which is very much of the moment. Know it one moment, you may not know it the next. But whatever his views, and whatever the views of his people – which let us suppose may be different from his – the fact is that Texas cannot annex the United States. It is the United States that will have to annex Texas, if annexation there ever is to be. Annexation requires a treaty. A treaty requires the consent of the United States senate. Is that possible? More than that – it requires a two thirds majority of the senate, and the northern states will not have annexation at any price. What would you, Captain Elliot, given all that, estimate the chances to be?'

Senator Clay did not expect an answer. Elliot took his leave and moved towards the door. Lucy rose to approach him. Each saw the other at the same moment.

She said, 'I am Lucy Moncreiffe.'

This man and woman meeting in a New Orleans sitting room were connected by one single circumstance, though that was of the greatest moment. This circumstance was an event that had taken place two and a half years before, and on the other side of the world. Richard Moncreiffe, having left Lucy to join his ship on the India station, had been immediately ordered to China where he died in the siege of Canton. In that action Elliot lost one of his officers, and Lucy her husband.

In the sitting room he took the hand she offered.

'Lady Lucy, I have known for six months that you were in Louisiana and then in Texas. Mr Addington wrote to tell me. I have left letters for you, which I suppose will be still waiting somewhere.'

'I received one in the city of Houston.'

'And one was returned to me the other day from Washington-on-the-Brazos.'

'Magnolias,' she said.

'Yes.'

Lucy and Charles Elliot stood in the busy room, and the minds of both were eight thousand miles away on the Pearl River. She saw that he was as distressed as she.

She said, 'Captain Johnson of the *Calliope* did write to me. He wrote very kindly about Richard, but said he could tell me little, because he was not there.'

Elliot said, 'Moncreiffe played a brave part.'

'You were there?'

She looked Elliot full in the face, and saw that he was more than distressed. He was swaying.

He pulled himself together, but when he spoke it was as if he had not heard her question.

'I am glad that you did at least get my letter in Houston. I heard later that you and your companions were with General Houston there. So the letter, yes. But there are some things one cannot write. Houston, yes . . . '

Lucy did not know what kept Elliot from speaking about her husband, but she saw the man's condition and said anything that came into her mind, to give him time to recover.

'He gave me an introduction to General Jackson. "Go up the Three Rivers,"' he said.

'Ah. And you have met Senator Clay?'

'I have sat and listened this evening.'

'You see, Senator Clay is the old America. Now General Jackson – he is an old man now, but he is the new America. He was the beginning of the new. He beat Clay for president what, eleven years ago. Everything changed with him, and will change more. I heard he was ill, but you should see him. Do go.'

'I think *you* are ill, Captain Elliot.'

Now he obviously was. He was feverish and put a hand on the wall for support.

'I think I may be. It comes.'

Mr John Twining had seen the meeting. He had seen Elliot's condition, but out of the delicacy of his feelings for Lucy, not wanting to intrude in any way, he hesitated to intervene. Now he saw there was nothing else for it. He took the captain's arm, Mr Lindsay Twining took the other, and together they assisted Elliot towards the door. A group of curious faces observed them.

As he was helped away Elliot turned back to Lucy. 'Sudden things, these,' he said. 'I have had them since China. Forgive me. But . . . '

'I think,' said the older Mr Twining to Elliot, 'that we had better be off. We will see you home.'

'Lady Lucy,' said Elliot, looking back and for the moment lucid again, 'there is a lot to say. May I call on you tomorrow? It will have passed by tomorrow.'

The two Twining men carried Elliot off in the hired carriage, leaving Adelaide and Lucy to wait in the hotel lobby for their return.

Out in the street a group of admirers waited to greet the senator when he should leave the hotel to return to his brother in law's house where he was staying. They were outnumbered by another crowd of Democrats who were there to hiss him. Democrats baited Whigs. The Clay men retaliated by singing an old campaign song about Prince Hal, their Harry Clay.

> *Our noble Harry is the man*
> *The nation most delights in,*
> *To place him first is now the plan,*
> *For this we're all uniting.*

This was met with Democratic laughter and jeers. After a quarter of an hour Senator Clay emerged, offering his hand to those who had waited for him at the hotel door. One man refused with contempt.

'I'd be soiled by it, Senator. I'm none of your people, and you're none of mine. I've earned every penny I have with my own sweat.'

The senator's companions fell on the man, grabbed him by the lapels, and were dragging him off when Clay stopped them.

'Sir,' he said to the man who had accosted him, who was now dusting himself down and rearranging his coat, 'Sir, I know my deficiencies. But among them is not that I was born to any great estate. Whatever I have, I have earned for myself as you have. From my father I inherited only infancy, a child's ignorance, and indigence.' He offered his hand again. This time the man took it.

'Well,' he told Clay, 'now that I've seen you, you may be a damned clever gentleman, and you may still be none of mine, but you've neither horns nor hoofs, as I'd been told you had.'

When the Twinings returned to pick up their women, Senator Clay had gone but his supporters were still relentlessly serenading the passers-by.

> *The great, the good, the valiant Hal,*
> *And shout whene'er you name him.*

Next day Captain Elliot was not recovered. The Twinings sent the same Edinburgh doctor who had attended Adelaide. Elliot was delirious, rambling on about opium. Was he addicted, asked the doctor. For himself he could see no sign of it, but felt it his duty to ask. Lucy told him about Elliot's China service, and about the chests of opium he had surrendered. The doctor nodded. He knew nothing about China, but gave his opinion that the captain was suffering from an intermittent fever, very like the swamp fever he had seen in southern Italy, in the Campagna. For that matter, it was not unlike the fever that flourished in the Mississippi delta. It was caused by the miasmatic exhalations of swamp and river water, which arose mostly in the heat of the summer. It was a fever that did not usually present itself in a Louisiana winter. He had, however, known fevers originally contracted elsewhere to recur in the coolness of winter. This was plainly the case with Captain Elliot. Medical opinion was not certain how or why this should happen. With careful nursing, which he could ensure, the patient should be out of danger in a week, and to some extent recovered in three. But as to a complete recovery, a long residence in a more bracing climate was essential.

Mr Lindsay Twining said, 'Captain Elliot is British chargé d'affaires in Texas.'

The Edinburgh physician shook his head. He would not advise another summer in such a climate as that.

That afternoon Lucy came to a decision. It grieved her to leave her friends, but she would not return with the Twinings. She was unhappy not to accompany Adelaide, but knew she was a good sailor and would be well looked after on the mail steamer from Jamaica to England, by her devoted husband and by the diligent woman stewards they had met on the outward passage. Nor, having disappointed Mr John Twining, could she easily spend another month in his company. Their solicitous kindness to each other since her refusal of his proposal was wearing to both. And she must talk with Captain Elliot. That had after all been part of her reason for choosing to make this grand tour of the Gulf. If she had not met him at all, she might have left. But now she had met him, she had to stay until he was recovered enough to tell her what she had to know. It was impossible for her to leave.

She did not ask herself if there were other reasons that weighed with her. But she would use the time Captain Elliot needed for his recovery to do as General Houston had asked her. She would visit General Jackson in Tennessee. Jeannie would stay and accompany her.

She told the Twinings. Four days later they departed. Mr John Twining made a brave farewell. Mr Lindsay Twining hugged her, which astonished and pleased them both. Lucy and Adelaide parted with a close and tearful embrace. Their adventure together was ended.

Lucy then made minute enquiries about the Three Rivers. As Sam Houston had said, anyone would tell her. She booked her passage up the Mississippi, the Ohio, and the Cumberland.

15

An Army from Canady

'Taken for a dancer,' said the old man propped up on pillows in the high wing chair. 'Taken for a dancer, were you? Well, I see it. I see how.' Andrew Jackson was happy to receive this young woman with her letter of introduction from Sam Houston. He was happy to imagine her as a dancer, disposed to see, in the modest way she composed her skirts around her as she sat, a flirt of petticoats.

Lucy's reputation had preceded her at the Hermitage. Coming up the Three Rivers, and disembarking from the riverboat at Nashville with a troupe of Italian dancers, she was mistaken for the ballerina by the mayor and his welcoming party. She had fallen in with the troupe on the river passage. They had little English, and were happy to find she spoke enough Italian to converse with them in their own language, and translate their needs to the crew. A week with them on the riverboat revived her Italian. She had first learned the language from her governess, and forgotten it. Then, during a long stay in Italy the year before her marriage, she had practised until she could make herself understood. But after ten days of constant conversation on the riverboat she had a fluency in the language which she had never attained before.

At the Nashville landing the mayoral party was assembled, the band played, a company of militia presented arms, and Lucy, disembarking first, was accosted, addressed, and swept up on to a low platform.

'No, no,' she insisted, 'it is not me you want' – but still she smiled at the mistake.

This was taken for the theatrical reluctance of a performer who protests for greater effect as she is dragged on for her tenth curtain call. The Italians themselves saw what was happening, entered into the spirit of it, and called out loudly to her, encouraging her to go along with the game. The welcoming party, hearing this, assumed the Italian company was showing its own approbation of the principal dancer, and treated Lucy with even greater gallantry.

She gave in and played the part.

'Che bellissima città,' she said, with a wide gesture of her arms. The gesture, and the words – when they were translated by the impresario of the troupe into broken but fulsome praise of the city – were well received by the gathered citizens. Jeannie, having been swept up with Lucy and also taken for an Italian, replied in broad lowland Scots to a remark about the capacity of her wide hips made by a sergeant of militia who did not expect to be so readily understood. Then Lucy, breaking into English, confessed that she was only a passenger, called forward the principal Italian dancer and presented her to the mayor, and all was set right.

It was true that the Italians could hardly suppress their mirth, and that the riverboat's crew, seeing what was going on, did not even try. The Democratic mayor was miffed. He bristled at the derisive howls of the crew, but did his best not to show his fury. The *Nashville Whig* reported that the Nashville School of Jacksonian Democracy had once again, and by no means for the first time, been led astray by the charms of a lady.

General Jackson, hearing about all this, was mighty amused. He had always thought the mayor an ass. When he received a brief note from Lucy, enclosing Houston's letter of introduction, he straight away asked her to call on him at the Hermitage, his plantation a few miles to the east of the city, and offered to send a carriage for her.

The carriage was not his but his nephew Mr Donelson's. The Hero of New Orleans no longer kept a carriage. Lucy had never seen a plantation house before, except those at New Orleans which she had viewed from a distance, across the Mississippi from the French quarter.

After the buildings of Washington-on-the-Brazos and Galveston,

the Hermitage was very grand. The gravel drive swung round in
front of a colonnade which rose two storeys high. But as the carriage
came to a halt she saw that the pillars were of wood, not stone,
and that the wood casing of the Corinthian columns had split in
several places to reveal the plain timber piles beneath. Fragments
of decorative carving had fallen from the capitals of the columns,
and had been left lying in the portico. Neither the pillars nor the
doors and windows of the house had seen any paint in years. She
had seen the like often enough in Scotland, at the grand houses of
the Scottish gentry which, like their owners, had fallen on hard times.

At the door she was greeted by George, Andrew Jackson's
black body-servant, and then by Mr Donelson, who conducted her
to his uncle. From the hallway they went through a sitting room on
the right, in which she saw a bed was made up, and then through
another door into the library. There Jackson awaited her in his wing
chair. One other gentleman stood beside him – a grey, unnoticeable,
angular man of middle height.

She curtseyed to the old man. She saw he was surprised by
this, but she had greeted him as she would any man of his age
and rank. He regarded her with his one good eye, had Donelson
bring a chair for her, and then, touched by the curtsey and having
closely observed the way she sat, told her he could well understand
why she had been taken for a dancer.

'I see it, my dear. I well see how.'

'Thank you, General. I have to say it was not a mistake I
greatly minded.'

He smiled at this. The gentleman standing beside him did not.
Then Jackson explained the newspaper's allusion to the Nashville
School.

'You are,' he told her, 'now in the presence of a good part
of that school. We are that school. It was a term of abuse, so we
promptly adopted it for ourselves. Always cherish a good term of
abuse. What is a Whig but a cattle rustler? And they seized on the
name. If they can seize on a name hurled at them, then so can
we. So the Nashville School consisted of me, when I was in the
White House, and of Mr Polk here – this is Mr Polk who has come

over from Columbia to see me – who was in Congress at the same time, and of Mr Donelson here, who was my secretary when I was in Washington. And of course there was young Sam Houston, whose letter you bring to me, who was a congressman from Tennessee at the same time as Mr Polk. Quite a school, that. And you could say the Nashville School has pretty well propagated itself. Why, four of Mr Donelson's children were born in the White House during his time there as my secretary. I always tell him that's one of my chief claims to having enlarged the political life of the nation. Did Sam tell you about Rachel?'

Lucy said he had not. This last short question, coming out of the blue, took her by surprise, as Jackson took many people by surprise in his last days. Most of the time he was as alert as ever, but he was now seventy-seven and in poor health. Sometimes his mind wandered, and often towards his wife Rachel, though it was fifteen years since her death.

'It was Christmas Eve, her funeral. Sam led the pallbearers. There were ten thousand here, mourners. You have heard me called a plain-thinking man, my dear?'

'I have heard that, General.'

'As I say, always seize a good piece of abuse. Hold on to it and cherish it. Now that was not kindly meant either, to call me plain-thinking. I reckon my opponents meant mule-stubborn. So I held on to it. But I am not sure that I *am* always plain-thinking.'

'How is that?'

'You see, when she died, I did not believe it. I had the doctor bleed her, but no blood came. Then I had her laid upon a table. And I said, "Spread four blankets on it, before you lay her down." So that if she came to, she would not have had to lie so hard on the table.'

Lucy said nothing.

'It was a delusion. I have thought about it since, as you hear, and I believe I always knew it was a delusion. There are necessary delusions.'

He paused. 'And that's not plain-thinking or plain-speaking at all, is it?'

'On the contrary,' she said, 'I think that's as plain-speaking as it very well could be, in any proper sense. You have said what you thought. What else is plain-speaking?'

Polk looked at her with his first glimmer of interest. Mrs Polk, who had unobtrusively slipped into the room during the last exchange, smiled to herself. Jackson nodded, conceding the point to Lucy.

'Well then,' he said, having briefly made Mrs Polk and Lucy acquainted with one another, 'how is Sam?'

She told him all she knew. He listened intently.

'And the last time I saw him,' she said, 'he was busy defending himself against a passionate accusation that he was being bribed by English gold to deliver Texas to Queen Victoria.'

'You come from Sam,' said Jackson, 'and if you know him, you will know also that he will keep Texas for us.'

Lucy had thought that her allusion to English gold would amuse the old man by its very absurdity. The idea was to her obviously absurd. She saw he did not find it so.

'I do not know that I can be said to have come *from* General Houston,' she said. 'Not in the sense that I am his messenger. Nor do I know him well, except that I can tell he thinks and speaks of you very much. I believe he loves you.'

Mr Polk's small, restless eyes came to a rest for a moment on Lucy's face, as if he were puzzled that a young woman should utter such reckless words.

'You have seen that?' said Jackson. For a moment he could not control his face, and turned it to one side. 'Then I am in your debt. Sam is a good man. He will keep Texas for the United States. Think what would happen otherwise. An English army from Canady, along our western frontier, could march through Arkansas and Louisiana, capture New Orleans, excite the negroes to insurrection, arouse the Indians on our west to war, and throw the whole west into flames that would cost us oceans of blood and hundreds of millions to quench and reclaim. Texas must be ours. We must have it.'

'I do not know,' she said, 'that we have much of an army in Canady.'

'*We*,' said Jackson. 'You say *we*. You, the English. And you are an English skirmisher sent to sniff out the ground, in the guise of an Italian dancer.'

'General, I am a Scot. And the Moncreiffes became the Moncreiffes, and acquired the Moncreiffe lands, because they were the more successful sort of cattle thieves along the border – thieves of English cattle, that is.'

'Ha,' said Jackson, and was satisfied. Lucy, watching both Mr Polk and Mr Donelson hang on his words, understood what it was in General Jackson that had made Sam Houston so devoted a follower of the man, and regard him as a mentor. And she knew Houston was his own man. So, she suspected, was Mr Polk, though he spoke little and was, she thought, unprepossessing. Jackson was still the chief. Chief was a word he liked to use, though not of himself.

'When Sam brings us Texas,' he said, 'his name and fame will be enrolled among the greatest chieftains.'

There was no ceremony about this. He said it chirpily. He was confident Sam Houston would be a chieftain.

Lucy left with a standing invitation to visit the Hermitage whenever she wished, and with a similar invitation from Mrs Polk to visit her during her stay in Nashville, which would be two weeks or so. She also pressed Lucy's hand in parting, and said they must talk about General Houston.

The old man could not rise from his deep chair, but his gaze followed Lucy to the door. She looked back and saw him perched on pillows and held down by blankets, stranded by his swollen bulk. The dropsy had spread even to his face. Only the high forehead, long nose, and plentiful white hair remained as they had been. She turned and curtseyed again. He raised one hand to her, and smiled with the one bright eye.

Mr Donelson, having business in the city, accompanied her on the drive back.

'You must accept Mrs Polk's invitation,' he advised her. 'She don't say much but she is a decent woman. She hardly says more than her husband, and he says nothing, but she is a kind creature. When Sam was here and in trouble, her doors were always open to

him when others would cross the road to avoid giving him as much
as a "Good morning."'

Lucy did not ask what Sam's old trouble might have been.
She did ask about Mr Polk.

'Polk, you could say, is in retirement. Was seven terms in Congress,
in Washington. Then came back here and was governor of Tennessee
one term. Then tried for a second, and was beaten. Then tried again
last August. Beaten again. So Polk's out to grass, unless the general
can do something for him. But the Whigs are on the up in Tennessee.
It does not help the old general's health to see it so.'

'I am sorry to see him so unwell,' she said.

Donelson said nothing for a long while.

'He has not been able to ride for months now,' he said. 'And
that for a man who was on a horse all his life.'

Lucy did not regret telling General Jackson that Sam Houston
loved him. She did not at all know why she had said so much after
so short an acquaintance. But she was glad she had. The wrecked
face had lit up to hear it. Now, she thought, listening to Donelson,
here was another man who was devoted to Jackson.

'His saddle mare has been sold from his stable. And now he
can hardly walk from his bed to his library, which is next door.'

'I do not think,' she said, 'that General Houston has any notion
of this.'

'I cannot think,' said Donelson, 'when Sam last saw him. He
is always asking after Sam.'

16

A Bride Adorned

Back in Nashville, Lucy found that her recent acquaintance with Sam Houston opened all doors to her. Where was Sam now? What was he doing now? Was he seen much with the Indians in Texas? Those who asked, also wanted to tell. There was no way of hiding from their confidences. The ladies of Nashville all wished to talk about Sam, and the tone of their conversation was close to that of Saligny's creole mistress in that box at the opera, when Lucy had first landed at New Orleans. Saligny's mistress had never met Houston. Everyone Lucy met at Nashville had known him, some very well. That was ten years ago, before he went to Texas. The story had become folk history. It was a history of love, longing, betrayal – of a bride betrayed or a man betrayed, according to which version was to be believed. It was a history of power gained and lost, and then of an unaccountable exile among pagan Indians.

'Is Sam,' she was asked for the tenth time in a genteel drawing room, 'is Sam much with the Indians these days?'

'I believe he visits the Indians,' she said. 'The first time I met the general was with friends from England, and he asked us all to go with him to the Cherokees, but we could not.'

With four pairs of eager eyes on her, Lucy did say that when the general first received them it was in an Indian robe. She did not tell them of her question to Houston – 'You will not receive us as you did Monsieur Saligny?' – but she found that the story of his greeting to Saligny, and his throwing open of the robe to show his naked wounds, had reached Nashville and had become part of the legend. It was a story thought by all the ladies to be indelicate, but they all knew it and somehow contrived to tell it.

'Of course,' said the mayor's wife, 'he was brought up by the Cherokees as a boy, and so it was natural that in his disgrace he returned to them. With Sam Houston, it was a short path from the governor's mansion to the wigwam, and he took that path.'

'Governor's mansion?' asked Lucy.

'My dear,' said the wife of a learned judge, 'he was governor of Tennessee, in the Jacksonian interest, naturally. Did you not know?'

'I knew he was in Congress.'

'And then governor. From Congress to governor. From governor's office to wigwam. How is Sam's new wife? We heard he had married again.'

'I have never seen her. I think she is often unwell, and stays at home while General Houston is either at Washington-on-the-Brazos or at Galveston. They have a child.'

'She has not left him yet?'

'No, ma'am,' said Lucy. 'She has not. But I know nothing of General Houston's private affairs.'

The mayor's wife evidently knew a great deal, and would not be stopped or snubbed.

'She is young, Sam's new wife?'

'I have heard very young.'

'That is Sam's taste. Eliza Allen was nineteen when she married him.'

'And still only nineteen when she left him,' said the judge's wife.

'Eighteen,' said a third, and it was then agreed, after some calculation, that Eliza Allen had been only eighteen when she was a bride, and only two months older when she ran from a husband she could no longer bear to live with.

'And he had known her since she was thirteen,' said the mayor's wife, capping the story. 'Five years he admired Eliza whenever he visited the Allen house, and he was in and out of that house often. Eliza a little girl still in short frocks, and he admiring her yellow hair and stroking it as a man may stroke a child's hair. And the Allens thinking him a great man and trusting him. When she was seventeen he asked for her. When she was eighteen he took her for his wife, and by then he was governor and the Allens were happy to see their Eliza become mistress of the governor's mansion. They set great store by Eliza.'

'Soon they were happy no more,' said the judge's wife. 'Not when she ran back home after two months, in the night, having been foully used by her husband. When she remained silent out of modesty there were even whispers that the blame lay with her. How could that be, with a wild man like Sam for husband? That was an imputation no gentleman in Tennessee believed.'

'Nor should any gentleman ever have believed it,' said another lady, the wife a minister of religion, who had just entered the drawing room to play her part in the mayoress's At Home. 'I saw a letter Sam Houston wrote to her father, the day she left him, when he was himself shamed into proclaiming her innocence. "If any mortal man dares to charge my wife or say aught against her virtue, I will slay him." Those were his words. So there was nothing against Eliza.'

'And everything against Sam,' said the judge's wife. 'That same night he wrote out his letter of resignation from the governorship, and would not be dissuaded by his friends, and took the riverboat into Indian country.'

'What a fall,' said the mayoress, 'for a member of Congress, a major general, and the governor of so respectable a state as Tennessee. *Sic transit gloria mundi.*'

'And that man,' said the judge's lady, 'rightfully abandoned by a virtuous wife, no longer governor but a vagrant and an Indian wanderer, making high-falutin' statements as he went. What statements they were.' Here she made an attempt at mimicking Sam Houston's voice: '"I acquiesce in my destiny."'

'He had better,' said the minister's wife, with a dark hint in her whole voice, utterance, and demeanour that for Sam Houston to have said anything else would have been to challenge the omnipotence of her Baptist God.

Lucy rose, leaving those virtuous Nashville wives to their chatter. At the Nashville Inn, Mrs Polk received her kindly. She was twice

Lucy's age, and their histories could hardly have been more different, but they were at once comfortable with each other. Lucy came with an introduction from General Houston, and that was enough for Mrs Polk. They first talked about Andrew Jackson, for whom she had grave fears. In the past year his dropsy had worsened, and weighed terribly on a man who all his life had been so active. When the talk turned to Houston, she was the first to say she was happy for him that he should have made a second marriage. She was the first not to enquire whether it had not already come to an end.

'You will,' she asked, 'have heard a great deal of talk about Sam in Nashville?'

'A very great deal.'

'It has become very decorated in the telling. You see, Sam always was a man to attract attention, whether he liked it or not. Sometimes he did not like it, but for the most part I have to say he did. Sam with that mysterious past, before I ever met him. But that really amounted to a year or two with the Indians when he was young and preferred that to standing behind a counter in his family's store. Plenty of boys would have done that. Plenty have. Then it was Sam the lawyer, Sam the congressman, and then Sam for governor. Sam on a grey dappled horse. Then Eliza. And whatever happened, and I do not know what happened – because he never told me and I never asked – it would all have been long forgotten if he had not been governor.'

A black servant, a young man in livery and white gloves, brought tea.

'My dear,' said Mrs Polk, 'you have been married. Sam told us that in his letter that you brought us. So you will know there are a thousand ways, and a thousand things that can happen, for better for worse, and most will be forgotten. But Eliza was both an Allen and the governor's lady. And the pride of the Allens – as General Jackson would tell you – is a mighty force in the land. Pride in their acres of bluegrass – miles of bluegrass. Pride in their daughter. Pride in their daughter as governor's lady, whose honour then became the more delicate because of the exalted position Sam himself had brought her. It was all worse because Sam was governor, and yet it might still have been forgotten if Sam had sat it out and *stayed* governor. She would have gone back to him. But for Sam to go off to the Indians again, for Eliza to be the estranged wife of a vagrant in Indian country – that was all too much for the pride of the Allens. I saw Sam and Eliza together often, mostly before their marriage, and afterwards too, and I could have sworn he cherished her. I never knew her mind, but she was a sweet enough girl. I do not know the half of it.'

'Strange,' said Lucy, 'to have resigned and left the same night.'

'Given Sam's temperament that's a very likely story,' said Mrs Polk, 'but it wasn't so. Sam stayed for a week, two weeks. He was often in my house. He stayed the last two nights with us here in Nashville before he left. The last night we sat late at supper. He excused himself early. His bedroom was right overhead, and as we sat we heard his footsteps above, back and forth, back and forth.'

The two women sat together while the sun set and the lamps were lit in the room.

'It should all have been forgotten,' said Mrs Polk. 'Later, a great deal was said here about Sam's divorce down in Texas, but even that was a blessing to the Allens, because very soon afterwards Eliza remarried, and lives out of state, and now has children. But everything conspired to make the whole affair conspicuous. I think the general was explaining the Nashville School to you the other day. Well, it was real enough. Maybe still is. You see, presidents of the Union came from Virginia. That was the tradition. Or from Massachusetts – the Adamses. General Jackson was the first man who was neither. When you have a president from Tennessee, suddenly the state becomes important. The governor of Tennessee, which was Sam, suddenly becomes a man known throughout the Union, which no governor was before. And of course, once General Jackson was in the White House, everyone casts about, asking who's in, who's out. And Sam is in. And soon talk had Sam as a possible successor in the White House. It was Sam for president one day – his name canvassed as I suppose the names of a hundred other men were canvassed, and it was all talk. Apart from anything else, I should think he was too young even to run for the office. But it all mounted up. Indian

youth, grey horse, Eliza's yellow hair, governor's mansion, the pride
of the Allens, Sam talked of for president, then she is drenched one
stormy night, then Sam is away on some business one evening and
Eliza is gone when he gets back, gone back to her parents and the
Allens are up in arms in defence of her honour. Then Sam resigns.
Then Sam on his way upriver to his Indians again.'

'Stormy night?'

'Sam said nothing. Not a word against his bride who left him. Not
ever. But he did talk about a stormy night – they had to put up at an
inn, on the Gallatin road I think it was. Nothing. His concern was
to keep her dry. She was mighty fazed because she got wet. That's
all I remember because that's all he said.'

'From the moment I landed in New Orleans,' said Lucy, 'and
throughout my time in Texas, everyone has talked about General
Houston as a legend. It is not kind of me to say it, but I don't think
he's above helping the legend on a bit here and there. Indian robes
and so on.'

Mrs Polk smiled.

'That's not unkind. I like Sam, but I can't disagree with that. I've
sometimes thought it's the showmanship of the shy. Two classes of
people always sought out Sam Houston – artists and women. There
must be three or four portraits of Sam here in town. As to women,
there was always talk, but he never sought them out. Gallantry always,
but that was all.'

Lucy looked up. The showmanship of the shy. She had thought
that of the man at their first meeting on the Brazos.

Mrs Polk said, 'A legend, yes, assisted or otherwise. Most of
all he's a legend to General Jackson. You will go to the Hermitage
again? He would very much like it.'

That night, as Jeannie undressed her, the talk was again of
Sam and Eliza. Jeannie's days in Nashville were not easy. Anywhere
else, even up to a point in Galveston, there was a society, which
instinctively formed itself, of other ladies' maids and of the upper
servants at the hotels. Even when she was not with Lucy, Jeannie
was not lonely. But in Nashville the maids were black slaves. Slavery
drew a line between black and white which Jeannie could not cross,

and was not permitted to cross. So her talk, while Lucy was at the Hermitage with Mrs Polk, was with the city's small tradesmen and their wives. She had heard the same talk as Lucy, with one notable addition, that General Houston was reputed to have returned to his wife's house, a year after his disgrace, and there bribed a slave to hide him in an outhouse, from where he could observe his beloved bride walking in the garden. Then he had slipped away unseen, but though he was unseen there were still vivid tales of Sam, variously dressed in black velvet and ruffs or an Indian cloak, wading the river at the foot of Eliza's garden and then vanishing into the dark forest.

Lucy visited General Jackson again as often as she could, driving in hired carriages the nine miles out to the Hermitage. The talk was always about matters of state. He treated her as if she, like Houston or Polk, were a protégée of his, to be taken into his confidence.

She told him about Senator Clay's soirée in the New Orleans hotel room. Jackson laughed at her account of the sycophantic company, and of the girl with bare shoulders who gazed in such adoration.

Then he said: 'Damn Whig demagogue.' He spoke with all the force of years of political enmity.

'I cannot say I saw him as any such thing, General,' she said. 'He went into the street at the end and shook a few hands. That is all.'

Jackson uttered a deep growl.

She did not pursue the matter, but repeated what she had heard Clay tell Captain Elliot, that two thirds of the American senate would never vote for the annexation of Texas, and that was that.

Jackson considered.

'Then,' he said, 'there must be other ways.' He did not explain himself, but reverted straight away to Houston. 'Sam will never become the dupe of England. Never. Nothing will seduce him from a just sense of patriotism.'

She was not going to talk patriotism with him, certainly not to the point of telling him that Sam Houston might very well now regard the object of his patriotism as Texas rather than the United States, but she did go back to the war of 1812. Jackson loved to talk about those days, and liked Lucy when she took for herself the freedom he would have expected from a well-liked niece. So she put to him General Houston's idea that those least opposed to the English these days, and least suspicious of English gold, were men who had fought against England in that war.

'Ah, ah,' said Jackson. 'Maybe.'

'But he said that you were an exception. He called you that.'

'Lucy, if there's any such rule – I hear you but don't admit to any such rule – and if Sam thinks I'm an exception to that unadmitted rule, then I'll tell you why.'

Jackson paused, looked down at the blanket tucked around his swollen body, and then at his withered hands lying on that blanket.

'See, Lucy, I have not always been like this. Will you believe I was a slender stripling? I do not think I have ever told Sam this. I may not have. I go back further than Sam. Two generations before Sam. Before Sam was born, long before, there was the first struggle against the English. Only they used Hessians to fight us, and Creek Indians to murder us. That was the revolution, Lucy, and I was twelve – a slender stripling. That was in North Carolina. Now they didn't kill my father. They couldn't, seeing he was dead long before. There was my mother, and my brother, and me – none of us likely to overthrow the British empire but all of us put in jail. I remember the red uniforms that lifted my mother and carried her to jail. And dragged me and Robert. We were not willing, you see? And my brother Robert died in that jail.'

She leaned across and took his cold hand.

'Old men weep easily,' he said, 'even for a grief nearly seventy years old.'

He gazed out of the window at a range of blue hills rising from a haze beyond the Cumberland river.

'Bluegrass,' he said.

'What is bluegrass?'

'Bluegrass?' said Jackson, suddenly restored. 'Bluegrass is Eliza Allen.'

Lucy was taken aback with surprise. 'Her?'

'I see you know of her. From Sam?'

'Oh *no*,' she said. 'No. Why should he tell me? It is everyone in Nashville who has told me.'

'Yes,' he said slowly. 'Yes. Well then, the Allens are bluegrass because they have miles of it, landscapes of it, horizons of it. People say Kentucky bluegrass. Tennessee has more than Kentucky ever dreamed of. The Allens on their own have more than the whole state of Kentucky, leastwise they'd say they have. Eliza was an Allen, an heiress to bluegrass. All bluegrass and pride, and yellow hair. Oh, you are thinking of what you have been told? See, Lucy, I don't know what happened. I don't know because I was not here. It was the year I went to the White House. So when I left Nashville, there was Sam about to be married to Eliza – a pleasing girl, an Allen with all that bluegrass, and him holding high office, governor here. I left him happy, and about to be married. What next? A letter from Sam in exile. Bride gone, governorship gone, and Sam on his way to conquer Texas. Some talk of him leading an army of Cherokees. Well, that was nonsense – turned out to be nonsense. He did take Texas, though not with Indians. But I was talking about bluegrass.'

'Yes. What is it we can see? What is it you saw when you looked out of the window?'

'Ah. Bluegrass. Well, where there's a divide between bluegrass and regular grass its so sharp you can see a line where the two meet. You could draw a line on the map of a paddock, supposing the line crossed it, it's so clear. Bluegrass doesn't die off. It's lush all year. Fine feed. And Eliza, I'd known her since she was a girl, all her life. Known the Allens, known her. Known Sam too. She just took herself off. Well, I would have given any odds against. Afterwards he just said a ploughshare had driven over him and laid waste to his hopes. I never made head or tail of it. And Sam, I heard, was burned in effigy in the Nashville square.'

Lucy said, 'I saw General Houston burned in effigy, at Galveston, long before I saw the man in the flesh.'

'Well, no man's much of a politician until he excites people's minds, and those he excites the wrong way, being unable to lay their hands on the man himself, burn him in effigy. That's the way of it.'

On her last visit to the Hermitage, Lucy found General Jackson in high spirits, having just received a letter brought to him by Houston's secretary, who was on his way to Washington.

'That was Mr Miller who brought it?' she asked. Miller had been present when she first met Houston.

'It was.'

'He did not stay?'

'He would not stay the night, though I asked him. He went back to the Nashville Inn, to be able to take the steamboat this morning.'

Lucy was puzzled. She was here because General Houston had begged her to come and see his old chief. Now he sent a messenger who brought Jackson a letter and did not ask after her, a messenger who even stayed a night at the same hotel and did not ask for her.

'Listen,' said Jackson. 'This is what he says.' And he read to Lucy large extracts from the letter which Houston had addressed to him.

'My Venerated Friend, My duty as president of Texas certainly might have excused or even justified a compromise on my part with the hope of securing for my country a respite from existing calamities. I am happy to assure you, however, that I have incurred no committal prejudicial to the interests of Texas or my own honour, and am free to take any action which her future welfare may require, and be perfectly vindicated from any imputation of bad faith towards any nation or individual.'

Houston went on to say that Texas had attracted useless loafers and restless demagogues from the United States who were a drag on the Republic. He wanted a permanent settlement before a September election when these men might be able to vote and impose their misrule for another three years.

Jackson read this over rapidly, interjecting, 'Yes, yes,' and then reached the part he had already read over to himself three times.

'Now, my venerated friend, you will perceive that Texas is presented to the United States as a bride adorned for her espousal. But if now so confident of the union she should be rejected, her mortification would be indescribable. It would forever terminate expectation on her part and it would then not only be left for the United States to expect that she would seek some other friend, but all Christendom would justify her in a course dictated by necessity and sanctioned by wisdom.'

Jackson turned a page. 'Then this. "This is all [Sam means annexation] of too great magnitude for any impediment to be interposed. That you may live to see your hopes in relation to it crowned with complete success, I sincerely desire."'

He folded the letter. 'There, what of that?'

'I do not see it,' she said. 'General Jackson says he has incurred no committal, but then calls Texas a bride adorned. For what? And what if Texas is presented and the Senate will not have her? What then? Indescribable mortification?'

She would say no more. General Houston was elated by his own reading of the letter. She knew this would be their last meeting. The old general, having taken some hot punch and put the letter aside, talked of remembered things. He was animated.

She had told him two days before that this would have to be their last meeting. Now she saw that he had forgotten. She did not remind him, and took her leave as usual. When she was at the door he raised one hand as she curtseyed and said goodbye.

Outside, the high wind of the night before had brought down more of the decoration from the Corinthian capitals. An acanthus leaf carved in cedar lay on the marble steps, intact but with its white paint long peeled from it by the weather, leaving the wood quite bare.

Lucy was sitting in the lobby of the Nashville Inn, waiting for the riverboat to discharge cargo before she walked down the path from the square to the river to go on board for the return to New Orleans. Jeannie was exercising her considerable natural authority

over two porters who were roping the baggage on to a handcart.
Then a lady descended from a carriage, helped by two slaves.
From the more than usually elaborate courtesy with which she
was addressed by the hotel owner, Lucy, sipping her tea, could
see that this was a person of consequence. She was dressed in
bright blue silk. She was in her forties. Under a hat which would
have seemed elegant even in New Orleans could be seen a head
of flaxen hair. The hotel owner, bowing to her, crossed the lobby
to Lucy. Mrs Grierson would be grateful for a word with her.
Lucy sent a return message asking the lady to take tea with
her.

'I had heard you were here, from some Nashville ladies,' she
said. 'I have come from Gallatin. I am Mrs Grierson.'

Lucy poured her some tea.

'You will take the riverboat?' said her visitor.

'I shall.'

'It is a steep path down from the square to the landing,' said
the lady.

'Indeed?'

'That is the path Governor Houston took,' said the lady, 'the
day he took the *Red Rover* – that was the riverboat then – upriver
to Indian country.'

Lucy put her teacup down and looked steadily at this woman
from Gallatin. She waited.

'My brothers followed him to Clarkesville and there demanded
that he should return and withdraw in the face of the world his
allegation that their sister had goaded him to madness. This he
declined. He has never made the withdrawal that might have been
expected from any gentleman.'

'Mrs Grierson, what has this to do with me?'

'Eliza Allen is my sister.'

'Even so, Mrs Grierson?'

'You have heard much from the ladies of Nashville.'

'I asked to hear none of it.'

'Even so, you will take back to New Orleans a character of
my sister which is sullied.'

'I shall take back nothing. I shall not so much as mention your sister. It is no concern of mine, and now . . . '

'No,' said Mrs Grierson, 'you shall hear me out. You have heard so much, you must hear the whole.'

'Must?' said Lucy. Her voice and her eyes would have caused any rational woman to retreat. But Mrs Grierson sat unmoved, unnaturally calm, and smiling as if she and Lucy were discussing some piece of needlework. She looked in the fierce Moncreiffe eyes, smiled again, and sipped her tea.

Lucy saw that Mrs Grierson was, though quite calmly so, out of her mind.

'Because you see,' said the lady, 'though Governor Houston was mad, it was not Eliza who made him so, not my sister who goaded him into it. She told me. He needed no goading.'

Lucy looked round. But the hotel manager was a wise man and had gone, and could not be called. Around her, Lucy saw the curious eyes of Nashville society which would observe all this and report it broadcast.

'We shall be heard,' said Lucy quietly.

'I intend we shall be heard,' said the lady.

'Then be quick.'

'Sam was quite mad. The fighter of duels. Bearer of valiant wounds got from the British – valiant wounds no doubt. He would say valiant. Since then I gather he has become the hero of San Jacinto, against the Mexicans. It is San Jacinto? But with my sister . . . '

'Mrs Grierson, is this not enough?'

'With my sister Eliza, this hero was afraid of the dark. He would cry out against the dark. He would weep to be alone in the nights. The governor weeping. He could not abide the spirits that were abroad. He was fearful as a girl.'

Lucy rose and walked towards the door. The porters came over to her, raising their caps. Jeannie glanced anxiously back at the strange visitor, who was still sipping her tea with an air of unconcern.

The hangers-on of Nashville society regretfully concluded that the show was over.

Lucy reached the door.

The calm voice of Mrs Grierson called over to her.

'It is important that you should carry with you a good character
of Eliza. She left him to save herself. Governor Houston was mad.
Mad in the dark as any Indian.'

17

The Texian
Legations

In a high hall of the palace of Neuilly, just outside Paris, Ashbel Smith strolled the length of the marble floor admiring the high polish on the boots he had only two days before collected from Lobbs, whose premises were conveniently next door to the Texian legation in London. The boots had been two months in the making. First there was the measuring of the feet. The height of his instep had been remarked upon by the shopman. Then the making of the last upon which the boot would be assembled. This last, in polished mahogany, was not only a facsimile of his foot, which as a medical man he took a great interest in, noting its anatomical accuracy, but also an object of beauty in itself. There were two lasts, one for each foot. As the shopman told him, no two feet on any one gentleman were ever identical. And the leather was more supple than any he had seen.

'But the leather, being so fine,' Smith asked at the third and final fitting, 'will it wear?'

This was a question the shopman had never before been asked. Those who had their boots made at Lobbs did not concern themselves with such matters. But Mr Lobb himself, hovering at the back of the shop and overhearing Mr Smith's enquiry, had come forward to give him an answer.

'Sir, the more supple the leather, the longer the boot will wear. That is the nature of suppleness.'

'Ah,' said Smith.

Mr Lobb took this for doubt, which gentlemen did not usually express in his establishment. But he was an easy-going man, sure of his genius for his trade, and he hastened to reassure a customer.

'In one recent instance, sir, I have even known a pair of walking boots to descend from father to son. That is to say, from a duke to his heir. I attended on His Grace the new duke only two weeks ago, and of course instantly recognised the boots he was wearing as those of the late duke – having made them myself. A good craftsman will know his own boots, though it is fifteen years since he made them. It was fifteen years, sir, as I remembered then, and later verified when I looked up the late duke's order in our ledger. They were the very boots, and will wear fifteen years more.'

'But,' said Smith, 'if no man's own two feet are identical, does it not follow that no man's foot will be the same as any other man's? So the new duke will not be fitted by the old duke's boots.'

'Alas,' said Mr Lobb, and he spoke the word from his heart, 'alas, that is so. From father to son, even, that is so. There may be *similarity*. But similarity is not a *fit*. Not a fit. I did tell His Grace the young duke so, but he is a man careless in such matters, and said his father's boots would do for any man, even for him. I could not in the circumstances disagree, though I did venture to demur.'

'And you are making other, new boots for His Grace the young duke, so that he will have at least some of his own?'

Mr Lobb bowed assent. Dr Smith came away with his own new boots.

Two days later, having crossed the English channel, Dr Smith, walking in marble halls at Neuilly, still glanced down now and then at his splendid new creations, the high shine of which reflected the gorgeous ceiling above him, which showed Venus in the act of failing to repel Zeus.

But it was not that happy reflection which caused Dr Smith to stop and look upwards. What took his attention was a display of flags of the countries of the world, hanging from the balcony at the end of the hall. Last night, as he well remembered, the state banquet had been given in this hall. This morning he had returned for an audience with the king of the French. While he waited he strolled in the hall and gazed at those flags.

Dr Smith was happy in his occupation, and happy in his life. The flags were those of England, Prussia, Venetian Lombardy, Russia, Switzerland, Hanseatic Hamburg, Portugal, Persia, and others he could not recognise. There was the double headed eagle of Russia on its golden ground, there the lions of Holland, there the leopards of England, there the castle of Hamburg on its azure ground, there the Persian lion passant on its golden sun. And among them all, among these ancient symbols of ancient cities and kingdoms, flew the new Lone Star flag of Texas.

He was a happy man. At an evening party at St James's Palace – a palace only a stone's throw from Dr Lobb the bootmaker's – he had engaged Albert the prince consort in conversation, Queen Victoria's husband, and assured him that annexation by the United States was an impossibility. The prince, in his guttural German, had earnestly hoped this was so. A few months before, on a visit to Rome, Smith had been received in state at the Vatican, and was one of half a dozen visitors given a place of honour at a ceremonial representation of the Last Supper. Next day the Pope granted him an audience, and the two men talked for thirty minutes in a mixture of ecclesiastical and medical Latin and in diplomatic French. His Holiness, having been informed of a novel by an English traveller which reported widespread banditry, was concerned for the spiritual state of Texas. Dr Smith had been unable to give him any reassurance that the Alamo, which the Pope well knew to have been a Roman Catholic mission rather than a fort, had yet been rebuilt. After that audience Dr Smith had written to Sam Houston saying he reckoned the Pope expected to pen them all in his fold eventually.

Then, having to visit the foreign minister of Belgium, he had taken the opportunity to wander over the battlefield of Waterloo. The memory of this visit was in his mind when a courtier came to inform him that Louis Philippe was ready to receive him.

As he was shown into the presence, Ashbel Smith, seeing the broad figure, reflected again that Louis Philippe looked more like a cattleman than a king, and that no one would have thought nine hundred years of royal blood ran in those veins.

The king was certainly a down-to-earth man.

'What is on your mind, Dr Smith, when my man goes to look for you and finds you gazing, as he puts it, into eternity or somewhere distant?'

'Waterloo, sir.'

'What's that? Waterloo?'

It occurred to Smith at that moment that a French defeat was no diplomatic thing to speak about to a French king. He was making a conciliatory gesture when the king understood him.

'Waterloo. A defeat for Napoleon, Dr Smith, not for France. So never fear. But what is there for you at Waterloo?'

'These places move me. Waterloo, San Jacinto, Bunker Hill . . .'

'San Jacinto I recall. You told me. I see you wear that green rosette of San Jacinto on your coat. It was San Jacinto? Yes, you told me. I recall. But Bunker Hill?'

'A battle in the war of revolution against the English.'

'All battles, Dr Smith?'

'As it happens, sir. It's the spirit of places where men before me have done great things – suffered much, achieved much. It elevates the blood in a man.'

Louis Philippe, who was not so much a peasant as he looked, was about to ask Dr Smith how, as a medical man, he would characterise the condition of elevated blood, when he stopped himself. He went straight to the point as he saw it. His foreign minister had talked to him about Texas, the United States, and annexation. The king followed the arguments. On the whole he would prefer Texas independent to Texas annexed, though he knew the whole matter was much more important to England than to France. France had no territorial interests in North America. She had no Canada, and no Oregon. For himself, the king saw it more as a matter between Texas and Mexico. Texian independence was buyable.

'Dr Smith,' he said, 'Mexico is embarrassed – put it bluntly, bankrupt. Would not a little cash . . .'

'Sir?'

The king made a gesture of the market-place, rubbing his thumb against the first and second fingers of his right hand.

'Smith, would not a little gift to Santa Anna ease the situation, and get you what you want? Put it this way – cash. Cash in the proper hands.'

'I do not know we have ever thought of it in that light.'

The king looked at him quizzically.

'Cheaper than battles, Dr Smith.'

'Very well, sir, but we do not have large lumps of ready money to dispose of. Though we might agree to pay reasonable sums at future dates.'

'Then I see your difficulty. Future dates may be of uncertain interest to Mexican presidents whose tenure is also perhaps uncertain. Do you know, Smith, some gentlemen approached me the other day, approached me indirectly but quite explicitly, with the proposal that I should give them a son of mine, a prince of Orleans, to place on the throne of Mexico. Which they said would ensure peace.'

Dr Smith did not know this and was eager to learn more.

'No, Smith, I cannot tell you who. I dare say I should not have told you at all. But I said they'd get no son of mine. Do you know what I told them?'

The king was now enjoying himself.

'Do you know what I said? I told them our cousin Victoria was yet again *enceinte*, and that if the accessions to her family were to continue as rapidly as they had so far proceeded, then there should be no difficulty in proposing to take a prince off England's hands. England might spare a prince, but they'll have none of mine.'

Jogging back from Neuilly to the Texian legation, Dr Smith wondered how best to convey to Sam Houston that the advice of the king of the French was a quick bribe. Then he put that out of his mind and left the letter until the next day. It was a lovely spring afternoon.

Back in his living apartments at the Meurice, where he had entertained Lucy and given her the passport she required, he saw the day's newspapers on the table. They could wait. He saw on his desk a letter with an inscription in a hand which he recognised. It was from Anson Jones, Houston's secretary of state, a man of eternal picayune diligence. Dr Smith walked across to open it.

The skeleton hanging from the ceiling of his bedroom clattered as it was brushed by the sleeve of a dress. He looked up knowing what he would see. There in the doorway stood Amélie. A hint of her scent reached him. She was a sturdy, dark-haired girl, with some of the peasant in her too.

He asked her: 'Do you know what the king of the French has just told me about the queen of England?'

'No,' she said. 'Come and show me.'

He put Jones's letter down. Amélie was a woman who elevated the blood in a man. It was a fine afternoon and he was the luckiest of men.

18

Last Shift?

'Annexation,' said Houston, pacing up and down, 'would annihilate us. We should become a mere territory, and of no political
consequence.'

'Allow me, then,' replied Saligny, 'to remark that the sacrifice
is as good as accomplished.'

It was a Galveston evening in mid May, still hot and as humid
as it had been all day. Houston was in shirt sleeves, Saligny in full
diplomatic uniform.

'As good as accomplished,' repeated Saligny. Houston swung
round intending to glare at the French chargé, but by the time
he turned to face Saligny he had tempered his expression to one of
sweet mildness. He hoped the fellow's high collar would choke him,
as in this heat it ought to. He wished the fellow would not pomade
his hair so that he was scented like a woman. He wished he were
dealing with Elliot, who was a man he understood. Then again, on
a moment's reflection, he was glad he was not. He and Elliot liked
each other. Elliot would never have addressed him in such terms.
Then again, he knew there was something in what Saligny said,
and his answer would for the moment have to be something less
than frank. So he was glad he did not have to make that answer
to Elliot, who had not fully recovered from his long bout of swamp
fever in New Orleans, and had left to spend the whole summer in
the healthier climate of a mountain resort in Virginia.

In any case, Houston knew he had brought this meeting on
himself. He had invited Saligny to call in order to tell him he had
received letters from Ashbel Smith, who, having seen the French

king and returned to Amélie, had later that evening, in a happy
frame of mind induced by the sum of the day's events, written that
relationships between France and Texas were more cordial than he
could remember.

Houston had summoned Saligny, whereupon the Frenchman
launched into a long lecture, relating how France had been the
first European power to recognise the independence of Texas,
how France had ever since given proofs of goodwill, sympathy,
respect, kindness, and so on and so on, but that he, as chargé
d'affaires, could only express his dismay at the intelligence, which
had come to him from many quarters, that Texian commissioners
had been negotiating with the United States. Furthermore, Saligny
knew that in expressing his own dismay he would be expressing that
of the government of the French king.

'If such is the case,' said Houston, 'then I am truly grieved.
You will readily agree, surely, that it is important to me that your
government should not doubt my candour, or think that I am playing
a double game.'

Saligny smiled a civil smile.

Houston wished heartily that he was not obliged by reasons of
state to keep his temper. But he knew affairs had moved on since
Smith's cordial audience with Louis Philippe.

He waved Saligny to a chair.

'Now I beg you to convey to your government that I was forced to
submit to circumstances beyond my control – circumstances which
I, more than anyone else, deplore – and that I am not to blame in
this affair.'

Houston studied Saligny's expression, and Saligny Houston's.

'You know my views on annexation, which are the same as
they have always been. You will have met General Murphy?'

Saligny had indeed. Murphy was, much to his regret, one of his
diplomatic colleagues. Ever since Murphy's arrival as United States
chargé d'affaires, Saligny had thought him a barbarian. Murphy
returned the compliment by openly calling Saligny a froggish fop.

'Well, sir, I break no diplomatic confidences when I tell you I
have made it plain to General Murphy that there is much more

in annexation for the United States than for Texas. I have told him
he only has to look at a map to see how unnaturally the continent
divides itself into two great republics – the United States east of
the Rocky Mountains, Texas to the south and west of them. He is
an army man, so he can look at a map. I told him he could laugh
at all that if he wished, but that it was none of my doing. It was the
God-ordained geography of a continent. It was destiny.'

Saligny waited for the president to continue.

'General Murphy can read a map. He can understand what a
map tells him. So he followed my drift. For the United States,
annexation would be a splendid thing, no doubt of it. But what
of us? Instead of being an independent nation with a promising
future, we should become an appendage. I have no wish to be the
president of an appendage.'

'It would be an appendage, General, which would have no
need of a president.'

This time Houston did glare, but he had to continue.

'Lately the United States has approached us, I have to say with
a persistence which amounts to importunity. I would have none of
it. For my part I held firm. I refused. I persisted in my refusal. But
Congress got hold of the affair and in a secret vote instructed me to
open negotiations.'

Saligny was satisfied that he maintained a mask-like countenance,
but he was mistaken. He uttered no word, but his silent face said 'I
told you so,' and this goaded Houston into indiscretion.

'I shall not,' he said, 'go into the considerations that may have
motivated our legislators, which were not always completely patriotic
and devoid of personal gain.'

Then he stopped himself. Saligny sat back happily, having heard
the president as good as confirm the many rumours which had come
to his ears that seven or eight Texian congressmen had bought for a
song millions of old and worthless Texas government bonds which
they hoped would be redeemed at par on annexation.

At this moment the door was opened, a secretary's head appeared
around it, a murmuring of voices was heard in the ante room
beyond, and Houston excused himself. The Tremont hotel was

built with wooden walls, and Saligny clearly overheard snatches of
a conversation in which the post of collector of customs at the port
of Galveston was solicited by a man whom he knew to be active in
the Houston interest.

The applicant was satisfied. The president returned. 'I am
ashamed to keep you so long. But the president is the servant
of the people, and is not even permitted uninterrupted time to
entertain the representative of a foreign power. It's a hard business,
having anything to do with a democracy. Now, do I need to say more
on annexation? It is a humbug, a last shift.'

Saligny played his ace. 'Permit me then to express my surprise
that, so far as I can see, the shift has been [the man used the word
again] *accomplished*.'

Houston was angry and wary at the same time. He circled
the room and then turned on Saligny.

'How?'

'How? Because there is even a treaty proposed between Texas
and the United States. It has proceeded as far as that. There is a
treaty.'

'Which the United States senate,' said Houston, trumping Saligny's
ace, 'will never ratify. D'you see?'

At which the president was interrupted by more office seekers,
and the French chargé d'affaires withdrew to write his despatches,
on the way back learning from an informant, a laid-off lieutenant of
the Texian navy, that Commodore Moore had at last been brought
to trial. The court martial was sitting at Washington-on-the-Brazos.

'Charged with what?' asked Saligny.

'Wilful neglect, embezzlement, disobedience, defiance of the country, treason, and murder,' said the grinning lieutenant. 'The court
is already dubious about the last two.'

'And piracy too?'

'Piracy's dropped,' said the naval man. The liquoring places of
Galveston were that night rocking with laughter at the news from
the capital that, having been charged on the indictments, Commodore Moore had promptly laid before the court, as a specimen of
the orders he received, one which stated, 'If you cannot with the

means at your command prepare the squadron for sea, you will immediately with all the vessels under your command set sail.'

The incompetent clerks of a navy department he had never wanted were adding to Sam Houston's present embarrassments.

Saligny's despatch to Paris said that he was inclined to believe in Houston's sincerity – though with certain reservations. After the letter had made its long passage to France, Guizot, the foreign minister, sat in his grand chamber overlooking the Seine and read Saligny's diplomatic guesses.

Perhaps, he suggested, the president had calculated as follows:

Suppose the treaty were rejected by the American Senate, then Houston could always put the blame on his opponents and say that, as for himself, he had always opposed annexation and had negotiated only under compulsion, and against his will. In such a case France and England, seeing American intentions thus clearly exposed, would do all they could to prevent a second and perhaps more successful attempt. An independent Texas would then have strong French and English allies, and Houston would get the glory for that.

Or, suppose the American senate did approve the treaty, Houston could say he had, against all odds, achieved the union of Texas and the United States, and take the glory for that instead. 'To say nothing,' wrote Saligny, 'of the rewards which would serve his private ambitions.'

And what, wondered Guizot, might those rewards be? Impatiently leafing through the pages, he wished Saligny would get on with it. But the very characteristics which sometimes made Saligny's reports valuable, also made them a trial to a man who had despatches to read not only from Texas but from Prussia, England, Naples, China, and the rest of the diplomatic globe. It was helpful that Saligny described Houston's moods and looks, and his pacings up and down, as well as his words. Elliot never attempted anything of the sort. On the other hand, Saligny went in for endless discursiveness.

'What rewards?' Guizot said aloud.

He read on.

'I have the honour to draw to the attention of Your Excellency a recent encounter of mine with Colonel George Washington Hockley – gentlemen on this continent often bearing Christian names which are presidential in their combination – who addressed to me the remark that General Houston had for two months dreamed of nothing but the presidency of the United States. It appeared, said the colonel, that the Hero of New Orleans [by which he meant General Jackson who defeated the British at the city of that name in 1814] has persuaded the Hero of San Jacinto that if he succeeds in achieving the incorporation of Texas into the United States he would have a very good chance of rallying the Democratic Party behind him, and therefore a chance in the near future of exchanging the presidency of Texas for that of the United States.

'For my part, though to such as him and to His Excellency such a prospect as was held out to General Houston might seem dim, far distant, and uncertain of achievement, I believed it well calculated to seduce Houston; indeed I feel that many others in the general's position would have yielded to it.'

And why, Guizot asked himself, could not Saligny put matters more simply? On the one hand, on the other hand. Suppose this, suppose that. What if General Houston were to have been led to speculate that, by a fragile and unlikely chain of distant and uncertain chances, he might become president of the United States? Suppose all that, why on earth should the man not hold on to what he had, and preserve the country he appeared to have created?

Guizot turned over to the last sheet of the despatch where, after reporting that the recent birthday of the king of the French had been celebrated in Galveston if not with brilliance then at least with the love and respect that such an event should not fail to arouse in the hearts of all good Frenchmen, as well as with flags and twenty-one gun salutes, and after announcing himself to be His Excellency's most humble servant, Saligny signed himself as comte Dubois de Saligny.

His Excellency took up his pen and scored heavily and with some pleasure through the word *comte*. The fellow was no such thing as a count.

19

An American Calamity

'But it is always dangerous,' said Mrs Consul Kennedy in Galveston, 'to bring servants from Europe into America. 'There are very few whose attachment and good sense are proof against the tempting charms and delusions of notional equality.'

Lucy hears her. The case is that Jeannie wishes to marry a young salesman of Mr Colt's revolvers whom she first met in New Orleans. His name, as Jeannie had told her, was Alexander Hamilton Treaze. Jeannie had first met him in New Orleans when Lucy was on her way up the three rivers to Nashville. She had met him again on their return to New Orleans. Now Mr Treaze had come to Galveston because of the thriving demand for his pistols, and in pursuit of Jeannie.

'It is the American calamity that afflicts us all,' continued Mrs Kennedy, 'this defection of one's servants. I have lost two that way, who have gone off for higher wages and for imagined freedom, the benefits of which I can only hope they enjoy. Though one doubts it.'

Lucy replied, 'Jeannie is also my friend. And she is not leaving me for higher wages. Nor for notional equality either, I'd say, since she's always known her own mind and has often let me know it. She is leaving to marry. I like the man, and having seen them together I can very well understand why she is taking him.'

It was in New Orleans, on the way back from Nashville, that Lucy had first seen them together. Or rather she had first heard them. She had returned to her room late. Jeannie was not there to undress her. This was the third time this had happened and Lucy,

determining to have a few sharp words with Jeannie in the morning,
unfastened her skirts at the waist, then untied her petticoats, and let
the silk skirt and cotton petticoats slip over her knees and then fall
in a circle round her feet. She was standing like this, wearing only
a bodice and with her hands raised to let down her hair, when she
heard a sound outside in the courtyard. Lucy was a Scot and liked
to sleep with a window open on the coolest nights, and at that season
in New Orleans the nights were cool.

Stepping from the circle of her discarded clothes she went
over to the window and looked down from the second floor into
the courtyard. She heard a rustling in the dark, and then stifled
laughter. In the dim light she saw a figure flit from a half lighted
doorway into the darkness by the wall, and then wait. A second figure
followed the first. More soft laughter. Then silence. In the shadow
by the wall she sensed as much as saw an urgent embrace of two
darker shadows, and then two shadows locked together, struggling
as one creature.

Lucy turned from the window and threw herself half dressed
as she was on her bed. As she lay she saw the window only as
a grey patch of quarter light. But through the open window she
heard, and did not stop herself from hearing, the barely audible
and secret sounds that were to her aroused senses clearly audible
and most open. She heard, and could not help but hear, each
exhalation of breath. Then an unstifled and exultant cry came from
the courtyard and then, after a silence, a man's voice speaking low
and unintelligibly, and then a woman's words in reply. Lucy could
distinguish nothing that was said, though the meaning of it all was
clear and the tones unmistakable. The woman's voice was Jeannie's.
As the cry came to her ears, Lucy, lying on her side, curled her knees
up to her waist and held herself with her arms wrapped round her
breasts for comfort, and rocked on the bed. It was some time before
she lay still, and half an hour before she became conscious that,
lying as she was, she was uncovered and cold. She covered herself
and slept, and woke next morning to find herself still wearing only
her unlaced bodice and to see Jeannie stooping down to pick up the
skirt and petticoats which still lay in a circle on the floor.

'Oh, leaving you to marry?' cut in the voice of Mrs Consul Kennedy, bringing Lucy sharply back to the drawing room in Galveston. 'Leaving you to marry an American?'

'Yes, and I wish her very well.'

'An American,' mused Mrs Kennedy. 'Is it not amazing, the power of a man over a woman? Of the lower orders, I mean.'

'Oh yes, always. But not surprising.'

'Lady Lucy?' Mrs Kennedy did not understand.

'It is always amazing, Mrs Kennedy, lower orders or not. But I do not find it surprising in the least. No more than the power of a woman over a man.'

'Really?'

Lucy realised that the consul's wife could not have begun to understand her when she spoke of the power of a man and a woman over each other, or when she said it was always amazing but never surprising. How could she have understood? Lucy had spoken with the sights and sounds of that New Orleans courtyard in her eyes and ears. She had spoken with all the memories, some most subtle and some most naked and direct, that had flooded her senses as she lay curled on that bed.

'And is he a presentable man?' asked Mrs Kennedy.

'Very much so.'

And so he was. Two days after the night in the courtyard, Jeannie asked if she could present Mr Treaze. He was a handsome man who talked much about the pawl, cylinder, and ratchet of Mr Colt's patent revolving pistol. He offered to let Lucy have one at the special price of fifteen dollars. She thanked him and declined. She observed the way he looked at Jeannie, and the way Jeannie chivvied him, and saw they were happy and well matched. Two days after that, Jeannie asked Lucy's permission to marry.

'Jeannie woman,' said Lucy, 'you ask *me*? You are your own woman to give to your own man. I was a child when you first maided me, and now you ask me?'

'At home I would have asked the Moncreiffe, ma'am.'

And so she would.

'Jeannie, you are not at home, and I am not my father, and you

are as much your own woman as any woman I know. So marry of
your own will, and you will do it with my love and my blessing.'

Letters had been waiting for her in New Orleans and Galveston.
First there was one from Captain Elliot apologising for his indisposition. He hardly needed to explain why he had been unable to
meet her. His shaky handwriting showed only too plainly that he had
no choice. He repeated that they had much to speak of, and hoped
that they would be able to meet on his return from the Virginia spa
where he was obliged to go to recruit his strength. Lucy did not see
how that could be, unless she stayed much longer than she intended.
Still, she would do all she could to meet him again.

   Then there were letters from her sister and father, both clamouring
for her return. Then one from Mr Addington in Downing Street,
which irritated her. He wrote that the Twinings had returned saying they had seen marvels, and that they and Lucy had been well
received by General Houston. He had heard that Lucy, wishing
to remain longer, had gone north to Nashville to meet General
Jackson. He did not know her intentions but, should she return
to Texas, could he ask her assistance? Captain Elliot's illness, of
which she would have heard, was likely to be longer-lasting than
they had hoped. Texian affairs were at a delicate stage. Mr Kennedy's
consular duties would keep him in Galveston. Downing Street would
perhaps think it necessary to send a man to fill Captain Elliot's place
for the moment, but that would depend on events, and in any case
could not be done immediately. Meantime, if Lady Lucy's travels
should take her farther afield in Texas, he would be grateful for her
impressions. He begged to remain her obedient servant, et cetera et
cetera.

   Such a letter, not from her uncle Aberdeen but certainly written with his knowledge, meant that she was being asked to do
what Her Majesty's principal secretary of state for foreign affairs
could not ask her to do – because the diplomatic policy of HM
government was always open, and could not even be thought to be
covert.

She was tart in her reply to Mr Addington. She wrote that she had no idea whether General Jackson still had the ear of the American government. He was an old and ill man. But she related his fears of an army marching south from Canada, and his determination to have Texas. She also said there were persistent rumours, of which Mr Addington would know the truth better than she, that the British intended to seize Cuba, thus commanding the American south. Then this:

'As to General Houston, he is canny by instinct but at times reckless by judgment – intending to speak or act recklessly, I mean, almost as if it were a matter of policy with him not to appear faultless. He greeted the French chargé d'affaires standing on a table wearing only an Indian robe which he threw open to show his wounds – or so the chargé says. Make of that what you wish, whatever you hear for or against him. As to Texas, whatever the true wishes of General Houston may be as president – and I have heard him speak well of England – I can only say that most Texians I have met came from America and probably still think of themselves as American. I have seen their like in New Orleans and Memphis and Nashville. Except for the flags on the post offices and city halls, a traveller would never know he was in Texas rather than in a state of the American union. This may change, and it is not true everywhere. It is not true here in Galveston. But it is broadly true.

'As to Lord Aberdeen, if you should by any chance see him [and she knew they would meet every day] please tell him that Senator Clay, whom I saw in New Orleans, is almost as learned about trees as himself. There was an ilex and cedarwood fire and he spoke with knowledge of the trees from which the logs came. The latest intelligence here is that my maid Jeannie is leaving me to marry, which I am told is an American calamity that besets English travellers, and should perhaps receive consular attention.'

Next day, declining to hire a slave, Lucy placed an advertisement for a maid in the *Galveston Weekly News*. This caused great hilarity. The advertisement said only, 'A lady requires . . . ' and asked for replies to be addressed to the newspaper office, and not to her by her own name but to Herriot – the river that ran through her father's lands. But on the evening of the day she placed the advertisement the news was all round the Tremont. Lucy heard this for herself when she dined there that night with the Kennedys and two of the city merchants who had shipped cotton to Liverpool.

Laughter came from a corner of the lobby where two Galveston ladies of fashion and their husbands were in conversation with the editor of the *News* and his wife.

'Why,' asked one of the ladies, 'can she not keep a black like all the ladies of the city?'

'Oh, the English will abolish slavery everywhere. That's why they'll buy Texas, to end slavery here and then, by creeping abolition, to free every black in the States.' This was the opinion of the editor's wife, who thought herself, by her intimate attachment to the Fourth Estate, better informed than any other lady in Galveston.

'But,' said another lady, 'I should not like it to be known all over town if I had placed a notice in your newspaper. I should not like my husband to know, for instance, that I desired a second carriage and had placed an advertisement for it. He might consider that extravagant. I should wish to keep my incognito, at least until he had to pay for the carriage.' The lady was one of the few in Galveston who possessed a carriage at all, and took every opportunity to remind her less fortunate friends of this fact. Here was such an opportunity.

'Dear lady,' said the editor, who had once gone so far as to fight a duel to prove his professional integrity, and had killed his man, 'dear lady, the Press lives by disclosure.'

'What you mean,' said a militia colonel who owned a large share in the *News* and was therefore safe from an editorial challenge, 'is that it is not in the nature of a newspaper to keep a confidence. Or in the nature of editors.'

The editor passed this off, but was wounded.

Kennedy's party heard this conversation. Kennedy apologised, and muttered something about making representations.

'About precisely what?' asked Lucy. 'And to whom?'

'Why, to General Houston,' said Mrs Kennedy. 'In Captain Elliot's absence, Mr Kennedy has free access to the president.'

Lucy hoped they both intended this light-heartedly, but with the Kennedys it was difficult to be sure.

'But he will be at Washington-on-the-Brazos,' objected one of the cotton merchants. 'In that God-forsaken capital of his.'

'No,' said the second merchant. 'He will be at Shoal City for the next few weeks. Then he comes on here. He wrote to me, saying he wants to interest me in the China trade. Says Captain Elliot has opened the China ports or some such talk, and wants the Texian flag to fly in the Canton river. Well, I'll hear him out, then ask him if the government pays. It won't, and that'll be that.'

Lucy did not want to hear talk of China. She immediately asked after General Houston, and the conversation turned to Sam. If you believed them, the merchants both knew him from childhood days.

Lucy listened. 'Then I shall go to see General Houston again at Shoal City,' she said.

The company assured her she could do this if she was set on it. It was half a day's sailing across Galveston Bay, and then a short ride. Not that there was anything at Shoal City but shoals.

'But there is General Houston,' she said lightly, and it was left at that.

So it was a fortunate evening. Lucy very much wanted to meet Sam Houston again. She had gone to the Hermitage because of him. Because she had been to the Hermitage, she must see him again.

The girl who served them was Helga, who overheard a great deal of their conversation. She also heard the talk of the newspaper editor's party. As she and the Kennedys left, Lucy asked Helga again about her man, and commiserated with her when she said he was still imprisoned in the fortress at Perote.

Now Helga did not read English easily and rarely looked at the *Galveston Weekly News*. She could not have written a coherent reply in English to the lady who advertised for a maid. She would not even have thought of doing so. But next day, having heard the talk in the Tremont lobby, and having seen Lucy, Helga Becker put on her best green satin dress and presented herself at Lucy's lodgings.

'Why should you want it, Helga? Are you not happy and settled at the Tremont?'

'I am that, ma'am. But you have always spoken kindly to me, and I should like to learn a new kind of work.'

Lucy looked at the girl. She was presentable. She was downright handsome. No one could replace Jeannie, but Jeannie could teach an apt pupil the bare essentials in a week or so. Helga might be an apt pupil. Besides, there had been no replies to the advertisement placed by Herriot. Galveston was not flush with ladies' maids. And Lucy liked the girl.

'You would have to travel,' she told her. 'When I go back to New Orleans I should want you to come with me. And I shall soon be going to Shoal City.'

'Yes ma'am.' Helga knew that, having heard it the night before.

So it was settled. Helga moved her few belongings from the attic room at the Tremont. And a week later, Helga having been taught the essentials, Jeannie married Mr Treaze, whose friends formed an archway outside city hall through which the newly-married couple ran arm in arm. Each of the friends held aloft a shining Colt pistol.

That evening Lucy was without Jeannie for the first time in seven years. She felt very much alone. She rang for Helga who undressed her and brushed her hair, one hundred long strokes as Jeannie had shown her. Lucy, sitting in her peignoir, closed her eyes and remembered the movement of the hand with which Sam Houston had touched her hair. Everyone who saw the gesture had thought it just a gallantry. She knew it was not. It had been an intimacy possible only in public, and the more an intimacy for that.

20

The Vermilion Edict

On a day in the early summer of that year, the two doorkeepers at the Foreign Office in Downing Street, having handed the visiting gentleman down from his carriage and shown him into the hall, returned to the street and looked the waiting carriage up and down. It was a gorgeous creation, all lacquer and gilt and drawn by two plumed horses. The richly uniformed driver sat on his box gazing directly ahead, not wishing to converse with the doorkeepers. A uniformed postilion held the horses' heads.

'What's the flag then?' asked the first doorkeeper, nodding in the direction of the bright and decorated tricolour which was displayed at the front of the carriage.

The driver affected not to hear. The second doorkeeper walked slowly across, stretched up his hand, and unfurled the miniature flag, so that its stripes of vivid green, silver, and bright red, were clearly apparent.

'Another eagle,' said the first doorkeeper to his companion, for there, on the central vertical stripe of silver, an eagle was depicted with wings triumphantly outstretched.

'And a snake in its beak,' said the second. 'It has scotched the snake.'

The driver looked down from his perch in dignified confusion. He did not know what to make of these two scoundrels who desecrated his flag. He spoke only a few words of English. This did not prevent him from suspecting that their enquiries were irreverent. He could very well understand the tone of their voices. And yet the two men looked respectability itself. Both were dressed in black, both wore top hats, and neither allowed his face to show anything but the utmost gravity.

The coachman uttered a couple of sentences in Spanish, and then looked straight ahead once more. The two doorkeepers exchanged looks, withdrew to their door, and stood in silence, which was broken when one remarked to the other: 'Eagle may have scotched the snake, but it's standing on a heap of prickly thorns.'

They exchanged a rapid grin, and then stood rigidly again, with features composed as if no thought that was not properly respectful had ever crossed their minds in the matter of the national flag of Mexico. That was what they knew it was, having been told that morning to expect the carriage of the minister of the Republic of Mexico. What they had seen on the flag was the Mexican heraldic eagle perched on a ground of heraldic Mexican cactus. The doormen stood stock still, every now and again exchanging remarks out of the corner of the mouth about the extravagant equipage which stood before them. The colours of green, silver, and red were echoed everywhere, in the uniform of the driver and postilion, in the plumes the horses wore, and even in the colour of the blankets which a second postilion threw over the horses' backs as they waited.

'The old Duke of Wellington rides up on his old mare on his own,' said one doorkeeper. 'And Don Whatsisname comes in the lord mayor's coach.'

'The less they 'ave to show,' said the second, 'the more they shows it.'

Inside the Foreign Office the Mexican minister, in full court dress, was wondering why he was being received this time by Lord Aberdeen himself. On previous visits he had been seen by Mr Addington, the under secretary, and on one occasion, as he well remembered, by the duty clerk. The minister's name was Don Thomas Murphy, an unlikely name for a Mexican, but then, as Aberdeen had been informed, Don Thomas was the nephew of an Irish general called Murphy who had done Mexico some service in its war of independence against the Spanish. This General Murphy had married the daughter of a Spanish Creole grandee whose family had lived in central America for two centuries, and into whose veins a fair amount of Mexican Indian blood had introduced itself over that long period. So Don Thomas was a fine mixture of Irish, Spanish, and Indian. He was short, dark, and shrewd. Lord Aberdeen thought it droll that he should possess the same name as he knew from his Texian correspondence was borne by the American chargé d'affaires to Texas. That Murphy was apparently an oaf. The man conversing with Aberdeen was evidently not. He was a man who had been obliged to treat for a hundred loans on behalf of his bankrupt country – loans from the British government, loans from merchants, loans from any bank that would lend – yet he still retained his dignity.

That morning he and the foreign secretary were still at the complimentary stage of their meeting.

'The tower that I see from my window is very fine, Lord Aberdeen.'

'Tower? Ah, the column for Lord Nelson? It is good of you to say so. Some have called the statue a little crude in its features.'

'They would have to be birds to get close enough to see its features, Excellency. From my windows I have as close a view of it as a man can get. I think it very grand.'

Aberdeen bowed. He had forgotten that the Mexican minister lived in Trafalgar Square, which was very new. Nelson's column was just completed. Murphy lived in the square in a house which was also new and twice as grand as anything in Downing Street. He was the minister of a country which could not pay its army and which had been for years in a constant state of revolution, but he inhabited a house half the size of a palace.

They sat. Aberdeen outlined his proposal. What he offered was a guarantee of Mexico's borders, on certain conditions, the first of which was that for its part Mexico should recognise the independence of Texas.

Don Thomas listened. 'This is a matter, Excellency, which touches the territorial integrity and therefore the honour of Mexico.'

'That is so. I would not attempt to put it otherwise.'

'But Your Excellency will be aware that Texas is a province of Mexico. How to preserve our territorial integrity by surrendering a province. Would it be proper for me – and I say this with the greatest respect – to propose that Great Britain should surrender Scotland?'

Aberdeen's smile conveyed to Murphy that this was a fair debating point. Then he said, 'But Don Thomas, there is *de jure* and there is *de facto* – the merely legal on the one hand and the real on the other. Your government will know better than I whether Texas could now be recovered. I will not presume to press my opinion of this matter upon you, though you will be aware that Her Majesty's government has for two years now recognised the Republic of Texas. I shall only say that the territorial integrity I have in mind is a very real matter. It is the integrity of your borders against the United States.'

Don Thomas was quick on the uptake. He appeared to consider. He looked first at Aberdeen and then at Mr Addington who, again quite exceptionally, had remained.

'I would,' said Aberdeen, 'urge it upon you and upon your government that the first duty of any government, in any country, is to ensure the integrity of its real borders. I may say the Duke of Wellington is always urging this upon me.'

It was Murphy's turn to smile at this allusion to the duke's preoccupations with France, which were well known to anyone who read the newspapers. He smiled also at the craft of Aberdeen who could appear to convey to him, as if it were a confidence among statesmen, information that could be bought for sixpence at any newspaper stall.

'And surely,' continued Aberdeen, 'the true preoccupation of a Mexican government must be with the security of its borders against the ambitions not of Texas but of the United States.'

Murphy knew this very well. He temporised. 'Excellency, you have talked about the legal and the real. What are the real interests of Her Britannic Majesty in this matter?'

Aberdeen, putting on his matter of fact, cards on the table manner, said one word. Aberdeen was an upright, honest man. Nobody had ever thought otherwise. But he had observed himself over the years, and seen that his one-word answers often told best.

'Cotton,' he said.

Don Thomas nodded, and then asked permission to send his

carriage away. What the foreign secretary had in mind would take a little time. A clerk was sent to convey instructions to the coachman. The two doorkeepers exchanged glances. Something was up. The Mexican minister had never before stayed more than the ceremonial fifteen minutes.

The deal was this. England wanted Texian cotton, which was as good as that from the southern American states but cheaper, since the Texians charged no duty and the Americans did. England could also send her manufactured goods either to Texas or through Texas to a vast market beyond, again without duties to be paid. England therefore did not wish to see Texas annexed to the United States. From the Mexican point of view, a Texas declared independent by Mexico, and with its borders guaranteed by England, would also be a convenient buffer between American expansionist ambitions and Mexico, a friendly state whose borders England would also, in those circumstances, be happy to guarantee.

'That, simply, is it,' said Aberdeen. 'It is a proposal in both our interests.'

Neither Aberdeen nor Murphy needed to enquire how such a guarantee could be enforced. The United States spent nothing on its navy. A single English frigate squadron in the Gulf would be enough, and frigates of the Royal Navy's America station were constantly exercising in those waters, out of West Indian ports. The matter of Mexican debts was delicately raised. Her Majesty's government would give every assistance to ensure the forgiveness of such debts. An accommodation would be arrived at. It would be quietly attended to.

English gold, thought Don Thomas, but kept that to himself. He did make one observation. England, for her part, would not be sorry to see the ambitions of the United States checked? He tossed in this question as if it were a formality, pertaining to something that could be assumed among gentlemen. It would dish the Americans, but neither of them would be so tactless as to say that aloud. Aberdeen replied, in the same spirit, that Her Majesty's government had always been opposed to the existence of any overweening power, on any continent. And besides, in this matter it was not a question of

England's interests alone. France had indicated that her interests were the same.

So it was agreed in principle that England, Mexico, France, and the United States should be invited to guarantee the present borders of both Mexico and Texas.

'The two European powers, Mexico, Texas, *and* the United States?' asked Murphy.

'Oh of course the United States also,' said Aberdeen.

'And what,' asked Murphy, 'if the United States does not consent?'

The two men had been speaking French, the universal diplomatic language. Both spoke the language as easily as their own, and although both could have spoken English they preferred French for their purposes that day. So to Murphy's last question, Aberdeen replied: '*Peu importerait à l'Angleterre que le gouvernement américain consentît ou non.*'

To be certain, Murphy repeated this reply of Aberdeen's in English: 'It doesn't matter to England whether America agrees or not?'

'Doesn't *much* matter,' said Aberdeen. 'Always provided France agrees. We know she does, although you will of course wish to assure yourself on that point.'

Murphy considered. 'But again,' he said at last, 'what if the United States won't agree? What then?'

'*S'il était nécessaire, le gouvernement de Sa Majesté britannique irait jusqu'aux dernières extrémités.*'

Murphy, wanting to be doubly sure, repeated this in English too. 'If necessary, England would go to the last extremities?'

It was agreed. Don Thomas's carriage was summoned. The two doorkeepers were amazed to see that not only Addington but old Aberdeen himself saw the Mexican minister to his carriage.

Back in the foreign secretary's room, Addington looked out of the window at the departing splendour of Don Thomas's equipage.

Aberdeen looked over at Addington.

'Now, what is it then?'

The two men had known each other for more than twenty

years. They knew every nuance of each other's moods. As he looked across at his junior, Aberdeen could read disquiet in the back of Addington's coat tails.

'What it is, sir, is that last question of Murphy's and your answer. *If necessary* England would go to . . . '

'If necessary, Addington. Those are the two essential words.'

Addington turned to face his master. 'You have often told me about Leipzig.'

'I have. I have often spoken of it in Cabinet. I have often remembered Leipzig.'

It was more than that. He had never forgotten. When he was still in his twenties, he had walked across the field of Leipzig the day after the battle. It had been a victory against Napoleon. If that was a victory he never wanted to see a defeat.

'I remember that day,' said Aberdeen. 'I remember the sights. I remember the sounds. I remember the men.'

'Then, sir?'

'Henry, what in this case do you think the chances of war to be? Put yourself in the position of the United States. A power on the American continent, certainly. But for the sake of Texas, could she fight a war against England, and France, and perhaps even Spain if that country were, for the sake of honour, say, to go to the aid of her former colony? But put Spain aside. Could the United States risk war with England and France together, and incidentally with Mexico? And we know the American senate will very soon vote that it wants nothing to do with Texas. Given all that, what are the rational chances?'

'Oh, *rationally*, sir – none.'

Later in June, when the news had been received in London that the United States senate did indeed want nothing to do with Texas, Aberdeen summoned Ashbel Smith to Downing Street.

'Two thirds would have been needed for annexation?' asked Aberdeen.

'And two thirds of the American Senate voted against,' said

Smith, who was already cheerfully convinced that Texas must go it alone.

Aberdeen made him the same offer he had made Don Thomas, this time stressing that what was to be guaranteed was first the independence and borders of Texas, and then incidentally the borders of Mexico. Texas, England, France, Mexico, and the United States would all be given the opportunity to be parties to the guarantee, which he would call the Diplomatic Act.

Smith then asked the same question as Murphy. What if the United States would have nothing to do with it?

'Frankly, Mr Smith, although the United States would be invited to participate, I should not expect her to accept that invitation. But that would avail her nothing against the combined determination of the other powers.'

'And what if Mexico would have nothing to do with it?'

'There is reason to believe she would. But if not, then if England, France, and Texas were to agree the act, Mexico would be obliged to abide by its terms.'

'The act, if passed by those three powers alone, would not be abandoned?'

'It would be maintained.'

Smith walked back from Downing Street to St James, turning the proposal over in his mind. It did amount to a perpetual treaty. He was a Texian, but was still enough of an American to suspect any European interference in the affairs of the American continent. And if this were to go through, it would amount to a Texian invitation to the two European powers of England and France to intervene in the affairs of the north American continent. And yet, what of that? The interests of Texas would be served.

When he returned to the consulate he found Amélie fretful. Smith found he had to spend half his time in England and half in France, and now brought her to England with him when he came. At first she had delighted in the shops, and in the dancing at the Cremorne and at Vauxhall gardens, but then she was lonely. She spoke no English and could not go out on her own. He could not take her to the receptions it was his duty to attend. So when he returned from

Downing Street she was fretful and possessive. All he wanted was to talk about the afternoon's doings. She resigned herself to listening. He sketched the terms out for her, to this girl who had never seen Texas or America and who before she met him had never crossed the English channel.

But she listened and then, with her peasant canniness, asked, 'What's the catch?'

Then Smith's mind went to Sam Houston demonstrating on a globe the vast extent of his Texian empire, stretching as far as the Pacific. If this Diplomatic Act were to guarantee the borders of Texas, they would be the present borders. Then he thought again. He had called it a perpetual treaty, but was there any such thing? A treaty could be abrogated, or modified. The present would be secured. In future years an impoverished Mexico would no doubt be glad enough to sell the uninhabited west to Texas. Or Texas could simply inhabit those western lands uninvited, and then what? He was sure Sam would find a way.

He took Amélie to Vauxhall. There, dancing with her under the thousand lights which were craftily arranged so as to create the greatest area of discreet shadow, and feeling her live warmth against him, he became more and more optimistic of the virtues of the Diplomatic Act, which he could not then know would become famous throughout north America as the Vermilion Edict.

21

Head Up,
Facing West

The party of three white men and three white women, and one black, were so completely surprised that there was never any hope of escape. The Indians appeared over the brow of the shallow hill and halted in line abreast. They had ridden carefully, stalking their prey, raising no dust. The whites, who were riding two and two, with Captain Carey out front alone in the lead, also came to a halt. Between Indians and whites there was at most four hundred yards.

'Who are they?' asked Alexander Treaze out of the silence.

'Comanchee,' said Captain Carey, the black. His lips were suddenly so parched with fear that his reply was scarcely audible. He was looking at a line of twenty Comanchee horsemen. The leggings, the feather headdress, the attitude – all were Comanchee.

Next to Carey a man in the dress of a sailor slid his hand across to his gunbelt. He was the boatswain who had bought a Colt revolver from Treaze two years before.

'No,' said Carey. 'Wait.' He looked round at the party. He was a hunter and had the two rifles he always carried with him in case he should come upon a deer. One was in its holster at his side, the other slung across the saddle in front of him. Treaze and the sailor had their Colts. The fourth man, a lieutenant in the Texian navy long since unemployed, had a pistol of sorts. That was all. The three women – Lucy, Helga, and Jeannie – were unarmed. They were on their way to Shoal City, Lucy to find General Houston, Helga with her, Treaze and his new wife Jeannie to see the country, and the two sailors for company and because they had nothing else to do. Captain Carey, the black who had saved a thousand dollars to buy his freedom, had hired them the horses at Galveston and come as guide. He was the only man in the party who knew the country hereabouts. He had known it since he was a boy. He also knew Indians.

Treaze edged up beside Carey.

'What do they want?'

Carey shook his head. Comanchees just might take a look, and ride away. He had known that happen. But he did not hope for it. The Comanchees were so many and the whites so few. They would want the horses, his rifles, the other men's pistols, and the women.

The boatswain eased his horse alongside Carey too. He looked back at the women. 'We make a run of it?' he asked quietly, so that they should not hear.

Another almost imperceptible shake of the head from Carey. He knew his horses. Mares docile enough for women to ride safely were useless when it came to running from the horses he saw on the hill. Comanchees were the finest light cavalry he knew. Besides, there was nowhere to run. The landscape was almost flat and, except for an occasional clump of oak, featureless. The only trees near them were two post oaks, both dead and without foliage, standing within a few feet of each other. The nearest trees which could have provided any shelter were over half a mile away, too far.

The women knew their danger well. Helga prayed to herself in German. Jeannie reached over and put a hand on Lucy's shoulder, by instinct comforting the woman she had brought up since she was a girl.

'What's to say to the women?' asked the navy lieutenant.

'Nothin' to say,' said Carey.

The Comanchees would want the women. Comanchees coveted children by white women. Sometimes a woman, who had been missing for years, would return white haired and broken to a Texian town, a woman for whom the Comanchees no longer had a use. There was nothing to say.

The line of Indian cavalry began to walk towards them. Of the white men, Treaze was ordinarily the most resourceful. The out

of work lieutenant had commanded a cutter. The boatswain had
survived a sea fight with a Spanish privateer. But it was Carey who
spoke up, and the others followed his lead.

'Nobody run. Just – get – down – off – the – horses, slowly
now, real slow.'

They all dismounted, the women sliding from their side saddles.

'Now listen good. So long as they walk t'wards us, stand. Stand
still. Maybe they'll talk. Ain't the biggest chance you ever had, but
it's a chance. But so happen they break out of a walk, and come for
us, lay your horses down if you can, but anyways lay yourself down,
and we'll pick 'em off as they come.'

Treaze put his arm round his new wife. 'Do like he says. Five
to one's fair odds, or I've said so often enough, selling pistols.
Now these heathens take me at my word. Now we'll see.'

Then hell broke loose. The Comanchees, who had advanced in
strict formation, became a howling horde, hurling themselves full
gallop at the whites. Only Carey had time and sense and knowhow
to force his animal to the ground, crouch behind it, and take steady
aim, first with one rifle and then with the second. He brought down
the two leading horsemen. Treaze and the boatswain threw the
women to the ground and then blazed away with their pistols,
thanking God for Mr Colt's five chambers. Between them they got
three of the raiders. The navy lieutenant did not get in a shot. He
was hopelessly overmastered by his own horse, which would not lie
down and dragged him screaming away, caught by the stirrup.

The loss of five men, and the mess of sprawling horses, gave
the party a breathing space. Carey reloaded both rifles. Treaze, who
glanced at him while he was reloading his own Colt, saw puzzlement
in Carey's eyes. Lucy screamed. A single Comanchee had broken
away and was coming straight at her. Carey cut him down. He
had handled a rifle since he was a boy. The game-shooting which
earned him his freedom had made him the best rifle shot for miles
round.

They had killed or wounded six men and lost only the lieutenant, who was now lying dead with his brains dashed out by
his own horse's hoofs. But the Indians were regathering. It would

still have been all up with them if a volley of shots had not at that moment come from behind. They all turned. More horsemen were riding fast towards them. All they could see was a cloud of dust. It might be fifty men.

Treaze groaned. 'More,' he said.

'Hang on in,' said Carey. 'Others, not more.'

He was right. In the mêlée that followed, some of the Comanchees made another chaotic attack which wounded Carey in the neck. Then the pursuing horsemen, emerging from their dust cloud, harried the Comanchees. It was all over more suddenly than it had begun. Eight Indians lay dead and two wounded. The rest had fled. The leader of the pursuers lay hurt in the side. Captain Carey lay in his own spurting blood. Jeannie tore a petticoat into strips to try to staunch his dreadful wound, but she knew it was useless. So did he.

'I was wrong,' he said. 'I had it wrong.' He died in Jeannie's arms. Lucy pulled her away. Helga put aside the canteen of water she had been hopelessly offering to the dying man. All three women were deeply stained with Carey's blood. He had led the defence. The slave who bought his freedom with a thousand dollars had kept his head and warded off the Comanchees until the newcomers saved them. Carey had done that, and he died saying he was wrong.

Their rescuers were a dozen men riding south to Galveston led by Major Pat Ferris. He was the only one of them who had been wounded. He had fought at San Jacinto.

The dead Indians were scattered around. The two wounded were taken prisoner. One was badly hurt, with his left arm smashed at the shoulder and hanging down. Six of the men who had saved them were German immigrants, and the rest Americans from the north. A drifter from Ohio wandered across to a dead Indian, looked curiously down, and then turned the man over with his foot. He called two of his friends over. They took one look, called their companions, and then all walked grimly over to the two prisoners. The Indians were jerked to their feet. An American spat full in the face of one, hit him hard, and then rubbed spittle and blood into the man's forehead and cheeks. The dye came off. The Comanchees were no Comanchees, only white bandits who had disguised themselves that way to escape

blame. It had been done before. In Texas it was a loathed and
detested trick.

In the middle of their small battlefield, Lucy and Jeannie stood
hugging each other, both bloody and both weeping. Jeannie said,
'My child, that I brought up from short frocks.' Lucy caught Treaze's
eye, and motioned him to come and comfort his wife, who was further
gone than she in shock and desolation. Helga knelt on the ground still
praying. The boatswain did his best to lay out Carey, straightening
his arms and legs and cleaning at least his face. There was nothing
to be done with the neck, which was open to the windpipe.

This was terrible enough, but then a new scream arose. It was
from the prisoner with the smashed arm as he was manhandled
to the dead trees. His fellow bandit was kicked and frogmarched
in the same direction. A single rope was thrown over a branch of
the first tree and then over a branch of the second. As it lay slack
between the two trees this rope was twisted twice round the throat
of each of the two prisoners. The two struggling wretches were held
at a distance of three feet from each other. Then both ends of the
rope were grasped by the willing hands of half a dozen men. They
hauled away and then the 'Comanchees' were swung up in a tangle,
suspended as if from a washing line between the two dead trees,
kicking at each other in their struggle. The man with the smashed
arm uttered a continuing throttled scream.

Lucy stood with her back turned to this spectacle. Pat Ferris,
who was lying within a few feet of her, saw her horror.

'Not pretty, ma'am,' he said, 'but too pretty for them. Your man
Carey, the black, what he meant was, when he said he got it wrong,
was he saw they was no Comanchees. Somehow, I don't know. Fool
anyone at first, but if they'd've been Comanchees there'd've been
nothing of you left by the time we got up to you. Saw some of it
from way off. Comanchees don't charge like a rabble. Don't run
neither. Comanchees would've gone through you and over. He
must've seen it then. That's what he saw. So don't you trouble
yourself with them,' – he jerked his head back at the hanging tree
– 'not them. Comanchees is wolves. But them . . . ' He turned and
spat blood at them.

That night Pat Ferris died too, from the wound in his side that had punctured his lung.

They straggled into Shoal City with their dead slung over saddles. Treaze looked after the women. Their baggage was lost. It had been strapped in panniers to horses that had bolted, and would not be recovered until it was light the next day. Their own clothes were caked with blood and ruined. The women of the town lent what clothes they could spare, and brought buckets of salt Gulf water to wash in. All privacy and reticence had to go. After a day of savagery the three women stood together. Lucy met the eyes of Jeannie and then Helga. All were bloodstained and filthy. The hair of each woman was matted with Captain Carey's blood.

'Let's go to it then,' said Lucy. She undid the laces of her drenched skirt. They helped each other tear off their clothes and throw them aside. All distinction and difference between them went. They sluiced each other down. Lucy motioned Helga to her. She doused the girl's head, unmatting the clotted hair with her fingers and then rinsing it, separating the gouts of blood from the long yellow hair. She wiped Helga's shoulders and back with a rag, and then the rest of her. Jeannie did the same for her, and then the two of them for Jeannie. The water in the buckets was all red with blood. Treaze brought more sea water and left it at the door. The three naked women finished the cleaning of each other's bodies as best they could. The three of them gleamed. The rush lights on the wall lit their limbs weirdly.

Jeannie had bathed and dressed Lucy for years, but there had never been such nakedness as this. Lucy had never seen Jeannie unclothed. As for Helga, she had never appeared naked even before a lover. There had always been darkness, and some covering.

Then they put on what the town women had brought them. There were no dressmakers at Shoal City, and no store-bought clothes. The women spun their own cloth from their own cotton, wove it themselves, and made it up into garments. Lucy stood in a linsey homespun dress, stained purple with berries. Then they ate what they could. They had not eaten for ten hours. Jeannie went to her husband. Lucy and Helga were given a bed to share. As they prepared to lie down for the night, Helga asked Lucy to sit on the one chair in the room. She had found a brush somewhere, and wished to brush her mistress's hair. It was the nightly routine. Both were dead tired. Lucy said no at first, but then told the girl to go on with it. After a day of savagery, it was a small approach to normality. Then the two women slept.

Next day the town buzzed as settlers came in from miles around, brought by the news of the attack and of Pat Ferris's death. Major Ferris was a man famous for the part he had played at San Jacinto. At midday the news was that Sam Houston had come to town. He was staying five miles out, and came for the funeral of his old comrade and of the other victims, which was to be that afternoon. When he heard the story of the attack, and learned that one of the women was Lucy, he sent asking to meet her. She was sitting in a rocking chair on the stoop of a clapboard house when he appeared, sweeping off his hat when he caught sight of her. He took the hand she held out to him in both his. She was sitting in the sun but her hand was cold.

'You are unhurt?' he said. She heard the alarm in his voice.

'I was lucky, General Houston.'

'I am ashamed,' he said. She saw that his emotion was real.

'Ashamed?' she asked. 'I am sorry for Major Ferris, who was your friend. He saved us, he and Captain Carey. And now they are both dead.'

'I am ashamed that this should happen to you in Texas. Ashamed that there are so many rogues, murderers, and worthless men. We are infested with such men from the north.'

The day before she had shaken with fear. She saw that Houston now shook with anger. He came close and sat gazing at her.

'I went to see General Jackson,' she said.

'I have heard you did. He wrote that you did. And you come back to *this*.'

'I was more fortunate than others.'

'But you were put in fear of your life.'

'Oh yes,' she said. 'And now I know what it is.' She spoke brightly, but she was exhausted in body and spirit.

'There is the funeral,' he said, 'which is soon, and I must go. May I come back to you after that?'

'General Houston, I shall come to the funeral too.'

He leaned forward earnestly. He told her she was in no state to come. He was afraid it would distress her.

'How could it not? But I must come.'

'Lady Lucy, it is not the custom in Texas for ladies to be present at funerals.'

'I am sorry for that. I do not wish to flout your customs. But I have mine too. Men died yesterday who saved my life. Forgive me, but I shall come.'

He looked at her dress. It was a far cry from what he had last seen her wear. She understood him.

'It is purple,' she said, 'which is a proper colour for mourning.'

She stood and smoothed out the rough cloth of the dress. It would not be smoothed. It was such a dress as a servant would not have worn back home in Scotland. But it had been lent to her in kindness.

She said: 'My father once told me clothes alone do not much matter – or not nearly so much as a certain carriage of the head. I shall try for that instead.'

Lucy stood there in front of Sam Houston, and would not be moved in her determination. There was nothing else for it, so he escorted her to the funeral. As he had said, she was the only woman. The graveyard was on the edge of town. On a sunlit afternoon they walked behind the cart carrying the coffins, to the slow beat of a single drum. Major Pat Ferris was interred first. The words of the English burial service were mumbled, a trumpeter played a few plaintive notes off-key, and then four men lifted the coffin.

She clutched at Houston's arm beside her.

'Easy,' he said, and glanced sideways to reassure himself that she was not faint. She had been steady so far.

She was not faint. She was taken aback by the actions of the pallbearers who, as she saw it, were just tipping the coffin into the hole. Then she realised what was happening. They were, with great care, sliding the coffin in feet first.

'What is this?' she asked him.

'Pat Ferris's wish,' said Houston. 'He always told me it was his wish. He told me before San Jacinto it was his wish.'

'What?'

'To be buried head up, facing west. Head up because he never in his life stooped to any man, facing west because all his life he travelled farther west. I said I would see to it for him.'

Then the navy lieutenant was buried. The government which had not paid him for two years provided at least a Lone Star flag to cover his coffin, just as it had for Ferris.

Then an immigrant from Ohio, one of Ferris's men, was buried. The preacher moved away. Lucy saw that was all.

'Where is Captain Carey?' she said.

'Captain Carey?'

'He is not to be buried?'

'Dear Lucy . . .'

'Is he not to be buried?'

'He has already been buried. It was done yesterday.'

'Yesterday? Not here?'

'He was a black. It could not be here.'

She turned on him in bewildered anger. 'And you, General Houston, tell me you are ashamed. Ashamed of murderers because they put me in fear. He was a man who saved us from those murderers, and they killed him. And you say he is not fit to be buried here?'

She withered him with scorn. He bowed his head. But then the press of events crushed her. The craven attack, the mortal fear, the murder of Carey dying in his blood, the savage stringing up of the wounded prisoners, and now this. He put out his arms to support and comfort her, and she did not want it but could not stop him.

Out in the scrubland Captain Carey lay in the grave Ferris's men had scraped for him. The horses for which, as for his freedom, he had worked and saved, were now other men's horses. They had caught his horses and taken them. Twenty yards from Captain Carey's unmarked grave the two murderers, still dressed in the remains of Comanchee rags, swung on their clothesline slung between two dead trees, and the scavenging seagulls from Galveston Bay jerked out and ate their eyes.

Lucy walked back into town with the procession. Houston held an umbrella over her head. Later she remembered a moment of irritation that he should have taken this on himself. The sun was low in the west and no longer hot on her head. There was no need. Jeannie, seeing her return, took one look, seized her from Sam Houston's side without ceremony and with no words said, and led her to bed.

Lucy fell into a long fever, nursed by Jeannie and Helga. They were exhausted too, but summoned up strength for what they had to do. Jeannie had disprized Helga when they first met, thinking her flimsy. Over the two weeks they nursed Lucy together, she changed her mind.

Lucy was young and vivid and strong. She was still only nineteen but had seen and known so much. In her delirium she saw herself and her husband Richard kneeling together by their bed, and then lying on the cloak on Lammermuir. Then she saw Jeannie dressing her in Paris, and her own parted legs wearing the grey ghosts of mourning, then herself and Ashbel Smith on that bright Parisian day, then her husband again, taking his leave of her, then her imagining of the manner of his death in China, then Charles Elliot, himself ill and swaying, about to tell her how Richard came by his death. She saw the Comanchees coming down upon her to kill her and then Captain Carey lying in his blood. She heard the exclamation of Jeannie with her man in that New Orleans courtyard. She heard the two bandits scream as they were hoisted up between the two dead trees. Then she was an Italian dancer on the steamer landing at Nashville. Then she and Richard were clasped together again, and Sam Houston was there holding an umbrella over them both to protect them from the sun that was not there. She saw, as if she were a spectator, three women washing blood from their gleaming bodies. Then, as she came to consciousness, she saw, mixed together in a tangle of silk, the discarded grey ghosts of mourning she had worn so long, and the stockings of netted Chantilly lace with which Jeannie had replaced them in Paris.

Through this silken tangle, Sam Houston raised his hand to touch
her hair.

When the fever went at last, she woke to see a face leaning
over her, and the hand that touched her hair was Helga's.

22

A Man Called Polk

When she was strong enough to travel, Lucy went back to Galveston, staying at the Tremont. Helga suggested that they should go there rather than take a house. She knew the hotel, knew its staff, and knew that such comfort as existed in Galveston was most likely to be found there. Lucy agreed readily enough. For the first time in her life she was listless. She did not leave the hotel but stayed in her rooms with the louvres left open to catch the sea breeze and create a through draught. When she was further on in her recovery she sat reading on the public terrace on the second floor.

One afternoon in early July she sat there alone. Jeannie would come to see her later. Helga had gone into the town to collect newspapers and to ask at the post office for any letters that might have arrived from her man in Perote. On the quayside Helga came upon a peculiar demonstration. Burnings in effigy had always been popular in Galveston. She had never before seen quite what she saw that day.

She encountered a parade of two hundred men marching, carrying at the head of the procession two flags. She stopped to watch it pass. One flag was the Lone Star of Texas, carried high. The other was the Stars and Stripes, but that was carried upside down as an insult, with the stars trailing in the dust. When they saw Helga the men broke into a ragged cheer. It was a cheer for a tall and handsome girl with golden hair, a cheer with a bit of bawdy hope in it since there was not a man there who did not admire the woman's splendid figure and wish she was his. But it was also a cheer for a woman they associated with the Tremont. She had worked there for two years.

The men who marched did not frequent the Tremont. The drink was too expensive there. The Tremont was for their betters, or at least for the men who employed them, the merchants and shippers of Galveston. By cheering Helga the marchers, in some part at least, were cheering the girl who served their bosses, and their bosses were men who had always stood up for Texian independence, the Lone Star alone. The sailors, porters, longshoremen, and day labourers who had shouted loudest for annexation and burned Sam Houston in effigy, had now turned on the United States because the American senate had showed it did not want them.

The parade halted on the quay opposite the point where an American sloop was anchored fifty yards out in the bay. Two sailors lounged on her rails, watching the scene impassively.

'Sixteen, sixteen,' the demonstrators yelled rhythmically. 'All they can raise are sixteen. To Hell with the States and sixteen.'

'Why sixteen,' asked Helga. 'What is sixteen?'

When Helga asked a question she could always rely on at least three willing men to go out of their way to answer it.

'Sixteen's all the American senators that voted to have us in the union,' said a longshoreman. 'Just sixteen. So we say to Hell with their sixteen.'

'More to the point,' said an attorney's clerk, who prided himself that he saw the finer points of politics, 'that thirty-five voted against.'

'Maybe, but to hell with their lousy sixteen if that's all they could raise,' said a third man, and the rhythmic chant was taken up again.

By then fifty of the sloop's crew, all of whom had wisely been refused shore leave by their officers, were lining the rails.

'Right, now show 'em their flag.'

The Stars and Stripes was raised in mocking salute to the American ship.

'And now show 'em what we do with it.'

A Texian sailor lit a taper and held it high, waving it at the American sloop. The American sailors, seeing what was about to happen, waved their fists and shouted defiance.

'Sixteen, sixteen,' yelled the mob, and then the taper was set to the flag. The Stars and Stripes was held aloft as it burned. It was a hot day, but the American flag had been taken from the locker of a Texian merchantman where it had been stored sodden with salt water. It took a long time to catch and burn.

'Strike,' shouted a voice on board the sloop. Two men ran to strike the Texian ensign which the sloop flew at its mainmast as a courtesy to the Republic in whose port she lay. But before they could do this an officer appeared on the afterdeck, and two petty officers with him, and together they forced the men to quarters. On board the sloop the lieutenant, the boatswain, the master at arms and two midshipmen stood at attention as the Stars and Stripes burned on the quay and its ashes were trodden into the ground.

Sam Houston, on his way to the Tremont, saw this from two blocks away but did not pause in his step. This was a mob that had once burned him in effigy and would now cheer him to the echo, but he wanted none of it. He carried on to the Tremont.

Since the day she had fallen into a fever after the funeral, Lucy had lived out of the world. Great events had taken place, but she did not know of them. Even those she did know of, she let wash over her. She did not know, and Texas did not yet know, of Great Britain's offer to guarantee the borders of Texas and Mexico against the world. She had dimly heard of the vote in the United States senate, but did not give it a thought. She had heard and understood the news of the coming presidential election in the United States, but that was only because it concerned Mr Polk, whom she had met at the Hermitage.

The Democratic party had made its nomination more than a month previously, before the senate vote against annexation. The convention at Baltimore voted seven times without any man getting the necessary majority. Fist fights broke out in the hall. A voice yelled, 'Give us Andrew Jackson again.' The convention adjourned for the day in a riot. Next morning, on the ninth ballot, James Polk from Tennessee was chosen. If he was not Jackson he was Jackson's friend, and obscure enough to have no enemies. Mr Polk himself said he had never aspired so high.

From Washington the British minister wrote to London, 'A Mr

Polk has been adopted, a gentleman hitherto little known in the political history of this country, but who appears to have found favour in the Democratick Party at the present moment by reason of his ultra opinions, more especially with reference to the annexation of Texas.' This was sloppy of the minister, who was too much a courtier to consider low politics of much interest, otherwise he could easily have discovered, by asking a question or two, that Mr Polk, though most recently defeated for the governorship of Tennessee, had once been Speaker of the House of Representatives in Washington. But that was before the British minister's time, and he did not think to ask. He said that the choice of a man called Polk demonstrated the sadly split condition of the Democrats, whereas, on the other hand, the Whigs had been solidly behind their candidate, and had chosen Mr Clay by acclamation. He took the opportunity to point out that the Democrats' choice of such an unknown candidate would enable Mr Clay to win even more easily than had been expected.

In this matter even Saligny, writing to Paris from New Orleans, knew better than Great Britain's man in Washington. Certainly, he said, no one had dreamed of Mr Polk before, except General Jackson and a few of his cronies. Mr Clay's chances would now be much increased, and with Clay as president annexation would be a dead letter. But he thought – and here he had a clear advantage in understanding over the British minister – that Mr Polk would be bound to stir up a commotion in what Saligny chose to call the Texian comedy.

Lucy, as it happened, knew Mr Polk better than either of the two diplomats. So it was natural, when Sam Houston walked into the Tremont on the afternoon of the flag burning, and mounted to the second floor verandah, that he and Lucy should talk about the new nominee.

It was the second time General Houston had called since she had come back to Galveston. In a strange way he felt easier with her now she had for the moment lost some of her vividness. He had been drawn to her by that vividness but all the same, in those days of her recovery, when she was paler, and sat quietly in a reclining chair, he could converse with her more easily and with less show.

They talked about her visit to the Hermitage. She told him of Mr Donelson's remark that General Jackson often thought of Sam, but that he could not remember when the old general had last seen his protégé.

'It is true,' said Houston, 'and the fault is mine. But I shall go to see him. When I can. As soon as I can.'

'I am glad of it. He talks so much of you.'

'Well, and you met Jim Polk.'

'I know Mr Polk a little,' she said. 'And I gather that to know him even that slightly is a rare distinction. I have not been out yet, but there is a joke among the hotel servants. They ask each other, "Who is Mr Polk?"'

'Yes,' said Sam Houston, 'and the answer is, I dare say, "The man nominated for president on the ninth ballot."'

'Yes. I cannot say, you know, that he said much when we met either.'

'He never does.'

'Mrs Polk spoke of you a lot, and spoke of you kindly.'

'She is a sweet woman. She was kind to me when I badly needed her kindness, many years ago.'

Lucy looked in Sam Houston's face as he leaned earnestly towards her. The chair was too small for him. He leaned forward almost anxiously, with his large hands spread on his knees. She wondered again, as she had often wondered since those days in Nashville, why he should have sent her to a town where she would be told so much about past events in his life which must be painful to him. She could not think why. She could not ask him. Perhaps he had not thought of it in that light at all.

'Mrs Polk did tell me,' she said, 'that you had at least three portraits of you done at Nashville.'

'True. And did she say one of them was of me as a Roman general?'

'She said no such thing.'

'Well, there is one. I can only say in my defence that the idea was none of mine, but the artist's.'

'She said artists sought you out.'

'Yes, Lucy, that is the truth. But it is not all the truth, not the whole truth. There has to be vanity in the sitter too. I admit it. But there have been no more pictures of me since – or only one.'

She smiled at this. 'What was that chanting and marching I heard in the town, just before you came?'

He told her.

'Not you burned in effigy this time? Only a flag.'

'Flags are more dangerous, Lucy.'

She had not thought of that.

'I have received a letter from Captain Elliot,' he said. 'He is doing well in Virginia, up in his mountains, and hopes to return to Texas by October.'

'Do you really think he will be able to?'

Sam Houston knew that her wish to see Elliot was one reason why she had stayed as long as she had.

'I think he will,' he said, and took his leave, kissing her hand and promising to return.

'Yes, I think he will,' he repeated at the door. At the moment he said those words, he meant what he said. If he had been asked later, or by someone with no interest in seeing Captain Elliot, he would have answered that he had no such belief at all.

As he left the Tremont he saw Helga approaching, up the broad street. She looked straight at him, and he at her. She asked him how he did. He raised his silver topped stick in acknowledgement. That was all; then he crossed to a cotton shipper who called out to him from the other side of the street.

Helga looked after him. Then she drew herself up straight and entered the hotel. She met Jeannie in the lobby, who asked what the matter was. Helga replied that there was nothing for her at the post office from Perote. They went up to Lucy together.

23

Crawfishing About

All over Texas, feeling against the United States ran high. Sam Houston's stock had risen high too. All that summer, no news came of his having been burned in effigy in any Texian town. But in the Mexican fortress of Perote, and much closer to home than that, there were men convinced of his treason to the Republic.

The closest to home of all was Anson Jones, the man Houston had himself appointed to be his secretary of state. In the heat of an August day, in his cabin at Washington-on-the-Brazos, he took refreshment with Colonel Bee. Bee drank whisky, Jones soda water.

'Not one of them here,' exclaimed Jones. 'Not Sam Houston, not one other single member of the cabinet either.'

Colonel Bee, who was lounging in a deep chair with his feet up on Jones's desk, took a sip from his glass and uttered a consoling grunt.

'I am alone,' said Jones. 'And the running of affairs devolves entirely on me.'

No response from Bee, who had himself only just arrived in the capital, on his way through to Galveston.

Jones took from his desk a handful of letters and waved them at Bee, who glanced at them and took another sip from his glass.

'Sam's hardly been here this year,' said Jones. 'All I see of Sam is his scrawl on papers I send him. I send him papers. Two weeks later, back come the papers with "Do This," "Do That," or "Tell Hill" scrawled across them.'

Bee grunted again, to show how well he understood. Hill was attorney general. He had never much liked the man.

Jones continued his litany. 'Well, how can I tell Hill? He's not here. The attorney general's not here. The vice president's not here. The secretary of the treasury's not here. Haven't seen him for months. The secretary of war's not here. The commissioner for lands is away, cultivating his own lands. You know what it's like.'

'What?' said Bee, and then recalled that he had once been secretary of state himself, five years before.

'That was under Lamar,' he said. 'Different man.'

'Same post,' said Jones. 'Secretary of state is secretary of state, though I suppose the times were easier. And it wasn't for long, was it?'

'Don't know about that,' said Bee, not wishing to admit that his own tenancy of the secretaryship had been any easier, and not volunteering the information that he had filled the post for just two months before both he and Lamar concluded, at much the same time, that the office was too much for him.

'There Sam is,' said Jones, 'making much of Elliot, while Elliot's here. Then as soon as Elliot goes he takes up with Saligny.'

'Didn't think . . .' began Bee, but then gave up the effort. He had been about to remark that he had never noticed Sam and Saligny got on well together. In this he was right, and showed he knew more than Jones. The truth was that in any large matters Houston acted as his own secretary of state, and kept Jones in the dark. He left Jones with only the minutiae of foreign affairs, but heaped on him the domestic business of the Republic.

'Now he treats that English woman as if she were chargé d'affaires,' said Jones. 'Tea with Lady Lucy, I've heard, at the Tremont.'

'Pretty woman,' said Bee, lost in thought of a woman of his own acquaintance.

'And now he's taken up with some German prince who wants to bring out immigrants. Passes the letter to me when the man writes, and I make a civil reply, and the prince arrives in Galveston, and the prince wants introductions, and I give him letters of introduction, and then suddenly Sam comes all over interested and wants to see the prince himself. And I dare say he will, and Sam will make foreign policy on the hoof, and make some bad bargain I shall have to keep.'

Bee removed his feet from the desk long enough to pour himself more whisky from a bottle on a side table. He put the bottle by his side on the floor, where it was to hand, and replaced his feet on the desk.

'Well,' he said, having taken two slow sips, 'you'll be president yourself soon enough. Please yourself then.'

This was true enough as far as it went. Sam Houston could not serve consecutive terms. The Texian constitution forbade it. So by December there had to be a new president. Jones's fear was that any new president would be president only in name, and that Sam's eternal influence would still be seen as the real power behind the throne.

'I have no expectation,' he said, 'that the presidential chair will be any other than one of thorns.'

Bee, leaning still further back, looked steadily at the unceiled beams of the roof.

'Nor,' said Jones, 'do I desire the office.'

'Your health, then,' said Bee, raising his glass. 'But I heard Sam was in Brazos and Harris counties rustling up votes for you.'

Jones glowered. 'I have lost more than I ever gained by my association with Sam.' He separated one letter from a pile and tossed it to Bee, who slowly read it.

'Why,' said Bee, 'what does this say but what I just told you? Sam's in Brazos. Says as much here in his own hand. Says he has heard nothing but good spoken of you.'

'Says he has *heard*. Doesn't say what he said himself. Crawfishing about, that's Sam, trying to defeat my election. Treason at work. But I'll be elected yet.'

'Your good health, then,' said Bee, draining his glass. He got to his feet. There was no reasoning with Jones. Besides, Colonel Bee never did trust a man who sipped soda water.

Jones waited until Bee was at the door. Then he asked, 'You see Moore?'

'Yep,' said the colonel, 'just as I was on my way to you.'

'Dress uniform and all?'

'Uniform anyway.'

'Dress uniform,' said Jones. 'With his commodore's two silver epaulettes. Hocked them at Hatfield's saloon when he came. Got them back when the court adjourned a while back.'

'So he's clear then? I didn't hear . . .'

'You didn't hear because you've only been in town two hours, and most of that drinking the state department's whisky. He's clear, and owed two years' pay. No surprise to me. He ate, drank, and shared a room with the president of the court, all seventy-two days that trial stretched itself out. Now he wants his pay. Won't get the pay until Sam signs the court's findings, which Sam won't like doing one bit. I told Moore that when he came to chase me for the pay. He asked for the navy secretary. Told him there was no secretary of the navy any more. That'll be more papers for me to send to Sam. Sam won't like this. But Moore's got his epaulettes back.'

In the fortress of Perote the Texian prisoners longed for the approach of night. The Mexican guards were themselves so enervated by the heat that they could not summon the energy to march their prisoners outside the walls to quarry more stone, and kept them all day pent up inside cells where the air was so fetid and bad that candles did not burn easily, and sometimes faltered and went out altogether. The Texians sat languidly, entertaining themselves with the louse derby that Feargus Mullin had devised.

'Now back home,' he had said, 'I was a great one for the horses. So, there being no horseflesh here worth the racing of, seeing the army of Mexico mounts its men on starved scarecrows of beasts, we must make do with what beasts we have. And I have observed, boys, that the national beast of Mexico, the beast that naturally flourishes in these parts, is your louse.' So he cut a circle from a cow's hide, eighteen inches across, inscribed a smaller circle inside that, and in the centre drew a cross. Then each man who cared to play provided his own louse – which he could easily find in his bedding, or just detach from his own person – and the assembled lice were nudged, spat at, and encouraged with the hot ends of burning sticks until one of them reached the centre and was the winner.

'The first whose beast finds salvation on the Holy Cross,' said Feargus, 'wins the jackpot.' The prize was a tot of mescal when they had it, or, when they had not, a handful of worthless Mexican coins. In this way they passed the heat of the day. In the cool of the evening they were allowed out into the courtyard. They talked about escape. The British minister from Mexico City visited them, and dissuaded them from this. He came because the foreign office in London had instructed him to do so, but he made an impression on the prisoners far greater than he could have imagined. They knew for the first time that they were not forgotten. They saw a man who came dressed in new clothes, clean shaven, and sure of himself in a way they had forgotten. The minister of France or the United States could have come, and the effect would have been the same. But it was an Englishman. The prisoners were tattered, bearded, and filthy, and they had begun to be afraid they would never leave this awful fort. Mr Bankhead, by his mere coming there, and by his sublime assurance, lifted them up. They saw the way he was received by the Mexican officers. The colonel in command came cap in hand to greet him, and Bankhead affably offered his hand. The colonel then explained that, although in any proper view of the matter, the prisoners were invaders of his mother country, he had used his discretion, had tempered vigilance with mercy, and no longer chained the men two and two during the day, only at night. Bankhead heard this impassively.

Then he turned to the men and shook hands with all who would. A few would not, loathing all the English. They were Irish. So was Feargus but he took the man's hand. They gathered round Bankhead and he talked quietly. He would not advise escape. He trod carefully among his words but conveyed to them that Santa Anna should be played gently. The president had imprisoned them. He knew the president had caused one in ten of them to be shot. This had been accounted savagery everywhere it had been reported, and Santa Anna was anxious to do anything to redeem himself from such a dreadful reputation. Bankhead could promise nothing, and said so, but gave his word he would do his best. For his part he would be grateful if they could go some way to assuring him that they would act with caution. He knew, he said, that this was asking a lot of them, but he did earnestly ask it.

There was a murmur of agreement. The few Irishmen who had not shaken his hand when he came could not lose face by accepting it when he left, but they no longer said anything against him. Feargus said to him, 'Some of us, sir, are British subjects, of Her Britannic Majesty as the phrase is.'

Bankhead smiled. He heard Feargus's Irish brogue, and knew very well that it was the Irish among them who were nominally British subjects, and that these were the very men who had refused his hand, most of them.

'I shall bear that circumstance in mind,' he said. 'I shall do my utmost for Her Majesty's subjects among you, as I shall for all the others.'

After he left, Feargus addressed them all. 'Now as an Irishman I have reason to loathe all Englishmen. Granted?'

This was readily granted.

'But what, I ask you, have I to lose by taking the poor man's hand when he offers it? The representative of the British nation is no small character in any part of the globe where the needle has turned. And no harm in it for us. He may do us a good turn. After all, what reply have we had to the letter we all sent to the United States, imploring the beneficent and mighty protection and aid of His Excellency the president?'

The Americans would not have this, so Feargus withdrew his imputation, readily agreeing that the letter might never have reached the president, or if it had that the reply might have been intercepted by the Mexicans.

'But then,' he said brightly, 'that in itself is an argument for taking help when it's offered, for taking a man's hand when it's offered. Now the president of the United States is too far off to extend his hand. Much as he wishes to extend it, he cannot. He's too far. Mr Bankhead's near. And he has the will, which is more than you can say for Sam.'

Every voice agreed with the last part of this statement. None of them had any time for Sam Houston. Not one. All were certain he had betrayed them.

And so the prisoners' greatest celebration of the year was on the fourth of July, the independence day not of Texas but of the United States. 'Boys,' said the Americans, 'we'll have an egg-nog tonight.' They spent what little money they had left on mescal, whipped this up with goat's milk and eggs, and prepared pints of the brew. The guards watched, sunk deep in lassitude. Feargus and Kurt Neumann approached the sergeant's lively wife, who not only supplied a little brandy but persuaded the other Mexican women to lend a dozen dresses. The prisoners found two fiddles, and then there was a mad ball, with everyone taking turns to dance with those of their number who had rigged themselves out in the women's dresses. The dance grew rowdy. A Texian let out a loud yippee, twisted his head clean round in his shoulders, made large eyes, and imitated the triumphant cry of a Mississippi owl.

The guards did not stir. A Mexican captain stuck his head round the door at the third cry, said, '*Telecote,*' and mimed to the prisoners that they were mad.

'What's he say?' asked an American.

'*Telecote,*' said Feargus. 'Mexican for screech owl.'

At the height of the excitement, Texians drunk on their mescal-laced egg-nog reproduced staggering caricatures of a drunken Sam Houston. 'Damn you Sam,' shouted a man from San Antonio who had served with Houston but now despised him. 'Damn you Sam for a craven liar.'

The drunken men echoed this heart-felt cry. Many fell asleep with that commination in their minds. They were left unchained that night because the Mexican blacksmith was as drunk as they were. Feargus and Neumann sat apart from the others, Neumann with a woman's dress in his hands, one of those they had borrowed for the ball.

'Helga?' asked Feargus, seeing his companion run his hand over the dress.

'Her,' said Neumann, beset with the high hops and deep doubts

which come naturally to a man who cannot remember when he last
held or saw a cherished woman, and cannot think when he next may.

'Come man,' said Feargus, 'think of it this way. I have never
seen your woman. But if she is one half what you have said, then
think yourself a fortunate man, having such a woman to stock your
dreams.'

24

Princeling and President

One evening that August, when a breeze had tempered the heat and humidity of the day, Lucy stood on a Galveston quay with Sam Houston and a stranger, watching a hundred immigrants disembarking from the brig that had come in that afternoon from Hamburg.

She was recovered. Houston, leaving his wife and one year old son up country, had come to Galveston to meet Prince Charles of Solms-Braunfels. Jones had been right when he predicted that Houston would want to deal with the prince himself. He had spent much of the afternoon taking tea with Lucy at the Tremont, and had then asked her to come with him.

'You will know the prince?' he asked.

She laughed. 'No. Not at all. Is it likely that I should?'

'But he is a cousin of Queen Victoria?'

'Something of the sort. General Houston, that's hardly the society I move in. I've never spent more than a few weeks in London in my life, and when I've been there I've never been asked to the palace. Remiss of them.'

'What do I call the man?' he asked after a pause.

She laughed again, amused that Sam Houston should concern himself with a matter of trivial etiquette.

'He could do great things for us,' he explained. 'He is bringing people.'

'Well. He'll be very formal with you. "Mr President", he'll say. I don't imagine you'll want to call him "Your Serene Highness", which is probably what he is.'

'What will *you* call him?'

'Nothing in particular,' she said.

Prince Solms did greet them with the greatest formality. Lucy returned his greeting with an inclination of the head. Sam Houston offered his hand.

'Fine people, Mr President,' said the prince, indicating the Germans who were disembarking. He was commissioner for a group of twenty-five noblemen, who, being reduced in fortune, were proposing to establish a German settlement in Texas. They had already bought land. Now they were bringing people. As Houston watched, he saw that they were all, even after a long passage, fit and sturdy. Each man carried a rifle.

'Population,' said Houston, 'is what we most want.'

'Then, Mr President, they will do admirably for you.'

Houston thought they might. They were not the ragged American drifters from the north whom he so much despised, adventurers who brought nothing except a taste for Mexican gold and then, when they were disappointed, turned into disgruntled loafers. He said as much.

'Each man,' said the prince, brings his own rifle, his own powder horn, his own game bag. His own tools to cultivate the land. They will rest two days here, and then go inland together. They are country people.'

Houston nodded.

'I do not like to let them see too much of the town,' said Solms.

'Galveston,' said Houston, 'is a trifle raw. True.'

'I would not willingly let them stay in any town,' said the prince. 'They are country people, who have worked all their lives in the country. They are simple, Godly people. They know farming. That is all most of them know. Hamburg is the only city they have seen, all but a few of them. And they were only two nights there, while they assembled. So we shall leave here as soon as we can. Country people need the country, and what I have seen of Texas has been magnificent. They will see it as one large farm, and rejoice at it. We shall go up the Guadalupe. There we have already built two large barns for them as shelter, one for the men, one for the women and children. When they get there, their first task will be to build their own houses, and then the barns will be used as barns for the first crop.'

At this moment two light cannon were swung up from the hold and landed on the quay.

'Four pounders,' said the prince. 'No great use as artillery. But of great service in making an impression, to protect a settlement.'

Houston nodded. He liked what he saw. Here were men well found, well armed, with their wives and children, ready to set off inland.

'People,' he said. 'People. See, annexation has failed. It is done with. And now that prospect is gone, the glory of the United States has culminated. It will grow no more. I have said so in as many words to the United States attaché. Or rather I told the man who did hold that office in Texas. When he heard annexation was defeated and was a dead letter, he said to me, "Well, General, then the tail goes with the hide," and took himself off home. Went to catch the first steamer to New Orleans. Though he never got there, poor man.'

'Indeed?' said the prince.

The man Houston meant was Murphy, who had been no adornment to the diplomatic corps, no credit to the United States, and an embarrassment to the Texian government. But still, Houston had not wished him dead.

'Died of fever here at Galveston,' said Houston. 'Do you know, Prince, three of the American representatives in Texas have died. First Judge Eve. Known him for years. Good man. Then Murphy. Then they sent a man to take Murphy's place and he's just died too. Didn't last a month. Three in a row. Now, Prince, do you see the hand of destiny in that?'

'No,' said Lucy. 'Just too much fever.'

'Ah,' said the prince, and diverted the conversation to the higher arts, indicating the harmonium which was being hoisted out of the hold. 'A patent new French thing. It is a small organ. After they have not heard music for such a long time, the settlers will be greatly impressed by an organ, no matter how small. They bring their music with them, as well as rifles and ploughs.'

Houston watched it as it was carefully landed on the quay. They all walked over to inspect this marvel.

In a minute it was out of its wooden case. One of the immigrants sat at the portable organ and pedalled until the bellows that worked the reeds were inflated.

'Mr President,' said Solms, 'would you do us the honour of playing the first notes?'

Sam Houston protested that he had never played such an instrument.

'Just a note, Mr President. If you will permit, the man will show you.'

'A chord,' said Lucy. She had never seen the like either, but the keyboard resembled a piano's. She took Houston's hands and placed the thumbs and fingers over the keys he should depress.

'Now,' she said. Sam Houston pressed down on the keyboard and a rich chord in C Major echoed round the quay. It was only one chord but the whole waterfront heard it, and the immigrants burst into a cheer. Houston looked round, nodding his shaggy head to acknowledge the applause of those who would soon be his new citizens.

Then the best player among the immigrants sat down at the instrument and played a diapason voluntary. The settlers stopped where they stood, and listened. The longshoremen ceased their work. The sailors stayed fixed in their positions on deck or in the rigging.

'By the youngest Bach,' said Solms. 'A noble harmony to expel from our souls all gloom and sadness, so as to raise and prepare our spirits.' And it looked as though it had. The new settlers, who had been cheerful enough before, now walked with a new spring in their step. A girl walked past singing, holding a child by each hand. Lucy watched her walk up to a young man, who took the children and lifted both in his arms. The girl stood with her hands on her hips, completely at ease, smiling up at the man.

'No American,' Houston said at last, laying a hand on the harmonium, 'ever brought such an instrument as this, or anything like this.'

Partly he was moved, but mostly this was intended as a piece of gallantry for Prince Solms's ears. Lucy sometimes thought – and had thought earlier that evening when he compared these new people with those he called drifters from the north – that Sam Houston was too much inclined to forget that in earlier times he himself, according to the accounts she had heard often enough at Nashville, had been one of these drifters into Texas, though a grander one.

So she said, 'General Houston, you come from America. You do appear still to be American. Say what you like, you do. Like it or not.'

'Lucy, I was born an American. I am now a Texian.'

She remembered Ashbel Smith, that day in Paris, expressing just such sentiments.

'And in the same way,' said Prince Solms, 'my people you now see on this quay are Germans. But soon, when they have raised their first crop, they will be Texians.'

'See, Lucy,' said Houston, 'that's it. I was American. I'm now Texian. A common origin has its influence as long as a common interest exists, and no longer. And there is no longer a common interest between the United States and Texas. Sentiment tells well in love matters, but in the affairs of nations there is no sentiment or feeling – or only one, and that is self interest. Nations have no friends, only interests.'

Solms gravely considered this.

'Where,' Lucy asked him, 'do *your* first loyalties lie, would you say, Prince?'

'Why,' exclaimed Houston, 'with England. You are a cousin of Queen Victoria, sir?'

'An uncle,' said Solms.

They parted. They were agreed. More immigrants would come. Land grants would be made. As Lucy and Houston walked back to the Tremont she took the arm he offered, and he could feel she was trying not to laugh.

'But the man is what he says?' he asked her.

'Oh yes, but he is German. It's true he's a grandson of George the Third, the king who lost the thirteen colonies, but then he was really

German too. He spoke German as his first language. Prince Solms
is a son – a stepson I think – of the old duke of Cumberland, about
whom nobody remembers anything except that a man once tried to
shoot him in his bath, and missed. The old duke lived in Hanover
or Hesse, one of those principalities, and the prince comes from a
village thereabouts. So does his name.'

'So he is not what he says?'

'Of course he's what he says. He's the queen's uncle, though
when he last met her would be difficult to say. If he ever did. But
he's first of all a German princeling, and German princelings are as
thick on the ground in German principalities as Moncreiffes in the
Scottish borders.'

'But he can deliver people?'

'As you have seen, along with what he calls harmoniums. He
will deliver people. That is how he hopes to make a living.'

So that was settled. Then Houston told her he was proposing
to make another visit to his beloved Indians, and asked her to
accompany him.

'My experience with Indians has not been fortunate,' she said.
That terrible day came back to her. He felt her hand tighten on
his arm, and looked down at her with concern.

'They were not Indians, Lucy. You saw that.'

She walked on with him a while, saying nothing.

He wanted her to come with him more deeply than he dared
tell her, but neither did he dare break the silence.

'They were not Indians,' she said. 'But before we knew that,
we were in great fear when we did take them for Indians. It was
not only my fear. Everyone feared them. They were all in fear of
their lives. And I was too. We took them for Indians and we were
all terribly afraid. Captain Carey, who knew the country best, was
afraid. And he took them for Indians.'

'He was not afraid because he took them for just Indians,
but because he thought they were Comanchees. Comanchees are
wolves. I would have no dealings with Comanchees. But there are
no Comanchees where we shall go. North and west of Washington-
on-the-Brazos is Cherokee country. I have never known Comanchees

there. I would never take you into Comanchee country. I would not go into Comanchee country myself.'

They walked on further.

'I have lived with the Cherokee,' said Houston. 'I trust them as I trust my own people. In some ways better.'

'I can imagine,' she said. 'I'll come.'

25

The Storm
in the Cherokee Town

So in late September, when the greatest heat of the summer was gone and at least the evenings were cool, Sam Houston and Lucy set out from Washington-on-the-Brazos with gifts for the Cherokees. They took one Chinese silken shawl, twenty-one silk handkerchiefs, three cotton shawls, seventy-five pounds of brass wire, ten dozen butcher's knives, eighteen looking glasses, seven dozen ivory combs, seven pounds of iron tacks, forty yards of unbleached calico, and thirty bars of lead from which to make shot. It took three mules to carry this. They were in all a party of nine – Houston; George Terrell, who was Texian commissioner for Indians; three men to handle the mules; an Indian half-breed who the muleteers swore was Houston's son; a French veteran of Napoleon's guards who after thirty years in Texas knew the trails even better than Houston; and Lucy and her maid.

The French veteran observed Lucy well. He was an old man now, but he knew her for what she was. That, he said to himself, is a rare creature. Strength of spirit made her bold, and this strength deterred any man who would have treated her lightly. Men recognised her strength, and took pleasure in it, and thought their thoughts if they wished – and then regarded and prized her, and admired her and took pleasure in her the more. A close woman friend of Lord Aberdeen, having once met Lucy and her husband early in their marriage, said to him: 'You know, that is a lucky girl, and her husband is a lucky man. A woman who's modest to the world, and a courtesan to her husband, is a woman of genius. And there's little enough genius about.'

Houston was happy with Lucy. No one else dared to be as sharp with him as she was at times – telling him it was fever and not destiny that had killed the United States' representatives in Texas, and laughing at him for mistaking Solms for an Englishman. No one else treated him like this, but he was now easy and happy and proud with her.

The day they set out for the Cherokees, Lucy's maid was Helga Becker. Houston was surprised to see her with Lucy. He ought not to have been. He ought to have known she was no longer a girl at the Tremont, but Lucy's maid. But he had never seen the two together. Helga had been out the first time he went to visit Lucy on the verandah at the Tremont, and had not come with her mistress to meet Solms. When Houston saw Helga there with Lucy as they assembled, he acknowledged her with a bare nod. She put a hand up to her yellow hair, held his eye for an instant, and then fell a few steps behind, watching Lucy and Sam together, unable not to watch them.

The first day of the journey was by river, up the Brazos.

'You told me the Spanish name,' Lucy said to Houston. 'River of the Arms of God. Lovely name. But what do the Cherokees call it?'

'I have heard the Kaddo tribes call it Tokonohono. But when I lived with the Cherokee it was far north of where they have now come to meet us. I do not know if they have a name for it.' Neither did Mr Terrell, but he said that when the Cherokees just wanted to talk of a long river without giving it a particular name, they called it the Long Creature. Lucy thought Mr Terrell unwell. He was tall and, though only in his thirties, already stooping, and had a constant soft cough.

They camped on the first night, left their two flatboats, and then began a half day's easy ride. Lucy had ridden since she was a child, across Scottish terrain wilder than this. Helga Becker was not used to horses but both women had docile ponies and the journey was taken at a walk. First they crossed rolling prairies, and then climbed into wooded higher ground, and then rode two by two along a path through a forest.

Lucy said, 'This is a friendly country to you then?'

The French veteran smiled and thought the better of her. Terrell took her meaning too.

Houston answered, 'They call me the Raven. I told you they are my people. If they were not, should I take a path through a wood?'

He understood her instinct too. The Moncreiffes from her side of the family had been soldiers for five generations. To ride a path through a wood, in a country that was not both friendly and well known, was a short way to ambush and slaughter.

From the woods came the cry of birds. One bird cried repeatedly, 'Sge, sge.'

After a sequence of three such calls, Houston replied, 'Sge, sge, sge.' He raised his hand and they stopped. In the silence before and around them three young braves appeared where a moment before there had been nothing, clear in the centre of the track. Houston waited. The first Cherokee approached, and gave him a scroll of parchment. Houston read it, and nodded. Two Indians ran ahead. The third stayed with the party.

'They can write English?' asked Lucy.

'They can write Cherokee,' said Terrell. 'They have an alphabet. All the nation can write it.'

'And all the women?'

'The women better. A Cherokee boy of ten will want to be out hunting. A boy is called a bow. A girl will stay at home. A girl is called a sifter . . .'

'And I suppose she sifts? Wheat? Maize?'

Houston heard the sharpness of her tone, and answered her himself. 'Both. But she will also be taught by the women, long after the bows have gone to the forests. So a girl learns better. I take it the Moncreiffes teach their girls?'

'So all of them write?'

'I tell you, yes, Lucy. Except the very old. Better than the white riff raff who drift south to Texas can write. The Cherokee nation had an ambassador at the Court of St James before the United States had one. Seventeen seventy something. And it took the Supreme Court of the United States in its glory, and not so long ago, to bodge together a convenient judgment that the Cherokee nation was not under the United States constitution a sovereign foreign nation. And then only by the voice of five justices to two. And then only to enable the state of Georgia to rob the Cherokees of their Georgia lands.'

'Georgia?'

'Georgia. Because gold was thought to have been found in Georgia. So the Cherokees were driven off the gold, and driven west, and have been driven west ever since. Last driven west by Lamar. But not by me, because I will not have it.'

'When I first came to Galveston, you had written a letter to a chief. I think his son had died and you wrote to console him. People call you an Indian-lover for doing that.'

'That was old Flacco. His son was young Flacco, who was a scout for the Texian army. Killed by Mexicans. And because the boy was dead, old Flacco could not bear to hear the name spoken again, and since his own was the same, he changed his own name. He wrote to tell me he was from then on to be known as Yawney. I wrote back to him as Señor Yawney. I have known him ten years.'

'Changed his name?'

'See, to an Indian the name is part of the man . . .'

'It is to anyone,' said Lucy. 'It is to me.'

'Yes yes. But when a man's name is wounded, the man is wounded. When a man's son dies, and the name is the same, the name is wounded, and the father cannot bear the wounded name because it is a wound to himself and to his spirit. To his soul – to his *andanta*.'

'I did not hear much about this *andanta* in Galveston. Only that the Indians had killed enough whites up country, even in Houston city, and when your letter to Flacco was printed in the newspapers you were not loved for it.'

'Madam,' said Houston, and this was a rebuke since it was some time since he had called her anything but Lucy, 'I have said that you cannot talk of just "Indians". There are many nations. They're different peoples. The Comanchees – wolves. And I have fought the Creek. I still feel a wound in the ankle I got twenty years ago from the

Creek. But I have lived with the Cherokees. To say just "Indians" is like lumping French, Germans, and Russians together, who were slaughtering each other in their tens of thousands a generation ago, in a murderous European war.'

'Look at us,' said Lucy, glancing back along the file of horses and mules winding through the forest track. 'No Russians. But a Texian, a Frenchman, the muleteer's American I think, a German girl, and I a Scot. Do you say that young Cherokee guiding us now, who came from nowhere out of the forest a mile or so back, distinguishes us one from another?'

Houston had no time to reply. At that moment, just as their guide had come from nowhere, so from nowhere appeared three horsemen, though how horses could have trodden silently in that forest Lucy had no notion, and then after a quarter of a mile the track opened into a clearing and they were in the Cherokee encampment.

When they arrived the instant centre of attraction was not Sam Houston, or Lucy, but the golden hair of Helga Becker. She wore a scarf against the dust. As she slid from her horse she loosened this scarf and let her hair fall, and an exhalation of wonder arose from the young men of the tribe. The Cherokee women ran to her, to touch this wonderful hair of a colour they had never seen. The girl stood very tall, a head taller than all the women round her, and did not flinch.

From the Cherokee chief came one word: 'Sge.'

This time it was not spoken softly as Lucy had heard it that morning, when she took it for a bird cry from the wood. This time it was a sharp command. The women withdrew. The young men took their eyes from the tall woman and turned, as it struck Lucy, into attentive courtiers as their chief greeted the great chief Sam Houston. They embraced. Mr Terrell, who had stepped forward with Houston, handed him the finest of the shawls, which he unfolded, revealing its pattern of formalised horses. Then he draped it over the chief's right shoulder. Houston himself then accepted a blanket, which he too took over his right shoulder. Then Houston turned to Lucy, who was still sitting side saddle on her pony, handed her down, and presented her to the chief. By instinct she offered her hand, which at home would have been all very well, where the chief would be presented to her. But she was not at home. The old man looked her straight in the eye. It took Sam Houston to save the day with solemn words and a grave mime of kissing her hand, at which the chief gravely took her hand himself and raised it to his lips, and spoke more solemn words. The chief then jerked his head towards Helga. Houston spoke as if to reassure him, and the chief laughed and uttered more rapid words, nodding towards the girl, and the two men embraced again.

Then they watched the game of the spirits, the play of birds and animals. Put plainly, it was a wargame of ten young men against an opposing party of ten, played in a grassed clearing in front of the sixty skin tents of the Cherokee town. Each man held a stick with, at its end, a mesh of leather thongs in which he could catch, hold, or run with a hard ball made of woven gut. Or he could hurl the ball. Lucy had seen her cousins play cricket, which is a subtle game, full of nuances, and yet a game for the vigorous and brave. She knew that she was seeing a game as subtle as cricket. She knew there were conventions and shades of meaning in the game which she could not understand, but she knew beyond a doubt that they were there. There was more to the game than any newcomer could hope to see. What she saw was beautiful. The ball was hurled the full length of the clearing and all twenty men were in rapid motion, and then suddenly the flying ball was arrested, held poised in the stick of one man, and the balance and pattern of the game were for that moment in that man's grasp.

It was the fastest game she had ever seen, but a game whose stillnesses mattered as much as its most rapid passages.

'It is beautiful,' she said to Houston.

'It is called anetsa,' he said. 'There are the birds, and there are the animals. The animals are the bears, who are the strongest, and the deer, who are the swiftest, and the young mountain lions, who are the bravest. The bear is the leader.'

A huge young man a few feet from them intercepted the flying ball by taking it full in his midriff. Lucy thought he must go down at

the blow, but he held his body in such a way that in one movement
he received the disabling blow and yet scooped the ball into the mesh
of his stick and flicked it to another of his party, a man more slightly
built, who ran flying off with it.

'The bear,' said Houston, 'who gave it to the deer.'

The deer hurled the ball high, and Lucy's eyes followed it till
she thought it must land among the tents, but a young man of the
opposing ten leapt after it, rising high into the branches of a tall
birch, and trapped it, and with a turn of his wrist gave it to a brave
who ran with it, evading three pursuers, clear up to the end of the
field, where he stood before the chief and bowed.

'The man who ran,' said Houston, 'is the squirrel, who was
rejected by the animals and so fights with the birds. And the man
who leapt for it was the raven, who leads the birds.'

'And the birds have won?' she asked.

'The birds have won the day.'

'And you are the Raven, yes?'

'Dear Lucy,' said Houston, 'it is done as a compliment and as an
honour to me. I am their guest.' Houston presented the raven of the
ball game with an ivory comb. The boy took it in both his cupped
hands, and then made a request. Houston called Helga Becker to
him, and spoke to her. Lucy could not hear what he said, but she
did catch Helga's reply which was a soft, 'Yes, if it will please you,
sir.' Then Helga took the comb from the boy, and, while he turned
his head sideways for her, she settled it into the long hair at the nape
of his neck.

'He is now twice a hero?' asked Lucy, when Houston returned
to her side.

'Yes he is. He has never seen hair of such a colour as hers,
and wants the comb fixed by her fingers, in front of all his equals.
Brave to ask for it. Twice a hero if you like.'

'Bold then,' she said. 'The game is beautiful.' She remembered
the raven leaping high into the trees.

'The French,' said Houston, 'were the first Europeans to see it.
They called it lacrosse, after the stick. Being subjects of His Most
Catholic Majesty the king of France, Louis the Fourteenth I think,

they naturally saw the stick as resembling a bishop's mitre.'

'And what,' she asked Houston, as they were escorted to their tents to prepare for the feast of the evening, 'what did you say to the chief when I offered my hand?'

'Told him you were a kinswoman of the great queen across the seas.'

'Victoria?'

'I told you the British once received an ambassador from the Cherokees, in London, as an equal. It is not forgotten.'

Lucy stopped in her tracks and looked at Houston in amazement.

'Well, Lucy, if Solms is the queen's uncle, why not . . . ?'

'And what did you say when the chief asked, as I think he did, about Helga? Just after you made me the queen's kinswoman. Did you connect Helga with the Electress of Hanover?'

'Something of the sort.' They parted for the moment. Houston had no intention of telling Lucy that the chief had remarked, of the tall girl with the shining hair, that in her height and complexion she resembled Tiana, the Cherokee quarter breed, three parts white, whom Houston, in his longest stay with the Cherokee, had lived with as his wife.

At the feast, blacks served the chief and his principal guests. Lucy had first seen slaves in New Orleans. She had seen them at Galveston, at Washington-on-the-Brazos, and wherever she had been in Texas. She had never seen them flogged and only rarely ill treated. But what she rebelled against was the absolute dominion of one man over another. But if that was it, if that was the flaw and the sin of it, why should she be more shocked to see that red men too had black slaves? She asked herself this question, and had no answer.

The sun of the afternoon had gone, but the heat remained, as it had not in the few previous days. The sky in the clearing above the Cherokee town was covered with high cloud. As the sun set, these clouds were dyed orange. The last speech was made, the last bowl shared between Houston and the chief. The wind fell, and then quite died away.

Sam Houston's tent was set apart from the others. To its left

lay the smaller tent occupied by the men of his party, and to its
right that occupied by Lucy and her maid. They said their good
nights. Cherokee girls brought cool water to bathe in. In the dead
calm, voices in the town carried far. At last light, thirty minutes after
sunset, the high clouds were underlit a vivid red. Lucy saw in her
mind the raven leaping again, in the beautiful game of the animals.
The dark came, and she slept.

She woke in silence and darkness. She did not know what had
woken her. There was not enough wind to rustle the leaves of the
trees. Then she knew what it was. It was the Herriot again, a river
by whose banks she had lived for years. Not the sound of the river
as she had often heard it as she lay in bed, but the clear scent of the
river – not of the grass on its banks but of the fresh water. She was
so accustomed now to salt water, which was the atmosphere of her
Atlantic crossing, and was in the air of New Orleans and Galveston,
that she no longer noticed it. She had almost forgotten what it was to
live near fresh water. She had never sensed fresh water so powerfully
as she did that night with the Cherokees.

   She heard a rustle of leaves, and felt the breath of a breeze come
in at the tent flap. And yet the heat that had been with them all day
was still there. Then a branch nearby stirred in what was more than
a breeze. One side of the tent moved, like a sail catching the first
life after a calm. She had known this once on Lake Geneva, when
she was ten years old. She had been afraid. Out of the calm had
come heavy gusts that threatened to dismast them. The hired man
and her father between them had been unable to furl the sail. Her
father took a knife and cut it away, and their boat drove before the
wind under bare sticks.

   Now, in the Cherokee town, a growl of thunder came out
of the west, then a glow of lightning. She could call it nothing
else. It was not lightning forking down, or sheeting across the
sky, but a glow that illuminated the skin roof above her and then
went. Then the wind struck. The tent shook, the lesser branches
of the trees struck each other as they were caught by contrary

gusts, and then lightning came that was no longer a glow but a crash.

Lucy was on her feet. Then there was a lull she could not believe. The wind dropped so that the tent no longer shook, and the leaves now only rustled on branches which a moment before were clattering wildly. She heard a voice raised in chanting lamentation. Then the rain began in a sudden downpour. The scent of the rain, falling sheer from the sky, was the scent of fresh water that had woken her while the rain was still far off. An explosion of thunder surrounded her, shaking the ground. Lightning lit the tent like day. Helga was awake and lying with terrified eyes. Light was all round them, coming from all directions, so that Lucy, facing Sam Houston's tent, saw in silhouette a man writhing in the slashing light, and then swaying back and forth with his arms raised.

The wind rose again, and as it did so the darkness fell for an instant. In the blackness, through the tent flap, Lucy saw the tops of trees glow with a dancing soft light, which then flickered to the ground and lit the tips of grassblades. The narrow, toothed leaves of a yellow wild flower, a goldenrod, two feet from where she stood, were delicately picked out and edged by this glow. Then the lightning returned, and showed her the swaying man again. She stepped out into the open.

When she lay down to sleep she had taken off her red cotton riding dress of the day. Now she stood in her chemise and russet petticoats, holding a blanket over her head. She was barefooted. Houston's tent was five yards away. As she ran that distance the pelting rain turned to hail, which slashed at her bare arms. Then she was in Houston's tent. He was standing with his back to her, neither seeing nor hearing her, and addressing the storm in Cherokee:

'Sge – you, storm, are coming in rut for my life, but you shall not track me. I shall show you my footprints, but they are where you cannot go. I point them out to you, but you cannot follow. My path stretches out past the tree tops to the high mountains. You, wind, let your path go where the waving branches meet. Sge . . . '

And then, in another flash of lightning, he saw Lucy's shadow pursuing his on the skin walls of the tent, and turned with both

hands raised to strike. She stood still. He found not the spirit of the
storm stalking him, but a girl standing in russet petticoats heavy with
white hailstones the size of pearls. She found a man beyond himself.
She did not know whether he recognised her or saw a devil out of some
dream.

He let his hands fall to his sides. She went to him and took his head
in her hands. He trembled.

'Tell me what it is. What are you saying? Tell me.'

He shook his head, but she held him and then he did tell her a
part of it, about the storm that pursued and tracked him and would
kill him if it could.

The appalling lightning surrounded them both again and she
held him the closer.

It went and they were in the dark. She said: 'I know something
like this. Something the same. Our ancient enemies in the Borders
are the McGregors. There was a McGregor who killed an ancestor of
the Moncreiffes, and threatened his children and their children. Tam
McGregor. And whenever Tam came, in a storm, the Moncreiffe
would stand on his battlements and defy the McGregor. "Who's riding
round my house the nicht? None but bluidy Tam. Away wi' bluidy
Tam."'

She did not know whether Sam Houston heard, because he
began his chant again. Now she understood the talk in Nashville.
She understood how Eliza Allen had thought Sam Houston mad. She
understood what his young wife had meant when she said Houston
feared nothing by day, but feared the night and the storm, and lived
in terror of being alone. Well, she would stay with him. In the flashes
of the now receding lightning she could see he was wearing the old
Indian robe in which she first met him. She held his head and then
lay her head on his shoulders, and gradually the trembling stopped,
and his heart did not pound so. He breathed more evenly. The height
of the storm was past. She still held him.

He turned away.

'No, no,' she said, and, since he would not turn back to her, she
went to him again. She held him closer, coaxing him to hold her,
folding herself against his body, and found him erect. 'Then,' she

said. She took his hands and placed them at her waist. His head
jerked back, then she slid her hands down to open the robe, and
he stood before her with an arching prick.

She led him to the fur bed, lay down with her body already
moving, and held out her arms to him. 'Then,' she said. 'Oh, come
into me. Come into me.'

He held back, but he was only a man. He knelt before her, touched
her lips with the fingers of his right hand, looked in her steady eyes
— and then threw her petticoats round her waist and entered her with
a cry of 'Sge.' It was not gentle and she did not want it gentle, and her
Scottish ancestors, looking down on this scene of lovers, would not
have been surprised that a girl of the Moncreiffes, a girl modest at
heart, found good Scottish words to encourage her man. He came with
a cry of her name. They held each other and he repeated her name like
a litany — Lucy Lucy Lucy.

The thunder had gone to the east and was a growl in the
distance. The lightning was no longer above and around them, but
only an occasional glow in the east. The wind had steadied, merely
waving the branches which at its height it had clattered together
and threatened to wrench from the trees. Lucy Moncreiffe and Sam
Houston lay together in the tent. She comforted him, stroked his
hair, and murmured reassurance. He was a big man, and lying as
he did he was heavy on her. But all the power was hers. She had
gone to him, she had held him when he was mad with fear, she had
coaxed him, and she had enclosed him.

In time he did recover his senses. He realised that her clothes
were still round her body, and soaking wet. He lifted her with one
hand, drawing the petticoats down over her hips and knees and feet.
The chemise was laced at the back, and the sodden laces difficult to
untie. She showed him how, but the cotton tore.

She showed him where to tear the rest.

He did. Then he dried her shoulders and all the rest of her in
his cloak. This drying of her was his first caress — other than that
touching of her hair before all the world in the hotel lobby, long
before. The darkness was broken at intervals by the now distant
lightning. They slept for an hour wrapped in each other and covered

with a blanket.

Before dawn, as they lay apart, awake and facing each other, Sam Houston spoke again in Cherokee. This time he was calm, and she listened for a while to the sound of the words.

Then she asked, 'What is it you are saying? Tell me.'

'I cannot describe what sort of thing it is.'

'Then tell me what the words are.'

'It says, "Serene woman, you have made the path for me. I shall stand up straight. You have made me a white man . . . "'

He hesitated, so she asked, 'White?'

'It does say white, but the meaning is, oh, peaceful, at peace.'

'And then what does it say?'

'That no one is lonely with you. That you are beautiful. That I stand with my face towards the sun. That your soul has come into mine. That no one is lonely with you.'

No one lonely with her. This touched her heart. They lay together quietly. She knew it would soon be dawn. The lightning and the storm had gone altogether. She could make out the shape of the tent flap by the first grey light.

'What is this word "Sge"?' she asked. 'I heard it in the woods yesterday. You kept on saying it in the storm. You said it to me.'

'So many meanings. "Look", or "Listen," or . . . '

'Or what?'

'Or "Behold,"' he said.

'Many meanings then.' She was happy and a bit shaken. Sge was the word he had hurled at the storm – 'Listen.' And it was what he called out when he entered her – 'Behold.'

It was now just light enough for her to make out the shape of the discarded bundle which she knew must be her petticoats. Another ten minutes and the eye would be able to see it was a bundle of clothes. Ten minutes after that, the eye would see the clothes were coloured. And ten minutes after that, what the colour was.

She must go now. She kissed Sam Houston's forehead. She stood, took a blanket to wrap round herself and cover her head, and picked up the russet petticoats from the earthfloor of the tent.

He reached out a hand, found her ankle, and held it.

'Oh *yes*,' she said. 'Beyond any doubt, I'd say.'

She stood for a moment looking down at him, and then slipped away to her own tent. She saw no one. Her figure was seen by a hundred Cherokee eyes, who wondered only why the woman left the Raven so soon.

26

Houston Has Done It

The departure in mid-morning, in the clear light of a brilliant fall day, was all formality. The chiefs and the young men took leave of their guests. Houston received in public the chiefs' assurance that the war whoop would be heard no more on the prairie. He promised the same. This was translated into English by Mr Terrell, who would be staying a week to settle the details of this pact of peace. He was glad to stay, hoping to recover from a slight fever which had come upon him. As Lucy heard, listening to him translating between smothered coughs, he had got worse overnight, and was even paler.

In matters of state, as she also heard, Houston referred to himself in the third person. 'Never,' he said, 'has grass grown in the path between Houston and his red brothers. Houston will return again in the spring.'

After Houston, it was Helga who was made most of by the young men, who sang for her a song to the woman whose hair was smiled on by the sun. Helga, who had been silent, was cheered by this demonstration and by the extravagant words. Then the old chief, who had seen Lucy's delight in the ballplay of the day before, gave her a woven strip of cloth depicting the spirits of the game – the bear and the deer, the raven and the squirrel.

At dawn, after she went back to her tent, Lucy had slept deeply. When she woke the russet petticoats had been washed by the Cherokee women, dried in the sun, and returned to Helga. When Helga came to see her mistress, she raised her eyes from the clothes she was laying out and regarded Lucy as she stretched. Lucy caught the girl's direct look, and returned it. Then she cut the moment short.

'Now,' she said, and they got on briskly with the day. No more than the everyday words of rising and dressing were exchanged between the two women. When Sam Houston handed Lucy on to her pony as they left, he glimpsed a flurry of russet beneath her skirts, the russet petticoats of the night before. She saw that he did. He stepped back and bowed his courtly bow.

Not a word was said about the storm. On the way back Houston said nothing about the ballplay, or about anything touching the Cherokees. As they came down from the wooded slopes into the level prairie what he talked about was the country – the richest soil in the world.

'And this bride,' he said, 'thus adorned, has been declined by the United States, and declined for the last time. I have seen to that.'

Bride adorned. She remembered Houston's letter to Andrew Jackson, which the old man had read to her in Nashville.

'What have you seen to?'

Houston told her about Aberdeen's offer to Ashbel Smith, whose despatch had arrived in Washington-on-the-Brazos only three weeks before, having taken nine weeks from London.

'It is everything,' he said. 'Or it is enough. Her Britannic Majesty – your kinswoman, Lucy, remember – offers to guarantee us against all comers. Against Mexico. Against the world.'

'English gold?'

'No gold, either way. None asked, none offered. It suits Texas. And the English want it. Twig that!'

She had been riding thoughtfully, but at this phrase she looked up at this man whom, in one day, she had seen in so many different ways. Now he was boyish.

'People will say English gold,' she said. 'And what of Mexico? How can you be sure of Mexico when Santa Anna cannot be sure of himself? Can he answer for Mexico? If he could, would you take his word?'

'Lord Aberdeen says Mexico will not object, or have the means to object. If she does, she will be made to submit. England and France are perfectly agreed on it.'

'Won't the mortification of the United States be perfectly indescribable?'

Houston looked at her sharply. She was quoting back at him his own phrase to Andrew Jackson, when Houston had written that Texas, if rejected by the American Senate that summer, would be indescribably mortified.

She said, 'General Jackson read me your letter when I was at the Hermitage. Mr Miller brought it while I was in Nashville. I was not sure what it meant. General Jackson was. He was certain. You said you were keeping Texas for the United States. Something of the sort. He was perfectly sure.'

They rode on steadily.

'I have fought with General Jackson. I revere the man.'

She looked across at him. 'I know.'

Then Houston said, 'He is not well, Lucy.'

She waited for him to continue. She knew General Jackson was not well. She had seen him very unwell. She knew this was a matter close to Sam Houston's heart.

'In his last letter he said he was growing weaker every day. His shortness of breath was worse. It was a letter he had to dictate to Donelson. It came to me in Donelson's handwriting. That has not happened before.'

'I am sorry,' she said. She was sorry. She had taken to the old man at the Hermitage.

'I will put things plainly,' said Houston. 'After San Jacinto, we were all for annexation. We were American through and through, in heart, in sentiment. That was what we wanted, pat. We were denied. It was only on his last day as president that General Jackson recognised even the fact of our separation from Mexico. That was all he could do. The American Senate of those days did not want even that. Why not? For fear of offending Santa Anna? I never knew. Whatever it was, it was a flat No. I wanted annexation then because I did not believe we could stand on our own two feet. When we were denied, we had to. We did, and now we can. Two months ago the American Senate says No again. Well, a fair number of men in Texas were mortified then. You saw it. You saw the Stars and Stripes burned at Galveston. So now we are rejected a second time. And now England offers us what we want. The grandmother is kinder to Texas than the mother.'

'For her own reasons, perhaps?'

'For her own reasons I don't doubt. But England's reasons don't hurt me. It is enough.'

'And what does Dr Smith say?'

'He goes along. He says we should consider, look at it every which way. He says it would amount to a perpetual treaty. I don't see how any treaty can be perpetual. It can be revised, renegotiated. I never knew a treaty without protocols added. Events supersede treaties. Then Smith says that to confer on European powers the right to interfere between American countries might be awkward this side of the Atlantic. I see it. But I should be conferring no general right. It is not in my power to confer such a right, or in any man's. So I should not be doing that. I should be making a particular treaty. Smith and I have known each other for a long time. I sent him there. But he goes along with the offer.'

'And you go along?'

Houston did not answer directly. He said: 'I will tell you something I have told no one else. I said General Jackson wrote to me – the letter he had to dictate. He wrote after the news came to him that the American Senate had declined us again. He begged me to stay with annexation, to persevere in the hope of annexation, even after that. And he warned me against England. He does not mince his words, but he has never spoken so strongly. He said England was aiming at the overthrow of the republican system in the new world. He said all the skill and strength of England would be put to undermining the United States, and into keeping the States and Texas apart. All the diplomatic skill of England would be put into that effort.'

He hesitated, so Lucy said: 'If that is so you will have seen it, because that diplomatic skill will have been exercised on you, won't it? But Captain Elliot has not even been in Texas for months. He is at his warm springs in Virginia. That leaves Mr Kennedy at Galveston. Has he been entrusted with any such delicate instructions? Not likely, I'd have thought. But you'd know.'

Houston stared at her. 'General Jackson said England would tempt me, tempt me in a hundred ways.'

At which Lucy, the woman who had come to Sam Houston the night before, met his eye. She had the beginning of a smile on her lips and in her eyes, and the smile was asking, 'I am one of those ways? You think that?' Houston took her meaning. At that moment he saw her again as the woman of the night before.

And so, riding behind them, watching them, seeing their eyes meet, did Helga. She held her yellow head higher.

Houston lowered his eyes, avoiding Lucy's smile, and shook his head. 'No,' he said. 'No.' Then he plunged on with his account of Jackson's advice. 'Depend upon it,' he wrote to me, 'England would tempt me. She would deceive me. If Texas made an alliance with Britain, in three years Texas would lose her liberty. Lose her liberty and become an instrument in the hand of European monarchy to destroy the voice of the American and Texian peoples. And Sam Houston – these were his words to me – would become a subordinate governor in a remote English colony.'

He had evidently finished. Lucy made no immediate reply. Then she asked if Captain Elliot had ever suggested or hinted at any such thing.

Houston shook his head. 'Lucy, what do you think of this matter of a colony?'

'How could I know?' she said.

She did know, however, what England's reply had been when Mexico offered California three years before, to pay off a debt. She knew because Lord Aberdeen, the day she visited Downing Street to tell him about her plans for a grand tour, had happened to mention it to her as a matter of little importance. She could not tell Houston how she knew. She had never told him Lord Aberdeen was her great uncle and a man she had known all her life, though only as a child and a young woman know a much older man. But she did say: 'As to Texas, again, how could I know? But it is well enough known that England did not want upper California when it was plainly offered. The colonial office did not want new and distant colonies. Last thing. I remember that. Always having to send a frigate or a regiment to protect settlers who've tangled with some local grandee. Too expensive and too much trouble. I've said I'm a Scot, so I disqualify myself from speaking for the English, but English ambitions for Texas – that's wild, I'd say.'

'As to your being Scottish,' said Houston, 'so's Lord Aberdeen. Which disposes of that, Lucy. But wild, yes. I did think General Jackson was wild in his fears. It grieved me. It was a heavy thought for me, a heavy thing for me to decide.'

'So,' she asked again, 'you go along with the English offer?'

'Smith said in his letter, "Consider." He was always telling me to consider. Well, I have considered. I've chewed it over with Jones on the Brazos. Most of all I have chewed it over with myself. Jones'd be chewing still, but I settled it.'

'You will do it?'

'I have done it. It is done. Before I left the Brazos I told my secretary of state, "Jones, do it." You remember I kept you while I signed a paper as we were leaving?'

She did remember. They were mounted, ready to start. Houston had stopped the cavalcade outside the clap board house where the secretary of state had his office. 'Jones,' he called out. Anson Jones had appeared. Houston dismounted. He said a few words to Jones, who made no reply. On the verandah outside Jones's office, on a rough table, Houston took a sheet of paper, dipped his pen, and wrote a letter. He wrote as he stood, not sitting down. Then he signed the letter with that flourish she had seen before. She had seen his signature and its extraordinary rubric, but she had never seen him make it. It was not a scrawl. It was not rapid. It was deliberate, and executed with a slow flourish. He held the paper up, to dry perhaps, but it was also as if he were showing it to the world. Then he folded the paper and addressed it to Jones, though the man was standing beside him, and there and then and in the presence of them all handed it to him. Lucy remembered the show of it all.

'So that is what you signed.'

'That was it. An order to tell Smith to settle with England on the terms they proposed. As long as the border with Mexico was the Rio Grande, and that would be no trouble. To get it signed, sealed, and done with. It was not something I decided easily. For three weeks I carried Smith's despatch and General Jackson's letter round with me, on my person. I read them both a hundred times. No, I read General Jackson's two hundred times until it was in rags. But then I decided, and once I decided it was better done quickly, better done with. Now it is done.'

He was lighthearted again. The telling, like the decision, had been a burden to him. Now he was free of the burden. He broke into a trot and then a canter, calling back to her, 'So it's done, Lucy. Done. Houston has done it.'

He wheeled round, slowed to a trot, and returned to her.

'See, it's the start and birth of a new empire.'

She reined in and sat upright on her mount in the middle of that rich prairie, and did not look after him as he wheeled off again.

Helga came up level with her, but Lucy shook her head and the girl dropped back.

So much for the storm and for the whole night and its events. Lucy knew that Houston had only for a moment that morning seen her as the woman of the night before. She knew where his mind was. She knew that the prairie – the countryside, the whole vast territory – was the bride he had adorned, and that he had adorned it for himself, as his own bride.

PART THREE

27

Tea and Destiny

Then events moved fast. Houston had done what he had done, but in the United States Mr Polk made the expansion of the Union, and the annexation of Texas, the theme of the Democratic presidential campaign. The Senate might not have wanted Texas, but let the people speak. From Nashville an old friend wrote to Sam Houston – a friend whose son was Sam's godson – saying he and his companions had no doubt of carrying Tennessee for 'Polk, Texas, and Victory,' which was, he said, their rallying cry. Houston read the letter with a face that showed nothing, and then put it aside. Mr Polk's Whig opponents campaigned confidently for 'Clay, the Union, and Liberty.' Sam Houston read all these reports, and said nothing. A letter from New Jersey written in an unknown hand, one of many such from the north, begged him always to protect the bright lone star of Texas against the foul, inglorious plot of an insatiable union to destroy its freedom and seize its lands. Houston read these letters too, and said nothing.

Annexation became a woman, whose draped figure was the centrepiece of processions conducted by both political parties. In the anti-annexation north, Texas was represented on floats by a woman dressed in deep mourning – for annexation would be an occasion of mourning, illegally expanding the Union's territory against every intention of the Founding Fathers, extending slavery in the Union, increasing the debt of the United States, and bringing inevitable war with Mexico. Did not the United States already have more land than could be properly cultivated and more people than could be harmonised each with the other? So in the north, annexation was a woman swathed in deepest black. But in the annexationist south, the figure was that of a young woman, the prettiest girl in town, decked in white and covered with flowers – for annexation would protect Texas from the rapacity of Mexico, bring America all the trade of the vast rivers of the west, and, besides, deter the British from taking Texas as they would surely soon take Cuba. Was it not the destiny of the American nation to grow until it filled the continent, and did not the United States have a duty to defend its own wider borders as it would the chastity of its daughters?

Sam Houston read all these reports too, and said nothing.

Meantime Downing Street quietly awaited the reply to its Texian proposals, Lord Aberdeen agreeing with his minister in Washington-on-the-Potomac that, since any British intervention might excite American national fervour and perhaps to some small extent preju-dice the expected victory of Mr Clay, the best policy for the moment was silence. Dr Smith's reply would come soon enough. When that time came, Great Britain would act. Until then, silence. So Lord Aberdeen, who had never seen an election, not even a Scottish election, since he held his seat in the House of Lords by hereditary succession, read the reports of the presidential campaign in the London newspapers, and said nothing.

In Galveston, Houston and Lucy sought each other discreetly, meeting at the Tremont, where Lucy had taken rooms again. They met at tea time – an innocent hour. It was, besides, an hour when he had called before, when Lucy was ill earlier in the year. So there was nothing unusual in his visiting her. And anyway the managers and waiters, the barmen and chambermaids were all used to Sam, who used the Tremont as a second home. He had for years been in and out of the place whenever he was in Galveston – Sam holding court in the lobby, Sam addressing dinners that went on late into the night, Sam holing up in this or that room, striking deals with men they knew or with strangers they did not. And Sam and the lady had been seen together too often to make it remarkable. 'Taking tea with Lady Lucy,' Anson Jones had scornfully pronounced, and the jibe had become known, and then so familiar that it became innocuous.

The first time Sam Houston called they talked small talk. Helga served tea. They watched another group of newly-landed German immigrants pass in the street. This was a good season, late in the year, for immigrants to arrive. It was cooler now. There was no fever. They would have time to settle before the rains of February and March made the roads impassable. Houston and Lucy admired the strength and preparedness of these newly arrived people. They asked Helga to translate snatches of conversation in German which drifted up from the street. Most of the newcomers were sure they had found a fine new country. Lucy recalled the Prince of Solms and his harmonium, and they laughed at the recollection of the instrument being winched out of the ship's hold and landed on the quay, and then at the fine brave chord in C major Sam Houston had played.

They laughed, but there was the greatest tension between them. The night of the storm in the Cherokee town, and its immense events, lay between them. The very events that now brought them inexorably together, lay between them as they sat taking tea and admiring the fortitude of the German character. Houston had not come to see Lucy until ten days after their return, and for both of them it had been an age.

So mostly it was small talk, that first visit, though at the very end of his stay Lucy spoke about the ballplay of the spirits and the animals they had seen in the clearing.

'I remember the raven,' she said. 'Oh I remember it all, but perhaps most of all the raven, leaping high into the branches of the birch trees. Up like this.' She took up the strip of woven cloth the chief gave her when they left the next morning and held it up over her head. She was sitting on a sofa. He was standing in the window. She let go the cloth. The vivid colours fell into her lap. She longed to run across to Sam and embrace him. Neither moved. When he left, five minutes later, his visit had lasted perhaps forty minutes. The nights were closing in. At just gone half past five, in those southern latitudes and in late October, it was already dusk.

That evening she sent him a note hoping he might care to take tea at the same time three days afterwards. When he came, she said, 'Helga has gone for the day to one of the families who came in from Hamburg. I sent her.'

He stood and could say nothing. She held out both hands to him, and led him to the door of her bedroom.

Later, as she lay beside him in the dusk on her high feather bed, both of them looking up at the tall ceiling, he said, 'Lucy, before today I have never . . .'

'Never what?'

'Never seen a woman entirely unclothed.'

She heard from his voice that he wanted to confide in her.

She said, still gazing upwards at the ceiling, 'You were some years with the Cherokees.'

'But not with the Cherokees either. See, Lucy, you must not think of engravings of noble savages and open forests, not a Cherokee garden of Eden. That is not the way.'

'You mean not in open day?'

'Not in open day. But never open in the night either. A man and a woman are always so close to others, do you see?'

She heard from his silence that he wanted to go on.

'Well then, your days in Congress, at Washington?'

He did not reply for a long time.

'See, Lucy, there and at Nashville, there were ladies I wooed. I had a name for it. That is what you have heard. But the ladies I wooed I did not get. After San Jacinto, after the fight, the first letter I wrote . . .'

'Tell me. I think I have heard, but tell me.'

'I do not think you will have. It was not to General Jackson, though that is often said, but to a lady I admired, who taught me what Spanish I have. I sent her some leaves I gathered from the ground straight after the fight, and made into a garland. But then I was backward in wooing her, do you see? I sent messages to her by a friend. He was a man I made secretary of state.'

'What, Dr Jones? Him?'

'Before Jones. When I was first president. My first term. A man called Irion.'

'And the woman?'

'Married Irion. She married the messenger. Fact is, she eloped with him. Then they named their first child after me. Sam.'

At this Lucy turned to Sam Houston and saw he was smiling, and then she laughed.

He turned towards her, took her head in his hands, and kissed her forehead. She folded him in her arms.

'You must have inspired the girl, anyway,' she said, 'though you did not get her. To name her child after you? What about that?' She laughed again.

'Dear Lucy,' he said. 'Dear woman, this amazes me. You amaze me. This is abandoned and entire.'

As he held her she stared over his shoulder, remembering those words. Abandoned and entire. She pulled a light cotton wrap around her. He stood. She saw the republican wounds he had displayed to Saligny.

She had carefully not asked him about Eliza, not about his lost first wife. Nor about his second wife, Margaret, though that was another matter. She was again at home, up country. Neither would mention her. That was understood. Lucy had never seen her and knew nothing of her. She did know a great deal about Eliza, and guessed she was still close to Sam Houston's heart, an old sorrow of the past and sometimes of the present. All she knew of both Eliza and Margaret was that both were wives he had never seen entirely unclothed. He had not meant to tell her that. He had meant to express his delight in her. But in doing that, he had told her.

The next week, as they lay making lazy conversation, he told her Donelson was coming to Texas, having been appointed American chargé d'affaires.

'To fill the vacancy caused by destiny?' she said.

'He writes to say he's anxious to talk about old times and General Jackson, and guesses the American election will be close.'

'If you will talk about destiny,' she said, 'what about this? Mr Polk, who when I met him was out to grass and was thought to have a hard time finding any other place, now has a chance of becoming president. And Mr Donelson, who when I met him was

doing nothing much in Nashville – and it was he who told me Mr
Polk was out to grass – will now be the American minister here.
And Mr Polk, and General Jackson, and Mr Donelson I take it,
are all your friends, your old friends, and all will oppose you, and
all want Texas for America. Destiny?'

'Can't be, if destiny assumes success. Texas is not to be had.'

Next day Galveston learned, first through Helga, that the Perote
prisoners had at last been released. The bells of Galveston Island
pealed out, the steamboat sirens screamed, and it was a holiday –
all on account of a letter from Kurt Neumann, reaching Helga by a
Spanish brig from Vera Cruz, telling her that all were free and about
to take ship for New Orleans. The letter was only two weeks old. That
same afternoon, when the city was already well gone in liquor, official
confirmation of the news arrived by an American naval schooner. It
had been a dying wish of Santa Anna's late wife that they should be
let go, or so the Mexicans said.

'Ma'am,' said Helga with shining eyes, 'I must go to him.
You will let me go to him in New Orleans? I have enough for
the passage money.'

'Yes, yes,' said Lucy. 'Of course you shall go. You will not
need the passage money. I shall go too, and you'll come with
me. And then I suppose you will wish to leave me?'

'If he will have me, ma'am.'

'If he will have you? Since when were you so timid, Helga?
And the man has done nothing but write to you since he was
taken. I have never known such a faithful correspondent.'

Helga was elated. The whole town congratulated her. Everyone
knew her story. Everyone knew of that faithful correspondence.
Everyone knew she had got the news before the American cutter
brought it. Everyone knew and recognised her yellow hair. That
day even those few who did not know her stopped to say a few
words, wish her well, and enquire if she was going to New Orleans
to meet her man. She was, and for the first time in many weeks
she was happy. The ache of seeing Lucy with Sam Houston, and
of the general taking no more notice of her than he would of any
acquaintance, was soothed.

She had been faithful in her way too. She had never spoken a word to anyone about the night in the Cherokee town, or about General Houston's teas with Lady Lucy. She was glad to save her fare to New Orleans, but knew this was because Lucy had already expressed a desire to see an American election, and because Sam Houston, as she also knew, was obliged to spend three weeks in the interior, with Margaret in the Houstons' new house at Huntsville, and then on the Brazos. Lucy was for that reason free to travel to New Orleans.

There was another matter of which Helga knew nothing. The American schooner which had brought from Louisiana the confirmation that the Perote prisoners were indeed released, had also brought letters for Lucy. Her father and sister again wrote, saying she was now so distant and her whereabouts so unknown that they had to address their letters, in hope and at a venture, to the St Charles Hotel in New Orleans. 'What are you doing?' demanded her father. 'Shall we give you up for lost,' asked her sister, 'or take it that you have emigrated? Do let us know which. If lost, prayers shall be said for you in church and in proper form. A line will be enough to tell us which, and then I'll tell the parson.' Lucy heard her sister's voice speak through the written words, and smiled to herself.

There were two other letters. One was from Captain Elliot. He feared he might have to stay away from Texas longer than he had expected, and might not return that year. She had asked him about her husband. He would much prefer to have told her in person but events had made this impossible. So he must write. At the time of the siege of Canton he had sent skirmishing parties to take certain landing places and forts which commanded the Pearl river. One of those parties was led by Lieutenant Moncreiffe, who was killed in the ensuing action. The men he led had all spoken of the courageous manner in which he comported himself. Moncreiffe had been in China only a week, but in that short time Elliot had formed a high opinion of his abilities. It was because of this that he had put him in charge of the party. The order sending him was Elliot's own and, since he was relieved of his appointment the following day, it was one of the last orders he gave in China.

He could only express the utmost regret that he should in this way have been the unwitting instrument which brought about the death of a gallant and most promising young officer. He felt it deeply. He offered his condolences.

Lucy read and reread this letter. She wept for her husband. She felt for Captain Elliot. She was grateful to him for writing, but there still remained in her mind, she did not know why, a sense that there was more to know, and that she had not been told everything.

The last of the letters awaiting her helped to raise Lucy's spirits. It was from Adelaide Twining.

'Lucy, we have a son. He is said in his eyes and hair to resemble me, but though the eyes won't change from their blue, unlike kittens', Mr Twining clings to some hope that his mouse hair may change to the Twining black. The physician is tactful and does not discourage this hope. In his names he will be entirely Twining – to be christened John William Lindsay, Lindsay for his father, John and William for notable Twinings past, who have all been in divinity or in tea, either bishops or tea merchants in India or in the City. Lucy, I told you how wonderfully we had been drawn together, Mr Twining and I. I would not then have believed it could be closer, but John William has made it so. Oh and I must tell you that Mr John Twining, after three months grieving over your refusal, grief which all the world knows he resolutely concealed from it, has married a Miss Rombout, whose family is, you will never guess, in coffee. His brother tells me, for my ears only, that tea and coffee is a bold though unlikely union. Do tell me where you are, and when we shall see you – John William and I. How I remember our talk on that bed of woodshavings we shared, though I have forgot the name of the place. Lucy, tell me you will be back soon.'

It was this letter, rather than her father's or her sister's, that brought back to Lucy the memory of home, and the realisation of where and what she was. Adelaide, with whom she had first seen Texas, and first seen General Houston, had for many months been home in London and now had a new baby. She turned over the letter and glanced at the endorsements on the address. There were the smudged frankings of the post offices at Kingston, Jamaica,

New Orleans, and Galveston. The letter had been sent from London in late July. That was almost two months before she had gone with Sam Houston to the Cherokee town, almost two months before the night of the storm. She and Adelaide were in different worlds.

28

Vote Early, Vote Often

Helga and her man were reunited on the gangplank of the Mississippi riverboat *Planter*.

At that time of year the steamers between Galveston and New Orleans ran erratically, so Lucy and Helga did not arrive in Louisiana until the day after the election.

'You missed a fine day, ladies,' said the porter as he trundled their luggage the half mile from the river quay to the St Charles hotel. 'And a fine night.'

They could see that for themselves. The streets were still festooned with the bunting of the day before, there were no cabs to be had because their drivers were still recovering from the roistering of the night before, and as they walked they trod on the broken glass of that night's celebrations.

'Where are the Perote men?' asked Lucy. 'They have arrived?'

'Arrived,' exclaimed the porter. 'Arrived they have, and all did a fine day's work yesterday. *There* was a proper spirit, you could say. Proper men, every man jack of them, and a proper day's work they did, every man jack of them. And proud I was to drink with them, every man jack of them.'

'Did you see a German,' asked Helga. 'Name of Kurt. Kurt Neumann?'

'An Irishman there was,' said the porter, who had himself come in as an immigrant from Ireland only eighteen months before. 'Now he was a spirit, a *leading* spirit if I ever saw one. Feargus. He knew Cork in the old country. We drank to the old country, he and I.'

'But did you see a German?'

The porter, who was wheeling his trolley in such a high spirited way that the two women had trouble keeping up with him, pressed on at the same rate. 'German? All Americans now. They were all naturalised, do you see? There was a Frenchman, and several Irish, and several that was Texian but cried out aloud that they would be Texian no longer, and the judge swore them all in. Hands up all together, he says. Swear the oath all together, he says. Then Amen says the judge, and it was done. All together they were made American, and swore allegiance, first morning they was here.'

'What for?' said Lucy. 'Why the first morning?'

'Why, to do their duty as true men, and vote. How they voted. A fine day's work.'

'But did you see a German?' Helga persisted, and launched into a description.

The porter caught her tone at last. 'You are after the man? Would he be your sweetheart you are asking after?'

'He is my man.'

The porter stopped. 'There was a German, or a Dutchman, that was with Feargus. And I drank with the both of them. And they damned the Mexicans, and they damned Sam Houston, and they drank to Polk, and they did talk of a girl. I remember there was a girl in their talk.'

Helga looked at the man beseechingly.

'I should be pleased to tell you I'd seen your man that you're asking after. And the Dutchman or the German, whatever he was, did talk of a girl. But I would not thank myself for raising your hopes wrongfully, Miss – for, you see, they all had a girl in their talk, most every man of them. As they would, being men of spirit.'

Helga dropped her head. The porter started off again, at an even greater rate.

'But I do recall,' he said, 'it does now come to me, that they drank a toast – they drank a hundred toasts you see, but there was this one among them – a toast to a girl with a sash at her waist. A red sash.'

'Then it's Kurt,' exclaimed the girl. 'That's my sash at the Tremont. Ma'am, I must go to him.' She was trembling with hope,

fear, and excitement. She wanted to dash into the dark and run all
over the town until she found Kurt.

They were now at the door of the St Charles. Lucy asked the
hotel people where the Perote men could be found. They did not
know. It could be in one of a hundred liquoring places, or worse.
Probably in the French quarter, said the major domo of the hotel,
who was all attention to Lady Lucy and had a low opinion both of
the Perote men and of the French quarter. It was again the Irish
porter who came to their assistance. He might have an idea. He
would not tell them what. It was not, they would understand, something generally known, but it could perhaps be found out. Lucy gave
him two dollars, promised him five more if he could find Kurt, and
insisted that she and Helga ate and rested and warmed themselves
by the cedar fire in her parlour. The girl calmed down, and obeyed
her.

Two hours later, just as they were resigning themselves to
learning nothing that night, and just as Lucy had shaken her hair
loose and was about to insist that both should go to bed, a servant
knocked. The porter had reappeared in the lobby asking for them.
They went down. The man had found the Perote prisoners on a
riverboat, which had steam up and was departing in an hour's time.

'At night?' said Lucy. 'At this time of night?'

'That,' said the porter, 'being the way of things. They having to
be where they are going betimes tomorrow, not first dawn but early
rather than late.'

'Going where?' asked Lucy.

'Which I cannot say,' said the Irishman earnestly. 'Which they would
not tell me, although a man may form his own notions.'

The porter had procured a cab, which on that day and at
that time of night showed earnestness on his part. She looked the
man in the eyes and believed him. She would take the chance. The
major domo thought her a mad Englishwoman, going into the city
and down by the river at such an hour. Lucy insisted.

So they set out and at half past nine came to a quay not
two hundred yards from where they had disembarked earlier in
the day, and there was the riverboat *Planter* with steam up, and

brightly lit on all three decks. From her saloon came the sound of a hundred men carousing. The porter signalled them to wait, went on board, and two minutes later appeared at the top of the gangplank with Kurt Neumann.

Looking out of the light into darkness, he could not at first make Helga out. She took two steps forward on to the foot of the gangplank and he saw her yellow hair. She looked upwards. 'Woman,' thought Lucy, waiting behind and watching, 'why don't you go to him?' But there Helga stood timid with fear and hope, and it was Kurt who ran down to her.

Helga was a tall girl, taller if anything than Kurt, but after their first embrace he swung her into the air, and held her up by the waist. His friends, who had straggled out after him on to the deck, broke into laughter and cheers.

'No sooner out of one lot of shackles,' called an Irish voice from the upper deck, 'than you're finding yourself some others?'

Laughter and more cheers came from the gathering crowd on the decks of the riverboat.

Kurt lowered Helga to her feet, and turned to acknowledge the ribald applause. She twined her long arms round his neck and buried her face in his shoulder.

'So, Feargus,' said Kurt, replying to the Irish voice from the boat. 'Shackles, you say. Shackles of a softer kind.'

He led Helga by the hand up to his friends. She whispered something to him, he conferred with a man in a greasy yachting cap who was the steamboat captain, and then Kurt came down to Lucy, presented himself, thanked her, and asked her to come on board. She congratulated him on Helga, and asked him where the riverboat was bound and why.

'Pipe-laying,' he said.

'Pipes for what, Mr Neumann? And at this time of night?'

He smiled. 'Helga tells me that you wanted to see an election, that you came to New Orleans to see the election but were delayed?'

'I'm afraid so.'

'Come with us and you will see an election.'

Lucy went on board.

The pilot was confident of the first few miles of the river passage, even in the dark. The boat was an island of light and made a confident progress up the broad river. Then they encountered mist. They slowed to half speed, then quarter speed. Then they only crawled forward. By three in the morning a thick fog surrounded them. It was impossible to see from the wheelhouse to the bow, the engines were stopped, and they lay near the left bank of the sluggish river. Helga and Kurt had vanished long before into some corner of the ship. Lucy retired to the cabin from which the captain had ejected four men to accommodate her. The men, as she saw, were all rather more than half drunk, and the night was damp and cold, but they gallantly surrendered the little room to her, murmuring that it was only proper that a lady should have a warm and decent place to rest. A woman purser made her up a bed and brought her coffee. She slept for three hours but then woke suddenly. All was silence. The fog was lifting but she could still not see beyond a boat's length. She found the captain and one of his officers gazing astern. The *Planter* gave a mournful blast on her steam siren, which was answered ten seconds later by a distant siren in a higher key. The two officers looked at each other. The younger man held out his right hand. Lucy saw by the light of a lantern that in half a minute a dozen black specks settled on his palm.

'Closer than she was,' said the young man. The captain nodded.

They saw Lucy did not understand, and explained to their guest.

'It's not the other steamer that's coming up in company with us,' said the captain. 'That's her siren you heard answer ours, and she's too far off. So these black specks on Mr Mate's hand here, the question is, whose are they? And where is she? She's close.'

Lucy glanced up at their own stack. It was high and its top was lost in the mist, but she knew it was making some smoke. She could hear and feel the *Planter*'s engines idling below deck.

'No, ma'am, those smuts are not from our smoke. What wind there is, it's aft of us and taking our smoke for'ard.'

They listened. There was no sound of a paddle wheel, not a mechanical sound anywhere on the river. That was strange because that other ship, wherever she was, would be as full of noises as the *Planter* when she was under way, however slowly.

'Not a voice neither,' said the mate.

The captain grunted. 'And that's strangest of all, ma'am,' he said. 'They'll hear us, not our words but something that'll tell them there are voices here, quiet as we are. If a man turns in his sleep here, they'll catch the creak and rustle of it. A man can hear for miles on the river. It carries. She's close.'

'What is she?' asked Lucy.

'Lord knows, but she's close, and keeping silence, and it's her smuts falling on us.'

They listened and waited. In half an hour the fog lifted a little more, the sky lightened in the east, and they saw, outlined against the obscured sun's dim glow, a much smaller steamer lying on the right bank of the river. She did not reply to their whistled signals.

The *Planter* got under way. At nine o'clock she was lying off Plaquemines. On a bend stood a shack, two hundred yards from the river bank, and from it flew the Stars and Stripes. The men were now roused and breakfasted. Neumann, Helga, and Feargus had reappeared. As the steamer came into her landing the men crowded to disembark, and she listed, at first slightly and then alarmingly. The captain roared. His officers and men took up the yells. 'We'll careen over, blast you.' Helga, who had returned to attend to Lucy, fell against her as the boat listed. For an instant before she regained her balance Lucy felt the warmth of the girl against her side, this girl who had spent the night with her lover, though only in some warm corner of the crowded and dimly-lit saloon. At that moment Helga's eyes were on Kurt. He was with the rest of the Perote men who were being cursed, persuaded, prodded, and herded until they arranged themselves half on the port side, half on the starboard, so that the ship could balance herself. As they drifted in to the landing all the men took up the cry of 'Polk, Polk, Polk. Polk, Texas, the Union, and Liberty.' Lucy, looking across the river, saw on its eastern bank the small steamer that had shadowed them in the night. The vessel was a hundred yards off, but she could have sworn that there, standing in the bow, was a tall, stooping figure she knew but could

not place. The *Planter* came to the landing with a shudder, and tied
up. Then her passengers disembarked on to the jetty, ten men from
the starboard, then ten from the port side. All then formed two lines
and marched up to the shack flying the Stars and Stripes. This was
the polling station for Plaquemines parish, Louisiana.

'But the election was two days ago,' said Lucy. 'I was told
I missed the election.'

The sheriff of Plaquemines looked with amusement at this
strange woman with her strange accent and her even stranger
scruples.

'You're not from round here, lady. Can tell that. Now voting
was Monday in New Orleans, I have heard. But we being kind
of distant to reach, we reckoned three days was fairer. Gives an
opportunity – for such men as your pipe-layers, see?'

He laughed. The nature of the pipes to be laid that day at
Plaquemines became rapidly clear.

'Name?' said the sheriff to the first man who presented himself. A
name was spoken in reply, the man was given a voting ticket, marked
it, and handed it to the sheriff who, after perusing it, stuffed it into
the ballot box.

'Name?' This was the only question asked of any man, though
why even that was asked was not clear, since it was checked against
nothing. There was no register of names to check it against. No
register had ever existed. Nor did the sheriff even listen to the
names the men declared. His question was a matter of form, and
the only shred of form there was to this polling.

'Name?' Feargus Mullin and Kurt Neumann gave their names.
O'Keefe, O'Malley, Springstein, Lacoste, Crève-coeur all gave theirs.
All were thereupon given tickets. Crève-coeur folded his and made as
if to stick it in the box himself. The sheriff caught his hand.

'Now, friend, I don't think it right in my precinct that any
man, even with a fancy name like that, should vote a folded
ticket. We're plain with each other in my precinct, gentlemen. Plain
and open.' At which he unfolded the paper, saw that the vote was
for Polk, held it up for the others to see, and placed it in the box
himself.

'Name?' And so it went on.

A second riverboat, the *Agnes*, the steamer whose siren had answered the *Planter* in the night, came up to the landing, and her freight of pipe-layers lined up to give their names. The *Planter*'s captain brought Lucy some coffee and observed the scene with detachment. 'Two dollars a day to each man to lay a pipe, and a fine cruise up the river for him.'

'Who are *they*?' asked Lucy, indicating a group of six men who were standing twenty yards off, just watching. None of them had come up to vote.

'Off the small steamer that followed us in the night. We caught her smuts, remember? Knew she was there, though she lay quiet. She was watching then, as those men are watching now. Their ship's anchored on the right bank, across from us, see? Then they rowed across this morning in a boat, and was seen off by the sheriff. But then they said they had a right as American citizens to watch. So long as they don't come close, no one'll rough 'em up, ma'am. Let 'em watch.'

It was still only mid-morning, in winter. The sun, what they could see of it, still lay low behind the watchers. Lucy thought she saw again the tall man she had seen standing in the steamer's bow earlier in the morning. She had seen him somewhere, but could not place him.

A boy presented himself at the ballot table – a boy, aged perhaps fifteen and small for his years, straight from the engine room with an oily rag in his hand. He asked if he too could lay a pipe. The engineer pushed him forward to the sheriff who looked evenly at the boy.

'Name?'

'Jack, sir.'

The boy Jack was given a ticket.

'Say, sheriff,' said the engineer of the *Planter*, 'now I've a gentleman on board has worked as a steward on Red River boats for ten years. He'd like a ticket if you'd permit it, sir, if that's lawful?'

Now the engineer was known to the sheriff to be a firm Kentuckian Democrat whose word he would take for anything. So the sheriff considered. 'Sure Jimmy, that's lawful in my precinct,' he said, and the steward was produced. But when he voted he did the unthinkable and put his mark against Clay. This ticket was scanned by the sheriff, who held it up for the pipe-layers to see. 'Shame,' they cried. The Kentuckian engineer was as much taken aback as the others, and ashamed as a true Democrat to have lost face with the crowd. He berated the Red River steward, who did not comprehend the enormity of his offence. The sheriff then consulted with his deputy, and then addressed the crowd. 'Gentlemen, I'm now of the opinion that in the matter of a Red River man I'll have to take advice, and the nearest advice is three hours' ride away, and three hours back, and I can't start off till this evening, which'll make it tomorrow before I can rightly say.'

But, said the steward, still not understanding, he would be back in New Orleans by then. The sheriff considered this too, and then said well, he didn't see a case of any injustice there. The man would suffer no disadvantage by being at New Orleans, seeing the polls at Plaquemines would be closed by then anyways. This was considered great fun, and raised a good laugh. The steward was pushed aside.

Feargus Mullin voted a second time, giving his name as Clay. Loud laughter. Kurt Neumann announced himself the second time round as Sam Houston. More hilarity. Then the sheriff, his deputy, and the two gentlemen who had chartered the *Planter* and the *Agnes* put their heads together and decided that, after the long tradition of Plaquemines parish, the poll might as well close at a convenient hour, say 10:30am. This was disputed only by a few who had been unable to register a second vote and thereby earn another dollar. They were outnumbered by those who thought it convenient to take dinner early, and then start back early for New Orleans. The electoral tickets were thereupon counted on the spot, a few brought in from neighbouring precincts the day before, and the majority those given that morning at Plaquemines. The result was declared to cheers. For Clay, 44 votes. For Polk, 1,283. Then the sheriff and his deputy, the organising gentlemen from New Orleans, Feargus Mullin and Kurt Neumann, the two ships' masters, the engineer, with Lucy

Moncreiffe and Helga as their guests, sat down to dinner at which spirits flowed freely.

In early afternoon the riverboats departed, the *Agnes* carrying back those citizen tradesmen of New Orleans who had already voted in their own city on the Monday, and the *Planter* freighted with the Perote prisoners who hoped, by having voted diligently for Polk and annexation in New Orleans on the Monday and in Plaquemines on the Wednesday, to have done all in their power to dish Sam Houston, whom they hated. When it was dark again, and they were approaching New Orleans, and much more liquor had flowed than even at dinner, the chief organising gentleman announced, to howls of laughter, that in no previous election in Plaquemines had more than 340 votes, in total, been cast for all candidates, of all parties, added together. Now today there were 1,283 for Polk alone. Such was the inevitable march of progress. (Laughter.) Such was the go-ahead spirit of the day. (Howls of mirth.) It was agreed that, all in all, they had put in a fine day's pipe-laying. And, said the organising gentleman, to put the matter in a finer light, they had put in a fine day's ballot-stuffing – the sort of stuffing, said he, carving himself another slice off the turkey, which imparted, as the gentlemen would all agree, a fine relish to the meat.

Three days later Lucy said goodbye to Helga. The girl was happy with Kurt but sad to leave Lucy. They had endured the attack at Shoal Point together. Helga had nursed her in her illness. Lucy liked and trusted her. The girl had been discreet about General Houston. She had been loyal, but they had never been close. Lucy could not think why that was. Now she was happy to see Helga happy, though, in losing her second maid, she suffered what she supposed she must call a second American calamity.

'You have been kind to me, ma'am,' said Helga, as they said their goodbyes. 'You took me to the quay last night, and found me my man.'

'I could not very well have let you go on your own, Helga.'

'But I would, ma'am. I would have gone out in the dark on

my own, and it would have made no sense. I would have done it. You saved me from that. You were kind then. You have always been kind.'

Then Lucy prepared to return to Texas. She knew she ought to go home to England. She knew there was no sense in her staying. She knew she stayed for Sam Houston.

On the steamer landing, as she was preparing to embark alone for the passage back to Texas, Lucy saw the tall figure of George Terrell at the ticket office. She had not seen him since their visit to the Cherokees.

'I did not know you were here,' she said. 'I am sorry to have missed you. You should have been at Plaquemines. Such sights.'

'They were,' said Terrell, and then Lucy realised that it was his tall figure she had seen on the steamer, and later watching by the ballot table. Now she saw him close up and in broad day she knew he was the man.

'We caught your smuts,' she said. 'The captain knew your steamer was there.' She told him the story of the mist and the silent river.

'So you were there that night and that day?' he said. 'You saw all that happened?'

'I was there, right by the table where they voted their tickets, and was openly told it was ballot stuffing, by those who were doing the stuffing. They are all at least frank about it. No one could accuse them of subterfuge.'

He nodded grimly.

'Such sights that day,' she said. 'Fascinating for a political man, too, I'd say.'

'I could think of other words. I went up there on that steamer with a group of Clay men, who had wind that the two riverboats were going upriver. They were right. But there is nothing to do. You know Polk took Louisiana?'

'I have heard by seven hundred votes.'

'Fewer than that,' he said. 'Across the whole state. And the majority at Plaquemines was twelve hundred. So we saw Louisiana won for Polk, you and I.'

'But it was open fraud. It was Vote Early, Vote Often. They were paid. It was so open you had to laugh. They did laugh. Surely the Plaquemines ballot will be overturned?'

'I do not think so. Polk has won the entire election. He took New York by five thousand, and more than that were naturalised in the city the day of the election, so they could vote. New York state gave him the election, along with a few more Plaquemines here and there. Polk will be president.'

There was no more to say about it. The Plaquemines story had been all over New Orleans, and men had laughed at it.

She said, 'Shall we be taking the same steamer to Galveston?'

'I fear not. I am on my way to England.'

'England? Are there Indians in England since I was last there?'

'I am no longer Indian commissioner. General Houston and I go back a long way together. We practised law together in Tennessee. When he was governor there he found a use for me as attorney general. When we both came to Texas we happened to see eye to eye on the Cherokees, so he found a use for me as commissioner. Now there is a use for me in London.'

'But what of Dr Smith?'

'You know him?'

'We met in Paris. He gave me my passport. He is ill?'

'Well enough as far as I know, but he is recalled.'

Lucy's mind went back to the day of the return from the Cherokees, and to Sam Houston's exaltation, his cantering round her, and his cries of, 'Houston has done it.' By now it should all have been done. By now it must have been done. So what on earth could Dr Smith's recall mean?

'You go as chargé d'affaires?'

'I do. Jones was not wholehearted in making the appointment. I can tell you that and break no confidences, since the word was all over Texas when I left. No, Jones was not sure, and he havered and hesitated for weeks, even after my commission was signed. In the end I said, "Do I go or do I not?" As you see, now I'm on my way.'

'You and General Houston saw eye to eye on Indians, Mr Terrell. Do you see eye to eye on England?'

'I never asked him in as many words, but yes we do. Now Donelson, whom I think you've met . . . ?'

She nodded. She had told Terrell.

'Well, I met Saligny last night, and the word from him was . . . Or perhaps you will already know? You have met Mr Saligny?'

'I have met him, but not this time. He is not a man I seek out.'

'No. Well, I met him and his lady, whom I must call handsome, a beautiful woman, but . . .'

'No doubt of that, Mr Terrell. She is certainly a beauty.'

'Yes. Saligny was saying that Donelson is now going round New Orleans like a proconsul, saying the American people have spoken – I suppose he means in that election you saw so splendidly won at Plaquemines and no doubt in other places like it. And the people having spoken, Donelson says – or Saligny says Donelson says – that it is treason, or unnecessary, or inappropriate, or unpatriotic, or all four, to utter a word against annexation.'

'Was that,' asked Lucy, 'Mr Saligny's account or his lady's?'

Terrell smiled. 'Both. He may have adopted some of her emphasis. I take your meaning. But however that may be, Donelson is off to Texas, where he'll get short shrift with that sort of talk, if he *was* talking that kind of talk.'

'Mr Terrell, the last talk I heard, before I left Galveston, was that annexation was a dead cock in a pit, something elegant like that.'

'But there are those who would go for it if it were offered even now. Polk may find a way of offering it again. There are the men who think it would turn earth into gold. Then there are those members of the Texian congress who still hold government stock which is now worthless, which they sincerely expect that the United States government, once possessed of Texas, would redeem at par. That's a chimera. I think it all a chimera.'

Mr Terrell's ship did not leave for two days. He had come to make sure that some of his heavier baggage, which was being sent after him from Texas, arrived on the Galveston steamer, the one Lucy would take on her passage back. The steamer was late and there were a few hours yet to wait. Terrell offered to take any letters she had for England, and she did write notes to Adelaide and to her father and sister. To Adelaide she sent her congratulations and love. To her father, an assurance that she had no plans to become a citizen of Texas, a prospect which he had laconically assumed, in his last letter, that she must be contemplating, since her long absence could, he feared, hardly mean anything else. To her sister she wrote, 'Not lost. No prayers yet,' and then gave her news, or that part of it fit for an unmarried sister to hear. She entrusted these letters to Mr Terrell, together with introductions to two cousins of hers who lived in London, but not to Lord Aberdeen. He would meet Aberdeen in any case, and she did not care to tell him of her connection with him. He waited with her until the Galveston steamer came in.

'You are looking well,' she told him. 'Much better than in the early fall.' This was true. He had lost his chronic cough and much of his pallor.

'The Mississippi air?' he suggested. 'But yes, I am better. And the sea air of the Atlantic passage will help no end.'

Lucy wished Mr Terrell well in London and Paris. He stayed on the pier until the steamer taking her to Galveston backed with a noisy churning and frothing of paddles into the central channel of the river, and then disappeared round a bend in the Mississippi, leaving the beautiful crescent of New Orleans behind.

29

The Safety of the Future

By early December Charles Elliot was at last back in Texas. There on the quayside at Galveston he was accosted by a hearty gentleman who had been superintending the unloading of small trees from the deck of a German brig newly put in from Hamburg.

'Have I the pleasure of addressing Captain Elliot?' said the stranger.

Elliot raised his floppy white hat, and admitted that was he.

'And I am Carl Solms,' said the prince, for it was another of his ships that had just arrived. 'I did myself the honour of leaving my card at your lodgings. I have much looked forward to meeting you. We have interests in common, Captain.'

Elliot excused himself. He had seen the card only on his arrival the evening before. He had not yet had time to give himself the pleasure of replying to the prince, but was delighted to meet him now.

'You have been in the United States, Captain Elliot, and at Washington? On the Potomac I mean. And you are recovered?'

'Mostly in Virginia, but that was near Washington and I passed some time with my colleague there, the British minister. And I believe I am recovered. The fever is gone.'

'You will have seen something of the late presidential campaign there?'

'Very little, Prince.'

'You will forgive me if I suggest you have perhaps seen more than you are at liberty to admit? It is a diplomatist's duty to observe, yes?'

Elliot smiled at the question and at the way it was put. It was the first indication to him that this man, with his perfect English, was for all that a German.

'That is a question you cannot with propriety answer, Captain? I understand. But you will have met Mr Polk?' And here the prince recited the old saw. Someone asked who was Mr Polk. To which the only reply was, the man nominated on the ninth ballot.

'But now,' said the prince, 'I believe it goes a new way? There is a new way of saying it? The question is the same, "Who is Polk?" But now the answer runs, "He is the man just elected president of the United States." And that is all anyone knows, yes?'

'What,' said Elliot, looking steadily away at the German brig and at the cargo it was unloading, 'are those trees, Prince?' As he spoke a parcel of trees, being swung over their heads to land on the quay, deposited on them a shower of pine needles.

'Those trees, Captain, are in a sad way. I would have to admit that.' And so they were. They were small firs, about four feet high, and most were evidently dead. The roots were intact, but the branches of many were almost bare. Those branches not yet bare were shedding needles rapidly.

'I have been bringing in settlers, Captain. Now when a man emigrates, he leaves home. I have been at some trouble to impress that simple truth upon them. They come here with a view to live and die here, to establish their families here. They will be Texians. But that does not mean that I have not brought out with them some reminders of the old country. I brought music out to them, which much cheers them in the hard first few months. You will have seen the harmoniums I have brought in as cargo?'

Elliot did not know the word.

'A kind of organ. For sacred music.'

'I see.'

'And the trees are for Christmas. Or were for Christmas. It is a custom in the old country to decorate such trees. They have not prospered on the voyage. Every care should have been taken. The horticultural instructions to the ship's officers were precise. But I see we shall have to use the trees of the new country.'

'They are plentiful.'

'Captain Elliot, I have been up-country, viewing the settlements we have already made in Texas. We have been warmly welcomed by the old settlers wherever we have gone. The mayors and officials come out and place themselves at our disposal. In fact, everybody acts like possessed. I could say that.'

'They are friendly people.'

'I say I have been up-country. The last time I was on this quay was with General Houston, when we watched some earlier immigrants disembarking. That day we landed a harmonium, the instrument I have described to you, and the general played the first chord that sounded from it on Texian soil.'

'I did not know General Houston was musical.'

'It was a countrywoman of yours who assisted him, pointing out the keys. A Lady Lucy I believe.'

Lucy Moncreiffe. Elliot remembered her.

'When was this, Prince?'

'Perhaps four months ago. Between three and four. General Houston expressed himself much pleased with the spirit of the immigrants he saw that day. "Population," he said. He repeated that word several times. Population was what his country required. He is right, Captain. And in this matter of population lies my business with you, and I believe with Her Majesty's Government.'

'I shall be glad to be of any service I can.'

'You have heard Mr Polk declare that during the presidential election the question of annexation was put nakedly to the American people, and that the American people have spoken decisively in its favour? So now he will be president, we may expect him to seize Texas in the name of the people?'

'I have not heard it put in quite those terms. It would take a treaty. Any treaty would be a matter for the American Senate. And I do not think, on balance, that Texas would wish to be annexed.'

'I have seen Mr Polk's words often reported.'

Elliot bowed. Let Solms have it his way.

'Captain Elliot, would you not agree that mediocrity has become almost a quality without which, in the United States, one is not entitled to aspire to the highest offices in the land, since those offices are elective, and to be elected a man must please the people, and to please them must resemble them? Would you not agree that such are the fruits which the radicalisation of democracy has ripened and brought forth? If I were to say that nine tenths of the virtue, intelligence, and respectability of the American nation had voted for Clay and against annexation, that would be an exaggeration. But how much of an exaggeration would it be? Without any doubt, Mr Clay would have been the victor if the votes had been weighed, that is to say given their true worth.'

'But votes are not weighed but counted,' said Elliot. He was no friend to democracy, particularly not to what he called pure democracy, where each man, irrespective of who he was or what he had done, had an equal voice. He could not understand, and few Englishmen of his class could have understood, how any rational government could be carried on under such a system. He was honest in his grave doubts and sure of the probity of his reasons, and therefore did not wish what he saw as the overwhelmingly strong case against democracy to be weakened by the too-extravagant and intemperate condemnation of such a man as the Prince of Solms. Besides, he could not discuss the internal affairs of a foreign power with any man.

'True,' said Solms. 'Counted not weighed. But, in any rational view, what should the votes of the poor white trash of the south weigh, in a metaphorical sense if you wish, against those of the farmers of New England? How should those of the Irish day labourers of the northern cities, who voted unanimously for Polk, weigh against those of the merchants and manufacturers who employ them?'

'If you will forgive me . . . ' murmured Elliot, about to take his leave, but the prince would not let him go.

'Dear Captain Elliot, it is I who should ask your forgiveness. Allow me to leave that vexatious matter and come to the point. Let me come to my people. Given the character of the Americans as we know it, and their appetite for new territory, can any European power stand indifferently by? While there is *any* chance of Mr Polk's designs on Texas coming to fruition, can a European power stand

by? I think not. And if not, how can such a design be prevented? It
seems to me that there is a very obvious step to be taken, and that is
to fill Texas as soon as possible with a large number of Europeans.
This is after all what General Houston has expressed a desire for.
"Give me population. Population is all that is needed." He has told
me.'

'Suppose that to be so,' said Elliot. 'How could it be done,
what you propose?'

'I believe the German immigration society could be of great
use in the matter. Should the government of Her Majesty the
queen approve the idea, it would be easy to send, even by the
end of next spring, some twenty or thirty thousand people, well
armed and equipped, to this country. English and German ships
could carry them here. Able and active young officers of every arm
would accompany them. Most would be retired English officers.'

'Who would then all become Texians?'

'Indeed yes. I do not propose an invasion.' But what the Prince
of Solms proposed, though neither he nor Elliot could know it,
was no less than a European counterpart of the retail invasion of
unoccupied north American tracts which Lord Aberdeen believed
was already being carried out by the United States.

'We Germans,' said the prince, 'fought well alongside your countrymen in the Peninsula against Napoleon, under Wellington.'

'That was war, Prince.'

'And this is peace. Peaceable English and German settlers would
do as well as any army to stop American encroachment towards the
south. In fact, Captain, once that force was established – twenty or
thirty thousand men and women brought out in German and English
ships – I would pledge my word for the safety of the future. You will
see that these proposals are communicated to your government?'

'Of course.'

'I will assist you by incorporating them into a memorandum,
which I shall deliver to you.'

Elliot bowed again, and cordially accepted a cordial invitation
to the prince's for dinner, being careful however to fix no date.

'A standing invitation,' called the prince, moving off to demand an explanation from the ship's master for the lamentable condition of his Christmas trees.

Elliot stood looking out over the harbour. He had received orders, while in the north, to make himself amenable in every way to the Texian government. Texas needed population, the prince was right in that. He had no doubt General Houston had said the same. And the prince's plan, stripped of its rhetoric and of its regrettable reference to the Peninsular war in Spain, was workable. All the same, he had orders to do nothing to excite the United States in any way, and such proposals would be dangerous written down. If an uncle of the queen offered them in the form of a written memorandum, Elliot could not discourage him. But he would destroy the original once he had encoded a copy to send to London. Such a task he could perform only himself. No clerk could do it for him, and Elliot knew it would take the better part of a day.

He turned away. As he did so another load of baby fir trees was swung out high over his head, scattering a thousand dead needles over him. He brushed them from his hat. He was not a cursing man, but he did put it forcefully to himself that he could do very well without the Teutonic assistance of Hessian princes.

30

Mighty March of Empire

Charles Elliot had arrived back in Texas in time to see the Prince of Solms's dead Christmas trees unloaded, but too late to reach Washington-on-the-Brazos to see Anson Jones take over the presidency from Sam Houston. The presidential election in Texas had been overshadowed by that in the United States, but Jones had won the palm. He had achieved his ambition and should have been delighted, but continued to be soured in his mind, taking particular notice, and taking it as an affront that whenever he and Sam were seen together it was Sam men noticed and Sam they addressed.

And this, to Jones's disgust, was most of all true when Donelson came to present himself and his credentials. It was not Jones he sought out but Houston. But Houston for his part avoided Donelson, and they did not meet until the morning of the transfer of office to the new president. Then it happened this way. As the members of the two houses of the Texian congress were assembling, and as Anson Jones was crossing the porch to welcome Donelson, who had come as a spectator, Sam Houston disengaged himself from a group of friends and imposed his great presence between Donelson and the approaching Jones. It was masterly. He had cut out Jones, and was seen to have done so. And by meeting Donelson in public, and saying what he wished to be heard in public, he had deprived the American chargé d'affaires of the deep confidential conversation he wanted.

Donelson was taken aback and surprised. His prepared subtleties fled his mind, and he was left uttering public platitudes.

He was happy to meet Houston, whom he trusted he might still claim as an old friend.

Houston beamed, and waited.

He looked back with delight, said Donelson, on the intimacy of their earlier days in Tennessee. He was now honoured to renew a friendship with a man distinguished by the common consent of the world. He saluted the Lone Star which the Texians had set up in the hallowed sky of their victories.

Houston beamed again.

And, continued Donelson, he trusted that the light of this Lone Star would blend its rays with those of the many stars which hung over his own beloved union of the United States, making a greater light which, he firmly believed, would never be extinguished.

These sentiments were uttered on an open porch, overheard by lounging congressmen and senators. Houston waited. Donelson had finished.

Well, said Houston, putting an arm round Donelson's shoulders, he was mighty glad to meet an old friend again, and a friend who was a pupil, as he had been, of that illustrious patriot the Sage of the Hermitage.

An approving murmur arose. A reference to General Jackson was always an occasion for applause.

'And if,' said Houston, 'in my somewhat eventful life, I have done something, however insignificant, which has helped in however small a way, to add a new nation, this lovely land, to the family of free nations of the earth, then I shall retire content from my duties [here he beamed again, this time at the assembled congressmen and senators] and embrace instead the quiet and seclusion of private life.'

Then, still talking of patriotism and the general sum of human happiness, he swept Donelson inside, saw him to a good seat, and left him.

Then President Houston delivered his formal valedictory.

'Gentlemen, the attitude of Texas is now, to my apprehension, one of peculiar interest. Let her maintain her position firmly as it is, and work out her own political salvation. Let her legislature – that is to say you, gentlemen – proceed upon the supposition that we are to be and remain an independent people. Let us proceed upon that supposition.'

He paused and surveyed the gathering. No one gainsaid him.

'But if, gentlemen,' he continued in a tone which no man could have argued was not sweetly reasonable, 'if, gentlemen, the grounds for that supposition should one day appear less evidently substantial than they must now appear, *if* the United States should *soon* open the door to Texas [this with a nod towards Donelson] and, on proper terms, bid her enter the United States and become, I say on proper terms, a member of that great union, then you will have other conductors better than myself [a gesture here towards Anson Jones] to lead you into the beloved land from which we have sprung – the land of the broad stripes and bright stars. That is an *if*, gentlemen, which we have all considered and which it behoved us to consider.'

The Congress he was addressing was not on the whole friendly towards him, and Sam Houston knew this. But many of the members were newly elected and were awed by him, seeing and hearing him for the first time. And even the oldest, most experienced, most sceptical, and most opposed to him could hardly suppress a grin when Sam Houston pointed out Anson Jones as the more able man. And only young Senator Kaufman, among those gathered there, calmly returned Houston's gaze when it fell upon him. Kaufman was the arch annexationist, certainly an able man, and Houston knew it.

As for Jones, he sat silently as his old chief went on, complimenting all, heaping encomium after encomium on the legislators of this lovely land, and when Houston was about to come to his peroration, Jones knew it first. He knew it because Sam dropped his voice, looked around him, hesitated and then lifted his head, as Jones had seen him a hundred times hesitate and then lift his head, and then, after another pause, speak more softly than ever, compelling the attention of his auditors.

'If,' he said at last, 'if we remain an independent nation, our territory will be extensive, unlimited. [Another pause.] The Pacific alone will bound the mighty march of our race and our empire. We have our destiny, gentlemen, in our own hands.'

When the buzz had subsided, Jones took the oath of office, kissed the Bible, and then read at length from a prepared script about reducing expenses, encouraging agriculture, building jails, and ameliorating the condition of their red brethren. That meant moving them on again. Bridges were to be built and land disputes settled, and on and on. Finally he called on Providence to watch over Texas.

This last sentiment was answered with an audible whisper of, 'Which with you we'll need.'

Then Houston was being gracious again, and Jones, the new president, was left for a moment standing quite alone, clutching the text of his speech, until he was approached by the first of the many who sought offices of profit under his administration.

That evening, to the distant tune of a polka, Donelson composed a letter to General Jackson reporting the day's events, saying he was uncertain of Sam Houston's true state of mind on annexation. The sooner another Bill was brought before the United States Congress, the better. He feared the influence of the European powers upon General Houston, particularly that of Britain. He sat writing late into the night, and did not appear at the inaugural ball in the big room over Hatfield's saloon.

At the ball, the Texian legislators were suffering from a lack of partners. Few had been able to bring their wives, or even the women reputed not to be their wives. But all the ladies of Washington, the wives and daughters of the saloon keepers, farmers, and owners of livery stables, had been pressed to come, and had needed no second invitation to what was the social event of the year. Still there were not enough ladies to go round, so by nine o'clock Lucy felt that she had danced for hours. She had come up to Washington from Galveston with Captain John Tod and his wife. Tod was commander of the naval station at Galveston, which by then consisted of a few sailors looking after a few rotting hulks. The sloop *Austin* still lay there, having attracted not a single bid at auction. One of the few political ladies present was Sam Houston's wife, Margaret. Earlier in the evening Captain Tod had presented Lucy to her. It was the first time she had met Margaret. She saw a woman she knew to be scarcely more than two or three years older than herself, but who was already lined round the eyes. Margaret talked about her son to Lucy and to a small group of other ladies. There seemed at first nothing to distinguish Mrs Houston at all.

Her voice was undecided and her eyes as faded as her gown – and yet those eyes lit up when she talked about her determination to see her husband received into the Baptist Church.

'You will perhaps not believe it, ladies,' she said, 'but General Houston was confirmed as a Roman Catholic.'

'Indeed?' asked a shopkeeper's wife.

'Before the revolution, you see, the Mexicans insisted that everyone coming to Texas should be received into their faith, but that was mere form. I have been urging that on my dear husband, and earnestly begging him to be received into my own church. It would be a great consolation to him, as it has always been to me.'

'Confirmed into the Roman Catholic church?' said Mrs Hatfield, of the gambling saloon. Her tone showed that such a thing was inconceivable to her. She was herself also a good Baptist.

'It was the custom. But a mere form, as I say. Why, the general was received as a Papist under the names of Samuel Pablo. Pablo, a name he never has borne, a name for that occasion only, and Samuel too. He is always Sam to me. I have never heard the general called anything other than Sam, by any lady or gentleman.'

Then Lucy saw that Margaret Houston did have some distinction. It was not just her determination, which showed itself in her wish to convert her husband to her own true faith; it was also her hair. It was not hair of any striking length or colour. It was mousy. But that for Lucy was the distinction. Her friend Adelaide's hair was mouse, and Lucy had seen Adelaide bloom under her eyes into a loving and beloved wife. This similarity between Margaret and Adelaide, whom she had loved, stirred Lucy in a way she did not welcome. She was about to excuse herself and move away when Margaret turned to her.

'I believe I have something to thank you for?'

The innocent words cut Lucy. Here was a woman she had wronged. In any ordinary sense she had wronged her.

'I do not think . . . ' she said.

'But Sam told me of it. You showed him how to play the prince's harmonium at Galveston, on the quay. When he told me, I urged upon him again to promise that he would have my pianoforte brought over from Houston city, so that I could continue the instruction you had started. I cannot remember how many times I have asked him to do that, but at long last he has consented. I do think that was some of your doing. Do not protest, I do think so. And so you see, I owe you my thanks. And General Houston's. He has several times spoken of the occasion at Galveston.'

Lucy hid her confusion, but was grateful when Captain Tod rescued her by asking her to dance. 'Now Sam's speech today,' said the captain, 'was unlike Sam.'

'What?' said Lucy, whose thoughts were still on Margaret.

'Unlike Sam whenever I've heard him. Sam sober was always for annexation, leastwise whenever I heard him. And Sam drunk – I beg your pardon ma'am, but it used to be so before he married Mrs Houston – why, Sam drunk was always for independence. Now today it's *if* the United States shall open the door on the one hand, and *if* we remain independent on the other. The glorious union on one hand, or the mighty march of empire on the other. Neither fish nor fowl.'

Then Senator Kaufman begged a dance. He danced well, holding her lightly in the dance, and talked well, not holding her at all lightly in conversation. He talked with some learning, so far as she could remember afterwards because Margaret was still at the front of her mind, first about annexation and then about the wild flowers that would coat Texas in the spring. She had mentioned Dr Smith's wild flowers to him, those he had told her about in Paris. After the dance he fetched her a cool drink, and they sat talking. Mrs Houston left soon after, and many of the ladies with her. The ball became rowdy. A senator and his ample partner stomped too gaily on a loose board, the plank collapsed, and both senator and partner tumbled over in a whirl of lace, white thigh, and petticoat. Through this chaos and beyond, on the other side of the room, Lucy saw Sam Houston surrounded still by his political admirers. He had not danced because of an old wound in the ankle. It was a wound she had seen. She was rising to leave, picking up her shawl and fan, saying a few polite words to Senator Kaufman, and looking for Captain Tod to escort her from the ball, when Sam Houston came over, bowed, and sat beside her. The senator returned the bow and left them.

'The ball,' said Sam Houston, 'is hot work, even for someone
who does not dance. I have not. But I have seen you dance and
talking with Kaufman.'

'The senator is very agreeable.'

'A man given to cleverness. A damned Princeton University man.'

'Then my father is a damned Aberdeen man. He never thought
it did him much harm.'

Houston growled.

'General Houston,' she asked immediately, 'where is Dr Smith?'

'Smith?'

'Do you remember the day you told me, "Houston has done
it"? You will remember that day?'

They were in public. They appeared a couple civilly conversing.
She was speaking low and keeping her face impassive, but he heard
the feeling in her voice.

'I do remember that day, and I shall.'

'Yes. Houston had done it, you said, and Dr Smith was to
accept Lord Aberdeen's proposal. It was done, you said. You had
done it. And now Mr Terrell tells me that he has Dr Smith's place.
I met him in New Orleans – while you were at Huntsville with your
family.'

She was ashamed of the words about Huntsville as soon as
she had spoken them, but there was no retracting them now.

'Lucy, it is true Terrell goes to London and Paris. Dr Smith
asked for leave of absence months before the English made their
proposal. He was given it, and Terrell sent in his place. But he will
have received the order before he returned. He may return with the
treaty signed. He may have it in his pocket. Or he may have left it to
be negotiated by the consul in London, who in his absence has full
powers. It was only in late September the order was sent. It is eight
weeks there by the fastest route, and another eight back. Sometimes
ten. And that is not yet. D'you see?'

'I see.'

'Dear Lucy . . . ' he began, but she would have none of it.
What he told her was reasonable, but he did not understand – as
how could he? – that it was not the diplomatic act that concerned

her but rather that Houston, having told her what he had, and told her in the circumstances of that day and of the night before, should since have told her less than the truth. That he should have told her less than the truth during the time when they had been lovers. This discovery also came at a time when Elliot's letter had brought her husband vividly back to her mind. And now, on top of all that, she had seen Houston's wife, a sweet and diffident woman who reminded her of Adelaide.

'Your wife tells me,' she said, 'that she is grateful to me for the small part I played with that harmonium of Solms's. Placing your hands on the keys. She is grateful.'

Sam Houston raised his hands in front of him, as if he were about to strike a grand chord, and with force. He did not. He looked at his hands and groaned.

She rose rapidly. Nothing inclined her to remain.

'And Mrs Houston wishes to introduce you into the Baptist church?'

He was foundering, but could let his face show nothing.

'Then let her,' said Lucy, and was gone.

It was not an estrangement she allowed to continue. At the Christmas races at Washington-on-the-Brazos, Hail Storm won from Red Rover, Mary Bowles, and Big Drunk. She watched the race in Sam Houston's party.

Later, lying on a bed of woodshavings, she said, 'I talked to their trainer, after the race.'

He took her meaning.

'Then I am a proud man.'

'Ought to be too. Who sired Big Drunk?'

'A large black horse, name of Sam Houston.'

'And who sired Mary Bowles? And Red Rover?'

'The same black horse,' he said. 'Same horse, same name.'

'And who sired the winner? Who sired Hail Storm?'

'Same name, same horse.'

'Who,' she demanded, 'named that large black horse Sam Houston?'

'I did.'

'I knew it.' She laughed. She told him to lie still, and picked the wood shavings, one by one, from his hair.

Late that night she lay in his arms and he, thinking her asleep and sitting up beside her, lightly touched her forehead, her lips, and the dark hair between her legs. Then he spoke softly and intently in Cherokee. She listened with closed eyes. If it had been lighter he would have seen the beginnings of a smile on the lips he had just touched.

He was saying, 'Never let this woman think of any other place, or any other man. Never let her soul leave mine. There is no loneliness where we are. Bind her to me with black threads.'

She waited, and then demanded to know what spirit he had asked to perform what this time. She was content, happy, and drowsy. She accepted his explanation that these words also, like those he had spoken in the night at the Cherokee town, were to prevent loneliness. He did not tell her that she was bound by black threads to him and him only, or that what he had pronounced was a Cherokee chant by a man to his woman, to insure himself against her adultery.

She was still drowsy. She said, 'It is loneliness you are afraid of most?'

'Because I have been lonely.'

'And that night of the storm . . . ?'

'Yes?'

'The night of the storm, the words you spoke to me that night, and the words you said just now, when you thought I was asleep, did you speak those words to your first wife Eliza?'

Lucy listened in the darkness to his breathing.

At last he said, 'Yes.'

'And there was a storm, with her?'

Another silence.

'Yes.'

That was it. He had spoken those words to Eliza, and she had thought him mad.

In the dark, Lucy reached up and brought him down to lie beside her again. She drew his arm across her and they slept.

31

The Halo of
San Jacinto

George Terrell was shown into an ante room at the Foreign Office in Downing Street, where he exchanged bows with an older gentleman who was waiting there before him. They sat on either side of a bright fire. Terrell leaned forward to warm his hands. It is difficult for two men to sit alone in a room in silence. The older gentleman, seeing Terrell lean towards the grate, and having noticed the heavy greatcoat the porter had taken from him, broke the silence by a diplomatic remark about the weather. It was, replied Terrell, difficult for a man to come from Texas to London in January and not feel the cold. He would be going on to Paris and hoped he would find the climate milder there. His predecessor had told him that it was.

'I hope it may be. But I think perhaps your colleague was thinking of Paris in the summer or at any rate in spring. Paris can be brisk in the winter. I should go prepared for, how shall I say, snaps of cold. It would be the same with most continental cities. Drier than London, but colder.'

Terrell thanked him. They were exchanging desultory remarks about the fine parks of London when a messenger appeared. The older gentleman rose. The messenger spoke a few words to him in a low voice Terrell could not hear. The gentleman resumed his seat. The messenger turned to the Texian chargé and conducted him into the presence of Lord Aberdeen.

Terrell presented his credentials, which Aberdeen immediately handed to a clerk. The government of Her Britannic Majesty would naturally take a man to be what he said he was. His commission would

never be as much as glanced at in his presence. Later it would be
minutely examined, but only later. Lord Aberdeen then presented
Mr Addington, who had just entered.

Terrell launched into apologies for delay – at Galveston, at
New Orleans – but Aberdeen waved them aside.

'Ah, these distances. Do you know, Mr Terrell, that London is
now little closer to Athens – in time taken to travel from one to the
other, I mean – than it would have been when Pericles was ruler of
that city? Not that he would have wished to make the journey since
there would then have been nothing here for him to see. He was the
leader of what one could loosely translate as the democratic party in
that city, as I take it Mr Polk is these days in the United States?'

Addington enquired after President Houston, recalling their early
days together in the United States.

'President no longer,' said Terrell.

'But still,' said Aberdeen, 'a man of the greatest consequence
in Texas.'

'Indeed.'

Dr Smith was enquired after, and it became clear that Mr
Terrell knew no more of his movements than they. Aberdeen
mentioned a conversation he had with Dr Smith at the time of
his recall – a conversation in which Smith had explained with
some difficulty why he had not yet, and that was at the beginning
of December, received a reply to the proposal made by Great
Britain in June. Distances, delays – all this had been plausible in
December but was puzzling now. Not that Aberdeen revealed that
he was puzzled. He made his indirect enquiries of Mr Terrell with
polite obliqueness. But it became apparent to Terrell that he was
expected to be the bearer of a reply. But a reply to what? He did
not even know that. It became clear at much the same time to all
of them – to Aberdeen, to Addington, and to Terrell himself – that
the Texian chargé d'affaires lacked the clear instructions he should
have received from President Jones.

Aberdeen glanced at Addington. During the American election
it had suited Great Britain's interests to require no answer, indeed
not to press the matter at all. But now Polk was home and dry, it

was necessary to act rapidly. As to Mr Terrell's evident lack of information, both Aberdeen and Addington had known this before. They had known ambassadors to lack instructions. In such a case it was necessary first to save the ambassador's face, since it was through him that any progress would be made.

'As you will know, Mr Terrell,' said Aberdeen, 'it was throughout the last year our view, and remains our view, that the independence of Texas is necessary to the political balance of the American continent. We have viewed with concern any contingency which might be incompatible with the continued dignity of Texas as an independent nation. In view of recent events in the United States, these considerations have pressed themselves upon us with fresh force, and we should desire to convey to you the strength of our sentiments in the matter.'

Terrell saw what was happening. He was being gently told what he ought to have known. He listened as Aberdeen repeated to him the offer of the Diplomatic Act, the guarantee of independence against the world. He heard that the governments of England and France were ready at any moment to sign such an agreement.

Terrell inclined his head.

'It is unnecessary for me to impress upon you, Mr Terrell, that it now rests with Texas herself whether she will remain an independent nation, or merge her existence with another. For ourselves, we should go the whole way . . . '

The eyes of both Terrell and Addington were on Aberdeen.

'I shall make myself plain. I say again, the choice is for Texas to make. If that choice should be for independence, then for our part we should have an indefeasible right by the law of nations to do what we have proposed, and in doing so we should infringe the rights of no other nation. And if the United States chose to make this the cause of a quarrel with us, then we should be ready to abide the consequences.'

Terrell digested this. England was willing to go to war. What other interpretation could he put on Aberdeen's words?

Aberdeen, having made his point, waited.

'There is,' said Terrell, 'another matter. The matter of slavery.

There is an apprehension that any closer connection with England would bring with it an English demand which would affect the rights of those in Texas, and in the southern states of the Union, who own slaves.'

Aberdeen, who had been standing, took a seat facing Terrell and put the tips of his fingers together. 'To most Englishmen, almost to any Englishman, slavery is unthinkable. But this evil – for I do consider it an enormous evil – was not of America's seeking. Let me first think of the United States. Slavery was introduced into their country, against the wishes of its inhabitants, by a British government in the time of an earlier British empire, which is now gone. Now Her Majesty's government – regarding slavery I say as an evil – nevertheless sees the difficulty of its extirpation and will do nothing which will affect the interests of the slaveholding states in this particular. That is how things stand.'

'But,' said Terrell, 'I have Texas particularly in mind.'

'That is your duty, Mr Terrell. And my answer with regard to Texas is the same, only more emphatic. It is the more emphatic because the time for Her Majesty's government to make any representations on slavery to the government of Texas was when Texas asked for recognition as a sovereign nation. We made no such representations. We recognised the sovereignty of the Texian nation as she was. Consequently we now have no right to interfere in the matter, and we shall not. You may assure your government that we shall not bring the subject of slavery into any negotiations between our two countries. Mr Terrell, you see I am open with you. Is there any other matter on which I may reassure you or your new president?'

'Not so much the president or me, sir. But any evening, in any liquoring place in Galveston, you will hear talk that England is after a Texian colony, with General Houston as viceroy.'

Aberdeen smiled. 'Rest easy on that. We have several colonies now we would be glad to get rid of.'

'Glad to get rid of if you could keep their trade?'

'That's it. And what we ask of Texas is a liberal trade. Every time an English manufacturer sends to the United States he has to make his goods jump over the American tariff. Over they go, up goes the price, down goes the profit, and the only gainer left is the United States. What we want with Texas is a free trade with no tariff to jump over.'

'And if you had Texas as a colony you would be glad to get rid of her?'

'I have heard,' said Aberdeen drily, 'that some of you are a restless lot, and rough hands to deal with.'

At which they laughed, and parted on cordial terms.

Aberdeen saw him to the street door, and then hurried back to the gentleman in the ante room.

'Who,' asked Terrell of the porter who helped him on with his greatcoat, 'is the gentleman who was waiting when I arrived?'

'That, sir,' said the porter, 'is His Grace the ambassador from the Austrian empire, who's been there an hour.'

Terrell hunched up against the cold and walked back to his hotel in St James's. It was a short walk but the wind cut him.

When the afternoon's business was over at the Foreign Office, and Lord Aberdeen had apologised to the Austrian ambassador for having had to detain him, explaining that some quite unforeseen matter had arisen which demanded his immediate attention, Addington stayed late with a clerk, drafting a despatch to Captain Elliot. The letter told him to renew with fresh force the proposals of the British government to that of Texas, addressing himself as to an independent nation which should bow to none in regulating its destiny. The despatch was sent that night.

While Addington was labouring late in Downing Street, Terrell sat close over the fire in his parlour, pondering the despatch he also had to write. He had been received before the Austrian ambassador, who had been kept waiting. For him, that was quite enough evidence of English urgency in the matter. The long conversation had been more than enough to tell him that he did not know what any chargé d'affaires should have known. He had known there was an offer from England. He had never known exactly what. The possession of that exact knowledge was a matter that could sway the future of Texas one way or the other.

He sat until late trying to read from a volume of Gibbon's *Decline and Fall of the Roman Empire.* It was a work he read and reread, taking one of its many volumes with him wherever he went. But he found it difficult to concentrate, and towards midnight found he was turning the pages without in the least comprehending the familiar words.

He put the book down and wrote with a troubled mind to the Texian chargé d'affaires at the Hague, who was an old friend from army days. He wrote that he had left Texas prosperous and Sam Houston well sound and hearty. 'But it is poor encouragement to know that this beautiful country, now of such high promise, may yet be merged within the national limits of another, and that the halo which encircles the heights of San Jacinto may be doomed to droop and wither and fade, and that Texas itself may be doomed to fill about half a page in the works of some future Gibbon of the Americas, and in a few more ages to be entirely lost in the mouldering ruins of extinguished nations.'

Terrell sealed the letter. One thing was clear in his mind. He was new to diplomacy, but was sure Aberdeen had been straight with him. He turned the day's conversation over and over in his mind and could see no other interpretation. Aberdeen had been straight with him. But someone at Washington-on-the-Brazos had been far from straight. He could not for the life of him think why.

32

Treason and
the Within Order

By the late January of 1845 Ashbel Smith was in New Orleans, near the end of his leisurely trip back to Texas. There, in the narrow streets of the French quarter, he was approached by a man whom he believed he recognised, though he could not remember from where or when. This person told him that if he cared to present himself at such and such an address he would hear something to the possible advantage of himself, and of his country and its friends. He knew the address given to him was on the same block as the house of the Mexican consul general. A time was suggested.

Smith kept the appointment. He was led through a narrow gate, across a secluded courtyard, through a passage connecting two houses, across another courtyard, and then up one storey into a large room whose windows were elaborately shaded against the weak winter sun. He did not know the figure who rose to shake him by the hand, nor did the man introduce himself. Smith, who had dealt with Mexicans before, kept his incognito too. They sat. In the shaded room Smith's eyes grew used to the dimness and gradually made out the features of the man opposite him. He had a splendid beard of shining black, and rings on the fingers of both hands. In impeccable French, and stepping with the greatest care between his words, he outlined to Smith the manner in which the Republic of Mexico might find itself able to come to an accommodation with Texas. He spoke in a manner which was almost detached, as if the matter were one of academic interest being discussed by two gentlemen, as they might have discussed the tooled leather bindings of the books Smith could see in the case behind his companion's

fine head. The gentleman did not refer to Texas straight out as the
Republic of Texas. But neither did he refer to it as a province, as
every Mexican had done in every previous communication. All things
were possible, he was saying, given good faith on both sides. It might
be that matters could be viewed in a different light now that those
two distinguished generals, General Antonio Lopez de Santa Anna
on the one hand, and Sam Houston on the other, were no longer
heads of their respective, ah, governments.

Dr Smith inclined his head gravely. It might be so. He had
heard in Memphis that Santa Anna had been deposed and was
now himself a captive in the fortress of Perote from which only his
merciful disposition, prompted by the dying wishes of his late wife,
had released the Texian prisoners. The two men – Smith and the
person who did not introduce himself as Mexican plenipotentiary or
hint that he had any kind of authority to pledge Mexico's word for
anything – sat obliquely, each in semi-profile to the other, discussing
hypothetical matters of state which were most real and which for ten
years had been the cause of sporadic bloody war between their two
peoples. This shaded discussion lasted three hours. What emerged was
that it was no longer inconceivable that Mexico might be induced
to recognise the independence of Texas. Shadowy words sketched
shadowy proposals.

The two gentlemen parted as they had met, neither revealing
his identity or making the slightest enquiry as to the other's.

When the last shadowy words had been spoken, each bowed to the
other. Smith was conducted across the two courtyards and out into
the light of the street by the same man who had earlier approached
him.

'My God,' said Smith, having emerged from that three hour
minuet of Latin diplomacy, 'all it needed was masks and we should
have had a masked ball.'

A passer-by looked at him strangely, and he realised he must
have spoken his thoughts aloud.

Back at the St Charles hotel, sitting over coffee and pondering
the matter again, it came to him clearly that what he had heard put
most subtly and deviously was the result of what Lord Aberdeen had

put to him plainly and bluntly when he called at Downing Street to take his leave back in early December. If Mexico were to decline to make peace, if she were to invade Texas, if there were to be any further incursions, and if for whatever reason or in whatever way this were to involve Mexico in war with the United States, whose troops would necessarily have to cross Texian soil with all the dangers to Texian independence that would bring, then Mexico could expect from England neither aid nor countenance. He remembered that phrase. As he saw it, the representations of the British minister in Mexico and the fall of Santa Anna had brought Mexico to the point where a minuet could be commenced. That is a dance in which each dancer must respond most strictly, and with the greatest elegance, to each movement of the other dancers.

At Galveston he was met by Sam Houston in the rooms he now kept at the Tremont, and that was no minuet.

They embraced.

'You have it in your pocket then, Smith?'

'Why, yes. I can't say it's the first thing that comes to my mind when I meet you again, General, after so long an absence. But yes. I have in my pocket Jones's offer of the post of secretary of state. And I suppose I shall take it. That was pretty well your doing?'

'Well, so it was. But the treaty, man? From London.'

Each looked at the other in amazement. In that moment Smith saw Sam Houston's face change. It was as if he had been struck a blow, though Smith had not yet said a word in reply.

'I have no treaty from London.'

'Then you left it to Terrell?'

Houston asked this question but already he saw in Smith's blank face that nothing had been done.

'Would England not stick to the terms she proposed? The terms of last July, man.'

'General Houston, I had no instructions. England would have stuck to those terms. It would have been done in a day. But I had no instructions.'

'I wrote, in my own hand, an order in plain words to complete a

treaty with England and France on the terms proposed. I gave it to
Jones myself. Put it in his hands.'

Smith said quietly, 'I received from Jones, towards the end of
November, a leave of absence to return home. Nothing else. Before
I left England I visited Lord Aberdeen, and wrote to Jones telling
him Britain was willing to act promptly. Just before Christmas, when
I had reached Boston, I wrote to Jones again, to emphasise what I
had said before and tell him where I was. In reply I received a note
telling me to take my time returning home. I had asked if I could
make a detour to visit my family in Connecticut and Tennessee. He
replied that nothing urgently required my presence in Texas. In New
Orleans I found another letter offering me the state department. That
is all.'

'You had no order from me?'

'Not a word.'

'Nothing from Jones conveying an order from me?'

'Nothing.'

Houston stood still a moment and then brought down his fist
on the mahogany table. He did this with such force that it jarred
him, and he put up a hand to that old wound in his shoulder. It
was throbbing now.

'Treason,' he said.

All evening the two men remained in that room, Smith piecing
events together while Houston paced up and down. Events fell into
place. Houston now knew why Jones, in his inaugural speech as
president, had bumbled on about jails, bridges, and petty economies
but said not one word on annexation. He understood why George
Terrell's departure had been delayed – something he had learned of
only by accident. Smith for his part told Houston about the minuet in
New Orleans. Mexico was fishing for terms. He told Houston why.
He talked about his journey south from Boston, how he had found
in Washington that many American senators still doubted if Polk could
assemble a majority for any new proposal of annexation, or whether
anything at all could be agreed. A dozen bills for annexation had been
brought forward, and their different proposers agreed on precious
little. McDuffie of Georgia had a bill. Benton of North Carolina

had a bill. Ingersoll, from which state Smith could not remember, had a wrecking amendment. And so on. They would never agree.

Houston would not be comforted. 'It was the *time*,' he said. 'The time was ripe. When I wrote that order it was the right time. The English treaty would have been received with joy and acclamation. D'you know, Smith, to myself I called it the Treaty of London. It was the time for it. Now there will be a struggle. Treason. Flat treason.'

'Then,' said Smith finally, 'I cannot become secretary of state in any administration of Jones's.'

It was this remark that sobered Houston from his rage.

'This is just the moment, Dr Smith, when you *must* become secretary of state.' The old fox was thinking politically again. That instinct reasserted itself. His first instinct had been to take Jones by the throat and shake him. But an evident split, a fight between Sam Houston and the man whom he had – though against his better judgment and for want of a better man – supported as his successor, would be exploited by those who wished to fly into the arms of the United States on any terms. They were now many, since American commissioners were already offering to bridge the Brazos, the Colorado, and the Trinity rivers, each at different points to satisfy different interests. Railroads were confidently touted. A road would be built from San Antonio to Houston, and from Houston to the gulf. Deeper channels would be dredged in Galveston harbour, to the great advantage of the shipping interest. All this besides the general scattering of promises. The laid-off, unpaid, and impoverished officers of the Texian navy would be commissioned in their present ranks into the navy of the United States. Five men already firmly believed they had the postmastership of Galveston safe in their grasp, once Galveston was a city of the Union. Houston knew one man who had bought a fine pair of carriage horses, and a carriage to go with them, so certain was he of that sinecure.

Well, Sam Houston was certain too. Smith must become secretary of state, dealing with England, France, and Mexico. Smith must become the central figure of the administration. Smith must discover, as quietly as he could, why that order had been disobeyed. Smith

must discover how far Jones had proceeded in any understanding
with the United States. Smith must be the eyes and ears of Sam
Houston. The two men sat up late, Houston drinking the first
whiskey he had tasted since he gave his word to Margaret. He
drank deep but remained stone cold sober, deadly in his hate of
Jones, but calm.

In the silence after the town clock struck eleven, Houston said:
'Jones has acted the serpent. Now we must scotch him.'

Before he went up to Washington-on-the-Brazos, Ashbel Smith spent
a day in Galveston unpacking the books he had brought from Europe.
He sorted the medical textbooks in English and French, the editions
of Virgil and Livy he had purchased in London, the novels he had
brought from Paris. He picked up his New Testament and read a
chapter of St Luke in the original Greek, but the familiar consolatory
words brought him no peace. He read again through the despatches
he had received from Anson Jones and found memory had not played
him false. There was Jones, as secretary of state the previous March,
saying how happy he was with Smith's conduct of affairs in Europe,
and that as long as the 'Old Chief' remained in office, or for as long
as he, Jones, had any control of the matter, Smith could remain as
long as he wished. Then there was the note recalling him, which
he now saw had been left undated. Then there was the note from
Washington-on-the-Brazos, dated December 21 last, just when
Smith would have been landing at Boston, saying Jones was happy
for him to spend some weeks with his relations on the way back,
there being 'no urgent cause' requiring his immediate presence. It
all amounted to a policy of omission and delay on Jones's part, and a
deliberate frustration of Houston's orders. But Smith was far from
clear in his own mind. He had never known Jones well, but they had
met as physicians and as members of Houston's first administration.
He and Jones were never likely to be close friends. Jones was a water
drinker. He was also, as Smith now recalled, one of those men who
had confidently predicted that Houston's second marriage would
never last six months. Jones was not a congenial man, but Smith

had never thought him dishonest. So it was in some turmoil of mind that he presented himself to the president's office on the Brazos.

Jones greeted him with as much warmth as he ever displayed.

'A pleasant voyage, I hope?'

'Rough. Seventeen days Liverpool to Boston. We were posted overdue. I became alarmed at one point when the master saw fit to assure us, when the ship was pitching into great troughs, that Samuel Cunard, whose steamer it was, had never in the history of his line lost a single passenger at sea.'

'But your family were well when you visited them?'

'My father well at Hartford, and my brother George, whom I hope I have settled in medical school in New York. And my brother Henry well in Memphis. But I now have a lively feeling I was wasting time dawdling back south as leisurely as I did.'

'How is that?'

'It is a feeling I have had since I met General Houston in Galveston.'

'We have not met since the inauguration. He is well?'

Jones's coolness astonished Smith.

'He was surprised – no, he was outraged – that I had not received an order which he gave you in September.'

Jones was not taken aback, not alarmed, not put out at all. In a matter of fact way, adjusting his spectacles, he said: 'I had for more than a year been vested with a free hand in the discharge of the executive. I was alarmed at his course when that order was given, and felt obliged to avoid a compliance with it. It was my duty.'

'But he did not know. You did not tell him?'

'I felt at liberty to take the course I did. I very much fear I have given mortal offence to General Houston by saving his administration. I must prepare for his revenge.'

Smith listened with dismay. He would have said as a physician that here in Jones was a man suffering from deep delusions. But that man was president.

He said: 'The order was to conclude the Diplomatic Act proposed by England?'

'Oh, just so. But you will remember that you wrote yourself, after your interview with Lord Aberdeen at the time, that it would amount to a perpetual treaty?'

'So I did. But that was one matter among many for you and General Houston to consider. Sam did consider. If you had passed on his order to close with the English offer, the negotiations would have been completed at a single sitting. The act could have been forwarded here as soon as the clerks had time to prepare copies.'

Jones said nothing.

Smith continued: 'It would have been done in a single sitting. Then both houses of the Texas Congress could have been convened, and they would have approved the treaty. I was not here at the time, but in the short while since my return, gentlemen of all persuasions have told me that an honourable treaty bringing peace – and this at a time when the prospects of annexation appeared hopeless – would have been received with shouts of joy.'

Jones listened calmly. 'This is men saying now what they would have done then. But they speak upon hypothesis. Hypothesis upon hypothesis. They would have done such and such *if* peace had been offered. But was it peace that was offered? And how can they know *any* offer was made? Only you and I know that.'

'And General Houston. And we all three know it was disobeyed.'

'I felt at liberty to suspend the order. General Houston was absent and could not have known the consequences of his order.'

'Absent? He put it into your hand.'

'And then departed to visit his precious Cherokees. He was mounted and ready to go. He dismounted to write the paper. He gave it to me, and then mounted again and rode off. It was an unconsidered order, which it was my duty to suspend. I had been in virtual charge of affairs, and you must remember I was to become president in two months' time.'

Smith's instinct was to throw his new commission as secretary of state in President Jones's face. But that would, as Sam Houston had said, reveal to the world that the Texian government was hopelessly split. All prospect of a treaty with England would go and with it all hope of independence. In the confusion, Texas would throw itself into the arms of the United States on any terms. It was, thought

Smith, his duty at least to get the best terms if annexation should be offered. More than that, it was still his duty to try to bring about an English and French treaty, particularly since Mexico was now at last ready to concede independence.

So he told Jones about the meeting in that shaded room in New Orleans.

Jones again listened with that unnatural calm of his.

'Perhaps,' he said, 'it was hardly fair of me to deprive you of the honour of negotiating a treaty in London, but the negotiation should take place here now, and you, as secretary of state, shall conduct it for Texas.'

Smith swore to himself that he would do just that. Then he bowed stiffly and left.

Jones stayed at his desk looking straight ahead. Then he took a paper from a drawer of his desk. It was Sam Houston's order of September, written in his own bold hand, directing Jones to accept the English and French terms. Jones did not read the order itself. He turned to the endorsement scrawled in his own spidery hand on the back:

> The within order cannot be obeyed for it would either defeat annexation altogether, or lead to a war between Europe and America. Besides it would directly complicate our relations with France and England, produce disturbances & revolutions at home and probably render it very difficult if not impossible for me to administer the government of Texas. General Houston has furnished no explanations of his motives for this course of policy. If they be to defeat annexation, produce a war, or break down my administration (about to commence) I cannot favour any of these objects & can conceive of no other.

He read these words slowly, convinced of the rightness of his own reasoning and of the probity of his action in suppressing the order. Now, he thought, he would have two birds in the hand. The first bird was annexation, if the United States should offer terms profitable to Texas. The second bird was independence, if Smith could negotiate that with the European powers and Mexico. Then he could choose.

He stayed at his desk for another half an hour, turning over in his mind the events of the last few weeks. On the whole, he had been right to pay as much as four hundred dollars for the Negress Mary. It was a large price, but she was young and strong, trained as a house-hand but also useful in the field when the cotton crop had to be got in. The yoke of oxen he had bought for forty dollars had been a distinct bargain. He and his wife were settling well into their new house at Barrington. And his trip to Independence to buy fruit trees had gone well. He was glad to say his affairs were flourishing. Then he noticed that he was still holding Sam Houston's order in his hand. He put it back in the drawer, telling himself he had been abundantly right to recall Smith. He was quite certain of it.

33

Bridal Dress
Tattered and Torn

In the United States Congress the proposers of different bills to annex Texas eloquently denounced one another. The more scrupulous demanded to know how the thing could be done at all by a resolution of both Houses, which needed a simple majority in each. This was what Congress was now attempting to do. The scrupulous asserted this was unlawful. If the unlawfulness were brushed aside, as there was every sign it might be, then the thing was still impossible in practice. Even suppose the House of Representatives passed the bill, would the Senate, which only the year before had voted two to one against? But the House did the impossible, and passed the bill. Then annexation was in the Senate, where, surely, it was safely dead. The bill before the Senate was promptly nicknamed Lazarus. The Senate was not expected to raise Lazarus from the dead. Then the bill was in Senate committee, which meant it was deader than Lazarus. The committee produced a report that took a week to plough through, and was reputed to have been read only by the printer's proof reader. Anyway, no one could understand it. Then the bill was miraculously on the floor of the House, but that would be an end to miracles because it would for a certainty be filibustered to death. There would be no end to the speeches, and no vote would ever be taken. But a vote was taken. By twenty-seven votes to twenty-five, the Senate passed the bill. Had one senator voted the other way, it would have been a tie and the bill would have been lost. The senator who did vote the other way was from Louisiana, a man who had often and vehemently declared that annexation was against his conscience. He changed his conscience. The vote came after a night sitting. 'The deed,' said the New York *Tribune*, 'was done in darkness, as was meet.'

Old John Quincy Adams, who had been president twenty years before, and was himself the son of a president, was incensed at the dark deed. He was a man who had negotiated Florida from Spain and warned Russia out of the Pacific northwest – a man, then, who had thoroughly supported expansion – but he damned the annexation of Texas as an apoplexy of the constitution. In extending the slave-holding parts of the Union, the bill was the first step towards a slaveocracy, towards the conquest of all Mexico, towards a maritime, colonising monarchy. Besides, by what possible constitutional authority could the United States annex to itself the territory of another sovereign nation? It had never been done before. Which clause of the constitution allowed it?

But legal or not, the bill existed. It needed the concurrence of the president. Tyler signed it three days before leaving office. It also needed the concurrence of the Republic of Texas. That was more problematical.

When, within a week, Polk came to office as the new president, he inherited all this – everything he had campaigned for. For the United States to enlarge its limits was, he said in a long, rolling speech, to extend the dominion of peace over additional territories and increasing millions. The title of numerous Indian tribes to vast tracts of country had been extinguished. New states had been admitted to the Union, and new territories created. Foreign powers should look on the American annexation of Texas not as the conquest of a nation seeking to extend her dominions by arms and violence, but as a peaceful acquisition by consent. No one could fail to see the danger to American safety and future peace if Texas remained an independent nation, or became an ally or dependency of some foreign nation more powerful than herself. Was there one American citizen who would not prefer perpetual peace with Texas to the occasional wars which so often occurred between bordering independent nations?

When Sam Houston, taking tea with Lucy in Galveston, was brought a newspaper report of this speech he was beside himself with anger.

'The pacific extinction of Indians? The danger of Texas independent? The dominion of peace? And I thought I knew Polk.'

'He is now the man who is president,' said Lucy. 'You did not know that man.' She remembered the quiet, unspeaking figure at the Hermitage, the man Donelson said was out to grass.

'And Texas to be engulfed by a mere resolution – by a majority of two, got at night – when the most trivial of treaties demands a two thirds majority in the Senate. Lucy, I have been at Washington, as congressman from Tennessee, when the settlement of some herring fishing squabble with Denmark failed because it could not command a two thirds majority in the American Senate. Herrings need a treaty. An agreement with any sovereign nation needs a treaty. Texas is a sovereign nation. Nothing can be done except by treaty. Nothing can purport to be done except by treaty. It shall not be done. I will not consider the principle of annexation because I will not have it, but I will damn the manner by which it is proposed to be carried out. And I damn this Will of the People that Polk chants on about. It is not the people's will. It is Polk's.'

'I saw the election at Plaquemines,' she said. They had often talked about the voyage of the riverboat *Planter* and that day's adventures.

'And that gave Polk the state. And he took New York in just such a subtle way. But that's not it, or it's not all. Will of the People, he says, but will for what? The American people have voted for annexation? Have they? Were all the Irishmen off the boat in New York, voting the Tammany ticket to damn their Whig bosses, hell bent on annexing Texas? Those men could not point out Texas north, south, east, or west. The people have spoken in the states? Have they? Even suppose you swallow the rigged votes, all those stuffed ballots, still only fifteen states voted for Polk. And since when are the states empowered to instruct the legislature? Not in my days on the Potomac. It is a nonsense.'

Lucy did not reply. What could she say?

'So,' said Houston, 'given all that, and even conceding, which no honest man will, that herrings rate a treaty and Texas doesn't, if Texas were to be dragged into the United States in such a fashion, her bridal dress would be the tattered and torn constitution of the United States.'

'Bridal dress,' said Lucy. 'When you wrote to General Jackson, the letter he read me at the Hermitage, you talked of Texas as a bride adorned for her espousal. Why is it always a matter of brides, espousals, wedding gowns? When men talk about nations, it is women they think of. Brides.'

'It is natural.'

'Why? Senator Kaufman – you did not like it when I danced with him before Christmas . . . '

'It was his principles I did not like.'

'Nor the dancing neither. He danced well. And he was talking – I hardly listened at the time but bits of it came to me later – he was talking about the consummation of a union between Texas and America. More bridals.'

'Kaufman is your annexationist *in excelsis*. He would think that.'

'It is not that. It is the *words* he uses. There would,' he said, 'be no force, no rapacity. I remember saying I was glad to hear it. I do not think he quite took my meaning.'

'It was my impression, watching the two of you, that you were understanding each other perfectly well. You tell me I did not like his dancing with you. Well, I admit it.'

'Admit what you please. I am glad you didn't like it. But he was going on about brides too. He said independence was not always a blessing. He meant not necessarily a blessing to Texas. Then he said dependence was frequently appropriate, beneficial, and comely. As in a woman, he meant. As in the dependence of a woman on a man. His entire metaphor was drawn from women.'

'And what did you say to that?'

'Nothing. Looked comely. Then he went on as if Texas and America were already one, and said what God had joined let no one put asunder. At any moment he would have been talking about one flesh.'

'And then?'

'Nothing. We sat down. He fetched me something to drink. You came over and he went away.'

'The man talks like a fool.'

'That is just what he is not, and you know it. That is the point, that he was not talking like a fool, just in the way men thinking of countries talk about brides. Bridal gowns, espousals, no force though, no rapacity, just comely submission.'

'I did not say that.'

'No. *You* said bridal dress tattered and torn.'

'Very well, so I did. They were words that came to me.'

She paused and turned away to the window. 'I remember when I first saw Dr Smith in Paris I caught a sight of his commission, which he had hung upon a wall, over his skull. His anatomical skull he had as a doctor.'

'I know that skull. I have lived in a tent with him and that skull for company.'

'Well, I looked at parts of his commission. You know, special trust was reposed in his Patriotism and Fidelity and Skill, and then it recited that he was to Have and to Hold all honours and perquisites due to his office. Have and to Hold. You see? More comely submission.'

'I see.'

'When you say bridal dress tattered and torn, you are saying Texas is *your* bride. That is it.'

'Lucy, it may be.'

She saw that he was tired. She went over to him where he sat, and put her hands on his shoulders. He let his head fall on to her breast.

She said, 'How is Dr Smith doing on the Brazos?'

'As well as any man could, with Jones and with Donelson.'

She had heard Donelson had been ill at Washington-on-the-Brazos. He had feared he might make the fourth American representative to die in Texas.

'Dr Smith,' said Houston, 'found himself playing physician to the plenipotentiary of the United States. And cured him, it seems. He's gone back to Nashville to recover. Smith has worked on Jones too. That fellow, having first rallied to the cause of annexation, or to some cause of his own whatever that was, is now a somewhat changed

man. Having read the terms of the American proposal, he has told
Saligny, and Saligny has told me, that America is being kind enough
to invite Texas to commit suicide. All public edifices, fortifications,
barracks, navy yards, ports, magazines, arms, armaments, and other
property pertaining to the defence of Texas to be handed over. It is
a ransom. And now, only now if you please, Jones calls it a suicide
demand.'

'Do you believe Saligny? Do you believe Dr Jones said that?'

'Why not? Jones will be busy seeing two sides to the question
now to save his skin.'

'So he may. I know very little about Dr Jones, but it does occur
to me that he may have had reason for wanting Saligny to believe
he is disenchanted with annexation. Dr Jones will not wish to fall
out with France, whatever he is really up to. Have you heard from
Captain Elliot?'

'Captain Elliot is a friend. Nowadays, since I am no longer the
executive, I do not see him. Since he returned he has been on the
Brazos and I have been here or at Huntsville. I hope he has been
working on Jones. I am sorry I do not see Elliot.'

She said, 'I hardly know the man. I have met him to talk to
once. Since he came back I have not seen him at all. I hope I
shall.'

'But as to Jones,' said Houston, 'I wish he'd thought of suicide
earlier. It would have saved a great deal. And even if he calls it
suicide now, he may find a way to shrug off that conviction. I will
not rely on the constancy of his judgment.'

Donelson, back in Nashville, was expressing much the same
opinion of President Jones. He wrote in a letter to Polk that
he considered Jones malleable and easily changed. 'Houston,' he
wrote, 'is the one to watch. He is now a private man, but he is the
power behind the throne, and greater than the throne.'

34

The Three Red Seals

The loungers on Galveston dock watched Captain Elliot and Count Saligny, and those two gentlemen watched the Gulf, strolling on the quays and often looking out to sea. They had been seen strolling there, together or apart, at frequent intervals in the previous few days.

'Unholy alliance, that,' said a longshoreman to his mates as they paused in their unloading of household chattels from another Bremen brig. She was the second to put in within fourteen days, carrying still more German immigrants.

England and France did make an uneven pair. Elliot was tall and spare. Saligny was shorter and more active, a man who liked his food and whose temperament was much the more volatile. When they conversed Elliot stood very still and Saligny seemed to dance round him. What they had in common was orders from their governments to work together. London and Paris had not said precisely in what manner. For this they awaited further orders. They knew despatches would not be entrusted to the American mail, but would come by a British or French vessel. So they watched.

Elliot, who was scanning the horizon with a telescope he had possessed since he was a midshipman, picked up the sail first. He identified the vessel and then handed the glass to Saligny, indicating the direction.

'A pretty corvette,' said Saligny.

'Sloop,' said Elliot. She was Her Majesty's ship *Electra*, twenty guns, a week out of Kingston, Jamaica. She took four hours to work into Galveston under topsails. Her captain, a young commander,

came ashore with the orders himself, one package with the seal of
Downing Street for Elliot, another with that of the Quai d'Orsay
for Saligny.

The three men went to Saligny's quarters, which were the
more comfortable. The two diplomatists read their orders, and
then compared them. The French orders were more elegantly put,
and longer. The substance was identical. The naval officer stood to
one side. The *Electra* was his first command and, in those days of
peace, he knew he'd been lucky to get that. He was awed by his
mission and by Elliot, whom he knew to have been plenipotentiary
in China and who was also – something much more important in
the young officer's eyes – a post captain in the Royal Navy and a
senior one at that.

'Let us,' suggested Elliot when he had digested the orders,
'take a celebratory glass of wine at the Tremont.'

Saligny's astonishment showed. Elliot had never made such a
proposal before. The Tremont was conspicuous. Both he and
Elliot were well enough known, but there was no point in courting
unnecessary attention by *showing* themselves together, and surely not
in the company of a British naval officer in uniform.

'The Tremont is perhaps somewhat public?' said Saligny.

'Oh?' said Elliot. 'But the wine is good.' And the three of
them walked there, seen by the whole town. It was the end of the
afternoon, and the Tremont was filling up as it always did at that
time. Captain Elliot exchanged casual greetings with the editor of
the *Civilian*, and then took a table in the open foyer and ordered a
bottle of a decent red Bordeaux. He proposed a toast to the *Electra*,
which was lying splendidly in full view – a lovely, trim man o'war,
exciting the admiration of even the most patriotic American seamen
who saw her. There was something of a competition, in those years
on the America station, as to which vessels were the more impeccably
turned out, the British ships from the Kingston squadrons or the
occasional United States men o'war. The British vessels outnumbered the Americans by more than ten to one, even in those waters,
but on both sides there was a wary respect for the seamanship of the
other. The honours were generally admitted to be about even.

'What ships did you see from Kingston?' asked Elliot. The commander of the *Electra* named American and German merchantmen.

'Yes? Any American men o'war?'

Saligny was caught with his glass poised half way to his lips. Really, Elliot was abandoning all prudence.

The English commander looked Elliot straight in the eye. Elliot returned the look with innocent blue eyes, making it clear to the young man that he required a reply.

'The *America*, sir.'

Now the *America*, though an old ship, was a powerful frigate of great beauty, and with her fifty guns was a match for any frigate ever built.

'Saw her once off Curacao,' said Elliot. 'Beautiful thing.'

All this was heard by anyone who cared to listen.

'Shall you stay at Galveston long?' asked Elliot, knowing perfectly well that the young officer had orders to wait as long as he was required to wait and sail wherever Elliot required him to sail. 'Because if you designed to stay in these waters for a week or so longer before sailing north, I should be much obliged to you for a passage to Charleston, in South Carolina.'

The commander of the *Electra* murmured that he was intending to cruise off Galveston. His ship was newly commissioned, the crew newly signed on at Kingston, and many of them pretty raw. So he had planned to exercise their gunnery in the gulf, tracking back and forth along the coast until they knew it like the backs of their hands. He would be in sight of Galveston for at least a week, and would be happy to accommodate Captain Elliot when he proceeded to Charleston.

'Much obliged,' said Elliot. 'My wife is there. I have promised a visit. She will thank you for bringing us together rather more quickly than I could have contrived by steamboat to New Orleans and then pot-luck onwards. Last year it took me an unconscionable time.'

On the quay the commander saluted, and climbed down into his ship's boat, whose immaculate crew were poised with oars held vertical while the coxswain stood erect in best blues and white wideawake hat. It was all too spic and span, too Britannic, and a few of the hangers on laughed aloud.

'Go it then, the Milliner's men,' shouted one sailor from a scruffy Texian brig. Queen Victoria was known as the Milliner on account of her taste in hats. The *Electra*'s boat shoved off and rowed impeccably back to the sloop. The Royal Navy and Her Britannic Majesty's chargé d'affaires had between them put on such a show that no one in the town could have failed to see or hear of it.

Back at the door of Saligny's lodgings, Elliot said, 'Well, shall we say a dawn start tomorrow, Count?'

'Sunup,' replied Saligny, whose English had been perfected in the American-speaking parts of the world. He turned away, feeling he had to say to himself that he had never, before this afternoon, seen his English counterpart act in such an indiscreet and ill-advised manner.

Their orders were simple. Her Britannic Majesty and His Majesty the king of the French being strongly impressed with the importance of establishing and preserving a lasting peace between the Republics of Texas and Mexico and with the establishment and preservation of Texas as an independent nation, their said Majesties authorised their respective chargés d'affaires to use their best exertions to this end. The two European powers would spare no appropriate measure to induce Mexico to recognise Texas, and this should be presented by the respective chargés d'affaires to the Texian government as a conclusive reason to renounce forever the idea of annexation. In other words a simple deal would be done. Texas would renounce annexation and Mexico in return would recognise the independence of its past province. To propitiate Mexican ideas of honour the approach would be made by Texas, assisted in every way by England and France. In this manner the European powers would preserve the independence of Texas, which they had long wanted, and Mexico would be saved from the prospect of the United States as an immediate neighbour.

That was the purpose. How to bring all this to fruition was left to the ingenuity of Elliot and Saligny.

'If we do not bring something off,' said Saligny, 'then Texas is done for.'

Elliot grunted. They certainly had little time. Since those orders had been sent off on their long Atlantic passage, the American Congress had made its unexpected offer to Texas. This was known all over Texas from the newspapers, but no formal offer had yet reached Galveston or Washington-on-the-Brazos. Whatever Elliot and Saligny did, they had to do quickly. If they reached the capital before the American offer, then they could bargain for time in which to obtain for the Texian government a Mexican admission of Texian sovereignty. Then Texas could stand on her own two feet.

On their two days' journey to Washington-on-the-Brazos, the two men discussed this endlessly. Or rather Saligny talked endlessly and Elliot answered laconically, but their strategies were much the same. Provided they could reach the capital first, and provided Jones would give them time, what was above all important was that the Texian Congress should not be recalled. Because the Congress was almost to a man in favour of annexation and would very likely take the American proposals as they stood.

As Saligny repeatedly said, no restraint could be expected from the Congress. Its members were elected annually by universal suffrage, and were therefore practised demagogues. They would run with the fashion, and the fashion was annexation. They were men of no substance with little to lose and everything to gain by the dissolution of their country. Here Saligny emphasised again the great number of congressmen with worthless Texian stock which could only appreciate on annexation. And, he said, many of them were scoundrels anyway, who embarked on political careers because they could make fortunes in no other way. The better and more intelligent men did not seek election.

Elliot agreed with much of this but did not like to hear it put so coarsely.

'The question,' said Saligny, as their horses struggled through wet ditches, 'is how.'

'If President Jones will accept our good offices, then I shall

myself go to the City of Mexico to obtain the Mexican consent
to their part of the bargain.'

'But, Captain, will you not be off to Charleston? Your wife?'

'That,' said Elliot, 'is what Galveston is quite convinced of.'

When they rode into Washington in mid afternoon on the second
day, filthy and exhausted, Jones was not there. Ashbel Smith was.
He listened, hearing recited to him the essence of the Diplomatic
Act proposed by Aberdeen nine months before. That was in Downing
Street. Now he was in a shack, and the act had been frustrated by
Jones, the very man Elliot and Saligny now had to convince.

'The president is ill,' said Smith, but he sent word to him at
his new house at Barrington. Then, during the long evening, while
they waited, he told them that the country, wherever he had seen
it, was hot for annexation. He was not sanguine.

Next morning Jones came to town running a fever. Then what passed was surprising. The bitterness that Jones had shown to Houston
over the past year, a bitterness so deep that it looked half demented,
was only between him and Houston. They brought out the worst in
each other. But Jones and Smith had always been civil, and now they
found they had common ground. Neither wanted an unconsidered
handover to the United States. Both wanted to approach Mexico.
Neither liked the terms proposed by the United States. Texas was
to hand over everything but remain responsible for its old national
debt? Jones went so far as to call this humbug. And then there was
Captain Elliot. He had been much closer to Houston than ever he
was to Jones. He would have said he hardly knew Jones. But Anson
Jones, when Mrs Jones had eighteen months before borne him a
second son, had proposed to name the child Charles Elliot Jones,
and wrote to Elliot telling him so. The surprised Elliot had replied
that it would surely be better to call the child Anson Elliot Jones,
giving him at least one of his father's names, but Jones had insisted.
He was strange about his children's names. He had christened his
first son Samuel Houston Jones, which he now regretted.

So there it was. Jones respected Elliot. He listened while Elliot
and Saligny told him what they knew from their governments –
that Mexico showed every sign of being willing, and that their

governments would use all good offices with the new Mexican government, with all fresh force. This chimed in with what Smith knew from his shadowy meeting in New Orleans. So Jones was willing to approach Mexico through the representatives of England and France. Jones was willing to agree that, if Mexico should concede Texian independence, Texas on her part would assure Mexico that she would never annex herself to the United States. The European powers were offering their mediation. Jones could accept that. Neither Elliot nor Saligny pointed out that the word *guarantee* was no longer used, their governments having felt it unnecessary to go so far, not wishing in the present delicate situation to provoke the United States and reasoning that once Mexico had accepted Texian independence, no guarantee would be needed. The omission was not noticed.

Then came the matter of the Congress. That was nearly the sticking point. But Jones agreed at last that for a period of ninety days his government would enter upon no negotiations in the matter of annexation.

'There is your breathing space,' he said.

'Time for even Mexico to bring itself to agree?' said Smith.

Elliot and Saligny assented.

The Texian cabinet was twice consulted. Next morning, on their third day at Washington, Elliot and Saligny went for their final meeting with Anson Jones and Ashbel Smith.

Jones spoke. 'I have to ask you, Captain Elliot, if you would yourself undertake the journey to the City of Mexico to present this proposal to the government there. This is something that needs more than a courier.'

Elliot, who had been screwing himself up to offer that service, promptly agreed. He then asked if he could make a suggestion. He had heard that Mr Terrell's nomination as chargé d'affaires to England had not been approved by the congress which had lately dispersed, and that consequently he would be recalled. Jones said that was true. Then, asked Elliot, could he suggest – and this would of course depend upon Mr Smith as well – that Ashbel Smith should return to Europe. He was well known and liked, and if the Mexican treaty should turn out as they wished, then it would be essential for Texas to have an experienced representative in London and Paris. Jones glanced at Smith, who assented, and the appointment was made.

At one o'clock they signed the document to be taken to Mexico. Smith unfolded the parchment and laid it open flat on the table. Across the full width of it he signed first, as secretary of state, for Texas; then Saligny for France; then Elliot for England. Then each impressed his seal. Smith held it up to dry. The three red seals marched left to right across the instrument which, if all went well, would secure the independent future of the Texian republic.

So it was that Anson Jones, who had frustrated an alliance with England the year before, now set in train Elliot's mission to Mexico. And it was Ashbel Smith, whose previous efforts had been frustrated, who now insisted on the agreement of them all to a separate memorandum in which he set out that if, whatever happened in Mexico, the people of Texas should in the end prefer annexation, then the government of Texas, without any breach of faith, should be at liberty to consummate the national will so expressed.

The signing was at one. At two o'clock Elliot and Saligny rode out of Washington on the road back to Houston. At six o'clock they encountered a man riding in the opposite direction. It was Donelson, whom Polk had sent back to Texas with the formal American offer. He had come by steamboat from New Orleans to Galveston.

'When will Congress be convened?' he asked.

'It has not yet been called, I believe,' said Elliot.

'Where is General Houston?'

Both Elliot and Saligny replied that they had not met him since Anson Jones became president.

The three diplomatists parted with civilities.

'That's dished him,' said Saligny.

He and Elliot rode on towards Houston and then Galveston, making the best time they could on the appalling road. Donelson pressed on the ten miles to Washington, arriving in the dark. Smith was affable, but regretted that he was about to go on leave and that the president was down with a fever. He said Mr Allen would be taking over the state department for the time being. Donelson swore. Ebenezer Allen was a firm opponent of annexation. Nevertheless he sought Mr Allen out, only to learn that he too had gone on leave. The secretary of the treasury had also gone off on urgent business to his property on the Red River. No one knew where Sam Houston was.

Donelson swore again. 'Hide and seek.'

During the negotiations at Washington, Houston had been at Ashbel Smith's estate opposite Galveston island, near the shores of the Gulf. The grand house Smith wished to erect on his land was still only a plan, but there was an existing frame house, stables, and kitchen. It was a prudent place for Houston to stay when, though he might be the power behind the throne, he had no wish to make any public statement. Above all he had no wish to meet Donelson. Donelson would want assurances. Donelson, passing through Galveston on his way to Houston city and then the Brazos, and bringing confident news of annexation, had spoken openly of Sam Houston as a likely candidate for president of the United States not just one day, but in 1848. It was true that Mr Polk had only just taken office but, said Donelson, he was set on being a one-term president. Polk had work to do, he would do it, and then he would stand down. Donelson carefully put it about that Sam Houston was firm for annexation. Then why, he was asked, didn't old Sam speak up. Because, Donelson said wisely, Houston was now a private man, who wished to let Jones speak first. But if Jones did not speak soon, then let them be assured Sam would. Donelson had stayed in Galveston only two hours before he set off north for the capital, but he used his time well.

A day after Elliot and Saligny returned to Galveston, Smith came too. To everyone who asked he replied that No, he regretted that he had not seen Donelson, though their paths must have crossed. No doubt Donelson would by now have sought out President Jones. He was repeating such assurances to a group of ardent questioners when Lucy appeared on the steps of the Tremont. They had not met since

Paris. She saw a man who had aged since then. He was as slim as
ever, and his hazel eyes were as alert as she remembered them, but
his face bore lines it had not had, and there was some grey in his
chestnut hair. He saw a woman who was freer than she had been. As
she entered from the street alone, she swept off her wide brimmed
hat and shook out her hair. It was a gesture that would have been
impossible to her in Paris.

Smith embraced her, kissing her on both cheeks. It was the
custom of Paris, but a salutation not often seen in Galveston.

'You have become American,' he said, indicating with a sweep
of his hand the sweep of hers with which she had removed her
hat.

'Ah. I would not see such things in myself. You are right.'

'And cotton, Lady Lucy?' He touched the wide skirt of her dress.

'Cotton. Should I wear silk in such a climate? They say silk
is cool. It is not. And you, in Europe, you have seen great things?'

'Courts. If courts are great things.'

'And Godoy?' She remembered the day they had seen that
extraordinary old man.

'Still Prince of Peace, still gazing in shop windows on the
boulevards, still asking after you. He did the week before I left.
But you must tell me about your own adventures. I've been told
you have at least met General Houston, whose signature you met
in Paris.' Smith had heard of Houston's teas with Lucy.

'The signature is like the man, or the man like the signature.
You were right.'

Ashbel Smith was anxious to convey to the passers-by at the
Tremont that he was a man with nothing pressing on his mind.
He was delighted to meet Lucy for herself, and also glad to be
seen publicly in leisurely conversation with her. He remarked
that she was alone and unattended. She told him about her two
American calamities, the loss of her two maids. 'Now,' she said,
'I have learned to put up my own hair, and how to shake it
out.'

Would she, asked Smith, care to visit his small house, where
she would also, at the moment, find General Houston? She let her

face show nothing but a smile. They fixed on the afternoon of the following day.

The evening before that, *Eurydice* came in sight – a British frigate out of Vera Cruz with despatches from Mexico for Elliot and Saligny. She waited until first light before putting in to Galveston, and there was a sight for the town.

'The British are coming,' yelled one man, and the onlookers burst into gales of laughter. But there *Eurydice* was, a handsome frigate of thirty-four guns, and she was putting a boat ashore. And out in the bay cruised *Electra*. It was another show, though the frigate captain, being himself post captain, made a more modest show of it and sent his first lieutenant. This time neither Elliot nor Saligny went to greet the officer who stepped ashore. He was shown to Elliot's quarters. The chargé d'affaires read the papers, which conveyed nothing unexpected. Her Britannic Majesty's minister in Mexico wrote reassuringly of the new government's apparent willingness to conciliate England and France. The lieutenant, seeing Elliot's hands tremble as he read, asked after a while if he were not ill. 'Nothing,' said Elliot.

But when Ashbel Smith took Lucy to meet Sam Houston that afternoon, he carried the news that it was more than nothing. It was the old China fever, more moderate this time than it had been in New Orleans the year before, but still the same old fever, probably brought on by the fatigues of that long ride to Washington.

'He will be able to sail?' asked Houston.

'It is suggested,' said Smith, 'that Saligny should go instead.'

'That is Elliot's suggestion?' Houston asked unbelievingly.

'No, he insists he will be carried on board if need be. It is Saligny who insists he will go himself.'

'Never on my life.'

Lucy listened to this exchange. She did not know what Elliot had proposed to do. She did not know what Saligny now proposed to take upon himself. She did know she would have entrusted Saligny with nothing of any consequence.

'Lady Lucy,' said Houston, 'Captain Elliot is to go to Mexico to negotiate a treaty.' He did not tell her what treaty.

'I see.'

'Would you entrust Saligny with that negotiation?'

'General Houston, you have just exclaimed that it would be over your dead body, so you cannot need my opinion.'

'All the same?'

'Well then, my father would not have trusted Saligny with the care of an avenue of elms. Or the planting of a clump of firs.

'No,' said Houston. 'So Captain Elliot must go.'

'You are cavalier with the man's life,' said Lucy. 'Is that an easy passage? Would he not certainly be better at home in his bed?'

'He is a sailor. That is his profession. The ship has a surgeon.'

'I am glad you are so solicitous of him.'

Smith stood aside and watched this exchange. He knew what Houston wanted, and knew that unless Lucy were a woman of quite remarkable spirit she would do it. Houston got his own way where his political interests were at stake. Smith had seen it before. He did not always like this streak in his old friend.

Houston said, 'Captain Elliot is set on going.'

'As you, I see, are also set on it.'

'He is set on going. Will you go with him?'

'What for? What could I do?'

'You are his countrywoman.'

'If he proposes to take one of the British ships in the bay, then all the officers are his countrymen, for what that matters. Will a fever take that into account?'

'You are a woman and would comfort him. He would get well the sooner for that.'

Smith, who knew Houston of old, heard him in those last few words talking like an Indian. Lucy heard the same thing, heard it and knew it for what it was. Hers was a shorter but much more direct knowledge than Ashbel Smith's. She knew the Indian in Houston better than any other man or woman.

'You are saying,' she said, 'that Captain Elliot would not be lonely? Something of that sort?'

Sam Houston avoided her eyes. He nodded his head.

'So be it,' she said, and Smith, listening, and seeing Houston get his own way, could have sworn it was Lucy Moncreiffe who had imposed her will upon Sam Houston.

35

The Man in the
White Hat

Next morning *Eurydice* slid out of Galveston harbour with no ceremony, watched longingly by a group of Texian sailors and two long-stranded and unpaid lieutenants of the Texian navy who now had no ships of their own that were in any state to put to sea. Three of the English frigate's officers had come ashore the day before, had met the Texians in the Tremont, and commiserated with them. Officers in the Royal Navy lived from one ship to the next. *Eurydice* was a new commission so they were safe for a year or so, but after that there was the ever present fear of no other ship to go to, and of long months spent ashore in Jamaica on half pay. So they felt for their Texian counterparts who had no ship and no pay at all, and the Texians, watching the frigate sail, longed to be aboard her bound for Vera Cruz, to which port she was returning.

In the afternoon these same Texians watched *Electra* work in. They saw Captain Elliot, in a shaky state, helped into her boat and then, out in the channel, helped on board the sloop. The boat then returned for the Englishwoman and her trunk. So she was off to the north too? The Texian lieutenants knew Lucy. She had been in that party attacked by bandits the year before, by the gang dressed as Indians. One of their own colleagues had died in the affair. They knew her and liked her, and waved her off. She waved back. So there was Elliot going off on leave to see his wife in Charleston, and Lucy perhaps bound there too, or on her way home. They watched *Electra* ease out of harbour bound for the north, and continued to watch her until she was hull down over the horizon.

Out of sight of land, just before sunset, *Eurydice* and *Electra* made their rendezvous. Captain Elliot and Lucy were transferred from *Electra* to the frigate. The seas were light, but it was not an easy passage between the two men o'war. A lady was not expected to climb, and Captain Elliot was too weak. Each was swung up the frigate's side in a boatswain's chair. *Eurydice* with her new passengers continued south, for Vera Cruz. *Electra* sailed east. She would speak any vessel she encountered, making sure her passage east and north would be well noticed.

On board *Eurydice* the officers asked no questions. Her captain had plain orders from Jamaica to do whatever was required of him. He turned the first lieutenant out of his quarters and gave them to the lady. He shared his own great cabin with Elliot, who was delirious for much of the time. *Eurydice*'s surgeon reassured his captain. It was nothing that would infect the men. It was an intermittent swamp fever. Captain Elliot had suffered from it before. He would recover, though a man's health could take only so much of this relapsing and recovering.

'Damned tropics,' said the surgeon.

'Damned China,' said Lucy.

It was a passage of eight days, and not difficult. Lucy was some use to Elliot. He had consented surprisingly easily to Smith's suggestion that she should accompany him, though his state had been such that she had doubted if he fully knew what he was doing. He was in the surgeon's care and that of the surgeon's mate, but he took a little food from her when he would take none from them, and in his coherent intervals he talked with her, mostly about his wife whom he would not now see for some time, and once about the paper with the seals that he carried with him. She knew what it was. He had told her once before, on the first day out, though in his fever he had forgotten that. Smith had told her too. The only other person who knew was the ship's captain. In the case of Captain Elliot's death the paper was to be got somehow to the British minister in Mexico.

The officers entertained her, but left her alone when they saw she would prefer that. On the last evening before they were due to sight Santa Cruz she was gazing out to sea from the quarter deck.

The young officer of the watch stood apart. Then the captain came
on deck and she moved to the windward side, giving the captain the
lee side of his own quarter deck as one of his own officers would
have done. He came across to her. How did she know this piece
of seagoing etiquette? She had naval connections?

'My husband was a sailor, Captain. The China station. He
instructed me about ships, before we married.'

'You were on board, ma'am?' This was asked in surprise. The
wives of junior officers were not usually suffered on board queen's
ships.

'No. He instructed me with ships' models. And he talked, oh he
talked a great deal, about the voyages he made. But I have never
been on board a man o'war before.'

The captain did not press her. Lucy stared out to sea again.
This passage brought back to her the memory of her husband and
their short marriage. He had walked on quarter decks such as this.
Why had she come? For Richard's memory, certainly. Because Captain
Elliot was a member of the same service. Because he had been on
the same station with her husband. Because he had written to her
sympathetically about her husband's death. Because she might con-
ceivably be able to help him. She had instantly understood General
Houston's conviction that somehow the presence of a woman might
help the spirit of a man recover itself. It was one of his Indian ideas.
Others derided them. She did not. She had felt the force of them.
She had come for the memory of her husband, for Captain Elliot,
for Ashbel Smith even, because he had wished it too, but most of
all for Sam Houston. She did not delude herself, and knew she had
come most of all for him. For his sake she was on her way to a
country her uncle Aberdeen had warned her not to go to. 'Lucy,
Lucy, think. Yellow fever often, bloody flux always, roguery and
bandits everywhere, and fifteen revolutions in the last twenty years.'

By the time they were in sight of land Captain Elliot was
no longer delirious. He was coherent, able to walk, and insisting
they should go on. He did not now want Lucy, and was privately
amazed he should have consented to her coming in the first
place. He did not want to put her at danger in Mexico. He

also did not see what on earth she could do. He put this mildly to her.

She said: 'I am here. A woman and a man travelling together are less conspicuous than a man alone.'

Elliot saw the sense of this. He also saw there was no leaving her behind without raising questions he did not want to raise in the mind of *Eurydice*'s captain. If Captain Elliot and the woman did not go on together, why should she have come at all? So Elliot agreed she should continue, but they would take one of the ship's lieutenants with them as well.

'*Two* men and a woman,' she said. 'Very well.'

They found a broken down carriage and a broken down horse. Vera Cruz saw two men, one young and fresh, one older and a bit ravaged, and both in mufti, set off with a young woman in a cotton dress who was carrying a parasol. It was a journey of three days to the city of Mexico. They looked unlikely prey for bandits, but that was only to English eyes. On the second day they were languidly stopped. The two men were relieved of their silver watches, a few sovereigns, and a pistol they wisely did not attempt to use. Lucy's silk purse was taken, the only thing of silk she had about her. The thieves required Elliot to hand over his white hat, examined it, tossed it about, laughed at it, and gave it back as not worth having. Then they languidly waved their victims on. The chief bandit spoke a few words of parting.

'What did he say?' asked Lucy.

'Go with God,' said Elliot.

Next day in Mexico City they were cheerfully received by Mr Bankhead, Her Britannic Majesty's minister.

'That road?' he said. 'A constant scene of robbery and murder.'

Elliot, who seemed to have survived both the journey and the banditry well, took off his spurned white hat and observed that on the way to the legation they had been obliged to pick their way round piles of rubble, even in the main square.

'An earthquake a week ago,' said Bankhead. 'Few dead. But there are some who take it as a sign that they should not after all invade the United States. After it was known that the American

Congress resolved to annex Texas, some regiments of the Mexican
army resolved on their part to march on the District of Columbia
and burn the capitol. This sort of thing has been resolved on before
in Santa Anna's days. Anyway, the earthquake has unresolved them.
Not that they could pay an army. They could not pay a platoon. There
is not a dollar in the treasury to pay them.'

'And no money to clear the rubble,' said Elliot.

'That won't take money. Much of it's already gone. The rest will be
gone in another week. The scavengers will do it, when they summon
up the energy. Stone to build houses with is not easily come by. So
chunks that have fallen off palaces will be carted off on the backs of
donkeys. Our trouble is that the hills of Congress have been badly
damaged. The Senate is undecided whether it would be proper to
permit Congress to meet in the Senate chamber.'

'A matter of punctilio?' asked Elliot.

'Pride and punctilio. But until they meet somewhere, they can
consider nothing, and that is what touches us, because they must
meet to consider your proposal.'

Strategy was then considered. Cuevas, the foreign minister, had
made it known indirectly – as indirectly as the Mexican plenipotentiary had to Smith at New Orleans – that an approach would not be
rebuffed. But it was important that the *iniciativa* should come, and
be seen to come, from Texas. Bankhead thought the tone of the
agreement sealed on the Brazos was satisfactory. The reality was
nothing of the sort, but Mexico must be able to see herself as the
parent country and Texas must seem to present what was virtually
a petition – though that petition happened to be supported by the
power of England and France and, in his indirect way, by Cuevas
himself.

The next day both Bankhead and Elliot presented the document
with the three seals to Cuevas. Bankhead remarked that he did not
need to tell Señor Cuevas that the great advantage of such a treaty
to Mexico would lie in interposing between herself and the United
States a strong barrier in the form of an independent Texas. Elliot
observed that England was now commending to Mexico an action
similar to that taken by England herself when in 1783 she had

recognised the independence of her thirteen American colonies.

Then they withdrew. 'The treaty will be signed,' said Bankhead. 'When?' asked Elliot.

Bankhead shrugged. It was with the Congress now, who had at last found somewhere to meet. 'It is also important,' he said, 'that we allow these *valientes* to talk a little about *patriotismo*.'

After the first meeting with Cuevas, the negotiations were left to Bankhead alone, this being the protocol. Elliot had presented the petition in person, which was proper. Now it was proper that he should withdraw. He could not even leave the legation. Her Britannic Majesty's chargé d'affaires to Texas could not be seen wandering round Mexico City. So he remained in the legation while Lucy, escorted by the lieutenant from *Eurydice*, walked amazed round the tremendous cathedral and the Palacio Nacional. Not since Paris had she seen such grandeur.

'Where have you been?' Elliot would ask.

And she replied, 'Where Montezuma was.'

Three times Cuevas told Bankhead, 'Tomorrow. It will be decided tomorrow.'

But what the Congress decided was that it had a duty to examine the history of the whole affair. The debates ranged as far back as the conduct of the Duke of Alva in the Low Countries.

'That,' said Bankhead, takes them back to the sixteenth century. 'And the duke's conduct was atrocious. Sixty men hanged from each tree.'

'I suppose,' said Elliot, 'they see that as going to establish Spanish title to Mexico and therefore to Texas.'

'As to Texas,' said Lucy, 'if they are going to consider the title to Texas they had perhaps better take into account Godoy's title.' And she told the story of his asserting that title to her one spring day in Paris.

Then for the fourth time Cuevas said, 'Tomorrow.'

At dinner that night Bankhead entertained them with his account of the downfall of Santa Anna at the end of the previous year. 'At three o'clock in the afternoon an alarm was given, and the palace gates were closed. That is normal. There are always alarms. Then

there was a bustle, which is also normal, but then the flat roof of the
palace was occupied by troops. Now *that* is not normal. That is the
usual preliminary to a revolution. So from then on we took notice.
A few insurgents were killed. Then the grenadiers, some sort of a
guard, turned out, and we knew it had to be a revolution. The guard
rarely gets itself together. Then it was quiet, which is another bad
sign. Then the president tried to escape, and they kidnapped him.
That is how it goes.'

Elliot did not join in the laughter. He waited, and then said in a
strained voice, 'Bankhead, Cuevas says tomorrow. When is tomorrow?'

It was three weeks since they had arrived. The fallen stones
from the earthquake had long before been carted off on donkeys.
Lucy had watched Elliot. At first he had recovered. Then the strain
of waiting irked him. His demand, 'When is tomorrow?' was the first
time she had seen him lose his usual coolness.

'Tomorrow,' said Bankhead, 'is *mañana*. But I am sure it will
come.'

When Elliot had retired to his bed she took Bankhead aside,
and told him that unless Captain Elliot had somewhere to rest,
and soon, he would very likely relapse into fever.

Bankhead saw her grave face. 'I believe you. You must forgive
me if you will. In this place one becomes used to *mañana*. One also
has to delude oneself with a certain jollity or one would go mad. It
does not always succeed that well. So I am sorry for that wretched
tale about the revolution.'

'Fifteen in twenty years, I've been told.'

'I've seen several. But you see, this Texian business will take
time here. These people feel it deeply. It was their province. A few
foreigners there seized the country, seized a large part of Mexican
territory, captured their president – I mean Santa Anna, years ago
– and then if you please let their president go. That rubbed salt
in the wound, as if they could do what they wanted at will. Then
they established a new country. On top of that they succeeded in
persuading England and France to recognise that new country. The
people are a proud lot here, and all that loss of territory and loss of
face is fearfully trying. D'you see?'

'I do see that, and so I dare say does Captain Elliot. But all the same...'

'Yes. It should not take more than, say, another week to finish this business. But I'll give you and Captain Elliot an escort to a place I have stayed myself. It's a convent in the mountains. It will be better.'

Elliot consented. The place Bankhead had in mind was on the way back to Vera Cruz. As soon as he had a decision from the Congress and the Senate he would send it on by the lieutenant from *Eurydice*. No time would be lost. So next day Lucy and Elliot, together with an escort of three men, started the journey to Jalapa, an old Aztec village where the air was clear and good and, at more than four thousand feet above sea level, cool and congenial to a European.

Back in Texas, meanwhile, Donelson had done his level best to find Houston, and Houston had eluded him. When he found no one at Washington-on-the-Brazos, Donelson wrote from that empty capital to the general saying all Houston's old friends – Jackson and Polk among them – looked to him for support. All he asked was that Houston should not commit himself: if he could not approve, at least let him say nothing against annexation. 'I say again, do not commit yourself.'

Four days later Houston replied that the United States seemed not to be sufficiently impressed with the importance of Texas. The subject was too vast to speak of in haste. The present excitement would calm down. Three days later he was writing again, telling Donelson that but for the rains they would have met and embraced, but that he could not get to Washington for another two weeks. But, as he saw it, annexation was undoubtedly more important to the United States than to Texas.

The excitement did not calm down. At a public meeting in the city of Houston the call was for annexation. One Senator Lawrence, who was strong for independence, rose to persuade his audience of the error of their ways. He was an eloquent man but that night had also drunk too eloquently. He rose, surveyed the hall, swayed, and then fell flat on his face. 'Gentlemen,' said the chairman, 'the senator has the floor.' The vote was for annexation.

Then, when Donelson pressed him again, Sam Houston wrote a thundering letter. He would not even glance at the principle of annexation, but he would say the terms were not such as could properly be proposed by one sovereign nation to another. Texas must have a say in these terms, and not be expected to pay a tribute to the United States for leave to surrender her independence. She would not be driven into servile submission, and pay a price for that humiliation. For Texas to submit on such terms would not only destroy her own future prospects but also convulse the Union. For the sake of liberty, and for the sake of the future tranquillity of the United States, annexation should be effected only by treaty. He had to confess he had not been free from embarrassment in writing as he did. He had felt so deeply for his venerated and highly valued friend General Jackson that nothing but the most sacred regard for Texas could have induced him (Houston) to write as he had. But General Jackson was so absorbed in his desire for annexation that he had, very naturally, not been fully able to regard Texas as a separate country with interests not entirely identical to those of the United States.

Still Donelson could not find Houston. Houston would not be found.

At Jalapa, Elliot slept for two days. When he woke at last, the sisters of the convent called Lucy to him.

'Is there news from Bankhead?' She said there was not, but told him to be easy. It would come.

'It is difficult for me to be easy. This is something of my doing, or rather something I did not do.'

'How can that be?'

'You will not know,' he said, 'that there was just such an offer made last year, an offer from Downing Street to Texas and Mexico.'

She said nothing.

'And I was not at my post. I was not in Texas. I was in Virginia, in the mountains, and was not back for another three months after that offer came. Had I been in Texas I believe I could have conveyed the acceptance of Texas. It would have been done. Things would not have come to their present pass.'

'You had a fever last year, as you have this. I saw it. At New Orleans, remember? You must not think of it.'

'But I do. When we met at New Orleans I had already written to Lord Aberdeen saying I hoped for a post in Europe, or in a milder climate. I was not in Texas when I might have been. Perhaps I should have returned earlier than I did. I have asked myself whether I did my duty.'

She said: 'Lord Aberdeen must think you did, or he would have recalled you.'

'But the question is one I still ask myself, and the conclusion I come to reflects no credit on me.'

'If you choose to believe that I cannot stop you, but on the other hand some might say you are now doing rather more than your duty.'

He waved that away.

They were together for three days at Jalapa. He recovered his strength gradually, and did not talk about his duty again. They sat in the gardens in the sun, she carrying her parasol and he wearing his floppy white hat. The height and the breezes made Jalapa cool. The sun warmed them but was not oppressively hot as it soon would be at Galveston.

Then a fine rain came. They sat on a covered, overhanging balcony. Beneath them they saw the red tiled roofs of the ancient city, and around them the five mountains of Jalapa. Shrubs blossomed everywhere. They drank excellent coffee.

'Cortez was here,' said Elliot. 'Three hundred years ago the Spanish silver fleets came from Cadiz to Vera Cruz, and took out their treasure through this town, on this road.'

Lucy held her hand over the side of the balcony to feel the fine rain upon it.

'*Chipi chipi*,' said the sister who had brought them coffee. That was the name for the rain.

'It is so fine it is almost English rain,' said Lucy.

'Scottish rain,' said Elliot, 'almost a mist. You are a Scot, Lady Lucy, and so am I. You cannot hear it in my voice. I have hardly lived there since I was a boy, but I am a Scot. An ancestress of mine wrote that lament for the Scots killed by the English at Flodden field. The Flowers of the Forest, she called them. The flowers of the forest had all gone away.'

'Jean Elliot?'

'She.'

It was among the most famous of Scottish ballads.

Elliot's anxiety had left him for the moment. They talked easily of this and that, and then about their passage on *Eurydice*.

She said, 'The officers appeared in some awe of you.'

He smiled. 'What they cannot know is that, oh, over any diplomatic post I might ever be offered, I would prefer the command of a frigate like her. I am a sailor.'

'Could you not have a frigate?'

'It would not do for the navy. As a boy I was in the Mediterranean, then on the Africa station, then the East Indies, then the West Indies. Then flag lieutenant to the admiral at Portsmouth. So that is a lucky run. Then I had command of a schooner out of Jamaica. Then I was made post, and from then on my employment has been settled for me by Downing Street rather than the Admiralty. So a frigate – impossible. But I did once have a schooner – *Renegade*.'

'You had a fleet in China, Captain Elliot.'

He looked out over the five mountains.

Lucy said: 'When you thought we had missed each other, and might not meet again, you wrote me a letter I received in Galveston. That was kind. But, forgive me, I think there may be more, something you did not tell me. How did my husband die?'

He said at last, 'I remember that it was on the queen's birthday, because we fired royal salutes before we went up river. That was May the twenty-fourth. Canton was there for the taking, but those who say that do not understand that it is a vast city. Take it and fly the Union flag over the city, they said. They might as well say, take Paris, or at least take a city as vast as Paris. What was the use of Canton? It would have cost ten thousand deaths on their side, and a thousand on ours. All that in order to fly a flag, when all we wanted was the trade, and a murky trade at that? I would not do it. We had burned all their junks, but we had to make another display of force, so that they could withdraw without too much loss of pride. Chinese pride is less flamboyant than Mexican pride, but just as tenacious. So we had to make a few forays. We sent boarding parties, to take an island here, to hold part of the shoreline in another place. Moncreiffe led one of the skirmishing parties.'

He paused. She waited.

'I sent him on that foray. He went on my orders.'

'You told me that when you wrote, Captain Elliot. But others also went on your orders, and the captain of his ship wrote to me at the time saying Richard volunteered to go.'

'He did. And he died an honourable death in the face of the enemy.'

'I still feel, and you must tell me if I am mistaken, that there is more to it than that.'

'I beg you to consider this: would it help if there were more?'

He said this gently, but her reply was fierce.

'Yes yes yes. How could I ask you if it would not? Why should I ask you if it would not? Richard was my beloved husband. We knew each other in every way – heart and mind and body and soul. It was all a wanting to *know*. And there is still a desire to know. That remains. That is why.'

So Elliot told her. 'It was a gate on the right bank of the Pearl river. There was a sort of customs post by the gate, and three cannon by the customs house. It commanded that bend of the river. Moncreiffe had been in China a week. He did not know the country. He went with a warrant officer who did, a man by the name of Groce. They went upstream in a cutter which was in charge of a major from an Indian regiment. Moncreiffe took a boat from this cutter and landed with ten men and the warrant officer. There were some Chinese soldiers with rifles on a bank behind the post,

a dozen men. The major later told me they were standing there
fanning themselves. Moncreiffe landed, and then Groce saw what it
was about. Half a dozen women were kneeling before the customs
post, by the cannon. Groce called to Moncreiffe to come back.
There were only the women. The Chinese soldiers made no move,
and Groce had seen the cannon were for ceremony, firing blanks.
They saluted any passing ship that carried a mandarin. So there on
the bank it was nothing but ceremony, and Groce knew what that
ceremony was going to be. He called Moncreiffe back. The major
in the cutter saw too, and ordered Moncreiffe and his party back.
It was very clear. The others obeyed. Moncreiffe waved, just waved,
and went on. Then the women drew out their knives. It was a ritual
suicide. We had it again later at Shanghai. Moncreiffe ran at them to
stop them.'

Elliot paused.

'And then,' said Lucy quietly, 'the soldiers shot him?'

Elliot waited. Then he slowly nodded.

'That evening the truce was arranged. The Chinese withdrew
their army from Canton. We saw a mandarin at the customs post. He
signalled to us. Moncreiffe's body was laid out on the water's edge,
and we sent a boat to bring it in. It was wound up in a yellow robe,
which is worn only by a prince, and on the feet were the purple satin
shoes of a high mandarin.'

'Thank you,' she said

Elliot had told her all he could bring himself to tell her. Now
she knew. He had not told her that the Chinese soldiers had done
nothing. He had not told her that when Moncreiffe tried to save the
women, one of them struck at him with her knife, in the throat, and
then, like all the rest, killed herself.

Next day *Eurydice*'s lieutenant reached Jalapa carrying the Mexican
act recognising the formal independence of Texas. The Congress
had at last conceded the province, the Senate had approved, Cuevas
had signed, and it was done. Texas could stand on her own feet. All
that remained was for Elliot to get the treaty back to Washington-on-
the-Brazos. Time pressed.

36

Europe versus Liberty

Elliot returned from Vera Cruz to Galveston in the French brig-of-war *La Perouse*. All the world believed he was in Charleston, and he hoped that by returning in a French ship he would in any case escape all notice. He did not. He was first alarmed when he saw no fewer than four American naval craft lying in the bay. Then the Galveston pilot steamer came out to greet the brig, and circled her. Two of the steamer's crew let out a derisive yell.

'What is it they say?' asked Elliot, who was sitting under an awning with Lucy.

She said, 'It sounds like "White Hat."'

So it was. He was still wearing the hat. The pilot boat was expecting Elliot, and looking for him. All pretence was now useless. There was now no point in rowing to an obscure jetty as Elliot had planned. He landed at the town quay, where he was greeted by more laughter and more cries of 'White Hat.' As soon as they were on dry land they learned that Elliot had been seen in Vera Cruz, and that the perfidious adventures of the Man in the White Hat had been reported almost two weeks before in the New Orleans newspapers. The *Picayune* congratulated him on having by his subterfuge confirmed the worst suspicions of England, and on having achieved more than any other man to ensure annexation. It was suggested he should plead idiocy in his defence.

He did not answer the taunts. Lucy took his arm and they walked through the crowd to the Tremont. He had done much more than his duty, not to mention much exceeding his orders, he had achieved the diplomatic coup of his life, and now it was all come to this.

'What will you do?' she asked.

'Go on to Washington-on-the-Brazos. The opinion of a quayside mob is not likely to be that of the Texian government.'

She hoped it might not be, but she saw that Elliot's face was grey.

He delivered the treaty. Jones immediately published it, proclaiming independence from Mexico. 'Now,' he said, 'my country is for the first time at peace with ALL the world.'

'And the Congress?' asked Elliot.

Jones replied that he had kept his promise as far as he could. There would be no action on annexation by his government until three months from the date of their meeting on the Brazos. But as president he was the agent of the people, and had been obliged to call Congress to meet in ten days' time. He would put to it both the new treaty with Mexico and the American proposal of annexation. There would be a choice, and the Congress would have to make it.

'Captain Elliot, you bring me peace with no conditions. I have published it. Peace with all the world. There are some who urge the opposite upon me. One of the American agents is a Commodore Stockton. His squadron lies on Galveston Bay.'

'I saw it.'

'He came to me. He told me there were also United States troops on our eastern borders. He suggested moving on Mexico. I told him No. I would not manufacture a war for Mr Polk.'

Elliot could think of only one man who could sway the course of events now. Like Donelson, he asked for General Houston. 'I don't know,' said Jones. 'He don't know himself where he is on annexation. So he is nowhere, unless he has taken to a tree.'

Elliot, who did not know it was Jones who had frustrated the diplomatic act of the year before, shook hands with the president, and left for Galveston again.

Lucy had remained at the Tremont, expecting to be sought out by Sam Houston, and expecting to see Ashbel Smith. Neither came. She learned from a waiter that Smith had left four weeks earlier for New Orleans and then, the rumour had it, for England.

'Now, ma'am,' said the waiter, 'if you ask me, that's for sure, since as he boarded the steamer they asked him what he was about, and he told them straight out, it was to fetch more English gold.'

She could hear Dr Smith's ironic reply, but talk of English gold was now again everywhere. *Electra* had brought gold. *Eurydice* had brought gold. *La Perouse*, since she had brought the Englishman in the white hat, was part of an Anglo-French plot, and she had brought a cargo of gold as well.

So it was not Houston and not Smith who sought Lucy out, but the Prince of Solms. He was returning to Germany and came to say his farewells.

'I see many Germans, Prince. So your immigration has thrived?'

'Tolerably. Many have come. They are good people. But there will be annexation. I made my representations to the English secretary of state, but there came no reply. There will be annexation.'

'You cannot be sure of that.'

'No? I can see what I can see. And hear what is said. Do you know Senator Kaufman?'

'I have danced with him. We met at President Jones's inaugural ball.'

'He danced well?'

'He did.'

'He speaks well. He has spoken and written often enough, and always against me.'

'I am sorry. I had not heard of it.'

'He speaks against the German immigration. He says they are honest, industrious men that come. He is right. But the greater the capacity of the men I bring, the greater is his fear. He says that so many Europeans will subvert what he calls the pure principles of republicanism. He says they will bring with them European ideas of subordination. From there he goes on to argue against a sovereign Texas, saying any country so influenced by such immigrants would produce the most disastrous consequences on its neighbour the United States.'

'The United States can look after itself, I'd say.'

'He has dark forebodings of irritations and heartburnings, and the end of republican liberties. He fears the establishment of a nobility. He fears the power of the church. I think he fears there will be counts of Galveston and dukes of Brazos. He sees treason in harmoniums. So, it will be annexation, and I shall go. It is a good country, but I shall no longer send so many.'

'He did dance well.'

'Ah, Lady Lucy, that brings to mind a woman who came to me two days ago asking for you. I did not then know you had returned. She was in some distress. She had been once your maid, I think.'

'Helga?'

'Helga Becker, the same.'

Helga was indeed in distress. She and Kurt Neumann had come back to Galveston set on marrying. But now Kurt would not have her because of tales that she went to Houston that night in the Cherokee camp. She came and poured out her story to Lucy at the Tremont.

'Seeing the Indians made so much of me, because of my hair. I tell Kurt it was because of my hair I was made much of, and was so much noticed. The Indians said my hair was smiled on by the sun or some such thing, and it is true I was proud. And it was because of my hair they wanted me to put the comb into the Indian's hair after the game, the one that ran fastest. I did that because General Houston asked me, and I loved to do it because he spoke to me and asked me, and took my hand and showed me how, but that was all. I am not sorry for doing what I did. I wish it had not been all, but it was all. That was before the storm. But Kurt will not believe me and says there is more to it. And someone has said they saw me come away from the general that morning, after the storm, and go back into your tent . . .'

Lucy looked at the girl who stood before her.

'I never said anything, ma'am, not a word, not to anyone. It is the Frenchman who says he saw me, the old guide who was with us. My Kurt hates General Houston. Kurt was in the fort at Perote and he hates the general for that. Now he won't have me for it. And I didn't go to the general.'

The girl was in tears.

'No, you did not.'

Lucy saw it all, the Frenchman, before dawn in the camp, in the quarter-light, had seen a woman leave Sam Houston's tent, a woman with a blanket over her head, and had assumed it was Helga.

'I never said anything ma'am. No one would credit what I said, even if I did. But I wouldn't.'

'Helga, I believe you would not.'

'And. . . there *was* a time I was with the general, once, when I was new in the country, here at the Tremont. It was only once but I never forgot it. There were songs, and I poured him wine, and he made much of me. And then I took him water because he was thirsty. And I went to him later because he wanted me. He never said, but I saw it, and he had me and made much of me. And then, later on, when I came to you as maid, I could not know. . .'

'No.'

'It was good being with you, ma'am. And the first time you ever spoke to me was outside in the street, when I was watching, and men were burning that straw man that was meant to be General Houston, and I was thinking of him then and remembering him. When I came to you it was good being with you, but after the Indian camp it was sometimes hard being with you. The general would not know me any more. He crossed to the other side of the street once when we met, and it was only a word I wanted. Because he had me, and made much of me, and I thought of him so. But I always thought of Kurt too, and now he will not take me. And that is hard, because it was not so at the Indian camp.'

Lucy stood up. 'I know. Will you bring Kurt to see me?'

When Helga did bring him, Lucy asked him to sit, which he declined to do.

'Mr Neumann, Helga has told me what you think, and I wish to assure you it is not true.'

'But you are a friend of old Sam's, and you *would* assure me, wouldn't you?'

'I am a friend of General Houston. That is true. And you are not, and I know why not. I am saying nothing about General Houston, one way or the other, and why would you want me to?

What's that to the point? I am telling you about Helga, and I shall
do it. I know because we shared a tent that night, and she did not
leave it.'

'Not while you were asleep?'

'There was no sleep. It was a storm the like of which I've
never seen or felt, or Helga. We were terrified, both of us, and
sodden wet, and we clung to each other stark under a blanket
and shivered ourselves warm.'

Kurt was almost convinced. A lady would not talk in this way
unless it were to prove a truth. He saw Lucy before him in a lawn
dress on a silk sofa, and then saw her stark, sodden, and shivering.
Her portrayal of herself in that way was so unthinkable that he was
sure it must be the truth.

But he was a strong-minded man. To survive Perote unscathed a
man had to be. So he said, 'But a man said he saw a woman going
back to the tent.'

'Yes, Mr Neumann. At dawn. The Frenchman? He saw *me*.
There are reasons why a woman leaves a tent at dawn and then
returns to it, sodden though she may be after the night's storm, and
still shivering with it. And even if she is next to General Houston's
tent.' Kurt Neumann retreated in confusion, offering apologies to
Lucy. Helga kissed her and went to Kurt. That was the last time
Lucy saw them.

The cry of English gold was all over town again. The English
mail steamers from Portsmouth to Jamaica were reported to be armed
cruisers, and to be that moment skulking in the Gulf. English plans
were revealed to send steamers up as far as Memphis to bombard
that city. Groups gathered on Galveston quay to read the *Picayune*,
newly arrived from New Orleans, which declared that Texas would
be the battlefield of Europe versus Liberty. The war would decide
whether America was to be ruled by the American people or by the
crowned heads of Europe. But the people would baffle any sceptre
raised in menace. If there was to be war, the sooner the better.
Anson Jones turned on Houston in his absence, saying Old Sam
had always lived and acted solely for his own political advantage,
and possessed to perfection the art of appropriating to himself all

the proper actions of his associates and of shifting on to them all the odium of his own bad deeds. This did not help Jones, who was seen as a tool of the British, and who was now in his turn burned in effigy in a Galveston which was already confidently celebrating its annexation to the American Union.

In the chaos, Elliot became less sanguine, but still hoped and still wanted to trust Houston. 'He knows his own people thoroughly, and when he seems to be running with them, he probably senses that opposition now would only provoke them. So he waits. He is skilful in delay.'

Lucy, to whom this opinion was addressed, said nothing.

It was Saligny who brought them the news that Houston had been seen in New Orleans, where he had stopped on his way to the deathbed of General Jackson at Nashville.

'He takes his infant son with him,' said Saligny, 'so that he may be blessed by the dying hand of the Sage of the Hermitage. I take this consolation, Lady Lucy, that when the Sage takes his leave of this earthly existence, Sam Houston will at last be shot of his influence and at last able to pursue a course of his own. But he must die quickly, or it is all up with Texas.'

That night, although Galveston did not know it for another ten days, Houston reached the Hermitage to find that Andrew Jackson had died three hours before.

With that news in the future, Lucy left Elliot and Saligny and walked from the Tremont one block to the seafront, along a street decked with American flags. Sam Houston had gone to General Jackson and taken his son to be blessed. Very well. But he had gone while Lucy was still in Mexico, on a journey he had implored her to undertake, which she had undertaken for his sake, and he had gone without leaving the slightest word for her. She dropped her head for an instant, and then lifted it and stared fiercely out into the Gulf of Mexico, whose dark waters were lit by the fireworks and rockets of the rejoicing crowds. And she damned Sam Houston.

37

The Peace of the World

'Write to Captain Elliot,' said Lord Aberdeen, 'that we approve of the course he took.' Addington, standing at Aberdeen's elbow in the foreign secretary's room in Downing Street had just watched him read twice through the despatches from Texas. In his experience, stretching back over more than thirty years, British diplomatic agents abroad were told their course was approved only when there had been some grave doubt if they had acted properly at all.

'Tell Captain Elliot, rather, that I approve of the energy which he showed in prosecuting our Texian policy. That is the least I can say.'

'Yes, sir.'

'Add that it would in my opinion have been better for him not to go in person, and better not to have gone secretly, and better not to have misled people into thinking he was off to Charleston, because all that was likely to give rise to a false interpretation of our motives and intentions. As it has done.'

'I think,' said Addington, 'that openness in this case would have defeated everything, since the whole object was to secure a treaty with Mexico before an American howl could be raised against the very idea of such a treaty. The treaty had by its nature to be confidential, and in this matter where is the line between confidentiality and secrecy?'

'Quite. That is why I tell him that we approve what he did. Write to Elliot as I have suggested, but put things perhaps less abruptly than I did.'

The fact was that Her Britannic Majesty's Texian policy was

in tatters. The Mexican treaty obtained with so much difficulty had been rejected out of hand by the Texian Senate. In the end Elliot had expected this. He had come to see that the whole climate had changed while he was away in Mexico. He had faced the wreck of his China policy and now he faced the wreck of all he had worked for in Texas. But of Charles Elliot and Anson Jones, Jones was the more distraught. He had expected to the last that Senate would at least use the Mexican treaty as a bargaining counter, saying to the United States that the terms of annexation offered were not generous, that the Mexican treaty on the other hand was there for the taking, and in this way forcing better terms from Polk. Simply, Jones asked, let the Mexican treaty lie on the table. Let it lie there so that we may pick it up again if we should wish to. The Senate would not do this, but threw the treaty back. The whole Texian Congress then took the American terms, gulping them down whole without negotiation. Jones was vilified, burned again in effigy, and left with the knowledge that he had brought himself to this pass through his loathing for Houston, and that within a few months there would be no country left for him to be president of.

The news had come to Downing Street that morning. Addington had rarely seen his master so affected. Having received his instructions in the matter of the Elliot letter, he waited. Lord Aberdeen said nothing more. Addington had his hand on the doorknob, on his way to the clerks, when Aberdeen stopped him.

'Can you call to mind *any* precedent, ancient or modern, of a sovereign state voluntarily merging its sovereignty in that of a larger sovereign state?'

Addington could not.

'Nor I. It does amount, does it not, to that retail invasion I so feared? You will remember that Mr McNeil, a friend of mine from university days, once wrote to me that America stole entire provinces as a cuckoo steals a nest. Americans settled whole territories, without title, and then took them. Retail invasion was his phrase. A very just phrase it now seems.'

Addington did not remember Mr McNeil, but did recall the phrase, which Aberdeen had adopted as his own.

'I thought,' said Aberdeen, 'that the peace of the north American continent materially depended on Texas remaining independent, and therefore the peace of the world. I still do think that. This aggrandisement of the United States will not contribute to their strength in any way I can think of. And now it has gained this new momentum, this lust for territory will not stop here.'

'I doubt, sir, if there are any real American ambitions for Canada.'

'For Canada? No. No more than we have our eyes on Cuba, as some of our American friends firmly believe. But that belief in itself demonstrates an American way of thinking. To be prepared even to contemplate Cuba, we should have to put out of our minds the small impediment that Cuba is a province of Spain. And suppose that we were, monstrously, prepared to put aside that small scruple, what use would Cuba be to us when we already have Jamaica? No. But think of the vast amount of English capital engaged in the United States. *That* is something to the matter. That touches our interests. If the United States country tears itself apart, what then? More to the point for the moment, what chance do you now give Mexico of remaining intact?'

'None, sir. A few years at best.'

'None. But Mexico's the least of it. What of the United States themselves? This aggrandisement – I have no other word for it – this aggrandisement they're hell bent on seems to me to place their internal peace in great danger. What use is an ever greater Union when every increase in territory brings with it an ever greater diminution in real unity? Think of the Roman Empire. What did Britain as a province, and Memphis on the Nile, and Rome itself – what real interest did they have in common? As much, I'd say, as Massachusetts in New England, and Memphis on the Mississippi, and now Galveston in Texas have in common. And Rome fell apart. The United States will have Mexico in ten years. There will be an attack, by force or fraud, upon California. The United States is vaster than Rome already, and Rome fell.'

'*The Times*,' said Addington, 'is putting it another way, saying that what we see in the United States is democracy run riot, and that it is a renewal of the French revolution, on another continent and in abler hands.'

'I wish *The Times* itself were in abler hands. It is not what it was. What is to be expected of an editor still in his twenties? What does the French revolution mean to him?'

Addington knew what it meant to Lord Aberdeen. His parents had died young, and as a boy Aberdeen had been brought up by two guardians, one of whom had been the younger Pitt, who was prime minister throughout the French revolution.

So Addington said he supposed the French revolution meant little to the present editor of *The Times*.

'Very little, Addington. But in this he may have a point — though he goes too far.'

'I am sorry for Elliot, sir.'

'I am sorry for Texas. What possesses men to think that the dignity and prosperity of their nation will be better served by their becoming one twenty-fifth part of a continental mélange. How many states has the United States?'

'I think twenty-seven.'

'One twenty-seventh part, then, or one twenty-eighth if this means Texas makes the twenty-eighth. What leads men to abandon the command of their own affairs, and all privilege? Does the State of Texas, as a one twenty-eighth part, imagine it will be as much considered at the courts of Europe as it has been used to? I am sorry for Smith, and for that man Terrell.'

'He was ill in Paris, sir. Several feet of snow and the coldest February for fifty years.'

'I am sorry for him. I am sorry for Texas. But most of all I fear for the United States. I see the Tiber flowing with much blood. The French revolution in another continent? I hope that foreboding is excessive. *The Times* is given to excess these days. But where's Lucy?'

'Captain Elliot did mention that she was in Galveston.'

'I saw that.'

'And would be returning.'

'I shall be glad of that.'

'He mentioned also that General Houston was believed to be
in Tennessee.'

'Yes. But do the movements of General Houston any longer
concern us?'

They did not. But before then, in Tennessee, having attended the
grand funeral of Andrew Jackson, and knowing that the Texas
Congress would accept terms of annexation that he would not even
glance at, Sam Houston recited darkly to himself:

> *The little dogs and all,*
> *Tray, Blanch, and Sweetheart, see, they bark at me.*

But he had kept his silence, and found that when annexation
was voted for by the Texian Congress, those in the United States
who had sought his endorsement and never got it still wanted Sam
Houston in their camp, because his name would give credit to the
whole proceedings. Donelson whom he had avoided, Donelson to
whom he had refused to speak, Donelson to whom he had written
that Texas would not be driven into servile submission and that for
her to enter on the terms offered would convulse the Union, that
same Donelson now wrote to friendly newspaper editors asking
them to put the best construction on the Mexican treaty, to take
care to connect General Houston with annexation, and to see that
his enemies did him no injury. 'There was no harm,' Donelson
assured the editors, 'in his wishing better terms for Texas, provided
you show that he was in favour of the measure in the abstract. You
may rely on my doing him justice, and not forgetting the testimony
borne by General Jackson to his motives.'

In this way Houston was done justice. President Polk himself,
anxious to hold the Democratic party together, expressed an earnest
desire that Sam Houston might become a senator for the new state
when Texas entered the Union at the end of the year.

In Galveston, Captain Elliot at first spoke a little bitterly about
unreflecting masses of people whooped up and made drunk with
senseless projects of aggrandisement, but to Lucy, as they both

waited to take passage to New Orleans, he spoke for the most part philosophically.

'I am not sure,' he said, 'that there is much difference in the end between the despotism of a capricious Asiatic emperor and the despotism of a multitude in possession of uncontrolled power.'

'Is it not far fetched,' she asked, 'this comparison between China and Texas? I take it you mean China?'

'I do. Oh, it would be far fetched if I were to make any wide comparison, but I do so only in this particular. You see, at Canton I dealt with mandarins and commissioners who were men who knew the interests of the province and the city, and moreover could see the fleet in the Pearl river, and these men were wise, reasonable. They were wise, and conscientiously agreed courses which were acceptable to both sides. But they were always overriden by the caprice of the emperor in Peking, who knew nothing of Canton and cared only for the preservation of a God-given omnipotence which was long gone. So these mandarins had a choice between a complete violation of their conscience and a complete loss of political prospect. There of course they would have lost their heads to the executioner. Here it is the same except that no heads roll. The power of the multitude here is just as arbitrary. President Jones had to fall in with annexation in the end or he would have been impeached. General Houston, being the abler politician, first said nothing and then left the country, because in the end he saw that to oppose the tyranny of the multitude would deprive him of all future prospects. There you have a despotic emperor, here a despotic multitude lashed into a condition of ever recurring excitement by eager rivals for their votes.'

It did appear that Houston had said nothing, but then the New Orleans newspapers reaching Galveston reported him as having made a speech in Louisiana, on the way to Nashville. In this he said that he had coquetted a little with Great Britain in order to make the United States as jealous of that power as he could, and in that way get better terms from America.

Lucy was angry. Sam Houston had implored her to accompany Captain Elliot to Mexico as part of a piece of coquetry? And having

used her as his coquette, he had abandoned her, leaving not a word
for her? She said nothing, but Elliot saw her anger. He was himself
sad. He had thought of Houston as a friend.

'When you were talking about mandarins,' she said, indicating the
newspaper report they had both read, 'you spoke of their complete
violation of conscience. Would you call this a violation of conscience
on the part of General Houston?'

Elliot considered. 'If the report is true,' he said, 'and we do
not know that it is, then he has a great deal to answer for.'

Next day Lucy took the steamboat from Galveston to New
Orleans on the first leg of her passage home. On deck she watched
the low coastline of Galveston island disappear, the last of Texas.

38

The Toga and the Torque

On a day in the early fall, Lucy and Mrs Alexander Hamilton Treaze laughed at their reflections in one of the famous great mirrors at the St Charles Hotel in New Orleans.

'Do you remember when we first came here?' said Mrs Treaze. 'And the ship's pilot told us about these mirrors, and said they were the largest in Christendom? And *how* he laughed, and it wasn't till later we knew why he laughed.'

'They were,' said Lucy, 'the largest sheets of looking glass I'd ever seen. I'd never seen three sides of myself at once, in any state. Let alone in all states.'

'There was a lady three months ago, from Boston, whose husband came down the first morning after they arrived and insisted on curtains being hung over all the mirrors. For his wife's modesty, he said. So the management hung the curtains. Then the story of the poor woman insisting on curtains was all over the city, and she was laughed at for that, which insulted her modesty further.'

'Did she insist,' asked Lucy, 'or was it her husband, he being from Boston?'

'I never knew, but the poor woman was laughed at all over the city, and after the third day they moved out to the old St Louis, which is more proper.'

'Poor creature,' said Lucy, but she and her visitor were laughing again. 'But I feel for her. You know, whenever I caught sight of myself in one of those mirrors, that first time, I heard the laugh of that man who told us about them.'

'And him picturing to himself the sight that presented itself to

you? Very likely he did. It's a harmless thing in a man. Anyhow, the
rooms where curtains were demanded, they've kept the curtains in
that set of rooms, and now they're known as the Boston rooms, and
in great demand. The curtains are red plush and hung so they can
be drawn, or opened, or not drawn or open, but draped half open
to arrange the view to order. The manager says that set of rooms
is in great demand, and for what he calls all the right reasons, not
Boston reasons at all. My Alexander knows him, and the man says
he aims to fix up other rooms the same way.'

Lucy's visitor was her former maid Jeannie, who had married
Mr Treaze of the Colt revolvers.

'Business has done well,' she told Lucy, 'and Alexander says
now there's bound to be war with Mexico and business will be
even better. But I've said what I want to do is open a shop here in
New Orleans – muslins, organdies, French lawns, Italian lustrings,
satins, lacings. Alexander sees the call for that too, and says he will
do it now he has the capital. He calls it our emporium.'

'You would do well with it, Jeannie.'

'Having dressed you, ma'am, I think I would. And I could
always say I had connections with Baudin's of Paris.'

Lucy smiled. 'So you could.' Jeannie's connection with Baudin's
of Paris was that she had accompanied Lucy there on two occasions
to be fitted for dresses. It was to that couturier she had slipped off
early one morning – a morning which now seemed long ago – to
bring back a dozen pairs of stockings in white Chantilly lace, the
day Lucy put her grey ghosts away.

So business had gone well with Jeannie, and so had her marriage.
She told Lucy so.

Lucy knew. 'One glance is enough to show me that, or to
show anyone, I'd say. But then I always knew things would go
well.'

'You did, ma'am?'

'Dear Jeannie, yes. How can I forget it? I was late back one
night, and you were not here but down in the courtyard with your
man, and my window was open.'

'Ma'am, I did not think . . . '

'You were intent on other things.'

'Lord, how I was too.'

And they laughed again. Before Jeannie's marriage they had been together for ten years. Jeannie had known her as a young girl, a young wife, and a young widow. They had discovered the new world together, made the grand tour of the spirit together, shared the terrible day at Shoal City, and in short knew each other as intimately as two women could.

Lucy was within a few days of returning to Scotland. Jeannie, seeing her name in a passenger list in the *Picayune*, had come to say her farewells, bringing with her the parting gift of a lace shawl, one of the delicate things she wanted to deal in at her emporium. The talk about mirrors had begun when Lucy was draping the shawl round her shoulders and admiring the reflection, seen from three directions.

Then Lucy took a purple and green peacock silk scarf of her own, a beautiful thing familiar to Jeannie for years, and gave it to her as a keepsake. It was Jeannie's turn to admire her triple reflection.

There was a knock at the door. One of the hotel servants brought a letter. Lucy glanced at it, opened the seal, read the first line, and then tossed it crumpled on to a side table. Jeannie, still standing and holding the peacock scarf against her, could not help noticing the bold inscription on the letter. Neither could she help seeing that the letter, as Lucy tossed it away, landed next to another which bore the same inscription and the same seal.

She recognised the unmistakable handwriting. She remembered Sam Houston as the man from whose side, and without a word to him, she had taken the exhausted Lucy after the funeral at Shoal City. She had not seen him since, but Sam Houston was now the toast of New Orleans as the man who against all odds and against all British plots had safely brought Texas into the Union. She knew nothing about that. But there now returned to her the sight of her mistress and General Houston in that crowded lobby at Houston city, before they had gone to Nashville, when he had touched Lucy's hair. That recollection, the tossing of the letter on the table, and the presence of the earlier letter, were enough. Jeannie did know Lucy very well.

'Then I must go,' she said, gathering up her things – her reticule, her parasol, and the precious scarf Lucy had given her.

'But I shall see you at the boat?' asked Lucy. 'You will come to the boat to say goodbye?'

'Girl,' said Jeannie, 'and is there any doubt I would fail to do that?' She no longer called Lucy 'Ma'am.' Lucy was 'Girl' again, and Jeannie was all at once the older and wiser woman, on whose judgment her young mistress would rely.

They were standing by the table on to which Lucy had tossed the letters. Jeannie asked nothing. Lucy took one of the letters up and then let it drop.

'It is General Houston,' she said. 'He wishes to make his adieus.'

'Aye, and you mean you do not wish it?'

'I do not wish it.'

'And *that* is what I see? Is it so? Is that what you tell me?'

Lucy did not answer. Jeannie recognised very well the stubborn, proud girl she had known in Scotland, whom there was no budging if she did not want to budge.

So she said, 'I see what I see. And if it's *that* great a thing to you, you must follow your heart.'

When Lucy was helped down by two black footmen from the carriage the St Charles hotel had provided, and stepped into the pillared foyer of the New American Theatre, Sam Houston was already the focus of attraction, standing out head and shoulders from the centre of a group of political gentlemen and their ladies. When he had written a third time Lucy had consented to see him, but only in a public place. She declined his offer to call for her, replying that she would make her own way.

In the vast foyer, which quite outdid any London opera house for size, expanse of gilt, and glittering light, she gave her wrap to an attendant and stood where she was. She did not need to wait. Houston had been waiting, watching for her while he abstractedly acknowledged the compliments of his admirers, and had seen her the moment she entered.

He detached himself and came straight to her. Each had dressed for the other. She wore a gown of emerald silk, cut high in the neck (whereas the fashion of the day was for a deep décolletage), fitting her body to the waist, and then spread round her in wide skirts. It was the simplest dress in the theatre, and therefore striking. Her only decoration was a torque made of twisted threads of silver, a Moncreiffe heirloom from three hundred years back, which she wore at her throat. As to Houston, he was in the black velvet coat and knee breeches fashionable when the United States was new. This was Sam Houston as Founding Father, but slung across his right shoulder he wore an Indian blanket.

Before the eyes of hundreds he bowed over her hand. Already a new group of admirers had assembled to watch their greetings.

'You dazzle us all, Lady Lucy,' he said.

'And you, General Houston, are dressed to have your portrait painted as a Roman general once again? You did once tell me you already had one such portrait done?'

'I did. But that was in Nashville, in my portrait days. But in any case,' he said, indicating his dress, 'how am I Roman this evening?'

'General, you are the only man I know who can wear an Indian blanket like a toga.'

The assembled United States senators, Louisiana state senators, judges, major generals, and their ladies thought this hit Sam off well. He took the compliment in great good humour.

'But,' he said, 'the greatest among us have declined to be thought of as Romans. General Jackson, shortly before his death, declined the honour of being entombed in the sarcophagus of the Emperor Alexander Severus, which was brought from Syria by a commodore of the United States Navy.'

The reply was applauded. Introductions were made all round. General Houston and Lucy were the guests of the governor and his lady, and the four were conducted to one of the grilled boxes Lucy had encountered on her first visit to New Orleans, when she had been the guest of Saligny. The governor was cordial. Toasts were drunk in cooled Rheims champagne – toasts proposed by the governor to his guests, by Houston to the governor, and by both of them to Polk and to Texas as the twenty-eighth state of the United States. The opera was well into its first act before these toasts were done with. The dimmed lights in the box were just enough to enable the governor to see their glasses as he refilled them. Through the gilt grille Lucy could see the promenaders in the auditorium, which was as brilliantly lit as the stage and stayed that way throughout the performance. The hubbub of conversation continued. The opera was played by an Italian company, something of Donizetti's, but what it was made little difference to most of those present, who could hardly say they heard it. In the corridor, petitioners trying to attract the favour of the governor and of General Houston became so clamorous that the old black footman locked the box to keep them away. In the house, the audience did not listen but still demanded encores of all the arias.

During the first interval, when they left the box for a brief promenade, Houston accepted several papers which were thrust at him, and was several times addressed as senator.

'I see,' said Lucy, 'that your talk of coquetting with England has served you well. You will be senator for Texas? You are once more American. Houston himself again?'

Houston looked round. The governor and his lady were for the moment engaged. He spoke quietly to her. 'I said *if* Texas had coquetted with England . . .'

'Oh I am sure you did. If. I can hear that. That is the way you would put it.'

'But suppose, Lucy, that a lady has two suitors. Suppose that lady to be Texas. Suppose that lady's favourite to be slow coming forward. If she is skilful, may not that lady flirt with the other suitor, making sure her other suitor knows of the flirtation, and bring him on that way?'

She was standing with her back to a pillar, and he leaning over her shielding her from the crowd around them. Both spoke softly, and the buzz around them ensured their privacy.

'General,' she said, 'all that is very likely, but you forget I know it is not the truth. What favoured suitor? I know the suitor you favoured. "Houston has done it," you said, as you cantered round me. You have forgotten?' She saw from his eyes that he had not, but he could say no more then because they were whisked away by the governor to entertain another group of New Orleans gentlemen, who openly spoke to General Houston of his becoming president after Polk.

During the second act the governor's lady, being afflicted with the heat of the theatre and with slightly more champagne than she was used to, retired to the chaise at the back of the box. The governor stood over his wife, fanning her. Leaning forward in their seats as if to gaze through the grille at the performance or at the audience, Lucy and Sam Houston continued their intent conversation.

'It was *if* and *if* and *if*,' he said. 'I could not know it at the time, but it was so. That was an order I gave to Jones to close with England at the very time, and as it turned out at the *only* time when it would have brought the greatest good to Texas. It was an if that Jim Polk was nominated. It was an if that he won the election . . . '

'I saw that *if*, at Plaquemines.'

'Had any one of those ifs gone the other way, affairs would have been settled. And then, even when the resolution was before the American Senate, if one man had not changed his mind, one man, the resolution would have failed. One man. That man was Senator Johnson of Louisiana, and he is here tonight. You met him here tonight, downstairs in the crush. Before the night of the vote he had always spoken against annexation.'

'I heard he changed his conscience, as you did yours. And what has happened now to your empire?'

At this moment the governor returned from attending to his lady, confiding to General Houston that she was somewhat indisposed, and asking his pardon and Lucy's if he slipped away with her. To tell the truth, he said, he was no great man for opera either. He trusted he would often have the pleasure of meeting Senator Houston again, and was glad to have been able to drink

to President Polk with him, knowing him to be an old friend of the
president's.

Sam rose to say his goodnights, the governor and his lady
took their leave, the second interval came and went with more
promenading by Houston and Lucy, and more congratulations
being pressed upon him, and then, at the beginning of the third
act, the black attendant moved more petitioners away from the box
and again locked the door against them.

Inside, the two of them alone at last, Lucy sat on the chaise
looking straight ahead, and Houston stood in the far corner of the
box pouring two more glasses of the champagne. He offered a glass
to her. She declined.

'What of Captain Elliot?' she said. 'He considered you his friend.'

'I considered him mine. I hope I still may. But he understands
that a nation's first principle is that of self-preservation.'

'I think he may very well think it your first principle. He
says you have a lot to answer for.'

'If . . . ' he began.

But she cut him off, and asked the one question that mattered
most to her.

'Why did you desert me? Why, having sent me off to Mexico, did
you go without leaving one word for me? I went only for you, and
you know it.'

It was a question that came from her heart, and he heard this.

'News came that General Jackson was dying. I went to him.
I loved the man.'

'Yes. Though I suppose if he had died sooner that too would have
made some difference to your matters of state? You would have been
freed from your loyalty to him? It would have made things plainer and
easier for you? You would not have had to finesse so much, and could
have spoken up plainly against annexation? But if that were so, what
of your loyalty to General Jackson on the day you told me, "Houston
has done it"? What loyalty were you thinking of then? Hardly to him.
And then, when it comes to Captain Elliot going off to Mexico, you
see me off with him, then ditch us in midstream to go off leaving no
word for me?'

'Lucy, because by then it was lost. It was lost before the treaty was ever signed in Mexico.'

'I think it was all for nothing. I think it was lost before Captain Elliot and I ever set foot in Mexico.'

'And I admit it may have been. It may have been. But I did not know that. When I asked you to go I still hoped, but very soon after that it was lost. I fought Donelson as long as I could. And then I knew that the Texian Congress was set on annexation. I saw Texas was lost. There was no speaking out against it then. I acquiesced. It is not a word I like.'

'No? But I dare say you will acquiesce in your becoming a senator? You will allow that to be thrust upon you because there is no avoiding it? Just as you have just acquiesced, I suppose, in toasting Texas not as Texas but as the twenty-eighth state?'

He bowed his head.

'But to go without a word for me?' She asked that question again.

'Lucy, because then it was lost. Because I did acquiesce. Because I could tell you nothing that would not shame me. So I shamed myself further by leaving no word.'

It was the truth and it proclaimed itself.

'Houston,' he said, 'was ashamed.'

She would have laughed at the form of words if it had not brought back to her the time in the Cherokee town when she first heard him speak of himself in this way. Houston, he had said of himself, would return to his red brothers in the spring. Houston, he had told her, had done it. The words brought that time back to her, and a rush of loving affection for the man.

She walked across to him, took the glass from his hand, and held him in her arms. He stood still, not embracing her until she took his hands and placed them at her hips. She leaned forward to kiss him. She held out one hand and led him across the box to the chaise. She sat looking up at Sam standing before her, smiled again at the shyness of this bold man, and held up her slender arms to him in invitation. He took her hands. She drew him down, until he knelt and buried his head in her silk lap. They rested like that for some minutes, neither speaking. The warmth of her body invaded the senses of the man. She raised his head, encouraging him, leading his hands first up to her face, then down over her throat, then to her waist, then to the silk of the gown, and then under the gown into the petticoats.

'Another,' she said, 'there's another one too.' She showed him the way to her third petticoat, and then the way beneath that. He stood holding her by her white hips, looking down at her.

She held out her arms to him again. Later she called out once, loudly enough for the footman outside to lift his head. Nothing, he said to himself, and was wrong.

Then, afterwards, she lay back on the chaise with her arms above her head, the odd phrase of Donizetti reaching her ears, and the folds of her silk dress spread about anyhow, creased and crushed by the weight of her lover. The torque of twisted silver bit into her neck, and she put a hand down to ease and loosen it. Her hand encountered silk, which was the hem of her gown where it lay against her cheek. She laughed. 'My skirts,' she said, 'and there's a proper place for them to be, I'd say.'

The man outside heard her long laugh. 'That's champagne for you,' he thought, and was wrong again. Sam Houston roused himself and stood beside her, looking down.

She lay as she was, to be admired, and then, seeing his diffidence even now, laughed again, this time with a quite different tone. She was amused.

'Cover me a bit then, if you like.'

He tried.

'Lift me first,' she said, and he did, helping her retrieve a fold of silk from here, a frill of petticoat from there. She stood, shook her skirts out around her, recovered her shoes, and assembled herself. She took his hands and kissed each of them lightly. In the mirror on the back wall, she saw the mark of the torque on her neck.

'That's for you,' she said.

After the opera was ended, the old black footman unlocked General Houston's box. He saw the general and his guest standing at either side of the box, in deep conversation. The general was asking something of her, but she did not reply. The footman withdrew but, as he did so, caught a few words from the woman, who said, 'What else should I do?'

Next morning Lucy left for Jamaica, there to take the West India mail steamer back to England.

PART FOUR

39

Sam Young Again

Early on a midsummer's day in 1866 a man of less than middle height walked into the shop of John Lobb the bootmaker in St James's Street, London. A shopman took his hat, his heavy grey cloak, and his silver topped cane. Mr Lobb himself, emerging from the back of the shop, paused and gave the slight bow which he made out of courtesy to all those who entered. It also gave him the few seconds he needed to remember the name of a customer he had not seen for a while. Mr Lobb prided himself on his memory. He did recall the name, and his customer smiled at the feat, and both were in great good humour.

'It has been a long time,' he said.

'A little while, sir, a little while,' said Lobb, then calling to his clerk, giving him the remembered name. 'Edward, bring the gentleman's book.' Many gentlemen came to Lobb's for their boots when they were straight out of school, and had their boots made all their lives by two or three generations of Lobbs. Some gentlemen left years between visits, before they returned one day from their sugar plantations in the West Indies, or from governing Bengal, or from doing nothing on their Irish estates. This gentleman spoke with an American accent, which explained his little while away.

The ledger was consulted, a reference number found, and the clerk despatched below stairs to find the numbered wooden last on which the gentleman's boots had been made. Meantime he sat at a small round tripod table, with the glass of claret and biscuit which were offered. He sat and sipped until the claret was almost gone.

The search for the last was taking a long time. Mr Lobb offered more claret.

'Thank you, no,' said the gentleman. 'But I have a professional interest in feet. The shape of feet. The disposition of the metatarsal bones, and of the extensor pollicis longus' – here he touched the instep of his own right boot. 'That is a muscle which presents a peculiar difference in development from one man to another.'

'Quite so,' said Mr Lobb. He had known medical gentlemen take such an interest before. They used Latin terms to describe features of the human foot which he had come to know by a different route, that of long practical experience.

'I have seen my own last, but never compared my own with others. Since your man is having some difficulty finding mine, may I go down and see?'

In the basement Edward was chivvying an aged man in a leather apron who was searching with the help of a candle through an orderly forest of lasts. Near the foot of the staircase the lasts were new and the handwritten labels clear. 'Richard Roberts Esq,' 'His Grace the duke of Montrose,' 'Sir Harry Llewellyn, Bart,' 'Lieutenant Walter Hand, RN' – only with this last one the rank of lieutenant had been scratched out, to be replaced by that of captain, and then in turn by rear-admiral. These were the lasts still in regular use. Further away into the shadows of the cellar the ink on the labels had faded. Then, farthest off, rose shelves of lasts whose wood, even in the dim light, could be seen to have darkened with age.

Mr Lobb handed the gentleman the late duke of Wellington's last, and he admired the extraordinarily high instep, and nodded understandingly when told that the great duke always said he could never get a decent boot made elsewhere, no one else being such a master of the instep as Mr Lobb.

'It was my grandfather,' said Mr Lobb, 'that he told that to. Though I fitted the duke often in later years.'

The ancient bootmaker was now searching in the farthest corner.

'Abel, where have you got to now?' enquired Mr Lobb, to which the quavering reply came, 'The Deceased, sir.'

'What?' asked the gentleman, half-hearing.

'Among those put away, sir,' said Mr Lobb confidentially, but the customer had now recognised the word he had heard uttered and was laughing.

'My feet put away among the deceased?'

But at that moment Abel emerged from the gloom bearing a last in his hands, and replying, 'Oh no, sir, among the Supposed.'

'Sometimes,' said Mr Lobb, 'Abel supposes a little prematurely.' He took the last for the right foot, glanced at the gentleman's right foot, ran his hand over the contours of the last, and announced that this was the one. He then glanced at the label to reconfirm his judgment, and they ascended.

It was twenty-one years since a boot was made on that last.

The gentleman ordered three pairs, and then, having been ushered out, turned left and took the few steps which brought him to Berry Brothers, wine merchants and shippers. He ordered twelve cases of Madeira, six of Sercial and six of Bual. The account in his name was still on the books. In London little had changed, in America everything.

He stepped into the street, and looked into a narrow passage next to the wine merchant's that led to a court of houses built late in the reign of Queen Anne. The mellow red bricks, the carved doorcases, and the sash windows painted with white lead, were all as he remembered them. It was as if he had never left the legation in London of the Republic of Texas, and as if that Republic once more existed and was represented at the Court of St James.

Dr Ashbel Smith walked quickly up St James's, turned left into Piccadilly, then worked his way through to Park Lane, and presented himself at the door of Lady Lucy Gordon.

When he was announced she ran to meet him, held out both hands, kissed his right cheek, and hugged him. His beard was now grey, he was thinner, and his face was lined, but the hazel eyes were not faded. And she? He had forgotten she was as tall as himself. He had never forgotten their first meeting in Paris, and here was the same warm girl again, only now a warm woman, and she had kissed him.

Not so slender now, he thought; and as he thought this she caught his glance, knew its meaning, and laughed. 'Dr Smith, I have six children, you see.'

She led him by hand into her sitting room, and they sat in two chairs either side of a bay window overlooking Hyde Park.

Lucy Moncreiffe had returned from Texas as a young woman of twenty, having in the previous four full years enjoyed a happy marriage, suffered widowhood, and then undertaken what her great uncle Aberdeen called her grand tour of the spirit. When she spoke of it, she called it 'My Texas time'. A year after her return she married James Stuart Gordon, Esquire, a young Scotsman with a few hundred acres on the Scottish borders, who admired her as she admired him. On her second marriage she took her old courtesy title with her willy-nilly, and her new husband's surname, and became Lady Lucy Gordon. Gordon had no fortune, or no more than was necessary for him to read for the English bar, at which he practised. They lived half the year on his acres in the Borders, acres which were most of them so nearly vertical as to be unfarmable, and half the year in London. The house in Park Lane was hers, or at any rate it belonged to a Moncreiffe cousin who hated London, never wanted to stay in town more than a week every two years, and let her the place as her own.

'Six children,' said Smith, who was unmarried and had only one child that he knew of, long ago. He wished there had been more.

And as if she read his mind – as each had read the other's in a long friendship of brief meetings going back many years – she said, 'Six. It is a fortunate marriage.'

'Lucy, it is in the nature of some women and some men to have fortunate marriages. They make them fortunate.'

'See the sixth,' said Lucy, turning as a nurse came in, leading a girl of three. 'This is Catriona. The children like stories of great magnolias ninety feet high over the Brazos, and wild horses for the rounding up, and wild grapes for the picking. Remember you first told me about those horses and grapes – and about champagne air, I think.'

'In Paris,' he said.

He leaned forward and told the child about his grapes.

'There are mustang, and muscadine, and summer grapes, and post oak grapes, and . . .'

'What are mustang?' the child asked.

'A mustang is really a wild horse. You have to catch and tame a mustang if you want to ride it. But it is also the name of a grape, because the grape is wild too. Why, it hangs in clusters from trees, twenty, thirty feet high. The birds eat them. You wouldn't like them, because they're not sweet enough to eat, but you can make wine from them. I make mustang wine.'

'Mama likes wine.'

'Not mine, I think.'

The child was taken away for her tea.

Lucy asked, 'How is the world with you?'

'I practise medicine. I grow cotton. I used to judge exhibitions, you know. There was a craze for universal exhibitions all over the country. We sent a lot to your great exhibition here. We won medals for Virginia tobacco, and Kentucky hams, and a small medal for Mr Colt's revolvers.'

'I had a maid I took from Scotland to Texas, who married a man who sold Mr Colt's revolvers. Jeannie.'

'I know him. He made a fortune from it. Your Jeannie and her husband have the biggest store in San Antonio – Italian silks, French lawns, English satins, and Colt revolvers on the side.'

'I'm glad for her. We were very close. She was my maid when I was a young girl in Scotland. She and I have kept up with each other, you know. We write perhaps once a year. She tells me she has the largest plate glass windows in Texas at her emporium, and four children as well. Then there was a German girl, Helga, yellow hair, very tall, used to work at the Tremont before she came to me. I've never heard from her.'

Smith remembered Helga Becker well. 'She married a German, one of the Perote men, who made his pile out of the postmastership of Mobile he got from Donelson. They fell out, and she went to Santa Fe. That must be fifteen years ago.' Smith did not say, and was soon glad he had not, that the falling out came after Helga was found slipping away from Senator Houston's room, and her husband would not listen to her exclamations of innocence.

'I remember her first at the Tremont,' he said. He paused. 'The Tremont was a hospital in the war, you know.'

The war.

The bay window was west facing. The sun from the south-west lit Smith's face and Lucy saw that he was deeply tired. It was the fatigue of long, hard, bitter years of civil war. She remembered the heavy grey cloak she saw him give to the footman in the hall as she ran out to greet him. The grey cloak of the Confederacy.

He gazed down across the room, as if estimating a distance. He was thinking of a stretch of road. 'At Vicksburg, there was a road. For two hundred yards the bodies lay so thick you could go the whole distance walking on them, not touching the road. I did walk down the road. The fact was, if you wanted to walk that road you had to walk on those men. In places you could not tread round them, they fell so thick.'

She said, 'Lord Aberdeen was always afraid of war between the States. I do not mean he just said he was afraid, though he did say it often. I once heard him say at dinner that war was the greatest folly and the greatest crime of which a country could be guilty. He thought it would overtake the United States. He said it often. But he did more than say it. You could feel he was afraid of the prospect of war, and for those who would die in it. He said it would come, after annexation. I did not know. But I did feel his fear.'

'Those weren't our dead,' said Smith, his mind still at Vicksburg. 'The bodies on the road, they were Union soldiers. But then there was the siege, and affairs took another turn. You slept in your cloak in a hole. And peaflour to eat, and bad cornmeal, and bad water. Then nothing. Bare feet. All eatables gone. Then . . . '

Lucy sat silently.

'Then surrender. Sam hated and feared the war. The whole war. You would not think it of the victor of San Jacinto, but he feared it, and saw it coming. He always saw it coming. And spoke out against it. I heard him once in Galveston, at the beginning of the war. "My

God," he said, "have the people all gone mad? Do they not know that the civil war now being inaugurated will be as horrible as His Satanic Majesty could desire? Let me tell you what is coming. Your fathers and husbands, your sons and brothers, will be herded at the point of a bayonet. You may, as a bare possibility, win southern independence, but I doubt it. I tell you, what I fear is the north will overwhelm the south." He talked about millions of treasure wasted, and oceans of blood. That was from the balcony of the Tremont. In that voice of his. They did not listen, and he was right.'

Smith did not go on.

Lucy tried to take him away from the war.

'When I last saw General Houston,' she said, 'there was talk of his becoming president after Polk.'

Smith raised his hands and said Sam was three times US senator, and was put forward for president often, but never nominated. As late as 1860 he failed by only a few votes at one convention, but the Democrats were hopelessly split.

'That would have been to run against Lincoln. But no. When war came he was governor of Texas, of the State of Texas. He did not want secession. He fought it with all his strength. When Texas did secede, he insisted that secession from the Union did not mean membership of the Confederacy, and that Texas was on its own again. Texas itself again, he said. He would not take the oath to the Confederacy, and was deposed for it. So he went home. His oldest son, Sam junior, volunteered for the Confederacy, served in my regiment. But to the end Sam Houston maintained that Texas having left the Union was Texas sovereign and independent again. Once when I was on leave he called me to him. I went to him at home. He had a plan all laid out, to preserve Texas. He said it was his duty, with God's help. He wanted to call Texian troops home, raise the Lone Star flag again, declare himself president again. After a while I said that as a soldier I could not hear him say such things, and went back to my regiment. To the end he would not let Texas go. It was Sam's Republic again.'

Smith was moved, and gazed out at the lush park. Lucy rose, rang for tea, and came back to him.

She sat, looking down at her folded hands in her lap, and said: 'He wrote to me sometimes. Not often. He wrote to tell me about children, and I wrote and told him of mine.'

'He and Margaret had eight. You knew Margaret?'

'I met her once. He was always away somewhere, always on the move, and she was always left at home. It was the children he wrote about, but not the last time. That was three years ago. He wrote about a Texian empire again, an imperial domain. It was not as if he were dreaming. It was Sam Houston again as I first knew him. He was drawing bold lines on maps again. He had plans for steam cars running from Washington-on-the-Brazos down to Mexico City. That was the last letter, and I could not reply in time. I had a letter from Mr Addington only a few days afterwards – Addington whom you would have known at the foreign office – and he told me General Houston was dead.'

'It was just after Vicksburg. I heard later from the nurse that his last words were "Texas" and "Eliza." She did not tell Margaret that. You knew about Eliza?'

Lucy nodded, seeing herself back in Nashville again, hearing talk of Houston and his fears, and then with Sam Houston that night of the storm in the Cherokee town.

A maid brought tea. Lucy was busying herself with teacups when a deep voice was heard in the hall. The door to the sitting room opened and a young man stood in the door.

'Jo, come in and meet Dr Smith, from my Texas time. Dr Smith, this is my eldest son, Jo.'

Smith rose, slowly offered the young man his hand, and gazed at him. He was well over six feet tall, with large features, chestnut hair, and grey eyes. And to Smith, the way the boy held his head was unmistakable. Smith could utter nothing beyond 'How d'you do?,' and the young man excused himself, saying something about a horse he must see to, and that he would meet them again at dinner.

'We call him Jo,' said Lucy, 'but his name is Joel. Joel Alexander Robert – I gave him a choice of Christian names – but Jo has stuck. He is always Jo.'

Neither Lucy nor Dr Smith was a devout Christian, but both

knew their Bible as well as any other educated man or woman of the time. Joel in the Old Testament is the son of Samuel.

Lucy looked up at Dr Smith, waiting.

'It is Sam's son,' she said. 'Do I shock you?'

'You surprise me. That young man astonishes me. I knew Sam as well as any man knew him. When we first met we shared a room for months, shared a house because there was only the one room in it. It is just that your son is Sam young again, and I loved the man. I did not know. Sam never said a word about the ladies. He knew?'

'Did General Houston know he had a son? No. I saw him last in New Orleans, and came back by way of Jamaica. So I did not even think it possible until I was in the English channel on the passage home. I did not know for sure until I was in Scotland again.'

'You never told him?'

'Oh, I thought and thought. But could he come to me, or I go back to him? There was Margaret. I knew they already had a son and a daughter, babies. So I did not tell him. If he had none of his own, I would have told him. But he had sons and daughters. He wrote to me about his sons and daughters.'

'But what of you?'

'I? No woman in her senses wants a child without a father. But I was with child, and then the child was born, and I had a son, and I was happy the son was Sam Houston's. It could be great trouble for many women, but I was fortunate. I was my father's daughter. He would not turn me out of doors, and if he would not, no one else would dare speak. He was the Moncreiffe. We are Scots, and some would say still a little feudal. Do you know the Scottish phrase, "An outside child?" My father said to me, in some irritation, that if I was going to get an outside child, I might at least have found an honest Scotsman to father it. I said I had, since General Houston was certainly a Houston of Hugh's Town, though a few generations back. Then, later on, when he saw the boy, my father loved it, and said well, he thought the better of any man who could get a child on me.'

Smith laughed. 'As I do; and the better of you for having a son by Sam.'

'It was not a light thing,' she said, 'between Sam and me. We were very much together in the last year, or as often as we could be. You may think the less of me for that, Dr Smith, to say I was with him whenever I could contrive it, but it was not a light thing. It was real.'

Smith had not doubted that. They were reconciled. There were things in their minds they could not tell each other. The bright day in Paris had remained as affectionately and deeply in Smith's memory as in Lucy's. He knew it would remain in his mind all his life, just as she knew she would always remember Jeannie dressing her in the grey ghosts, and then the boulevard and Smith and Godoy, and next morning twelve pairs of new stockings in netted Chantilly lace. It was Ashbel Smith who had woken her from out of her mourning.

'You will stay to dinner,' said Lucy. It was not so much an invitation as a statement. Smith excused himself on account of his clothes, having nothing to change into, but she disallowed that as a reason, and he consented. Before she herself went up to dress, she told him about her husband, so that Smith should know something before their meeting. The important part was again about Sam's child.

'Of course I told James. So he will know, if we talk of General Houston at dinner, as I expect we shall. You have heard of Highland flings? Well, the Moncreiffes are Lowland Scots, but they have flings. It was at such a fling I met James. It was wanting at first sight, for both of us. I was what, twenty-one years old? He knew there was my first marriage. He knew there was Jo. Put those two together in a woman, and you'd think a man could do better for a wife. I'd say a man could. I told him so. I sent him away. He came back. Now a woman in that situation is like a ship. If there is to be a contract – oh, it is more than a contract, but in part it is a contract, a sort of charter-party for life – then there must be a manifest. A ship or a woman must make known what she is and what cargo she brings with her.'

'That,' said Smith, 'would be difficult for some I have known, and hard on them too.'

'Oh, a woman has a discretion – as long as it's an honest discretion. So I told my suitor about General Houston. He knew of him. Houston was a myth in England, too, you know. Learned histories, sixpenny books, twopenny pamphlets – the Alamo, San Jacinto, Santa Anna vanquished. So I told my suitor. He thanked me and renewed his proposal, and I thanked him and instantly took him. Later on, a couple of years later, I did ask him why he took me, and he said a man with any sense chose his wife as a woman would her wedding gown – not for a fine, glossy surface but for such qualities as would wear well. Scotswomen don't just wear their wedding gown once; it serves as a ballgown ever after. I was not sure how to take that at the time. When you're young you don't want to think about wearing well. Now I take it as a huge compliment. Anyway, Jo has been brought up as our eldest son. He's now an ensign in the 13th Hussars. When he is twenty-one, which is next year, I shall tell him too.'

Lucy left Smith, sending her husband's valet to attend to him. As she went upstairs the words 'outside child' came to her mind, and so did the grilled box at the New Orleans opera, and the chaise, and Sam Houston, and the odd snatch of remembered Donizetti to go with him. Not, she said to herself – this happy wife, happy in her house, recalling that evening – not, she reflected, that there had been so much outside about it at all.

They were four at dinner, though Jo was late. Talk of the American war was avoided. James Gordon, having spent the day in court at Westminster Hall on some maritime case, chatted about that and the hodge-podge of probate, family property, and admiralty cases which were his living.

'I always tell Lucy it's wills, wives, and wrecks,' he said. 'And I never know which of those it'll be from week to week.'

'Wives' property?' asked Smith, explaining that in Texas a woman's property did not pass to her husband on marriage but remained her own – a concept then unknown to the Common Law of England.

'In that,' said Gordon, who held liberal views for a lawyer, 'the United States is more civilised than we.'

'Not the United States,' said Smith. 'Only Texas, so far as I
know. And if a man dies bankrupt, the homestead and two hundred
acres remain with the widow, not the creditors. That's the Texian
law. Women are still scarce in Texas, and therefore cherished.'

At which point, with the soup already gone from the table and the
fish being served, Jo Gordon made his entrance, booming apologies
about a horse, kissing his mother's hand, bowing to Dr Smith and
to his father, and then settling in the chair held out for him by the
footman and falling to his food.

James Gordon was an observant man, and guessed correctly
at the meaning of the glance exchanged between Lucy and Smith
when Jo bent to kiss his mother. For a start, there was the young
man's dress. He was gorgeously got up, not in any sort of evening
wear but in a kilt of the green and dark blue Gordon tartan, with triple
yellow stripes. His coat, of the same tartan but of a different sett, with
less yellow in it, was fastened with a silver brooch the size of a saucer.
The dress, and the manner in which he greeted his mother, were
pure Sam Houston. Gordon learned from that intercepted glance,
more clearly than ever Lucy had or could have told him in words,
that the boy was his father's son in manner, spirit, and everything.

'Dr Smith,' said Jo, when he had polished off two Dover sole
and they were waiting for the roast fore-rib of beef, 'mother has
often told us, my brothers and sisters and me, about her Texian
time. Catriona is now hearing the old legends again, even more
embellished this time I'd say.'

'Shame, Jo,' said Lucy.

'No, no, mother. Yours is such embellishment as gives added
grace to the real. But, Dr Smith, they all seem to have been a race
of giants. Hardly a small man among them, unless it's a man called
Jones.'

Smith smiled. 'I was one of them, and you see that I am five
feet six inches. Anson Jones – now he was no villain. I believe he
was honest in his narrow way, at least until his later days when he
was plain deluded, but in no way a big man – not in body, mind,
anything. Would you say, Lucy?'

'The last I saw of him he was still president, and busy asserting descent from Oliver Cromwell, having the Cromwell crest engraved on all his spoons. Who'd want spoons with a regicide's crest? I suppose he went to the American Senate?'

'No,' said Smith. 'I can vouch for the crested spoons. And crests on all his plate. I have eaten off it. But he did not go to the Senate; not a vote for him for senator. He expected it, and kept on expecting it. He went home, taking the state papers of the Republic with him, and defacing them over the years with endorsements he then claimed to have made at the time, all tending to show it was Jones and Jones alone who saved Texas from being sold to England for English gold. Proofs of treachery, he called them, hundreds of them. Poor man. Then he shot himself. But what of Captain Elliot, Lucy? I think you liked that man.'

'Mother's Mexico caper,' said Jo, drinking champagne from a silver tankard. 'One of the legends of the Gordon household. As told to six children, one after the other.'

'I did come to like him. He once told me, when he was ill, that what he most wanted was the command of a frigate. He never got that. What he got was Bermuda. You know he got Bermuda?'

Smith did know that, because Captain Elliot had been made governor of that colony in the same year Texas was annexed. The appointment was greeted in Texas as hilarious.

'The oldest colony in the empire,' said Lucy, 'and very grand. But he has fallen on hard times. True, he's an admiral now, and by now he's *Sir* Charles I should think, but he's never had a ship to fly his flag in.'

James Gordon confirmed that Elliot had received the knighthood which went with the rank of admiral. 'But now I think, and for some years, he's been governor of St Helena, which has to be the smallest, most inconsiderable colony there is, a thousand miles from anywhere, out in the south Atlantic.'

'I do not,' said Lucy, 'know what he did to deserve that. I hear he has planted some quinine trees, for the malaria he first had in China. He had it' – here she addressed herself to Smith – 'when he went to Mexico for you and General Houston.'

'When you went with him,' said Smith.

'The legend,' said Jo.

Lucy smiled. 'I have always remembered Mexico City. When I was there I told myself I was walking where Montezuma had walked. And I remember, about two years after I returned, seeing those engravings in the illustrated newspapers of American troops riding into that same square in front of the cathedral.'

'That was when America took California,' said Smith, 'and half the continent besides, that used to be Mexico's. All the territory that Sam hankered after for his empire.'

'His empire,' said Lucy. 'The last time I talked with General Houston he said he had fought annexation until the last, and then he acquiesced in it. I have to say I was pretty scornful at the time, and told him he had done well enough out of it. But he said No. He had fought until there was no point in fighting on, and then he acquiesced, and was ashamed he had. "Houston is ashamed," he said, in that way of his.'

Smith sat back and asked, 'Did you believe him?'

'At the time he said it, yes. Oh, no doubt of it. But with him the truth was always the truth of the moment. Next day, in another place, with someone else, the truth might appear differently. It was second nature to him, but it was *his* truth. I suppose that makes him a scoundrel in some ways?'

Smith nodded slowly. 'We knew the same man, you and I. The truth of the moment, yes.'

'And a rather *splendid* scoundrel,' she said.

'How close,' asked Jo, looking up from his roast beef, 'was Captain Elliot to making Texas an English colony?'

'Jo,' said his mother, 'those were different times. Nowadays colonies run in people's minds. Everyone picks up colonies now. Nobody wanted them then – except America, and America didn't call them colonies. I know Lord Aberdeen declined California twice when it was offered by Mexico. That was several years before the United States took it. He said he didn't want the trouble and expense of looking after British subjects so far from home, some such thing. Colony, no. But Dr Smith will know how close Texas was to being an empire.'

Dr Smith took himself back to the summer of 1844. 'The treaty with England would have been completed at a sitting.'

Lucy said, 'And I was there – my family know this, Dr Smith, but you will not. You were in Europe at the time. I was there when General Houston put the crown on his own head. I do think of it that way. He used to talk of monarchies.'

Smith knew this to be true, though how much of it was hyperbole neither he nor any other man could tell. He said, 'I fancy he talked about a crown because he was exasperated by a Congress whose acts he vetoed, and which then nullified his own appointments. He was much taken by the way an English or French minister could say he would do something, and then just do it. But when was all this?'

'On the Brazos, at Washington, in the fall of 1844, we were setting off to see the Cherokees. He asked us to wait a minute. We waited, and we saw him write out the order to accept the English treaty, and saw him give it to Jones.'

Smith nodded, little rapid nods, signifying that this fell in with what he knew. Then he said, 'I saw the order. Not at the time. Not until years after, when poor Jones was going manically through his state papers, justifying himself. I remember Sam Houston saying he signed that paper at the very moment, and the only moment, when it could have benefited the republic. Jones defied the order, and sent me a leave of absence instead. Brought me home at a time when it could all have been done in a day.'

'So,' said Jo, 'if . . .'

'Ifs and ands,' said Lucy.

'And so our independence was sacrificed as if on an altar,' said Smith. 'It was treated as if it were worth as much as our navy. I saw the navy sold. There were no bidders the first time it was offered, and precious few later. The sloop never sold. The Americans inherited her and broke her up. There were two good brigs. One went for four hundred and fifty dollars. The other fetched fifty-five. Fifty-five. A good brig.' There was a bitterness in his voice which Lucy had not heard before. Even talking about the war, when he was speaking of great evils, he had spoken matter-of-factly. But he believed that Vicksburg and the whole atrocious civil war between the states took its origin – in part, no one could say how large a part – from the events that extinguished the Texas Republic.

'Yes,' said Smith coming out of the reverie which his hosts did not interrupt, 'it hit Sam hard too, but he would not let it show. Much later on, when it came to the war between North and South, and before I went off with my regiment, he wrote asking me to visit him. He went all over it again, the last few months of the Republic. It came out as if he'd been telling it to himself for years, telling it over and over to himself alone. Now, he wanted to tell someone else.'

Lucy said, 'He was terrified of loneliness. But no one was ever lonely with him.'

She got up from the table, leaving the men to themselves. As she passed her husband she ruffled his hair. When she returned twenty minutes later Jo was holding forth about the bay mare that he and the groom were teaching to stand fire, not to be afraid of drums, gunfire, and other sounds of battle, so that when he rejoined his regiment he could take her as his troop horse. 'First you put a pistol and then a carbine in the manger with her feed, so that she can see them. Then show her the weapons, sometimes on one side, sometimes on the other, sometimes waving them around, until she is quite used to them and takes no notice. Then fire a blank charge outside the stable, but where she can see you. We have done all that, and she don't shy at all. Tomorrow, I shall fire a blank in the stable, then . . . '

He rose for his mother, which interrupted his flow, and James Gordon asked Dr Smith about remedies for snake bite. 'It is a true bite,' said the doctor, 'a bite by sharp teeth. Not just darting fangs. You think it is a wildcat but it is a snake, and if it is a rattlesnake the pain is terrible. Most bites are in the foot. A man will recover with iodine, if the leg is kept elevated.'

Jo came back to his mare, remarking that he would not allow her tail to be docked, as was the fashion, since a docked horse suffered so from flies, and when Dr Smith agreed, wanted to press him about cavalry actions in the American war. Lucy shook her head at Jo, warning him away, but he did not see her and exclaimed that he would have given a lot to see service there.

The men were now mellow with good brandy, but Smith stared into his glass. 'You would not say that if you knew.'

Only a very young man could have persisted, and even so young a man as Jo saw that the recent war was painful to Smith, and asked instead if he thought it would have come to war between England and the United States if Texas had accepted the English guarantee of 1844.

'Would war,' said Smith , 'have followed the passing of the Diplomatic Act? Would an attempt have been made by the United States to appeal to arms? No. The United States Senate had already spurned a Texian approach earlier that year. If there had been a war, they would have had to confront Great Britain and France, perhaps also Spain and Mexico. Individuals talk flippantly of war. There was much war talk from such people. But men at the head of affairs are conscious of responsibility, for a land destroyed, and all those men that will be broken – dead of typhus or scooped out by shrapnel.'

Jo was listening intently. Lucy was about to divert the conversation again, but her husband put a quiet hand on her arm, and she understood, and let Smith go on.

'And, if I turn my thoughts to much later, to very recent times, and think of the mightiest matter which has befallen the American people since 1776, I mean the war between North and South which ended last year, would a sovereign Texas Republic have been drawn into such a war of secession? Wouldn't there rather have been an exodus of people from those southern states to Texas, as to a promised land?'

Lucy sat with her eyes on Dr Smith, remembering her return with Elliot from Mexico, with a plain guarantee of peace. Smith was at that point too.

'In 1845, there it was, peace. Peace so long desired, peace and independence so earnestly prayed for. But events had moved fast, and Texas, which a few months before would have received peace from Mexico with joyful shouts, was by then frantic for annexation. There was no withstanding it. When it was a fait accompli I accepted it, as I would not be separated from my people, and all my friends.'

Lucy crossed to Jo and put an arm on her son's shoulder.

They had talked until after ten o'clock, but at that hour on a midsummer's day in London there is still light in the sky.

'But I must have done with it,' said Dr Smith. 'After all, individuals do not control great events in the history of nations. Such events take place when the time for them is ripe. So it was with annexation. The time for it had come.'

Lucy said: 'Whatever he thought later, the last time I saw General Houston was on an evening in New Orleans, after the opera. The stars and stripes were already everywhere, in the opera house, in the street outside, to celebrate Texas coming into the Union. As he handed me into my carriage he looked at the flags and said, "The fuss is over. The sun will shine tomorrow. What next?"'

A Note
and Acknowledgments

This is a novel, not a history, though I hope it catches something of the spirit of Texas and of an extraordinary period in its history. But though this is no history, the principal events of the story are based on fact. They happened. Sam Houston as president of Texas did order his secretary of state to accept the British and French offer of a guarantee of independence against Mexico, against the United States, against the world. Anson Jones disobeyed the order and concealed his treachery. Ashbel Smith, the Texian chargé d'affaires in London and Paris, did say later, when he found out, that the treaty would have been completed at a single sitting. Events then moved fast. James K Polk, having campaigned for the presidency of the United States on the annexation ticket, won a notoriously fraudulent election. An uncle of Queen Victoria did want to ship 30,000 immigrants to Texas to dish American ambitions. Charles Elliot, the British chargé d'affaires in Texas (whose previous posting was, as in the story, that of British plenipotentiary in China during the first opium war) did go secretly and incognito to Mexico City at the request of the Texian government and obtain Mexican recognition of the independence of Texas. By the summer of 1845 Texas did have a clear choice between continued independence as one of the nations of the world and annexation to the United States. And Texas was annexed by the constitutionally dubious method of a joint resolution of both Houses of the US Congress. If one senator had voted the other way, the measure would have failed.

The received historical opinion has long been that Sam Houston surreptitiously worked for annexation to the United States all along.

I have found little evidence of this. He certainly coquetted with
Britain and the United States, playing one against the other. To
such a consummate politician and instinctive fixer this was second
nature. But the fact remains that he did accept the British and
French offer of a treaty of guarantee. He railed against what he
called the mobocracy that wanted to throw Texas into the arms
of America. He told the French chargé d'affaires that annexation
would annihilate Texas, and that he was convinced not a single
republican government would survive in north America in fifty
years' time. He told the British chargé that the United States' love
of dominion was equal to that of Rome under the first Caesars. He
spoke frequently of his vision of a Texian republic stretching to the
Pacific and including most of what became New Mexico, Arizona,
Nevada, Utah, Colorado, and California itself. To the last moment
he opposed what he called the servile submission and humiliation of
annexation, and acquiesced in it only when to do otherwise would
have destroyed his political career. After annexation came, he tried
to take the credit for it and was encouraged to do so by Polk. But
others tried to take the credit too, and Houston was first and always
a politician.

I have read most of the Texian and British diplomatic documents,
in manuscript where I could, and much of the American, French, and
Mexican correspondence. I believe – and was astonished to come
to this belief but could not avoid it – that almost every member of
the Texian government opposed annexation. The people, of course,
wanted it. It is one of the great *if*s of history, but had Texas remained
independent she would have become the second great American
republic, sharing the continent of north America, and one of the
most powerful nations of the world.

Apart from this, and perhaps above all, Sam Houston feared that
the annexation of Texas would convulse the Union. He foresaw and
feared the American civil war, as did Lord Aberdeen, who was British
foreign secretary at the time of annexation. When civil war came in 1861
Houston was governor of the state of Texas. When Texas seceded he
maintained that by doing so she had not joined the Confederacy but
had become once again a sovereign and independent nation. He

wanted to bring Texian soldiers back from the war and raise the Lone Star flag again. He died soon after Vicksburg, in the middle of the slaughterous civil war which realised his worst fears.

In the matter of Texas, Great Britain acted out of self-interest, and never pretended to do anything else. Britain wanted Texian trade. And naturally Britain wanted to dish the United States, no more wishing to see north America dominated by a single power than she wished to see the same dominance in Europe. A great howl of English gold was raised in the United States. England was buying Texas and bribing Houston. This was nonsense. Not a penny was ever offered. And as for wanting Texas as a colony, all the papers, public and private, show Britain had not the slightest interest. Colonies were not the fashion. In the novel, Lucy says California was twice refused. This is less than the truth. From 1841 to 1846 the British government four times declined offers of that Mexican province.

Most of the principal characters of the novel – Houston, Smith, Aberdeen, Andrew Jackson, Jones, Elliot, Donelson, Saligny – were real people, and where I could I have used their words as spoken in speeches or written in letters, despatches, or memoirs. I have taken a few liberties. Both the British offer of a guarantee and Houston's acceptance of it were later referred to as the Vermilion Edict: I have used the phrase to describe only the British offer. And there were two French chargés d'affaires in Texas during the Republic: to simplify matters I have allowed Saligny to keep the post throughout that time. Lucy Moncreiffe and her friends are creatures of the imagination. The two letters to Lucy from her first husband are very like those of Charles Kingsley to his wife. Lucy's knowledge of the heart and soul of Sam Houston is imagined, but has a strong basis in fact. Houston had spent some years living with the Cherokees, both as a boy and then in his thirties. He did make a brief and disastrous first marriage to Eliza Allen, and was harrowed by it.

Because this is not a history I shall not append a bibliography. The reader of the novel does not want it, and the historian will not need it. But I must thank those libraries and other institutions in the United States and England, where I have read the letters and despatches of the principal actors in one of the most far-reaching episodes in modern history. I thought it a great thing, in Austin, to hold in my hand Houston's letter telling his secretary of state to conclude a treaty with Britain and France, and to read Jones's scrawled endorsement: 'The within order cannot be obeyed . . .' Houston was in every way a big man and Jones in every way a small man. *There* is an irony of history.

So I thank, in the United States, the Center for American History (formerly the Eugene C. Barker Texas History Center) at the University of Texas at Austin; the Texas State Archives, Austin; the Star of the Republic Museum at Washington-on-the-Brazos, Texas; the Sam Houston Memorial Museum at Huntsville, Texas; the San Jacinto Library and Museum, Texas; the Historical New Orleans Collection, New Orleans. And in England, the Public Record Office, Kew, for the manuscript Foreign Office and Admiralty papers; the British Library, Bloomsbury, for printed state papers; the British Library at Colindale for newspapers; and the United States Collection at the University of London Library.

Lastly, I must acknowledge the debt I owe to two printed works. There are hundreds on Texas history, though the international politics of annexation is strangely neglected. But one modern work, and one by Ashbel Smith himself, are essential. *The French Legation in Texas* by Nancy Nichols Barker (Texas State Historical Association, Austin, 2 vols, 1971 and 1973) is a transcription and translation of the French diplomatic correspondence during the Republic, and much more than that. It is a work of high scholarship which gives a detailed and living picture of Texas in the 1840s, and makes the importance of Texas to France and Britain clearer than anything else I know. Then there is Ashbel Smith's *Reminiscences of the Texas Republic* (Galveston, 1876), which is a transcription of an address to the Historical Society of Galveston. It was almost the first thing I read, and it is short, seventy pages or so, but after I had read all the rest it remained not only the most obviously authoritative single account, but also the most obviously honest of the contemporary works, and the most readable.